Praise for Kevin J. Anderson

"Kevin J. Anderson has become the literary equivalent of Quentin Tarantino."

— THE DAILY ROTATION

"Kevin J. Anderson is the hottest writer on (or off) the planet."

— FORT WORTH STAR-TELEGRAM

"The scope and breadth of Kevin J. Anderson's work is simply astonishing."

— TERRY GOODKIND

"Kevin J. Anderson is one of the best plotters in the business."

— BRANDON SANDERSON

"One of the greatest talents writing today, Kevin J. Anderson is a master of adventures that are filled with dynamic, unforgettable characters."

— SHERRILYN KENYON

Horror and Dark Fantasy Stories
Volume 2

Horror and Dark Fantasy Stories
Volume 2

Kevin J. Anderson

HORROR AND DARK FANTASY STORIES: VOLUME 2
Copyright © 2024 WordFire, Inc.

All rights reserved. No part of this book may be reproduced or transmitted in any form or by any electronic or mechanical means, including photocopying, recording or by any information storage and retrieval system, without the express written permission of the copyright holder, except where permitted by law. This novel is a work of fiction. Names, characters, places and incidents are either the product of the author's imagination, or, if real, used fictitiously.

The ebook edition of this book is licensed for your personal enjoyment only. The ebook may not be re-sold or given away to other people. If you would like to share the ebook edition with another person, please purchase an additional copy for each recipient. Thank you for respecting the hard work of this author.

EBook ISBN: 978-1-68057-717-4
Trade Paperback ISBN: 978-1-68057-718-1
Dust Jacket Hardcover ISBN: 978-1-68057-719-8
Library of Congress Control Number: 2024937274
Cover design by Janet McDonald
Cover artwork by Tithi Luadthong "grandfailure"
Ornamental Image by Freepik.com
Kevin J. Anderson, Art Director
Vellum layout by CJ Anaya
Published by
WordFire Press, LLC
PO Box 1840
Monument CO 80132
Kevin J. Anderson & Rebecca Moesta, Publishers
WordFire Press eBook Edition 2024
WordFire Press Trade Paperback Edition 2024
WordFire Press Dust Jacket Hardcover Edition 2024

Printed in the USA
Join our WordFire Press Readers Group for
sneak previews, updates, new projects, and giveaways.
Sign up at wordfirepress.com

Contents

We Get What We Deserve: The Pickpocket's Tale *(with Neil Peart)*	1
Scarecrow Season	16
Dark Carbuncle *(with Janis Ian)*	30
Bad Water	42
Notches	50
Bump in the Night *A Dan Shamble, Zombie P.I. Adventure*	54
Much at Stake	80
Church Services	98
Leatherworks	112
Surf's Up *A Joe Ledger Story*	118
Royal Wedding	142
The Fate Worse Than Death *(with Guy Anthony De Marco)*	148
Social Distance *(with Rebecca Moesta)*	158
Last Stand	202
Santa Claus Is Coming to Get You!	224
Deathdance	232
Fire in the Hole *A Dan Shamble, Zombie P.I. Adventure*	244
Redmond's Private Screening	268
Loco-Motive	284
Drumbeats *(with Neil Peart)*	298
Previous Publication Information	317
About the Author	319
If You Liked ...	321

My novel Clockwork Lives, *written with Rush drummer and lyricist Neil Peart, is like a steampunk* Canterbury Tales *filled with different stories braided together in an overall framework.*

This is the darkest tale in the book, a chilling story featuring one of our favorite scamp characters, Guerrero, based on a young man Neil met in his younger days as a struggling musician. I was faced with the challenge of developing a sympathetic, heart-wrenching story about a character who manipulates and takes advantage of people. Why would the reader care about someone like that? But, as one of my creative writing professors taught me, "No bad guy ever thinks he's the bad guy."

Rush fans will find numerous Easter eggs sprinkled throughout the prose in this story.

We Get What We Deserve: The Pickpocket's Tale
(with Neil Peart)

When *you steal, what is stolen from you?*
It was a necessary lesson, but not everyone learns a lesson in time—or at all.

I had been warned not to break into the old man's house. The other pickpockets on the streets of Poseidon City were terrified of the place. "That old man is a *necromancer*," one of them told me when I mentioned my plans. "He's an evil alchemist. And dangerous."

I laughed bravely, making the other boy feel like a fool. It is easy to laugh bravely when you are safe and far away ... and before you do a stupid thing.

"The Watchmaker in Albion is an alchemist, and he has more gold than any person can imagine. So, I hope the old man is an alchemist." I narrowed my eyes. "You will all remember the name of Guerrero. Oh, you'll never forget me!"

My friends were not laughing. "We'll remember your name, when we tell stories about what happened to you."

I brushed them off and made my own plans to break into the necromancer's house and rob him blind. I had been wanting to do that for a long time.

When I was just a boy, my father taught me how to steal, and he tried to teach me how to kill. He said I had great potential.

We were abandoned on the streets of Poseidon. My mother had died of a fever when I was but five years old—at least that's what my father said. He thought I didn't remember her, but I could recall my mother's face very clearly. I remembered a screaming fight, her shouting at my father, calling him worthless, and then she had stormed off. She left me there with him, and I never saw her again.

I don't remember her dying of any fever, but my father clung to that story with all the desperation of a broken man clutching his last few copper coins at the gambling table.

We lived on the streets, and I was always hungry. When I begged him for food, my father scowled at me. "If you want food, you have to hunt for it. Out in the wild there are predators and prey." He gestured to the crowded marketplace, the inns, the small houses of working people, larger houses of merchants in the hills that rose from the harbor. "Everything around you is for the taking."

He took me along the bustling streets, told me to keep my hands to myself but my eyes alert. "In the wild, a lion has to hunt his prey in order to eat. Do you want to be a lion, Guerrero?"

I didn't feel like much of a lion with my empty stomach and my dirty clothes, but I nodded.

So he taught me how to hunt marks in the city. I had heard him complain that I was an impossible burden on him, but he learned how to make use of me, too. He explained that some animals hunted alone, some hunted in packs. And we were a pack —him and me.

We would walk quietly together, studying the marketplace and the individual stalls. At first, because it was relatively safe, he would have me dart in and steal portyguls, pomegranates, or apples from Albion. I learned how to be fast and reckless. I could grab fruit and race away while the merchants bellowed after me (if they noticed me at all).

About half the time I got caught, and as I struggled and thrashed, sometimes dropping the fruit I had stolen, my father would come charging up, looking indignant and upset. "My boy, what have you done?" He would groan at all the onlookers. "Didn't I teach you better than that?" He would strike me on the side of the head, graciously return the stolen fruit, and drag me away from the fuming merchant. "I'll make him learn his lesson, believe me!" my father would growl, and we would get away with it.

And I did learn my lesson—I learned how to be more nimble and more adept at dodging pursuit.

If I escaped unscathed with my booty, we would meet in a prearranged alley. I'd hand him the fruit, and he would cut it into pieces, giving me my share, which was about a quarter of the take.

When my father needed to steal something more valuable, such as a stall vendor's daily money chest or a metalworker's jewelry, we used a different ploy. I would wander into the marketplace where jewelers sold gold chains or tourmaline pendants, pearls from the northern coast, fire opals from the alchemy mines. I'd wander in innocently, skipping along, then let myself grow confused. When I reached the proper spot, I would suddenly start wailing for my father. The "lost and panicked little boy" was an extremely effective diversion.

When the jewelers and the city patrol rushed to help the poor, terrified child, my father would snag a few gold chains or amethyst brooches. He showed restraint, taking only one or two amulets so the merchants didn't even notice they'd been robbed, at least not right away.

We learned the underside of Poseidon City, hidden places that no one saw, and no one knew about, except for people like us. There were abandoned buildings, empty basements, snug and sheltered alleys. Every night a different home.

"It's because we are free, Guerrero," my father said. "A new roof whenever we like, a warm home, and then we move on and find another." I learned later that we had to keep moving to avoid being caught. The justice of the city patrol was swift and meted out with clubs.

We would look at the lighted rooms above the shops, where families lived in their permanent homes. My father would laugh at how they were caged, and how we were free. But I thought the houses looked nice. Part of me longed to have a place like that of our own, but my father cuffed me when I mentioned it. "I didn't raise my son to be a fool. Worthless dreamers are *prey*, not lions."

But he started to gaze at the private dwellings as well, the mansions in the hills, and his eyes held a new gleam. We paid attention to the houses of the merchants, the landlords, the city's elite, and we resented the rich people who built extravagant dwellings and sprinkled gold on their food to flaunt how superior they were to people like us.

He grew excited when he learned that some of those mansions were unoccupied, filled with food and possessions that were left to gather dust while the landowners went to vacation in the countryside to lead decadent lives. Breaking into those houses was easier than stealing from marks on the street, with a far smaller risk of being caught. We would locate one of those empty homes, break a low window. I was still small enough and young enough to worm my way through the hole, then unlock the door and let my father in.

I remember that first house—I had never had such a feast! We ate salted ham, pickled eggs, cheeses, preserved fruit, honey, and smoked fish. My father found grime-encrusted bottles of wine so old he insisted they were valuable, so he opened one for himself and one for me, making me drink it. I don't remember much beyond feeling awfully sick and him laughing at me as I vomited on the rich merchant's sofa.

One looming house was set apart from the others on a steep slope—it looked ostentatious yet sinister, and as we watched night after night, we never saw more than one hooded light moving from room to room; occasionally, colored and stinking smokes wafted from rooftop vents. The house wasn't empty, but it seemed to exude mystery.

I looked at it with curiosity and fear, hoping my father wouldn't suggest we try to spend the night there. To me, the house looked haunted, or cursed. My father, however, looked at the mansion with avarice in his eyes.

We knew other street people like us—not friends, not colleagues, not even competition. They were a source of knowledge, however, and my father began asking them about the house. Most of them shuddered. "Dangerous, too dangerous! That man is a monster," said one. "A wizard," said another, while a third called the owner "an evil necromancer with magic prism eyes."

My father was not frightened, though. He stared at that mansion with an increasing hunger, and I knew he would not let go.

He obtained a large sharp knife—stole it, no doubt, although he said he purchased it—and he got a smaller knife for me. After he gave me the blade, he took me to where we could look up at the supposed necromancer's mansion. He said, "You're not ready yet, Guerrero. I need to teach you the next thing."

"You know how to steal, but it's long past time you learn how to fight," he said. "Because sometimes the prey fights back."

I was scrappy, but fighting was never the preferable tactic because sometimes the prey might win. Sometimes a lion was killed.

For my deeper training, we preyed upon weaker people in the streets. We would linger behind taverns and strike men who were so drunk they could barely walk. We rolled them and stole from them, but most had already spent the bulk of their money in the tavern. My father robbed several of them to show me how it was done, and then he made me do it by myself. In the garbage of an alley they were easy pickings, and I didn't see how this was preparing me to fight an evil necromancer (who was probably just an eccentric old man anyway).

Sometimes our targets yelled for help, and I learned to dodge and dash away, running with all my might before the city patrol came. Once, when I ran away with a disappointingly thin sack of coins, I bolted between buildings and emerged in a narrow side street with my father puffing to catch up. Unexpectedly, I ran into another gang of street kids who surrounded me—five of them—as if I had sprung a trap. They were predators too, hunting the weak, but these were a different kind of predator. Not lions. More like hyenas.

They reacted swiftly, viciously, when I burst in among them. Working together they grabbed me; one snatched the stolen coins out of my hand, and another shoved me against a brick wall, knocking the wind out of me.

"We've seen you," said one of them. "Don't like you." He punched me in the stomach with the force of a battering ram. I doubled over, coughed and retched. They took turns hitting, slapping, slamming me against the bricks. I flailed but could not land a blow. One punched me in the face, and blood poured into my eyes so I could barely see.

When I looked up, I saw my father come running up between the buildings. I knew I was saved. But as the boys kept beating on me, my father just watched.

After they had taken the few coins from me, I had nothing left for them to steal, and I provided little sport against five of them, so they eventually grew bored and went away, leaving me bleeding and groaning in the gutter.

My father stood over me, frowning in disappointment. I tried to speak through swollen lips, but there was too much blood in my mouth. I finally managed, "Why didn't you help me?"

He grabbed me by the arm and pulled me to my feet, despite my outcry of pain. I was sure several of my ribs were cracked. "You have to learn how to fight. Be a lion." My father wasn't sure I had learned my lesson, so he got even harder. "You have too many boundaries, Guerrero. We have to make them go away."

I think he was looking for the right opportunity.

Several days later, we attacked a staggering sailor who wandered the wrong direction away from a tavern. He looked like a poor mark, not quite inebriated enough to make him defenseless, and he was larger than the two of us together, but my father pushed me forward, made me try to pick his pocket. The sailor fought back; he bellowed as I grabbed his money purse.

My father rushed in to join the fight. "Stop him from shouting!"

I saw a flash of steel—his large blade—which he plunged into the sailor's side. The drunken man gasped and choked, initially in disbelief, and then the pain hammered into him. My father ripped the knife free and plunged it in again, higher, then withdrew and stabbed a third time. The sailor's screams were hoarse now, mere gurgles. He slithered to the ground as I backed away in horror, but my father wasn't finished; he was just building momentum. He pushed the sailor to the garbage on the ground and stabbed him more times than I could count. When the victim lay bloody and twitching, my father grabbed the money pouch and tossed it to me. When I caught it, blood got all over my hands.

"You ... killed him," I said, stupidly.

Sneering, he yanked my arm, and we ran away from the corpse. "And what do you think a lion does to his prey? He *kills!* That's what you have to learn—be a hunter, not a victim."

When we were in an open street under a full moon sky, he grabbed me by the shoulder, turned me, and pointed up at the looming house of the necromancer. It still looked so tantalizing on the hill, a shadowy hulk with a glimmering light in one window. "*There!* Remember that. You have to learn to do anything for *that*."

Our lives were focused toward that goal, but as he built the eccentric old man into a greater and greater nemesis, my father made my training harsher. Desperation leads to justifications.

Each day and with every scavenged or stolen meal, he reminded me that we were free, that we made up our own rules—but it was my father who made up the rules, and he forced me to do things that I did not wish to do.

After the third man he murdered in front of me, I realized that he liked using his large knife, and he egged me on, forcing me to draw my knife whenever we attacked, just in case I might need to use it.

On the last time, late at night, I was with him while he brooded, planned, and grumbled, searching for a new victim. A thin man with a small valise left a shop and locked it, turning down an empty deserted street. He was a tailor, I believe, not our usual victim, but my father grabbed him, dragged him into an alley. The man yelped. "I have nothing." He flapped his hands, dropped his valise. "Take my papers, that's all I own."

My father didn't want to believe him. "Hold your knife, Guerrero. Be ready."

I drew the knife as instructed, not sure what my father wanted. "But, he's no threat to us."

"Help me," the tailor wailed.

My father let go of the victim and shoved me toward him. "Kill him—you have to kill him, Guerrero!"

The thin man cringed. I had the knife, but I froze. My arms were shaking. "No," I said.

My father slapped me in the back of the head. "You have to kill him! He knows your name. He'll call the city watch."

But I'd had enough. I knew how to survive in Poseidon City, but I wasn't sure how much longer I would survive living with my father.

"Kill him! Be a lion."

I whirled with the knife and jabbed it at my father's face instead. "You want to feel my claws?" I darted the blade back and forth, as I yelled to the tailor out of the side of my mouth. "Run!"

He scrambled out of the street, arms and legs bouncing like a scarecrow blown away in the wind.

My father reddened, and he grabbed for his own large knife, but I slashed with my dagger. This time the blade bit more than just the air. I sliced across his cheek, leaving a bright red line. He had taught me to steal and tried to teach me to kill, but I chose to be a coward rather than a murderer.

I jabbed my knife at him again, and he backed away, shocked. As he pressed his palm against his bleeding face, I fled. My father had said it many times before, but now I felt the difference. Now I *was* free. Now I was truly a lion.

I survived on the streets, as I knew how to do so well. I used what I had learned from my father, and also the *opposite* of what he had taught me. I never spent time with him again. Didn't want to. Didn't need to.

I made friends, shallow ones, because I didn't know how to do anything else. Some friendships lasted months, some only a few days, but they were like bright burning stars. I left them when it became necessary. Fundamentally, though, I was alone—and meant to be that way.

I learned how to get what I wanted. I fought occasionally, but mostly I escaped. I was swift. I was clever. I was a *survivor* instead of a victor, and that was enough for me. Whenever I found a safe, empty house, I would slip inside, take from those who had too much, and use things that would never be missed.

But as the years passed, I kept looking at the old man's house. My friends on the streets also avoided the place. They told stories that reinforced the fears my father had ... but the wild and specific details were so similar that I realized they were simply repeating rumors my father himself had started. I laughed them off, because I knew the stories weren't true, and I knew what sort of man my father was.

In time, though, I realized I would have to prove it—as another way to be free of my father. The mansion crouched on the hillside like a hoarder hunched over some ill-gotten treasure. It was a sinister, intimidating place, and every night I saw that eerie glow wandering from window to window.

Then the necromancer's house went mysteriously dark, empty, silent—for weeks. I watched for several more nights. A chill went down my spine as I made concrete plans, for it is a frightening thing when a fantasy becomes an actual possibility. The necromancer had vanished, or died, or maybe been trapped in some terrible misfire of a spell.

I had to make my move.

I chose my night carefully, waited for the dark of the moon, when the necromancer's mansion was one looming architectural shadow. Holding my sharp knife and ready to fight, I broke in as I had done countless times at other homes, but this felt different. Infinitely different.

Dangerous ... and tantalizing.

The gloom inside the mansion was oppressive, like a strangler's silence, but as I crept forward I could see that this strange and mysterious man, whoever he was and whatever his powers, was as inconceivably wealthy as my father had claimed. That part of the legend at least was true.

Urns were filled with gems, as if for mere decoration. Gold glimmered from all furnishings; mirrors hung on the walls with gilded frames and blank pearlescent faces that looked like moonstone, rather than silvered glass. There were statues and candlesticks, many made of gold, but others of even rarer silver or platinum. Chandeliers hung from the arched ceilings, sparkling with memories of light that came from nowhere within the mansion itself. A polished marble fountain was filled not with trickling water, but with long quartz crystal prisms that showed rainbows in a spectrum of black.

With so much fabulous treasure, how could I be afraid? I could just grab an armload of gems and gold and run grinning into the night. But I didn't. I should have known better.

Breathing fast, I climbed a wide river of stairs that flowed from the upper level. I should have grabbed an armful of treasure and fled, but that wasn't why I had come. Though I resented him, my father had prepared me for this. If the evil wizard lunged out at me, I would stab him with the knife and dash away.

I moved cautiously, eyes alert, ready to run if I encountered some slavering monster or crimson-eyed litch intent on stealing my soul. I doubted I could fight a necromancer (if he *was* a necromancer, instead of just an eccentric old man).

When I reached the upper level, I found an immense gallery with fountains and basins, empty frames on the walls that seemed to be waiting for portraits. And more mirrors, including one large looking glass on a stand. I heard a muffled voice, a desperate cry that seemed to come from far away.

The voice came from inside the looking glass.

As I stared, a figure appeared on the other side of the mirror, a kindly looking old man with long gray hair and a voluminous gray beard. He was *inside* the reflecting pane, an image without an afterimage. "Help!" he said, but his cry was muffled through a thin pane of glass and however many dimensions there were between us.

I was startled. I wanted to grab coins, jewels, and golden candlesticks and run away, but curiosity got the best of me.

The old man pounded from behind the looking glass, and I heard only small vibrations. "Help! Please!" His eyes lit up when he saw me. "I've been trapped for so long."

A lion would not run, no ... but would a lion *help*?

"Are you the necromancer?" I asked, holding up the knife as if to impress him.

A look of alarm crossed the old man's face. "Is that what they call me? A magician, a sorcerer? I always thought of myself as a researcher in the arcane sciences. I constructed this mirror with alchemy, coated it with a sheen of quintessence, a recipe described in the most secret research from lost almanacs. The spell was designed for purity and hope, but something went wrong, and I became trapped in here. You must let me out. Only you can let me out."

I was afraid to take a step closer, remembering all the wild stories I had been so quick to discount. On the streets, I knew when to run from a fight. "Why should I do that?"

Desperation leads to justifications. The old man said, "If you free me, you could have all my wealth."

"You are in no position to bargain." I faced the mirror, straight-backed and cocky. "If you're trapped, I can take all your wealth anyway."

His expression became somber. "But could you live with yourself?"

When you steal, what is stolen from you? I hadn't learned that lesson yet.

I shrugged. "Probably. What does this mirror do?"

His voice remained distant. "It's a reflecting glass designed to trap evil, to drain it from the person who gazes into it. It's a cleansing spell, but I became trapped inside." He reached out to the edge of the mirror. "Just take my hand, pull me out."

The old man looked so desperate. His voice trembled. My father had painted him as a fearsome monster, and I felt I had to prove that he was wrong, as he had been wrong in so many other things. I was torn. Was I a lion? Was I prey? I steeled myself. I was *human*. And I wasn't afraid.

Hesitant and skittish, ready to jump away if necessary, I reached out to touch the mirror at the point where the old man's hand met the reflecting glass. "I can pull you out," I said.

As my fingertips brushed the surface, though, it was as if I had popped the membrane of a soap bubble. His fingers folded around mine—and then the mirror glass folded around my hand as well. The necromancer's grip became like a claw. "Or I can pull you *in!*"

He seized me, refused to let go. With a rushing astral wind, I felt something being drained out of me, as if an artery of my soul had been severed and the mirror was siphoning off the evil parts inside me.

"Let go!" I struggled, dug in my heels, but some part of me was gushing into the mirror, pulled through to the other side of the reflection. The mirror was designed to steal a person's *evil* ... and it had stolen the entire presence of the necromancer. Now it was draining me. Would there be anything left on this side of the mirror?

I thrashed and yelled, not caring if anyone out in the streets heard the struggle. The necromancer held tight, dragging me farther into the mirror. My hand already felt dead, my bones and skin turned to ice. His grip was like a manacle far more secure than any wrist-shackles the Poseidon City guard used on a criminal.

I yelled and kicked. The tall mirror wobbled but remained rooted to the floor. I could not break free, and I used all my strength to pull backward, to drag this evil man out into the real world again—or would that only be worse?

Dark rainbows flashed from the old necromancer's eyes, and a wicked grin stretched his wrinkled face as he tugged harder, trying to draw me the rest of the way into the mirror. I felt weaker every second, diminished. My entire existence was being drained away, flooding to the wrong side of the reflection.

As I fought and yelled, I heard another muffled voice and twisted my head to see a second mirror hanging from the wall, a golden frame around a silvered moonstone glass. *My father's face* was behind it—I could even see the scar on his cheek from where I had cut him. He pounded and cried out from far away, but he was lost inside the mirror—as I would be any minute now. My knees were already watery, trembling; my strength was waning.

"I am a lion!" I said in a ragged shout.

Somehow, I found the strength to lift my sharp knife. My hand had plunged inside the mirror, and the necromancer refused to release his grip. Crying out, not daring to think, I swung the knife down and hacked at my own wrist. It was the only way I could survive, before any more of my arm was pulled into the hellish looking glass. The sharp, bright lightning of pain gave me the strength to jerk harder, and the necromancer recoiled. But it wasn't enough. Another blow, and the pain was impossible, an explosion of brilliant agony through skin, tendon, bone. I don't know how many more times I chopped before I fell backward into the room, collapsing onto the floor with my wrist spouting blood.

I crawled backward, reeling, unable to think. The old man, still trapped in the reflecting glass, howled—and my instinct was to flee screaming into the night. But I had to stop the bleeding, and I struggled out of my shirt, wrapped the sleeve around my wrist and pulled it tight, trying to cut off the flow.

When I got back to my feet, wanting only to lurch away, I knew I had one last thing to do. Tucking my bloody arm against my chest, I used my good hand to grasp the frame of the looking glass, throwing my weight against it until I wrenched it off balance. The evil mirror fell face forward and shattered on the floor, breaking the trapped necromancer into a thousand sharp shards on the floor. I don't know if it killed him or just imprisoned him there forever.

I was gray and sweaty, ready to collapse, but I had to get out of there. Dripping blood and cradling the severed wrist, I staggered away.

From behind the mirror on the wall, I saw my father's face, furious then wheedling. He pounded on the glass. "Free me!"

But I didn't know how to do that, nor did I care to find out. If I shattered the mirror, it might kill him. Or maybe not.

Before I fainted, I drew a breath, swayed in front of him, and held up my bloody stump before the reflection. "You taught me, Father," I said in a voice made hoarse from screaming. "I am a lion."

When you steal, what is stolen from you?

I staggered down the steps and out of the necromancer's mansion, unable to think straight, foolishly neglecting to take so much as a golden candlestick or any jewels from the fountains. I fled the evil place, barely able to stand upright because the pain was so great, leaving the echo of my father with all eternity to reflect on what it really meant to be trapped.

Dipping back into my enigmatic Wisconsin small town, this was an early Tucker's Grove story, published in an obscure small press anthology. I still have a copy, but I doubt anyone else does.

Many years later I was invited to contribute a story for another dark fantasy anthology. The very insistent editor wanted a story from me, but I didn't have time to write something new within his time frame (too many novel deadlines). But I remembered this old story, and I knew it was a solid, chilling idea, even though the original writing wasn't quite adequate to the concept. I offered to rewrite it, and the editor agreed. (Nobody remembered the original publication anyway.)

This is the new version, much improved, and I think it's quite creepy. Be careful what you wish for....

Scarecrow Season

The scarecrow hung on a crossbar in the Indian Summer sun, clutching at the last threads of life. Crucified. His clothes were tattered, his hair tangled and askew, his skin sunburned and blistered.

He had endured endless days and nights while he sweated away his body's water until he was little more than a dry corn shock. For a long time, he had stared at the acres and acres of waving cornfields that stretched out in front of him. Then the crows came to peck out his eyes, and he saw nothing else.

Blood crusted his wrists. On the first day, he had struggled to wrench himself free of the ropes that held him to the rough, nail-scarred crossbar. He knew with a sick sadness, and also relief, that he wouldn't last another day.

A broad, flat fragment of bloodstained altar stone rested against the foot of the upright support bar, just beneath his bare feet. Nearby, in the branches of an ancient oak along the fence line, he could hear the deep croak of a huge crow with fathomless black eyes. The crow had perched motionless in the tree, watching him as he hung helpless. The crow barely moved its head, eyes shining in the sun, watching, waiting. Like a demon.

The man's last thought was a gibbering curse at the person who had done this to him. *Elspeth Sandsbury.*

Exhaustion, hunger, and thirst drove him miles deep into unconsciousness, so deeply that he did not even realize it when that awful woman came to finish him off....

Elspeth whistled a bright melody as she marched down the weed-tangled lane to the back field, the one far from the road leading to Tucker's Grove. She swung the newly sharpened sickle in her calloused hand.

Elspeth Sandsbury was a hefty woman—"big bones," she always said. A farmer's wife needed to be strong and healthy. Most people didn't suspect just how strong she had become after years of doing the farm work by herself, after her husband had died. When Elspeth decided to use her strength, it took most of her victims completely by surprise.

Seeing the gray, drawn skin on her new scarecrow, she hurried, hoping she hadn't arrived too late. The Dark Ones would not be pleased if he died too soon; she doubted They could be fed with any but living blood. "Don't you go and perish on me before I can properly conduct my sacrifice, Mister!"

A quick touch to the man's bound wrist reassured her that his heart throbbed stubbornly, but weakly. Barely alive. No time to waste!

She quickly recited the prayer she had devised. "Dark Ones! Hear me! I swear my solemn devotion to you. Hallowed be Thy Names. Though I walk through the valley of the shadow, Thy will be done. Blessed be the farmers ... for we worship Thee and bring Thee sacrifices like Thou used to get."

She reached up and drew the scythe blade across the scarecrow's throat as if she were carving a Thanksgiving roast for her dead husband Jaacob. The razor-edge parted beard-stubbled skin, sinew, and blood vessels all the way to his neckbone.

Blood gushed from the scarecrow's jugular and splattered on the rune-carved altar stone at his quivering bare feet. With a contented sigh, Elspeth propped the scythe against the altar stone and flung some blood in the air for good measure. With a fingertip, she traced a cross of blood on her forehead and continued her chant. She no longer needed to go to the church in Tucker's Grove.

"And we know that Thou makest my crops to grow with great abundance and ensure that my stomach is full and I am warm and well. When Thou sufferest the sacrificial Lamb to come unto me, I shall deliver him up to Thee right quick. Amen."

The large crow stared at her, as if it knew just what she was doing. Elspeth watched the bird, acknowledged its presence with a nod, then grunted as she knelt before the altar stone.

With the fresh blood, she drew strange symbols on the stone. The runes were different with each sacrifice, things she had seen on barns and graves, or just designs she made up. She didn't think the Dark Ones minded: They had never shown her the right way to conduct the ritual, after all. As long as she was sincere and did her best, she knew the Dark Ones would settle for what they got.

When the sacrifice was done, Elspeth cut the ropes holding the scarecrow to the crossbar and caught the body as he fell forward. It seemed appropriate to wait for the first sunset of the night of the full moon, but she had timed this one close ... too close. At least the man was unconscious when she'd cut his throat. She hated when they screamed and gurgled.

The black crow flew off silently.

As she lifted the ragdoll body over her shoulders, she made a mental note to do the washing as soon as she got back to the farmhouse, or else the blood would never come off her dress. She plodded down the lane toward the garden, where she would bury him with all the others in the tangles of the melon patch. Elspeth grunted with the burden.

Walking back to the house, she paused by the only two marked graves on the Sandsbury property. One rude cross said, "Isaac Abraham Sandsbury: Beloved Son."

He had limped home with a gunshot wound in the leg after a stupid hunting accident. Elspeth had taken Isaac to a hydropathist, who advised her to rinse her son's injured leg and soak it in warm water. He instructed that Isaac should drink only water, that he must be surrounded by steaming pots of water. And after the hydropathist took his fee and departed for Bartonville, Elspeth had been helpless as her son's gangrene spread and spread....

The other cross, cruder than the first because Elspeth had done it all by herself, read, "Jaacob Jonah Sandsbury: Beloved Father and Husband."

An insanely religious man, Jaacob had accepted his smallpox as no more than a Job-like test from his All-Powerful God. Jaacob had died, writhing and screaming, his flesh roiling with stinking pustules. He praised his Lord with his dying breath, neglecting even to say goodbye to his wife of twenty-five years.

Then the barn had burned down. And Elspeth, in anger and determination, stalked out to do the spring planting by herself, hitching their one horse to the plow and taking out her despair by tearing into the Earth.

But the plow struck something hard and immovable, long-buried in the dirt. The unexpected obstacle made the horse lurch forward and break its foreleg.

Rain had poured down as Elspeth unearthed the broken altar stone with her bare hands. The flat fragment was etched with strange runes and brown markings that looked like long-dried blood. Elspeth couldn't decipher the symbols, but in a flash—a vision—she understood the truth.

No God, not even Jaacob's God, could possibly be so cruel as to let her suffer all that had happened to her, not without good reason. And now Elspeth had found that reason. While everyone else went to the town's Methodist church to sing hymns to some gentle, peaceful deity, the Old Ones were lying here in the ground, forgotten. And they were not too happy about it.

As the altar stone showed, others had known the truth long ago, and they must have appeased the Dark Ones with sacrifice and worship. Now, even though they were all but forgotten, the ancient gods remained hungry for the sacrifice.

Elspeth had been given a second chance. She could appease them. *She* would be the one to gain their favor, no one else. The Dark Ones *did* exist; she knew it. Finding the altar stone in the midst of her tribulations had to be a sign!

And so, she made sacrifices. First was the horse with its broken leg, right there in the field. Then the dog, Jaacob's surly old mutt ... then rabbits and squirrels. But nothing seemed to have any beneficial effect on the crops.

She needed a better, bigger sacrifice.

Then that traveler had stopped, asking for directions....

Elspeth had never really kept a record of how good the crops were when Jaacob did the field work, but she was certain the yield had increased dramatically since she began making the human sacrifices. The Dark Ones wouldn't neglect their faithful servant. Why should she doubt them?

Besides, she had enough trouble just watching over the Grossnetz boys who came to do her harvesting. She took down the scarecrow pole when it was time for them to come, of course, and hid the altar stone, but Elspeth didn't want them to become too nosy. She was confident that even if the Grossnetz boys discovered anything dangerous, the Dark Ones would strike them down, but she was afraid the D.O.s (as she called them when she didn't think *They* were listening) would also punish her for being careless.

Back at the old farmhouse she washed her hands at the well. Since it was such a nice day, with enough of a breeze to chase away the worst of the heat, she decided to forego the washing chores. She discarded her bloodstained dress and changed into a fresh, clean flower print.

The weathered rocking chair creaked on the front porch as she settled her bulk into it. She rocked back and forth, humming a tune that vaguely resembled "Amazing Grace," but with words she had altered to suit herself. Elspeth wondered how long it would be before the Dark Ones sent another victim to her.

Maybe she would do some embroidery in the meantime.

He came striding down the dusty road that passed in front of the Sandsbury house. Long-legged to the point of being gangly, he wore rumpled city clothes in the noon heat. The grin on his bespectacled face made him look foolish, even from a distance. He waved to her in polite greeting, and Elspeth waved back.

He took it as an invitation and veered from the road to walk up to the house. "Can you tell me if I'm anywhere close to the town of Tucker's Grove, ma'am?"

She waited for him to come to the porch before she answered. "Tucker's Grove? Well, how close you be depends on how far you've come, now doesn't it? It's about an hour's ride from here, a day or thereabouts if you're walking."

He held out his hand, flashing a broad smile. "Andrew Danforth Johnson, ma'am." He bowed. "Dentist."

"Elspeth Sandsbury ... farmer's wife." She took his hand. "Pleased to meet you, Mr. Johnson. Would you care for a cold glass of water?"

Elspeth started for the well pump before he could answer. She drove the pump handle until a stream of cold water poured from the spout. She lifted the ladle toward the thin stranger, and he drank, thanking her more enthusiastically than was necessary.

He sat on the step of the porch after she had resumed her seat in the old rocking chair. "Tell me, Mr. Johnson, what brings you on the road to Bartonville, and *walking*, yet! Where do you hail from?"

"All the way from Boston, ma'am. I heard that these parts of Wisconsin are quite pleasant, especially the small towns. Just having finished my schooling as a dentist, I thought it'd be a good idea to come out here to set up my practice."

"You came from Boston to get to Tucker's Grove? Well, mister, if you'll pardon me for saying so, that's about the most pure idiot thing I ever heard of!" She smiled at him disarmingly, she hoped.

He laughed. Elspeth clapped her hands together suddenly, as if she knew exactly the thing the dentist was waiting for. "Say, have you ever tried gooseberry wine, Mr. Johnson?"

"Can't say that I have, ma'am."

"It's just what you need to improve your stamina, heighten your spirits, and get you primed for the last leg of your journey. Besides, it's the hottest part of the day out there. You just set here in the shade while I go pour a glass."

"Aren't you having one yourself, ma'am?"

"I don't drink spirits, Mr. Johnson. Not since my husband died, anyways."

She disappeared into the house, then returned with a crystal goblet of a murky, purplish wine. "Here you be, Mr. Johnson. Just the thing." She handed it down to him. "Drink up."

Then she rocked back in the creaking old chair, glancing down the road to make sure no one else might be coming in the hot, lonely afternoon. With a smile, Elspeth saw the comical shock on the dentist's face as the potent sleeping powders hit him.

Andrew Danforth Johnson pitched forward into unconsciousness. Elspeth grabbed his collar and deftly caught him just before his face grazed the dusty porch. It would have been cruel to let the man break his spectacles that way.

She took a long drink from the well herself, quenching her thirst, then turned to her new victim. Time to get to work.

After she had mounted the dentist up on the scarecrow bar, Elspeth spent the night in the intimate company of nightmares—visions of dark wings and expressionless ebony eyes, ominous shadows. She was convinced she'd received an honest-to-goodness sending from the Dark Ones but was at a loss to understand its meaning. She found it confusing.

Why didn't the Old Ones just speak in plain, simple English that a body could understand? They always sent murky images, dreams, flashes of inspiration ... if she hadn't known better, she might have thought they were just products of her own imagination.

Elspeth woke at dawn, her ample body tangled in damp sheets that weren't half as twisted as her stomach felt. She wondered if she had eaten something bad the night before. Or maybe the D.O.s were upset about something. Elspeth swallowed hard, trying to figure out how she could appease them. She'd better make the new sacrifice quick.

The man would be awake by now, stiff from hanging on the crossbar all through the night. When she had hoisted him up the day before, she noticed with some curiosity that all the crows but the big one, the leader, were watching from the oak boughs.

The dentist's gangly arms had flopped and flapped in all the wrong directions as she wrestled with his limp body. The strong sleeping powders had turned his bones to rubber. Nailing his wrists with more vehemence than was warranted, Elspeth had spat out some curses that would have offended her husband, if his ears hadn't been well insulated by layers of earth....

Now, as she dressed herself, her head pounded an independent rhythm to the queasiness of her stomach. With this headache, and the confusing flock of nightmares ... yes, something was definitely peculiar. The Dark Ones were not happy with her.

Maybe They were just hungry again. She usually let each scarecrow hang for a few days so that the old gods could have a good look at the offering before she spilt its blood (and also so the sacrifice wouldn't struggle and make too much of a mess).

But she had timed that last victim too close. Maybe the blood of a man so close to death contained no tonic for thirsty Gods. Maybe They needed healthy, fresh blood. That would neatly explain her throbbing headache, her black nightmares and twisted stomach. She had to fix it.

"Well, Mr. Johnson, there's one quick way to satisfy a herd of hungry Gods. At least it'll be quick for you."

She retrieved the sickle from the kitchen wash-bucket, put on an apron to cover her clean dress, and strolled out into the early morning sunlight.

As she walked the lane back into the cornfield, Elspeth stopped in shock as she neared her garden. My, the D.O.s had been busy during the night!

The two crosses that marked the graves of her son and husband had been torn from the earth and impaled upside down in the center of the graves. The unruly grass covering the mounds was now black and leprous. "Oh, dear."

All the plants in her garden were hunched over, withered and coated with dripping icicles, as if blasted by the arctic breath of the Dark Ones. Her neat rows of beans, peas, and carrots all lay destroyed. The rotting leaves of potatoes and turnips sent a foul stench into the chill air.

Elspeth swallowed hard, and she felt a cold fist wrench her stomach, as if the ancient gods were prodding her. Then the pain subsided, and she hurried to finish up the sacrifice before the D.O.s got any angrier.

But she got no farther than the melon patch, where the once-healthy vines lay dry and wasted over the unmarked graves of her previous sacrifices. The broad fan-shaped leaves stirred as round shapes moved beneath them. Elspeth put a hand to her mouth.

The firm, green melons she had nurtured all summer had now transformed into the severed heads of her victims. The round, grimacing heads sat propped on the ends of dead stems from the vines, mottled with decay. Each one of the heads turned to face her, watching her with ebony eyes that had somehow escaped putrefaction. They didn't blink—just stared with venomous accusations.

Elspeth gulped and waddled down the pathway. The dead eyes followed her as she ran....

Andrew Danforth Johnson was awake and wide-eyed as she approached him with the curved, razor-sharp harvesting blade. The lanky dentist looked none the worse for his night on the crossbar or the nails through his wrists, but he seemed to have lost his voice, for he said nothing as she approached. Maybe he was too frightened to whimper.

Elspeth looked up at the big oak on the fence line, where the crows still huddled. She was a bit disappointed that the big crow wasn't there to watch, but she had a feeling it was close by, waiting.

"All right, no time to waste, Mr. Johnson." With her bulky form, she began to dance around the crossbar. She chanted a dissonant song, imploring the Dark Ones to accept this new sacrifice and to make her headache and stomach distress go away ... and, if it wasn't too much trouble, to return the graves and her garden to their former conditions.

She halted in front of the crossbar and placed her plump hands on her more than generous hips. The gangly dentist just looked at her, his expression sour, more disgusted than afraid.

"Your blood is going to be swilled by the meanest, darkest Gods on the face of this Earth, Mr. Johnson. Aren't you afraid?"

She brandished the sickle in his face, but instead of the spasms of terror she expected, he just looked at her sadly. Disturbed, she drew back the blade to strike. When he simply flashed his foolish smile at her, she sliced hard, laying his throat open to the vertebrae.

But rather than bright arterial blood, molten yellow fire spat out from the wound. The cut healed itself before her eyes with a line of sparks like flames dancing along a firecracker fuse. Elspeth cried out and dropped the sickle, then sucked her burnt, smoking fingers.

"You've damned yourself to the last, Elspeth Sandsbury," the man said. His voice was husky and wolflike now. Not even a scar remained from the wound in his throat.

She gawked at him as the ropes binding him to the crossbar suddenly caught fire and burned to ash without marking his skin or scorching his clothes. The nails in his wrists shot away like lead pellets into the cornfield.

Andrew Danforth Johnson dropped lightly to the ground, straightening and dusting his black clothes before taking a step toward her. "Poor Elspeth—if the Dark Ones were as powerful as you imagine, do you really believe that They would have *allowed* Themselves to be forgotten?"

He didn't look at all frail anymore. The stranger seemed to possess a power that could have felled an oak tree. His black hair had become iridescent in the sunlight.

"Did you never think that there might still exist high priests in the world? Priests who carry out the proper rituals in the proper ways—and with the proper sacrifices?" He loomed closer, and Elspeth shrank back. "Did you think the Dark Ones would take kindly to an ignorant usurper like yourself, who knows nothing of Them, nothing of the old ways, yet does not hesitate to shed blood in Their names? If there's one thing the Dark Ones hate, it's amateurs!"

The stranger started toward her. She couldn't run. She tried to speak to him to offer up an explanation, but her tongue could only manage gibberish.

He caught her by the front of her dress and lifted her bulk off the ground with one hand. She squirmed, but a cold hand in her gut crushed her resistance, twisting her innards.

The dark man slammed Elspeth against the crossbar. He seemed much taller now, for he held her against the wood with his shoulder as he lifted one of her thick arms against the bar. He cupped one hand, and with the other drew a long strand of shiny barbed wire from the recesses of his fist, like a magician's endless handkerchiefs from his sleeves. He bound her arms to the crossbar with the barbed wire.

Elspeth whimpered, then gibbered, begged, and wept, until she finally collapsed so deeply inside herself that she could do nothing but watch and listen.

"Elspeth, hear me now. The time for violent rituals and bloody sacrifices is over. The Dark Ones have had to adapt to survive to the modern age. They've had to become more compatible with mankind's need, more accommodating to a civilized way of life." He smiled at her as she hung helpless, bound by shining barbed wire. "But even so, They do still enjoy an occasional, *special* sacrifice."

He bent down and picked up the broken altar stone as if it belonged to him and easily tucked the heavy fragment under his arm, though it had taken Elspeth ropes and a lever to move it.

The stranger turned and walked away down the lane without a backward glance.

From the fence line the crows set up a loud, squawking racket. The big crow, their black leader, joined them at last, but this time, instead of just watching, the birds flew down to feast.

Now for something a little lighter. I didn't know that legendary folk musician and Grammy Award-winning singer Janis Ian was a science fiction fan until I got to know her. And boy is she a fan! When she walked around wide-eyed at science fiction conventions, several of us took her under our wing and introduced her to luminaries of the genre. Janis would always insist, "Oh, nobody knows who I am!" until we mentioned some of her songs, and then eyes would pop, and jaws would drop. For nerds and outcasts everywhere, the amazing song "At Seventeen" summed up our lonely and hopeless childhood years. I sang along to it myself during numerous dateless nights in high school.

When I was editing my second Blood Lite anthology, Overbite, *I had an idea for a story about desperate fans so in love with a deceased one-hit-wonder singer that they raised him from the dead to perform an encore of his one famous song. With Janis's background as a famous musician who had performed before huge crowds, I knew she could help as a coauthor. It took some convincing to assure her that I really did want to write a story with her....*

Through my friendship with Neil Peart, I have seen Rush in concert dozens of times, and while I—as a big fan—love to hear my favorite songs, I wonder how a band can tolerate playing their greatest hits at every show for decades. No matter how wonderful "Tom Sawyer" or "Red Barchetta" might be, what does a person think when performing it for the 5,000th time?

Remember this when you keep playing your Greatest Hits.

Dark Carbuncle
(with Janis Ian)

A graveyard. Night. Lurid branches scrabble across the blood-red moon. Silence, whispers, then a hush of anticipation. Fifteen boom boxes encircle a grave. Giant woofers (removed just that morning from an unsuspecting car) sit with bass ends flat against the massive gravestone.

> **Here at peace at last lies Thor**
> **Troubled by the Dark no more**

The four aging fans in attendance for the midnight show—the ritual—had polished their studs, mangled their hair, added dye where needed and bleach where not. They wore their finest black leather, but left the jackets open to expose too-small T-shirts from concerts past, fabric memories that paid homage to their hero's mind-blowing shows, when he'd been alive. *Thor.* The writer of the greatest song in the history of mankind.

"Man, we really should have put a line from 'Dark Carbuncle' on his tombstone instead," Conk said. "I mean, so everybody could see his genius for all eternity." His given name was William, and he went by the handle of "William the Conqueror" from some impressive historical guy, though most of his friends didn't get it. They thought "Conk" just meant he liked to bash things.

"Anybody can hear his *genius* just by playing the song, shithead," said Kutfist, ending with the sharp sneer he'd practiced all week. "Trust me, we didn't want to deal with the rights issues."

"Yeah, but dude, 'Dark Carbuncle' is an awesome song, right?" said Dredd, and though he'd said it many times before, nobody disagreed. Especially not on this night of nights.

The lone girl in the group, swaying to the music of a silent song, twisted a lock of hair around her finger. "Kinda creepy, ya think?" Despite the spider web tattooed on her chin, Longshanks was always the first to back away from anything remotely disturbing. "I mean, we're *raising him from the dead....*" Her voice trailed off.

"God, lighten up, 'Shanks. You've been this way since grade school. What can he do to us? He'll be in our power." Sneering, Kutfist turned toward the others with a shrug. Women. Jeez.

"Yeah, and 'Dark Carbuncle' is such an awesome song ..." Dredd's usual sentence trailed off as a cloud covered the moon.

"It has to be tonight, on the anniversary," said Conk with finality as he connected the last of the speakers. The Wikipedia entry had been very specific on that point.

Kutfist scanned the graveyard in disappointment. "I can't believe we're the only ones here. Elvis gets *tons* of fans on his Death Day every year!"

"Elvis fans don't know that 'Dark Carbuncle' is an awesome song," Dredd assured him. "Or they'd be here."

Longshanks tugged harder on her hair. "And what's he gonna look like with a fractured skull, Kut? I mean, part of his head might be gone. *Ecchhh.*"

Kutfist pushed his trifocals further up his nose. "Shut up, 'Shanks. The man was a *god*. That last show we saw was *unbelievably amazing*. He'd never have killed himself, never. We can finally find out the truth now, so just stop worrying and shut up."

Nodding, Conk stood up. Brushing leaves off his hands, he pulled a few folded sheets from the back pocket of his jeans and handed them each a paper with the lyric printed backwards phonetically. That was the worrisome part. They knew the lyrics forward well enough to sing them the required seven times, but the backwards part made Conk nervous. "We've gotta get it right, or we'll end up raising Frank Sinatra or something. Seriously, you can't be too careful with the Dark Side. Don't screw it up."

With tears in his eyes and excitement in his heart, he reached down to the nearest boom box and pushed PLAY.

Thor opened what was left of his eyes and knew he wasn't in the Ritz. It had been a long time since he'd stayed in high-class hotels on tour, and now suddenly he experienced a flashback rush of the last images he remembered.

A motel room, after the show, his ears still ringing from feedback and amps turned up to eleven. Used to be his ears would ring from the screaming fans ... used to be all-night parties, used to be groupies and sex—but the groupies were not as attractive now, and Viagra could only do so much. Ditto the gigs, no more backstage excitement when Mick visited, no more telling the roadie to bring the chick from row five back to the luxe hotel. Now, a gig was just a gig, something to get through until he figured out what to do with the rest of his life.

He hadn't slept a full night in months—years—and now somebody was playing that damned song so loud it echoed right through the walls of this fleabag purgatory of a room. Where the hell was this?

Thorton Velbiss—Thorny to his friends (not many of those), Thor to his fans (not many of those either)—was not having a good day. First, that pounding bass drum was unacceptable. The only noise he wanted to hear with this kind of hangover was the sound of vodka over ice. Second, his fucking hit record from two decades ago was playing, with the bass booming so wide he could swear the damned thing was sitting on his face. The only time Thor would tolerate listening to "Dark Carbuncle" was on stage, during a show, when he lip-synched his way through it for an audience of haphazardly fat metalheads bent on reliving their youth.

I was ferocious back then, ya know? Really fero. And taller, I think. Maybe just skinny. Now I have to wear a corset. Still, I had a hell of a good run. Just one hit, but it kept me in chicks and booze....

Fuck, no, it's a horrible song. Piece of shit me and Dirk the Drummer whipped up one night while we were wanking off. Farthest wank got to title the song. He won.

I hate that fucking song.

'Sides, I can't hit that high note, never could. Brought a ringer into the studio, never thought it'd be a hit. We had great shit on the album, great shit ... and all anybody ever wants to hear is "Dark dark dark. Dark dark dark. Dark dark dark, I'm a da-da-da-da-carbuncle."

Makes you want to puke.

Gotta lip-synch it now anyway, can't even hit the low notes. At least I remember the words. Stupid effing words—even I don't know what they mean. Last time I saw the big El, Scotty Moore had to hand him the lyrics to "Love Me Tender." Speaking of hand ... Hand me that vodka, wouldya?

He'd forgotten there wasn't anybody here. What the hell, he'd serve himself.

He'd been an altar boy in his youth, a good little Catholic, though that was part of his own secret past. The headbangers would never understand it. He hadn't prayed in ... what? Thirty years? Not since he'd picked up a Les Paul, plugged it in, and let wail.

Now, as he felt around for the bottle, trying to shake the cobwebs out of his head, he wondered who'd have the nerve to play that scrotum of a song right on top of his room. *Boom boom boom.* Trying to shut out the sound, he drifted back to the last gig.

It was like reliving a nightmare over and over again, singing that song every night. His agent said this tour could maybe revive his career (but then, he always said that)—opening for some fifteen-year-old one-hit wonder. At least if there was any justice in the world, it *should* have been one hit, but the kid was coming off his fourth top ten record. Turned out he was a metal fan, though, and loved "Dark Carbuncle" (and wasn't *that* embarrassing) and demanded Thor as his opener (though what his Top 40 demographic would make of it, only God knew).

Thor had checked into the motel under a fake name, just in case anybody noticed. Grabbed a quick nap (not that the fans needed to know about that either!), packed his crotch, hit the lobby. Out by the kid's tour bus, a few rabid Thor fans began jumping up and down, one paunchy guy with dreadlocks yelling "Dude! Dude! 'Dark Carbuncle' is an awesome song!" Thor stopped to see if they wanted autographs and noticed two wore pizza delivery uniforms.

"How should I make this out?" he asked a girl with a weird chin tattoo. Glancing at her nametag, he hazarded a guess. "To Tiffany?"

The girl went beet red. "Uh, no, *Longshanks*—just make it to Longshanks."

He smiled inwardly, but outwardly gave her the long, slow, *I could change your life, babe!* look. She brightened and giggled at her friends. At least he'd made *somebody's* day.

On to the show, which sucked. Of course. How the hell can anyone play music at two in the afternoon, under a wide-open sky, looking out at a bunch of hayseeds whose big weekend excitement was probably going to be the pig race? Real waste of Oreos, that one. He sped through the set, not even bothering with the pyro at the end, sneering when people applauded the opening chords of "Carbuncle." Idiots.

I used to dream about being a Beatle, you know? Back in the day, I played the Garden. Twice. Well, only once as the lead act, but still. Alice Cooper, Ozzie, Rob Zombie, they had nothing on me. Eating a live bat, hell—I used to shove worms up my nose, just to line the coke! Now look at me ... playing some friggin' rodeo for a hundred bucks. Pathetic, that's what it is.

Why couldn't I have died young, in a private plane crash? At least that would be a respectable ending.

Afterward, back at the motel—still daylight out!—he drank

most of the quart of Stoli that Mr. Four-Hit-Wonderkid had nervously presented him at sound check. Scratching at his empty stomach, Thor decided to surf the vending machines for dinner. Peanut butter cups and a vodka chaser, the perfect road meal.

He barely registered the Muzak droning through the elevator speakers, until he caught himself humming along. Son of a bitch! Bland whiter-than-white harmonies accompanied by easy-listening strings. *Dark dark dark. Dark dark dark. I'm a da-da-da-da-carbuncle, hiding in the dark.* Unbelievable. His song. That frigging publisher had sold him out, turned him into effing elevator music, music for supermarkets and dentist's chairs. Fucking asshole. And his agent was probably in on it, too. Scum, they were all scum.

He'd show them. If he couldn't die young, at least he could die tragic. "Dark Carbuncle" as elevator music—the last straw of all last straws.

Thor stormed back to his room and grabbed the .38 he always carried. Flopping backwards on the bed, he spun the cylinder—five bullets, one empty chamber. Go out like a man, yeah, playing Russian Roulette. They'd all be sorry then, even those stupid pizza-parlor rejects. Barrel to the head, *click click* and it's over. Jimi, Kurt, make way for the next dead rock legend.

Thor raised the gun. Winced at the cold feel of metal against skin. Paused. Squeezed.

Click.

Click? A barrel loaded with Super-X 500 hollow points, and all it can do is go *click?* Unbe-fucking-lievable.

He tried again.

Click.

Hell, how could you *lose* at Russian Roulette? He hurled the gun across the room, where it skittered to a halt on the bathroom floor. Throwing his legs over the bed, Thor grabbed the vodka, took a long slow drag, and made his way to the bathroom, where he somehow managed to drop the bottle on his toe. Yelling out loud, he jumped—and landed barefooted on the gun, which spun crazily against the tiles while he fell backward.

Sickening crack of his head against the tub. He lay on the cold, hard floor, feeling his life ebb away. Frigging humiliating way to die ... for both a former choirboy and a former rock star.

On the other hand, maybe God wouldn't consider this a suicide. Good news. His last thought was that he'd finally be able to get some effing sleep. Safe in the arms of the afterlife.

Until some fuckheads called him back for an encore....

Graveyard, night, big speakers booming, a familiar chorus sung again and again with enthusiasm, if not harmony.

Mmm, I ain't no spoonful
Baby I'm a mouth-full
and I'm gonna tumble,
rumble crumble tumble
your Dark Carbuncle
Dark Carbuncle

Conk, Kutfist, Longshanks, and Dredd sang the beloved words seven times seven (almost as many times as in the actual song), and three times more backward, until they were hoarse with it. Conk finally signaled the end of the ritual by switching off the boom boxes. They reeled in the sudden hush, breathing heavily.

"How long is it supposed to take?" Longshanks whispered.

"Give him a few minutes." Conk tried not to sound uncertain. The Wikipedia entry had been unclear on that point. "He's coming all the way back from the dead."

Kutfist sneered. "He never started the concerts on time either."

"Yeah, I loved waiting for 'Dark Carbuncle.' What an awesome song," said Dredd. No one disagreed.

Suddenly, the earth began to tremble, and something stirred beneath the leaves. The ostentatious tombstone they'd banded together and paid for all those years ago pulled loose and tumbled backwards, leaving a gaping hole.

Five grime-encrusted fingers pushed through the soil, followed by a hand, then another, clawing at the dirt in slow motion. Finally, a body heaved itself out of the grave. Covered in dirt, putrid clothes, and rotting skin, Thor raised himself up and tried to wipe the crust from his eyes.

The four fans cheered, whistled, and applauded as he swayed. "Omigod, it's him, it's really him!" Conk dropped the papers and stared. What a Wiki entry *this* would make!

Longshanks was jumping up and down. "He looks just like he did on the *Avenger's Revenge* tour!"

"He's staggering like he did on that tour, too," Kutfist said, without the sneer this time. He looked nervously around. "C'mon, gotta get him to the van."

The undead rock star lurched and shambled, looking disoriented but not entirely out of character. "Come on, Thor!" Longshanks pleaded. She lifted up her T-shirt to flash her breasts; Thor had never noticed her when she'd done it at concerts, but this time he shuffled toward her, making moaning, sucking sounds from deep in his throat.

"Hurry up, get him into the van!" Conk said in an urgent whisper. "Before some other fans show up. He's ours!"

"Wait! We can't leave the speakers—I borrowed them from my uncle's catering company," Kutfist said. "He's got a Bar Mitzvah tomorrow, he'll kill me!" Fortunately, since Thor was having a hard time orienting himself toward a vertical life, they had plenty of time to retrieve the gear and pack it into the pizza van they'd "borrowed" from work.

Conk started the engine while Kutfist and Dredd turned in their seats to stare at Thor, who was crammed into the third-row seat with Longshanks. "Now he's with his true fans!" She sniffed, then frowned. "Is he supposed to smell this bad?"

"I think that's just an old pizza I forgot to deliver last week," Conk said.

As the van careened out of the cemetery, Dredd leaned over the seat and said earnestly, "Dude, 'Dark Carbuncle' is an awesome song!" He extended his hand, then thought better of it and withdrew.

They jabbered excitedly as they headed off to Conk's garage. "I'm gonna have him teach me guitar. We could do some killer riffs together!"

"I want him to sign some autographs—impress my girlfriend for sure," Kutfist said. "Hmm, maybe even sell them online."

Longshanks tentatively nudged one of the scraps dangling off Thor's ruined face. "Hey, we could sell pieces of his skin. Talk about a real collector's item!"

Kutfist returned to the sneer. "What are you thinking? Anybody who'd buy Thor's skin could clone him—then we won't have the only one."

Longshanks dropped her gaze. "Well, we'd still have the original. A clone is no better than ... a cover band."

"How about we just sell locks of hair?" Conk suggested. He didn't want them to argue during this ultimate moment of fannish glory.

As the van pulled up to the two-car garage, the undead legend seemed to be getting his bearings, croaking slightly more comprehensible words. "What ... happened? Where am I?"

"You're with us—your real fans!"

Parking in the dark garage, they opened the doors and helped Thor out of the van. Conk hit the button and closed the garage door, then triumphantly switched on the lights to reveal the setup waiting for them in the other parking space—a small stage, microphone, boom box, and guitar.

Herding Thor forward, Kutfist shouted, "We brought you back from the grave for this, dude!"

Thor automatically stepped onto the stage and into the light, then stared at them in confusion. Longshanks sprang onto the stage beside him and shoved the guitar into his hands. "Omigod, Thor—now you can sing 'Dark Carbuncle' for us, night after night after night!"

Thorton Velbiss fell to his knees and screamed.

Surely this was Hell. Surely.

When he'd emerged from the darkness, he'd wondered what the fuck was going on. Why was he covered in dirt? Some super-extravagant part of the stage show he couldn't recall?

Then he remembered, and now he knew exactly what had happened. This was truly eternal punishment. Every bit of his Catholic upbringing rose in his throat—the priests' lectures, the nuns' scoldings, the fear of damnation. It was too much for any man, let alone a dead one.

Rotting ligaments snapped as he dropped to his knees and began to cry. For the first time in years he prayed, and for the first time in his life he really meant it. He confessed, he repented, he begged forgiveness. He reminded God of his years as an altar boy, how he'd been in the soprano choir until his voice had changed. He also pointed out that, technically—though God seemed to have overlooked the detail—he hadn't committed suicide and didn't deserve damnation. It was merely an unfortunate accident.

"Just please get me out of here! I want to go to Heaven. I'll do whatever you say, you won't regret it! Please!" He put more soul into the request than he'd ever spent on one of his stage performances, but even Thor was surprised when the cluttered garage and tiny group of fans swirled away into mist.

The new place was bright and shining, filled with sunlight and rainbows. He saw smiling beings in white robes with wings gathered on a nearby cloud, and an impressive, bearded man on a gleaming golden throne in front of him.

Holy shit, exactly the pictures the priests had painted, down to the last cliché! Choking back tears, Thor knelt before Him.

"Welcome Thorton Velbiss, my wayward son." The Almighty smiled with a warmth that made Thor tremble. "I am so glad you are finally among us. We have prepared a heavenly reception for you."

Thor could only stammer, "Thank you, thank you, Lord!" He didn't know what else to say. Everything was so ... clean. So ... cheerful.

"Rise, my son. Rise, and greet your Father."

Thor rose and moved toward the throne.

"Later, there will be manna, and angel food cake," God promised, patting him on the shoulder. "But first, I have a small request."

God seemed almost shy as he said it, and Thor thought *I could really like this guy.* "Anything, Your Omnipotence. *Um,* Your Magnificence. Anything you want, just name it!"

Taking him by both shoulders, the Lord turned him toward the nearby cloud, where the choir of angels suddenly pulled back their wings, revealing the electric guitars they wore. One sat behind a drum kit.

Snapping His fingers, God materialized a 1959 custom Les Paul and held it out to Thor. "Play 'Dark Carbuncle' for us, my son. I have always loved that song."

Thor fell to his knees, screaming.

The isolated starkness of the desert seems to be in my blood, and I've drawn upon my many hiking experiences in Death Valley, Arizona, and Utah for several stories.

I was enlisted, along with several other writers, by the production staff of a Canadian animated television series to write a story based on the manifestations of primal beliefs, especially indigenous legends. With their broad and general guidelines, any imaginative writer could tell an interesting story.

For many years, I made an annual pilgrimage to hike and write in the desolate canyons and the expansive desert. The stark emptiness of the place, as well as the spooky history of the native Shoshone people, seemed just the right ingredients for this assignment. Those experiences seeped into my writing.

I actually dictated this story into my recorder while driving across the Mojave Desert on my way to Joshua Tree National Monument. I finished the draft on the drive, and that night, after I checked into a fleabag motel, I transcribed it into my laptop as I sat at the rickety laminate desk.

It all adds to the veracity of the story.

Bad Water

With the ease of an expert in the ways of the desert, he found a path down out of the rugged mountains the white men called the Panamints. He saw the huge, sparkling white basin of salt and poisonous chemicals. It was a bad place, even though it sparkled white, like the snow that dusted the tops of the mountains once or twice a year. This was not snow, but alkaline crystals puddled with water that bubbled up from underground, terrible to drink ... inciting madness.

Any wise person knew not to come here, but not all men were wise, and he came to look upon the strangers and fools.

He had taken the name of Kit Fox, though it was not the original name the Panamint Shoshoni had given him. Some of his people called him arrogant, but he didn't need them. He had learned well what the Earth had taught him. He knew how to make his way through canyons, how to find private springs, even when the valley seemed filled with nothing but death. Like his namesake, he could hunt, catch lizards or round-tail squirrels; he could gather and grind mesquite seedpods. He could be self-sufficient, and if that made him "arrogant," then his people simply used a poor choice of words.

No matter what Kit Fox thought of the stodgy and

unimaginative Shoshoni, however, at least they were not ridiculous. As he came down into the powdery white basin, he looked upon the fools out there. The white men. They never failed to amaze him with their outlandish ideas and stupid practices.

They had built a camp not far from the edge of the long-dead sea, dozens of men in their hot tents pitched far from the nearest drinkable water at the oasis their people had named Furnace Creek. And worse than their absurd settlement were their giant machines that belched smoke and steam, bubbling up foul-smelling chemical vapors from vats and boilers that cooked down the caked, powdery borax residue scraped from the lake bed. What were these fools thinking?

The white men had come from faraway lands, with their strange culture and impractical dress. They did not belong here—as the desert often harshly reminded them by killing entire groups of wayward and unprepared pioneers, or idealistic treasure seekers looking for a shortcut to the gold fields in California, or merely settlers duped by a promise of paradise just on the other side of the mountains. Kit Fox knew this land: Mother Desert was a stern parent, but fair to anyone who followed the rules of survival. The white men did not take time to learn; they tried to change the land to fit their needs, rather than vice versa.

The men wore heavy, dark clothes, broad-brimmed hats, and thick beards that made them look like animals. And they treated some of their workers as animals, too—smaller people with dark hair and a different yet equally strange style of clothing. Kit Fox had heard that these others were called Chinamen, that they came from even farther away than the white men did. They had come out to the alkaline desert to work all day long in the impossible sun, shoveling the white powder from the ground, building up "haystacks" of borax for the chemical works.

When converted and condensed, the borax was packed into iron-rimmed barrels and stacked high; the loads were so enormous that they required numerous beasts of burden, as many as twenty-mule teams, to haul them over the Panamint Mountains. Why did the white men want the poisonous powder? For what purpose? Maybe they should scrape away all the alkaline salts and make the bad-water lake into fresh water again!

Kit Fox decided to go back and visit his people after all, if only to tell them of the laughable things he had seen. Many of the Shoshoni might not believe him, but he hoped they would come and see for themselves before the desert killed these dirt-scrapers, ruined their camp, and frightened these people away forever. Someday, the Shoshoni would tell stories about the white men who had ventured where they didn't belong and perished.

He kept to cover, camouflaging himself in the land. As he watched their activities, he laughed silently to himself, wishing they would know that he was having a joke at their expense.

Kit Fox found a shaded spot and waited until nightfall. Under full dark, with just a fingernail of moon, he would leave some sort of sign to show them that he was there. It would be just one more thing about the desert they did not understand....

The bearded men had their own tents, with bright yellow lanterns and boisterous conversations as they played card games. The larger group of Chinamen was separate, quieter, and the men sat alone with their thoughts instead of raucous games and liquor.

Moving as quiet as a shadow—even though these invaders seemed deaf to the natural world—he completed his task just outside the range of their lantern light. He heard their conversations, their guttural words like rocks clashing together, but he scampered about, gathering stones of his own, laying out a pattern on the parched pale ground, a mocking symbol in his own language. They would never understand it, but the curse was there nevertheless. They would find the sign, wonder what it meant, but Kit Fox knew. And the Earth knew. Before he headed away, he took time to piss on the edge of their camp, then, grinning, he bounded away.

As he moved back to the dry lake bed, Kit Fox saw a silhouette of a lone Chinaman at the edge of one of the shallow seep pools that dotted the surface of the basin; he was smoking a long pipe. Intrigued, Kit Fox crept closer, moving with all the silence of his desert skill. Maybe he could sneak up on this stranger from behind, show him that there were people who belonged in this landscape, and yet the Chinaman lifted a hand in greeting, without turning, even though he couldn't possibly have seen or heard his approach. Kit Fox hesitated but did not want to give the impression he was afraid.

He barely knew any words of the white men's language, and he understood that the Chinamen spoke an even more alien tongue. But the stranger offered the pipe—communicating in a language that everyone could understand.

Kit Fox sat next to the stranger, and they both looked at the smooth mercurial pool of alkaline water that had puddled among the hard, white salt. The man looked dry and haggard, overworked, barely a ghost of a human being. With a start, Kit Fox realized he was still a young man—they were almost the same age!

The Chinaman showed him how to smoke the unusual device, and Kit Fox took the pipe and inhaled. He had never tasted such strange fumes before; the smoke made his eyes and his nose sting, and his thoughts went dizzy. Had the Chinaman scraped up some other alien chemical from the desert? He saw what looked like a hard, white ball in the bowl of the pipe.

Kit Fox gathered his courage and demanded, "Why do the white men take all this useless powder?" He picked up a handful of the crumbling borax. He knew this stranger did not speak the Shoshoni language, but he could not ask the question in any other way. "You don't understand how to live in the desert! This place will kill you."

As if he had understood perfectly, the Chinaman shook his head.

"And why would *you* come here? Are you being enslaved? Why would you come here willingly?"

The Chinaman took another draw on his strange pipe and handed it back to Kit Fox, then he picked up a pebble from the ground, considered it in his palm, and gently tossed it so that it struck the mirror-smooth pool. Ripples radiated outward, leaving in the wake ... *images*.

Kit Fox saw steep hills, green valleys, a land unlike anything he had ever imagined. Was this the Chinaman's home? Then the pool showed crowded villages, skeletal people, starving families, excruciating poverty—a concept that he didn't understand, even after a lifetime of accepting the austere bounty of what the desert gave him. Kit Fox felt a tug of the man's responsibility for a large family, the aching hope that by going away to this far-off land in this harsh desert to work with these white men in the borax fields would stop the suffering back home. Kit Fox had never imagined that the Chinamen might have come *here* because what remained for them *there* was even worse!

"The white men should go away. They should not be here. They are fools to dig the poison from the dirt. You should leave them—soon they will all die. You are wasting your time. Go back to your family."

The Chinaman shook his head again, either refusing to go home to his family, or refusing to believe Kit Fox's conjecture. He seemed to accept the inevitability of what the white men were doing, taking part because it helped him to survive, not because he supported it. How strange! Kit Fox remembered his old grandfather once shaking his head at the boy's intractability. "If rocks fell and an avalanche came toward you, you would be too stubborn to get out of its path!"

The Chinaman seemed to understand something he didn't. He waited for Kit Fox to inhale again from the pipe, then he tossed a second pebble into the pool.

The ripples created a new set of images, the first showing the loud and smelly borax works here, then a larger encampment by Furnace Creek, the mule teams hauling loads of borax on rutted paths that became wide roads and then paved roads. The white men didn't just come to the desert—they were *everywhere*. Camps became villages, villages became towns, towns grew into great and crowded cities with tall buildings made of glass and stone and metal, stretching higher than the mountains. Their behavior remained foolish and incomprehensible.

Kit Fox had seen the white men as unprepared, with foolish and silly ways that did not respect the earth. And yet instead of being squashed by nature, as would have been right, these visions showed them *thriving*, ascendant.

It was impossible! Kit Fox understood the smallest secrets of the desert, and yet when he heard guffaws and conversation from the lantern-lit camp tents as the bearded men continued their card games, he felt that these people were now laughing at *him*.

In the night shadows by the edge of the pool, the Chinaman sat there with his pipe and a faint smile of resignation, not horror at the nightmares he had revealed ... simply acceptance of the way the world changed, rising and falling.

Kit Fox lurched to his feet and felt as if he were floating, dizzy. He broke off a large, sharp-edged hunk of dry salt, squeezing so tightly that it bit blood from his fingers. He wanted to destroy the images, and therefore destroy that future. It was a bad omen, a bad dream. Maybe he was smoking some poisoned chemical, and he was succumbing to madness.

He hurled the chunk into the pool, eager to shatter what he saw. But the images remained undisturbed. Instead of a splash in the shallow puddle, he felt the ground crumbling beneath him. Kit Fox swayed but could not get his balance. His head and his body weren't right—and he fell into the pool.

But it wasn't just a sheen of standing water. He found himself drowning in it. He flailed and splashed, but the liquid pulled him down, feeling oily and cold. This was impossible! These pools weren't deep.

Kit Fox did not know how to swim—why would anyone who eked out a living in the desert know how to *swim*? But no matter how much he struggled, he knew it wasn't the bad water killing

Kevin J. Anderson

him; it was the implacable future. He tasted the chemical water filling his mouth and lungs, and his eyes burned from it. But what he could not survive was the progress of industry, civilization, population growth, technology. Though Kit Fox struggled with all his might, he would be suffocated in the undeniable reality.

He coughed and choked, and as he went under again for what he knew to be the last time, Kit Fox saw the Chinaman sitting on the shore, much too far away, smoking his pipe.

Another short thriller that I published in The Horror Show *magazine—a quick read, a little sexy, and with a nice surprise. Decades after this was published, I took a Flash Fiction class for my MFA, and I submitted it as a class assignment. Apparently, the work still held up.*

Notches

"What are all these notches for?" The young man fingered one of the thirteen marks carved in the wooden bedpost. He stretched, but clutched the sheet, shyly hiding his nakedness. The smell of sweat and sex hung in the air. The house was silent in the afternoon, a private time when they could slip away, when she could teach him the things he had imagined, even obsessed about, but never known. He lay flushed, embarrassed, still not sure of his prowess, but with a puppy-dog expression on his face.

"I think you know what they're for." The war widow looked at him with a slight smile that was hard as cement. Parchment-colored light seeped through the drawn shades. She sat naked on the corner of the bed, smoking a cigarette. She was ten years older, much more experienced, lonely and broken since the death of her husband ... but not without options. Not in this town.

The young man grinned stupidly and, trying to seem more worldly than he was, fumbled with the pack on the nightstand, lighting up a cigarette of his own. He clearly wasn't a smoker. He was still trying to impress her, holding the cigarette in his fingers as he had seen actors do on TV. She waited, knowing it would be only a moment before he started to cough and choke on the smoke. She was right.

The young man had been timid, overeager, terrified and

clumsy, giving her no pleasure at all. He had stared at her body in awe, the curve of her breasts, the pale skin, but she had needed to be proactive, to take this shy boy's hands and show him what to do. A novice, a fool, a disappointment ... Did he even know what harm a person like him could cause?

She drew in another lungful of smoke. For long months she had mourned the death of her husband over on a harsh desert battlefield, killed by an inexperienced American soldier too frightened to know the difference between enemy and ally. Oh, she had loved him, and he had been the perfect lover for her, passionate, skilled, attending to every detail like an expert.

And he had come home in a box.

But she was young, attractive, golden-haired. She missed her husband's touch, his kisses, his hard body, but memories did not satisfy her appetite. She had bounced back with a vengeance, and word passed through the grapevine with astonishing speed, alerting young inexperienced men of her willingness to help them into manhood.

He seemed fascinated by the notches in the wooden bedpost. "Are you going to make a notch for me? Number fourteen?" he asked timidly. Sweat plastered his hair against his freckled face.

She slithered across the bed, sliding against him again. "And where would you like me to put it?" She leaned over him to reach the nightstand. She reached into the drawer with all the paraphernalia she needed for her liaisons and removed a long-bladed jack-knife. She could see his nostrils flaring as the sluggish air of the bedroom drifted her body's musk toward him. With her red-painted fingernail, she flicked open the knife.

"Right here." He traced a line on the bedpost with his fingertip, then lay back languidly on the damp sheets, watching her. His pants, his shirt, his belt lay pooled on the floor.

She held the long knife and looked at him.

Young, inexperienced, frightened, clumsy men. The type that had killed her husband. Friendly fire. Frightened amateurs.

On the bed, he turned away from her, reaching for his pants and belt lying at the side of her bed.

Now her pulse raced more than when the young man had actually been inside her, groping, proving his dangerous clumsiness. Just like the others. She figured twenty of them would give her sufficient vengeance. The other thirteen lay outside, buried deep in the empty lot where they would never be found.

As he reached down to the side of the bed, innocent and unaware, she moved. With a quick flick of her wrist, she thrust the knife at him, the long steel blade aimed for his smooth back, the kidney, for a swift killing blow.

But he was already moving, bringing up the sweat-damp sheets like a net, swooping the fabric and tangling her arm. When he brought her forearm viciously down on his knee, a muffled crack signaled the snapped bones of her wrist. The jackknife fell silently to the mattress. Her mouth made an outraged "O," shocked even as the pain rushed to her face. It was his turn to smile coldly at her.

She couldn't recover quickly enough, lifting her useless broken arm to fend him off as he lifted his leather belt and encircled her throat, drawing it tight. "Slut! Just like all the others." He gave it a harder yank.

As her eyes bulged, and black speckles appeared in front of her vision, she noticed marks on the leather, up near the belt buckle.

Six notches.

Of all my characters and series, my absolute favorite is Dan Shamble, Zombie P.I. So far, I've written seven novels and many short stories with this wacky and lovable undead detective and his ensemble of oddball friends.

I put the series on hold for a few years after the original publisher dropped it, but the fans kept wanting more, demanding new Dan Shamble adventures. But it just didn't seem viable to publish them myself.

Then everything changed when I decided to put the fan interest to the test—by running my first Kickstarter to see if the readership truly existed. Boy, did it! The Kickstarter campaign funded at more than twenty times what I'd asked for. And a new Dan Shamble novel, Double Booked, was on the way.

As a stretch goal for that Kickstarter campaign, to reward the backers once we reached a certain amount of funding, I promised to write a brand-new, never-before-published Dan Shamble story, just for them. We easily achieved that goal, which resulted in me writing "Bump in the Night." It was later published in Pulphouse magazine, and it is collected here for the first time.

"Bump in the Night" asks the important question—what would scare the actual boogeyman?

Bump in the Night
A Dan Shamble, Zombie P.I. Adventure

—I—

When the Boogeyman—the actual in-the-flesh Boogeyman—comes into the office and says that he's scared, you'd better pay attention. I could tell this wouldn't be a typical case for Chambeaux & Deyer Investigations.

He came through the door with a cold wind and a ripple of dread. Now, when I meet a new person, my usual response is a polite smile and a nod of greeting. This time, as soon as the Boogeyman entered, I felt my skin crawl.

He was gaunt, pale, and hairless. His eyes were sunken into shadowed sockets, his cheeks puckered against his teeth. He looked like a living manifestation of that famous Edvard Munch painting *The Scream*, or maybe a necrotic version of young Macaulay Culkin's horrified gasp in *Home Alone*. He wore a trim black business suit with a narrow black tie, as if he worked for a government agency that was all letters.

"Help me, Mr. Shamble!" he said. His voice was like a hollow wind blowing through an ice cave. "You've got to help me. I'm terrified!"

For the first time in my career, both as a living detective and an undead detective, I was afraid to take the case—and I didn't even know what it was yet.

Sheyenne, my already-drop-dead-gorgeous ghost girlfriend, rose from the reception desk, and her ectoplasmic form shuddered. Her eyes went wide in instinctive surprise.

Robin, my human lawyer partner, stood at the filing cabinets reviewing notes from one of her upcoming litigations. Seeing the visitor, she reacted like someone who had stepped on a rattlesnake while simultaneously biting into too much mustard on a hamburger.

Alvina, my too-cute ten-year-old vampire half-daughter, jumped down from the worktable where she'd been posting SickTok videos and Monstagram images on her social media platforms. The kid is an indefatigable optimist, and she never fails to show her pointy baby fangs in a bright smile. She could be bright and saccharin to the point of causing low blood sugar.

Apparently, she had better defenses against the Boogeyman than I did. "I'm not afraid of anything," she said with a sniff. She came forward to face him. "Hello."

"Boo!" said the stranger.

It was like a panic alarm going off in the offices. I had to brace myself not to bolt and flee. When he saw all of us cringe, the Boogeyman raised his cadaverous hands like white surrender flags. "I'm sorry! I didn't mean to scare you. I meant Boo—that's my name. Short for Boogeyman. I was just saying hello. Wait, let me see if I can turn it down, control it."

He closed his sunken eyes and began to breathe slowly, concentrating. He inhaled through his slitted nostrils, calming himself, counting silently. My pulse wasn't racing, since I don't have a pulse, but I could feel the terror begin to subside.

Gathering our courage, Robin and I stepped forward to greet the prospective new client as Chambeaux & Deyer, shoulder to shoulder. "Professionalism beats panic every time," Robin said.

I cleared my throat. "How can we help you, Mr. Boogeyman?"

"Boo," he said, and we flinched again. "Please call me Boo. I'd like to hire your services. I'm ... afraid."

Robin gestured the Boogeyman into our conference room, and Sheyenne followed with a new client form. Alvina trotted along, as if her very cheerfulness would help us get through the meeting. Robin carried a yellow legal pad and I had my intrepid memory (although we relied on Robin's notes as a backup).

Robin got down to business. "What are you afraid of Mr. ... Boo?"

"The only thing to fear is fear itself," he answered. "And that's a lot to be afraid of—a lot of fear."

After the gaunt man took a seat, Sheyenne offered him water or coffee or an energy drink, but he shook his head. "Nothing with caffeine. It makes me anxious." Boo put his bony elbows on the table and nervously straightened his tie. "I want to go straight. I don't want to scare people anymore, at least not unnecessarily. There are enough things to worry about in the world, and everybody just needs to dial it down a notch." He wiped a hand along his sunken cheek. "I might give myself an ulcer."

"Tell us more about your job," I said. "So I can get a better feel for the parameters of this case."

"My current job, the one I really love, is as an insurance salesman. Life insurance and afterlife insurance, primarily, but I also handle general casualty and property insurance. I want to give people peace of mind, let them know they'll be taken care of, even if the worst happens—and I'm very good at helping them imagine worst-case scenarios." Boo shook his head. "So many things to be afraid of—all the monsters that have returned to the world, all the people who are afraid of the monsters, and then there are lightning strikes, car accidents, falling meteors. I'm an excellent insurance salesman."

He looked at us, and suddenly the back of my mind was crawling with paranoia about all the bad things that could go wrong in everyday life.

"But I want to *ease* people's fears, not increase them," the Boogeyman insisted. "I want to go straight!" He curled his hand into a sinewy cadaverous fist. "But they won't let me out. They say fear itself is the only thing that holds us together."

Robin paused in her note-taking. "Who?"

"My family!" Boo's expression fell into abject dismay, like a kid who had just been told he would never, ever, ever be able to pet a puppy again. "It's a family business."

—II—

We've taken on a lot of unusual clients, no questions asked—and then we start asking a lot of questions in order to round out the case. Sheyenne presented the Boogeyman with all the necessary forms to fill out: personal profile information, confidentiality releases, payment parameters, and a delineation of the services we would be expected to perform.

Robin planned to prepare preemptive restraining orders for the most pernicious members of Boo's family, while I would offer protective services, as needed. I'm a well-preserved zombie of average height; I wear a trademark fedora and a brown sport jacket with stitched-up bullet holes from one of my previous fatal cases. I'm not all that intimidating as a bodyguard. Boo could have hired contract golem security, maybe even a rock demon, but he wanted Dan Shamble, zombie P.I. I guess my reputation preceded me.

Ever since the world-shaking event known as the Big Uneasy occurred thirteen years ago, we had all learned to be afraid of many things: monsters under the bed, hobgoblins in the closet, things that go bump in the night.

But that's just everyday life, and here in the Unnatural Quarter monsters and humans have managed to get along, mostly. Even before the Big Uneasy, back when life was supposedly "normal," people fought constantly, with a plethora of lawsuits and divorces and family feuds. That's what kept my private investigation service and Robin Deyer's legal efforts in business, except instead of representing a couple in a bitter property dispute, we'd now been hired by the Boogeyman, who wanted to extricate himself from his family's expectations.

Boo hunched over the table, reading the fine print on all the forms. He wrote in careful penmanship on every blank line, though he asked to use a felt-tip marker. "It's soft and less hazardous," he explained. "Those pointy ends on pencils or ballpoint pens could poke an eye out."

"I've always been afraid of that," I said. "And running with scissors."

Boo finished the forms, checked them over, made sure all of the *I*s were dotted and the *T*s crossed. Relieved, he looked up at me with a face that only a nightmare could love. "Now we can get down to business."

That was when the absolute fear fest began.

First it came on like a howling, yowling, grumbling, whispering, shrieking thunderstorm that rolled down the halls—and I knew that thunderstorms were definitely not supposed to be inside the halls, particularly not on the second floor.

It sounded like a train wreck of evil cackles bursting through our door. Three separate black whirlwinds, cyclones of smoke and screams, each one capped with a demonic visage of disappointment and wrath. Their horrific faces would have made the Wicked Witch of the West consider an alternate career.

Alvina shrieked in terror, and Sheyenne swelled herself up to place her ectoplasmic form protectively in front of the little vampire girl.

Gooseflesh ran all over my skin. "What are you?" I shouted. I feared I might actually wet my pants for the first time since becoming a zombie.

The three demonic spectres spoke in unison with the voice of a stern teacher assigning detention. "We are your greatest fears. We are your nightmares!"

One drifted forward, her lips stretched over broken teeth. Her eyes blazed red. "We are what our nephew *should* be doing!"

Though scared, Robin was fundamentally unflappable. She seized the half-completed restraining order and flapped it in the face of the horrific spectral women. "I'll file this if you don't leave us alone! I swear I will."

The scary manifestations were not impressed.

Then the Boogeyman came to the rescue. Boo raised himself up, and his gaunt face turned into a shrieking death's-head. His neat *Men In Black* suit rippled out in black tatters like formal attire for the Grim Reaper. Waves and waves of irrational paranoia rippled off of him like an overworked air conditioner unit on a hot, humid day. *"Go away, Aunties!!!"*

Though the command wasn't directed at us, I wanted nothing more than to pack up my fedora, grab Alvina, and run all the way to one coast or the other.

"You, too, Auntie Em!" Boo added to the foremost spectre. "Can't you see I'm busy here?"

The hammer of fear was like a headwind that drove the ghastly women away. They flitted backward out the door, black smoke swirling and entwining like a nightmarish locomotive in reverse. The foremost female figure swelled up in front of the Boogeyman and cackled, "That's my boy. I knew you still had it, dear." She tangled and twisted and whisked her form as she retreated, following the others down the hall.

Boo sat back down, looking rumpled. He straightened his back-to-normal business suit and shook his head. "Do you see what I mean now? They won't let me alone. I can't have a day's peace just to go to my regular office job."

"Who were they?" I asked.

Alvina added, "You called one Auntie Em?"

Boo looked at the little vampire girl. "Em," he said. "Short for Embodiment of Terror."

"I can see why you'd shorten it," I said.

"My three aunts. They want me to carry on the family traditions, but I can't," the Boogeyman said. "I just can't! Now you see why you have to help me?"

"We do." Robin looked grim and determined.

I gathered my courage and placed a firm hand on Boo's forearm. "We'll get you out of this, one way or another."

Boo stayed long enough to provide the details we needed, even the address where the three Unnatural women lived. Robin walked him to the door. "It's a free country. You should choose your own career, even if striking mortal terror is the family business."

"My aunties have high standards, and unrealistic expectations," he said. Looking more relieved than when he had burst into our offices, Boo left humming "The Happy Song" under his breath....

—III—

The cases don't solve themselves. That's my motto.

I needed to get a clue—or several—and I began by wandering the mean streets of the Unnatural Quarter. OK, some of the streets are actually pleasant, but if Boo's aunties got their way, everyone would quiver in terror—in the Arts and Garment district, in the Old Town restaurants and galleries, in the sprawling suburbs where monsters and humans come home after a long work shift.

I tipped my fedora to a mummy matron setting up a dried flower stand. I passed a writers' discussion club at a Talbot & Knowles Blood Bar, where vampires sipped frothy drinks and debated the ideal number of adverbs per paragraph. Four deadbeat zombie teenagers were tossing dice against the brick wall of a dark alley, but they lost the energy and motivation to pick them up and look at the dots.

It was a pleasant, cloudy day with no undue gloom—just the way the Boogeyman wanted the Quarter to be. I was reluctant to get involved in family matters, but we needed to get the nightmarish aunties to back off, not just for our client's peace of mind, but for everybody.

Ahead I saw a beat cop who had waved over a long, old Lincoln sedan. With his ticket book in hand, the policeman leaned into the passenger side window as he lectured the driver, a sweet old spinster. She had hair in a bun, wire-rimmed glasses, a powdered wrinkly face, and a flowered bonnet. When the cop straightened, I recognized my best human friend, Officer Toby McGoohan.

"I can't let you off with a warning this time, ma'am," McGoo said. "Not with all the previous safety citations on your record."

"Please, officer," said the sweet old lady. "It would mean so much to me! Aren't you a good boy?"

"I'm a good *cop*," McGoo said, "and it looks like other cops have been too lenient ten times before. You need to learn how to drive better, if you're going to keep your license, ma'am."

I sauntered up, curious. "Everything all right, McGoo?"

He glanced over at me. "Hey, Shamble. I'm just keeping the peace ... and keeping traffic moving."

"But I was moving!" the old lady insisted. She gripped the wheel as if it were the only thing anchoring her in place. "Ten miles an hour is still moving, and I was being cautious."

"You were moving far below the speed limit, Miss ..." He looked down at the driver's license in his hand. "Miss Flora."

"Floraboding," she said.

The name was suddenly familiar to me. Floraboding, all one word, was the name of one of Boo's aunties, along with Em, for Embodiment of Terror, and Widdershins.

"There's such a thing as exercising a dangerous amount of caution," McGoo said, gesturing to the long Lincoln. "I watched you stop too long at each stop sign. You were going so slowly I caught up to you at a fast walk." McGoo tore off the ticket and handed it to her. "That's what the traffic court calls reckless safety. You make other drivers nervous; you scare pedestrians because you seem to be following them." His exasperated expression became a little more considerate. "Just be a little more considerate, ma'am. Drive faster and more recklessly from now on."

Floraboding frowned like a prune as she tucked the ticket and license back into her purse. Looking closer, I recognized parts of her frightening profile behind the sweet granny facade. "Aren't you one of Boo's aunties?" I asked.

She recoiled in alarm. "Such a good boy. Much too good!" I saw fear wash over her face. "Please don't tell him about the ticket. He can't know."

I saw my chance. "Then perhaps, ma'am, if you simply agree to—"

She pushed the button and rolled up the passenger window, cutting me off. She stomped on the accelerator, and the big Lincoln roared off leaving a rubber track on the street.

McGoo nodded. "That's more like it. People won't be so worried about her abnormal driving." He looped his thumbs into his beltloop, leaned back, and said, "Hey, Shamble, what do you call a monster made entirely out of blood?"

Thinking he had actually encountered such a creature on a case, I fell for it. "What?"

"A hemogoblin!"

I was anxious enough that even the stupid joke gave me a moment of relief.

We watched the Lincoln drive recklessly for a block, then Floraboding halted at a stop sign for so long she could have shifted the vehicle into park. Then she eased forward with immaculate caution.

McGoo shook his head. "Some people never learn."

—IV—

Sometimes you need to confront your fears head on. I did not know that confronting my greatest fears would entail a pleasant conversation in the sitting room with tea and cookies.

Since Boo had given us the address of his three terrifying aunts, that afternoon I dropped in for a surprise visit. I considered taking Robin with me so she could serve legal papers, but that would have made the encounter official, and I've found that an off-the-record conversation can accomplish more than getting lawyers involved—even my own firebrand lawyer partner.

I arrived at their old brick townhouse, a place with a lot of character and high rent. Potted geraniums drank up sunshine on the corners of the porch. A cross-stitched sampler hung on the door, "Home Sweet Home." I rang the doorbell, which buzzed like an electric chair.

A sweet grandmotherly old lady in a flower-print housedress came to greet me. Her gray hair was tied back with a gray ribbon, and she wore lipstick the color of rose petals. She squinted at me. "Hello, dear."

I pulled out my well-worn private investigator license and introduced myself. "Good afternoon, ma'am. I have a few questions on behalf of my client."

A second old lady bustled up to see who was at the door, then a third. I recognized Floraboding in the rear, and one of the other two reminded me of the horrifying face I had seen in our offices, Auntie Em. The third one must be Widdershins.

"We adore company, dear! We'd be happy to answer questions," said Em.

"My client is your nephew, Mr. Boogeyman."

The three old ladies lit up. "Oh, dear Boo! I wish he would come visit us."

"You visited him in our offices ... though in a slightly more menacing form."

"Only slightly?" Widdershins clucked her tongue. "I thought we were quite ghastly."

"We've had a lot of practice," said Floraboding.

Em nodded. "Only because the dear boy won't do his job."

"He has another job," I said. "One that he prefers over the family business."

Auntie Em gestured me inside. "Please, Mister ..." She took another look at my license. "Chambo."

"It's pronounced Chambeaux," I said.

Widdershins touched her ear and leaned forward. "What did he say?"

"Shamble," said Floraboding. "His name is Dan Shamble."

I followed them into the sitting room without continuing the argument.

"I'll put on some water for tea," said Widdershins.

"Good thing we have fresh-baked cookies." Em gave me a grandmotherly smile. "We bake a new batch every afternoon, just in case we have company."

The sitting room had a coffee table, sofa (with protective plastic on the cushions), and three rocking chairs, one for each of the deceptively non-terrifying old ladies. The sofa cushions crinkled when I shifted my butt. A grandfather clock ticked in the corner. The air smelled of mothballs. This was not at all the confrontational confrontation I had anticipated.

"If he's here for dear Boo, we have to be hospitable," said Widdershins.

Floraboding sighed. "I wish that dear boy would visit us himself. It's been ages, and his aunties are so lonely." She spread a doily on the coffee table.

Widdershins brought napkins and cups, and Em came in with the cookies and tea. They all sat down in their respective rocking chairs.

That's when the pleasantness ended.

"I came here in hopes of a peaceful resolution, before we file any ugly legal restraining orders," I said. "Will you please leave your poor nephew alone to live his own life?"

The three old ladies swung their sharp gazes at me like ravens that had just discovered a ripe corpse. "The boy has responsibilities," said Auntie Em. "He doesn't understand what he's doing."

"It's just a phase," said Widdershins.

Floraboding set down her teacup and leaned closer to me. "Think about it, Mr. Shamble. What would the world be like without irrational fears?"

I pursed my lips, considering. "Uh, a better world?"

Em glanced up to the window where the lacy curtains were pulled back to show a small back yard enclosed by a wooden fence. She suddenly sat up straight, and her eyebrows arched in alarm. "There's that pesky black cat again! Why does it keep hanging around here?"

I turned to see a large black cat strolling along the fence, peering into the window. It meowed, as if expecting attention.

Widdershins rose promptly from her rocking chair. "I'll take care of it." When the old lady approached the window, the black cat seemed happy to see her, but she looked flustered and embarrassed.

Auntie Widdershins transformed into a snarling, smoky, evil spirit, a black demonic form. Her eyes blazed, and her mouth dropped open to reveal sharp fangs. Noxious green fumes boiled out of her throat as she roared. "Get away!"

The cat's fur stood on end like a cartoon, and it sprang away with a yowl and vanished in a flash.

Widdershins recomposed herself into a sweet old lady, but I knew what terrors lurked inside her. She brushed down her housedress, flustered. "We mustn't let the neighbor animals get too friendly. We have a reputation to uphold, you know. It doesn't look good."

"It certainly doesn't," said Em in a stern voice.

"Absolutely not." Floraboding furrowed her brows.

I felt sorry for the cat.

Em turned back to me. "As you can see, Mr. Shamble, fear is a powerful thing. It unites people."

"We keep everyone on edge for their own good," said Widdershins, rocking in her chair. "Not just things that go bump in the night, but fears that make your skin crawl."

Em nodded. "Fear keeps everyone alert and wary, so they stay sharp."

"It's definitely not good to let people get too complacent," said Floraboding.

I looked at her, remembering McGoo's traffic ticket for dangerous caution. I wondered if the other two aunties knew how circumspect and safety conscious Floraboding was.

Widdershins got a dark gleam in her eyes, and again the three ladies rounded on me. I could feel the intense emotions boiling in the air.

"Here, let us show you," said Widdershins.

"Before you finish your tea," said Floraboding.

The three transformed into their demonic appearances, black skirling nightmares that filled the quaint sitting room. As I raised my hand trying to fend them off with a cookie, I was suddenly engulfed with pure dread.

I saw pinch-faced, shrewish Rhonda—Alvina's mother, McGoo's ex-wife, and my big-mistake brief lover—barging in to the offices and cooing over Alvina, insisting she had made a mistake and wanting her dear daughter back.

I saw sweet Alvina skipping along the sidewalk, humming to herself—and out of nowhere, a piano dropped from above and smashed on top of her.

Then I saw a nameplate on an expensive wooden desk in a fancy office lined with books and realized one of my other greatest fears: that Robin Deyer had left us to join a large, corporate law firm.

My blood and embalming fluid turned to ice, and I shook my head to get these images away. But more came.

I saw Sheyenne glowing with romantic energy, then flitting away, leaving me behind. She had found her true soulmate in another ghost, and they wafted off together, heading toward the light. "It never would have worked out, Beaux," Sheyenne said, just before she disappeared.

And, perhaps most frightening of all, I saw McGoo standing on a stage, grinning as he held a microphone. He was pursuing a career as a standup comic.

I lurched up from the old ladies' sofa, fighting off these nightmarish visions. I looked down at a big wet stain on my crotch. In the panic, I had spilled my teacup across my lap—I swear it was just tea.

The three aunties returned to their quaint, endearing forms. They sat back in their rocking chairs in unison, lifting their teacups. "You see, everyone needs a good scare, now and then," said Auntie Em. "But our Boo could do so much better."

The other two old ladies nodded as they rocked and sipped. "It's a family tradition," said Widdershins. "Boo needs to face his responsibilities."

"I wish he'd visit," said Floraboding.

I tried to retain my dignity and ignore the wet stain on my

pants as I hurried out of the townhouse. "You will hear from us," I said. These three aunties were going to be tough nuts to crack ... and they were indeed nuts.

—V—

"Maybe we do need some insurance around here, Beaux," Sheyenne said. "For the office, and the business. You never know when something might go wrong."

"Something always goes wrong," I said. "It's one of the things we can count on."

I was a successful zombie private investigator, but we did not have a lot of spare operating cash. Robin was a passionate lawyer with countless cases, but she accepted too many pro bono clients, which kept her heart full and our bank accounts empty.

"How do we afford insurance?" I asked. "We'll just live with the risk."

"We should at least get a quote," she said, making up her mind. "I'm coming along with you to see the Boogeyman."

And that was the real reason. After my horrifying tea-and-cookies encounter with the nightmarish aunties, I needed to learn more about the Boogeyman's perspective. My ghost girlfriend simply wanted to accompany me to Boo's Life and Afterlife Insurance offices, and I didn't mind at all. Whenever my beautiful ghost girlfriend is with me, my confidence increases, and I become a better detective.

Boo's Life and Afterlife Insurance offices were located in an old strip mall next to a pho restaurant, a tanning parlor, and an Egyptian-themed art gallery featuring "Canopic Jars through the Ages."

We found the very tiny business office, just one little desk where Boo served as the main insurance salesman and policy underwriter, as well as receptionist, accountant, and coffee maker. "Gives a whole new meaning to the term 'small business,'" I said to Sheyenne as we stood in the door. Fortunately, her ectoplasmic form takes up little room, and I loomed in the doorway.

Boo sat at his desk across from a pale young human couple who looked nervous and shaky. The Boogeyman saw us and raised a finger. "I'll be with you in a moment, Mr. Chambeaux." Then he turned his full attention to the couple. "Now then, Mr. and Mrs. Vinson, have you given thought to exactly how many terrible things can go wrong every single day? In every corner of your life?

"A meteor could strike while you're out shopping for groceries." He glanced at the sweating, anxious husband. "Why, you could buy a nice bouquet for your lovely wife and hidden in the flowers might be a ... *murder hornet!*" His eyes blazed with the possibilities. "A gas main could explode beneath your house, blowing you all to smithereens. An airplane could crash into the Quarter, wiping out block after block. And you think you're safe at home? You could slip on the wet bathroom floor and fall into a full bathtub—while carrying an electrical appliance!"

"Oh," said the wife. "I hadn't thought of that."

"What if a fire demon moves into the neighboring house and he falls asleep while smoking a cigarette in bed? Or what if a child comes running toward you while holding scissors?"

"So much to worry about," muttered the man.

"And I'm just getting started." Boo calmly pulled out several thick documents. "That's why we have insurance for every imaginable scenario—and I've spent a great deal of time imagining and even creating such scenarios."

"But how much does it cost?" asked the husband.

"You only pay for what you need, Mr. Vinson." Boo's eyes grew brighter as if they had ignited from within. *"And you need everything!"*

Mrs. Vinson reached for the policies. "Where do we sign?"

Boo flipped to the last page of the thick, legal-size documents. "If you can pay a deposit this instant, your coverage begins immediately. Otherwise ..." The Boogeyman shrugged his bony shoulders beneath his black suit. "Who knows what could happen when you step out of the offices. There used to be a blacksmith shop upstairs and occasionally an anvil would fall from above."

Mrs. Vinson dug in her pocketbook. "Do you take personal checks?"

"Why, yes I do."

As the couple furiously signed every paper Boo put in front of them, Mr. Vinson seemed in a panic. His expression fell when he glanced at me in the doorway. "Does this insurance cover zombie attacks?"

"Of course. It covers everything," said the Boogeyman. "Nothing to be afraid of."

Sheyenne and I smiled politely as the young couple fled headlong from the insurance offices.

After the clients were gone, Boo collapsed into a shuddering mass of fear. "It's hard to project professionalism when every moment you expect your life to be torn apart! Please tell me what you've learned so far, Mr. Shamble. Are the aunties going to leave me alone?"

"I've been to see them in person, but I don't think I scared them."

Boo's eyes went wide as I explained my visit to the three aunts. "You're a brave zombie."

"Either that, or reckless," I said. "Em, Floraboding, and Widdershins tried to terrify me—and they succeeded—but zombies are relentless, especially zombie detectives."

"I wish I'd gone with you, Beaux," Sheyenne said. "I could scare them right back."

"They're just lonely," Boo groaned. "And they take it out on everyone else."

"They did mention that you hadn't visited them in ages. They miss you."

"They must have terrified you greatly when you were younger." Sheyenne drifted closer, concerned. "Did they abuse you? Give you nightmares?"

"Worse," Boo said with a groan. "They cuddled me and hugged me and pinched my gaunt cheeks. They showered me with food and love and gifts—and there's only so much a person can bear! They're too sweet ... but only in private."

I recalled the ghoulish spectres that made my skin want to crawl right off my bones. "Too sweet? Not the impression they gave me."

Boo shook his head. "Oh, they wouldn't want anyone to know, because then no one would take them seriously. But when they're around their dear nephew ..." He visibly shivered.

Sheyenne remained perplexed. "But if they're really just softies inside, then why do they want you back on the job to strike mortal terror into everyone?"

"They just want to retire," said the Boogeyman. "They're afraid of not being feared."

As I considered their soft spot, an idea occurred to me. "I might know a way to scare them."

—VI—

Surveillance is one of the best ways to catch a bad guy in the act, or to dig up dirt on a not-so-bad guy. Or just to see what's going on.

In private investigator school, I took a full unit on Furtiveness. I learned a lot, though my grade was only mediocre because I covertly hid my work from the professor.

I couldn't stop thinking about Auntie Floraboding's odd behavior when McGoo had given her a traffic ticket for reckless carefulness. Shouldn't a manifestation of deepest fears, chaos, and mayhem be a little more laissez-faire with safety rules? Having seen the old lady in her most terrifying incarnation, I wondered if she was covering up her real overcautious personality.

Back at the aunties' cozy brick townhouse, I crouched in the neighboring hedges, keeping an eye out for unexpected social activities. I hid in the shadows during daylight, and I huddled in the gloom as darkness set in. It was a stakeout just like in countless movies, though without any buddy cop banter. And it was just as boring.

Finally, the front door opened, and one of the old ladies scuttled out, head down. She wore a dark shawl and a lacy hat pulled down to obscure her face. Though she had covered herself up well, I recognized Auntie Em. After what I had learned in the Furtiveness class, I immediately spotted suspicious behavior.

Em darted forward, crossed the street, then crossed the street again, clearly trying to remain unnoticed, but she didn't elude me. I followed at a safe distance. She could have traveled more swiftly if she manifested her demonic form and swooped like a howling wind through the streets. Instead, the old lady scurried along the sidewalk, moving from one seedy part of the Quarter to an even seedier part. I couldn't imagine what Auntie Em was up to. Off to provoke terror in some unsuspecting homeless camp? Or to startle bar patrons into spilling their beers? Or just to flit past children's windows to give them quick nightmares? Maybe to hide under their bed or in the closet?

No, Em made her way to a soup kitchen—Miss Clara Baxter's Respite for Unfortunate Unnaturals. That was unexpected, and it angered me that the Boogeyman's nefarious auntie would harass these already-suffering monsters. I imagined her swooping in to antagonize them, disrupt the food servers, knock the coffee urns over, and chase the homeless trolls, vampires, and zombies back under their bridges or dilapidated crypts.

I decided to confront Em before she caused too much trouble, but before I could make my move, the old lady entered the soup kitchen, removed her lacy hat, shucked off her shawl, and donned a white apron and gloves.

Amazed and perplexed, I peered through the open door as a werewolf with a sorry case of mange shuffled past me to get a hot meal. Auntie Em stood behind the food line with other volunteers, where she ladled soup and offered plates of bread. She was serving the unfortunate Unnaturals—with a smile!

I took furtive photos of her doing her part, sweet and attentive. I was so confused I tapped the bullet hole in the center of my forehead, but I found no thoughts or explanations there either.

How did this behavior fit with the manifestations of terror those three projected in public? Struggling to fit the pieces of the case together, I made my way back to the brick townhouse, wondering what nefarious, or unspeakably kind, activities the other two were up to.

It was full dark now, and I approached from the side of the building, hoping to glimpse the backyard. I heard someone make cooing noises as I crept up to the fence. A single yard light was on to illuminate the small, enclosed yard, which was only big enough for a few potted plants and a small table. Auntie Widdershins was bending down, whispering and whistling. She extended a saucer of milk across the ground.

The pesky black cat stood on the rear fence, his back arched, his ebony fur full and fluffy. "Here kitty, kitty," said Widdershins.

I wondered if she was luring the poor feral animal close so she could terrify it again. But the cat jumped down, circled just out of reach, then approached the saucer, where he began lapping up the cream. "Good kitty, kitty." The old lady reached out with a gnarled hand.

I was afraid she might strangle the cat or cause him some terrible harm ... but instead she scratched behind his ears, stroked him until he arched his back and then brushed against her leg. Even from my hiding place, I could hear him purr.

The cat swirled around, and Widdershins beamed. "Good kitty. Come back for treats whenever mommy calls you." The cat finished the cream, then bounded onto the fence and vanished off on his own nocturnal feline adventures.

Auntie Widdershins took the empty saucer and hurried back inside, thinking that no one had seen her.

I now had all the leverage necessary to get my client what he wanted.

—VII—

You've seen those old "scary" movies (now viewed as either comedies or documentaries) about rotting, brain-eating zombies terrorizing a town. Sure, under the right circumstances zombies can be terrifying and intimidating—but if I meant to intimidate the Boogeyman's three horrifying aunties, I would confront them with the scariest weapon in our arsenal.

I brought our lawyer.

Now that's intimidating.

Robin Deyer has a knack for making guilty parties cringe and reconsider their bogus pleas when she walks into a courtroom. She's beautiful, professional, and holds all the power because she *knows* she's right and has the passion to prove it to everyone else.

She wore a navy-blue blazer and skirt, white blouse, and carried a briefcase, which seemed as threatening as a mugger's gun. We were going to bring down some fear onto fear itself.

Together, we stepped up to the Home Sweet Home cross-stitched sampler hanging on the door and rang the bell.

Auntie Floraboding answered, glanced at the two of us, and her grandmotherly smile expanded into a more vicious grin. "Back for more, Mr. Shamble? One good scare deserves another."

"I believe we'll be doing the scaring today, Ms. Floraboding," Robin said.

The old lady tittered and let us in. "Delightful!"

While the three aunties bustled around as hostesses, Robin and I went into the sitting room. She set her briefcase on the coffee table, snapped it open, and withdrew a manila folder. When the old ladies sat down in their rocking chairs, she flipped open the folder to reveal papers that looked legal and scary. "This is a cease and desist restraining order, two for the price of one. You are hereby ordered to stop harassing our client."

"We're not harassing him," said Auntie Em. "We're helping him do his job."

"The boy must learn to take responsibility," said Widdershins.

"He's our dear nephew," said Floraboding.

Robin spread the papers on the coffee table, but I knew our real weapons were still in the briefcase. "You are interfering with Mr. Boogeyman's right to the pursuit of life, afterlife, liberty, and happiness."

"You can't threaten us," snapped Floraboding. "We're the most terrifying presences in the Unnatural Quarter."

"But we wouldn't have to be, if Boo would shape up," Em muttered.

"Oh, you'll want to comply," Robin said. "Once this paperwork is filed, it will become a matter of public record ... and we'll include certain documentation that you would not want anyone else to see."

"Documentation of what?" Widdershins asked.

I took my cue and pulled out the next folder. I shared the photos of Widdershins offering a saucer of cream to the black cat, followed by a shot of the cat rubbing against her legs, and, worst of all, Widdershins grinning with love and happiness as she petted him.

"That cat!" Auntie Em said. "You were supposed to scare it away."

"I ... couldn't," Widdershins mumbled.

"You're supposed to be terrifying," Em continued. "What will people think if they see a manifestation of mortal terror coddling an alley cat?"

"Indeed, what will people think?" Robin asked, dripping with sarcasm.

It was Em's turn. I pulled out the photos of her at the soup kitchen sweetly ladling food, helping out unfortunate Unnaturals.

"That's what you do with your evenings, Em?" Floraboding recoiled. "What if someone recognizes you? We'd be ruined! We're supposed to be mayhem and chaos and nightmares."

Before Em could make excuses, I displayed a copy of the traffic citation that McGoo had issued to Floraboding. "And that's a little hard to do when you're one of the safest, most cautious drivers in the entire Unnatural Quarter."

Em snatched the ticket and scanned it, then looked in horror at her sister. "You got a citation for being *too careful?*"

"And a special letter of thanks from the car insurance company," Floraboding said, casting her gaze down. "I don't like to make other drivers worry. I could get in an accident."

"None of this is an accident," I said. "It's all on purpose."

Robin had assured me that blackmail and bluffing was an accepted legal strategy. "The world will know that you're actually just softhearted, sweet little old ladies," she said. "Not frightening at all." Robin snapped shut the briefcase. "And that is just a sample of what we've uncovered. You wouldn't want us to reveal all the other deep, dark secrets we have on you."

"No," Widdershins gasped. "That will ruin our reputations!"

The three aunts sat back in their rocking chairs, looking extremely nervous.

Frowning, I whispered to Robin, "What else do we have on them?"

She lowered her voice. "There's always something. I'm just letting them play on their own fears."

I nodded. "Seems appropriate."

Em picked up the cease and desist restraining order. "Now, now, there's no need for you to file these papers. They haven't been signed or certified yet."

I said, "I came here the other day, hoping you would be reasonable. When that didn't work ... Maybe now you three will do the right thing because you're scared."

Robin said, "This all goes away if you leave Mr. Boogeyman alone, let him live his life, and cut down on the nightmares."

The three aunts rocked silently for a few moments, hanging their heads. They glanced at one another, then in unison let out a sigh. "Very well, if that's what we have to do," said Floraboding.

"But we insist on one thing in return," said Em. "Our boy Boo has to visit sometimes. He can't be a stranger. He needs to see his dear aunties."

Robin stood up, taking her briefcase and all the papers. "I think we can manage that."

—VIII—

The following Sunday, Sheyenne and I went out for a walk with Alvina, enjoying a pleasant few hours together. As we passed the townhouse where the three aunties lived, I was glad we didn't encounter any howling or shrieking or nightmarish activity.

The purring neighbor cat emerged from the bushes for some attention. Alvina bent under a ladder leaned against the building and petted the black cat, with one of her feet firmly placed on a crack in the sidewalk. My half-daughter is definitely fearless.

Sheyenne said, "Look, here comes Boo now. His first Sunday visit."

Striding down the sidewalk, the Boogeyman wore a clean black suit jacket and the same old thin black tie. He held a bouquet of wilted lilies in his hands. His skull-like face was pale as always, and he lowered his sunken eyes, as if nervous or guilty.

As the Boogeyman approached, the black cat hissed, arched his back, and sprang away.

Seeing us, Boo paused, drew a deep breath. "Now I have to face the music." He shuddered, looking at the Home Sweet Home sign on the townhouse door.

"It'll be a nice time," I said.

"It'll be a nightmare. Auntie Em will pinch my cheeks, and Auntie Floraboding will exclaim about how much I've grown, and Auntie Widdershins will insist that I need to eat more." His shoulders slumped, but then he raised his chin, summoning his courage. "But I can face this."

"It won't be so bad," Sheyenne said.

"Oh, it'll be bad, but I can give as good as I get." He spotted the black cat crouched by the corner of the townhouse and said, "Boo!" The cat yowled and bounded away. "I'm the Boogeyman."

He rang the bell as Sheyenne, Alvina, and I kept walking. We glanced behind us to watch the three aunties greeting Boo, hugging him, cooing over him, pinching his cheeks. They dragged him inside where he would have to endure the smothering kindnesses.

"Nothing to be afraid of," Alvina said.

I looked down at the kid. "Oh, there's plenty to be afraid of, but no need to worry about it."

The vampire girl skipped ahead, and I glanced up to make sure no pianos were falling out of the sky. I cocked my fedora and strolled along with my ghost girlfriend at my side. "Nothing to worry about," I said.

I went through a heavy Dracula phase, reading the original Bram Stoker novel (which is really quite good), watching all the movie versions from the silent Nosferatu *to Bela Lugosi, Christopher Lee, Frank Langella, and an excellent but underrated TV version with Jack Palance. That was the first time I saw the Dracula vampire tied to the historical Vlad Dracul, the Impaler.*

As I researched more about the real Dracula, I imagined what a fascinating meeting it would be to team up the historical Vlad the Impaler with Bela Lugosi, the man who made the most famous portrayal of Dracula. When I learned that Lugosi himself was a heroin addict later in his crumbling career, prone to hallucinations, that was the collision idea I needed for the story....

Much at Stake

Bela Lugosi stepped off the movie set, listening to his shoes thump on the papier mâché flagstones of Castle Dracula. He swept his cape behind him, practicing the liquid, spectral movement that always evoked shrieks from his live audiences.

The film's director, Tod Browning, had called an end to shooting for the day after yet another bitter argument with Karl Freund, the cinematographer. The egos of both director and cameraman made for frequent clashes during the intense seven weeks that Universal had allotted for the filming of *Dracula*. They seemed to forget that Lugosi was the star, and he could bring fear to the screen no matter what camera angles Karl Freund used.

With all the klieg lights shut down, the enormous set for Castle Dracula loomed dark and imposing. Universal Studios had never been known for its lavish productions, but they had outdone themselves here. Propmen had found exotic old furniture around Hollywood, and masons built a spooky fireplace big enough for a man to stand in. One of the most creative technicians had spun an eighteen-foot rubber-cement spiderweb from a rotary gun. It now dangled like a net in the dim light of the closed-down set.

On aching legs, Lugosi walked toward his private dressing room. He never spoke much to the others, not his costars, not the director, not the technicians. He had too much difficulty with his

English to enjoy chit-chat, and he had too many troubling thoughts on his mind to seek out company.

Even during his years of portraying Dracula in the stage play, he had never socialized with the others. Perhaps they were afraid of him, seeing what a frightening monster he could become in his role. After 261 sell-out performances on Broadway, then years on the road with the show, he had sequestered himself each time, maintaining the intensity he had built up as Dracula, the prince of evil, drawing on the pain in his own life, the fear he had seen with his own eyes. He projected that fear to the audiences. The men would shiver; the women would cry out and faint and then write him thrilling and suggestive letters. Lugosi embodied fear and danger for them, and he reveled in it. Now he would do the same on the big screen.

He closed the door of the dressing room. All of the others would be going home, or to the studio cafeteria, or to a bar. Only Dwight Frye remained late some nights, practicing his Renfield insanity. Lugosi thought about going home himself, where his third wife would be waiting for him, but the pain in his legs felt like rusty nails, twisting beneath his kneecaps, reminding him of the old injury. The one that had taught him fear.

He sat down on the folding wooden chair—Universal provided nothing better for the actors, not even for the film's star—but Lugosi turned from the mirror and the lights. Somehow, he couldn't bear to look at himself every time he did this.

Inside his personal makeup drawer, he reached up and withdrew the hypodermic needle and his vial of morphine.

The filming of *Dracula* had been long and hard, and he had needed the drug nearly every night. He would have to acquire more soon.

Outside on the set, echoing through the thin walls of his own dressing room, Lugosi could hear Dwight Frye practicing his Renfield cackle. Frye thought his portrayal of the madman would make him a star in front of the American audiences.

But though they screamed and shivered, none of them understood anything about fear. Lugosi had found that he could mumble his lines, wiggle his fingers, and leer once or twice, and the audiences still trembled. They enjoyed it. It was so easy to frighten them.

Before Universal decided to film *Dracula*, the script readers had been very negative, crying that the censors would never pass the movie, that it was too frightening, too horrifying. "This story certainly passes beyond the point of what the average person can stand or cares to stand," one had written.

As if they knew anything about fear! He stared at the needle, sharp and silver, with a flare of yellow reflected from the makeup lights—and Van Helsing thought a wooden stake would be Lugosi's bane! He filled the syringe with morphine. His legs tingled, trembled, aching for the relief the drug would give him. It always did, like Count Dracula consuming fresh blood.

Lugosi pushed the needle into his skin, finding the artery, homing in on the silver point of pain ... and release. He closed his eyes.

In the darkness behind his thoughts, he saw himself as a young lieutenant in the 43rd Royal Hungarian Infantry, fighting in the trenches in the Carpathian Mountains during the Great War. Lugosi had been a young man, frightened, hiding from the bullets but risking his life for his homeland—he had called himself Bela Blasko then, from the Hungarian town of Lugos.

The bullets sang around him in the air, the explosions, the screams. The air smelled thick with blood and sweat and terror. The mountain peaks, backlit at night by orange explosions, looked like the castle spires of some ancient Hungarian fortress, more frightening by far than the crumbling stones and cobwebs the set builders had erected on the studio lot.

Then the enemy bullets had crashed into his thigh, his knee, shattering bone, sending blood spraying into the darkness. He had screamed and fallen, thinking himself dead. The enemy soldiers approached, ready to kill him ... but one of his comrades had dragged him away during the retreat.

Young Lugosi had awakened from his long, warm slumber in the army hospital. The nurses there gave him morphine, day after day, long after the doctors required it—one of the nurses had recognized him from the Hungarian stage, his portrayal of Jesus Christ in the Passion Play. She had given Lugosi all the morphine he wanted. And outside, in a haze of sparkling painlessness, the Great War had continued....

Now, he winced in the dressing room, snapping his eyes open and waiting for the effects of the drug to slide into his mind. Through the thin walls of the dressing room, he could hear Dwight Frye doing Renfield again, *"Heh hee hee hee HEEEEE!"* Lugosi's mind grew muddy; flares of color appeared at the edges.

When the rush from the morphine kicked in, the pleasure detached his mind from the chains of his body. A liquid chill ran down his spine, and he felt suddenly cold.

The makeup lights in his dressing room winked out, plunging him into claustrophobic darkness. He drew a sharp breath that echoed in his head.

Outside, Dwight Frye's laugh changed into the sound of distant, agonized screams.

Blinking and disoriented, he tried to comprehend exactly what had altered around him. As if walking through gelatin, Lugosi shuffled toward the dressing room door and opened it. The morphine made fright and uneasiness drift away from him. He experienced only a melting curiosity to know what had happened, and in his mind, he questioned nothing. His Dracula costume felt alive on him, as if it had become more than just an outfit.

The set for Castle Dracula appeared even more elaborate now, more solid, dirtier. And he saw no end to it, no border where the illusion stopped and the cameras set up, where Karl Freund and Tod Browning would argue over the best way to photograph the action.

The fire in the enormous hearth had burned low, showing only orange embers; sharp smoke drifted into the great room. He smelled old feasts, damp and mildew in the corners, the leavings of animals in the scattered straw on the floor. Torches burned in iron holders on the wall. The cold air raised goosebumps on his morphine-numbed flesh.

The moans and screams continued from outside.

Moving with a careful, driven gait, Lugosi climbed the wide stone staircase, much like the one on which he met Renfield in the film. His shoes made clicking sounds on the flagstones, solid stones now, not mere papier mâché. He listened to the screams. He followed them.

He knew he was no longer in Hollywood.

Reaching the upper level, Lugosi trailed a cold draft to an open balcony that looked down onto a night-shrouded hillside. Stars shone through wisps of high clouds in an otherwise clear sky. Four bonfires raged near clusters of soldiers and drab tents erected at the base of the knoll. Though the stench of rotting flesh reached him at once, it took Lugosi's eyes a moment to adjust from the brightness of the fires to see the figures spread out on the slope.

At first, he thought it was a vineyard, with hundreds of stakes arranged in rows, radiating from concentric circles of other stakes. But one of the "vines" moved, a flailing arm, and the chorus of the moans increased. Suddenly, like a camera coming into focus, Lugosi recognized that the stakes contained human forms impaled on the sharp points. Some of the points were smeared with blood that looked oily black in the darkness; other stakes still shone wicked and white, as if they had been trimmed once again after the victims had been thrust down upon them.

Lugosi gasped, and even the morphine could not numb him to this. Many of the human shapes stirred, waving their arms, clutching the wounds where the stakes protruded through their bodies. They had not been allowed to die quickly.

Dim winged shapes fluttered about the bodies—vultures feasting even at night, so gorged they could barely fly, ignoring the soldiers by the tents and bonfires, ignoring the fact that many of the victims were not even dead. Ravens, nearly invisible in the blackness, walked along the bloodstained ground, pecking at dangling limbs. A group of the soldiers broke out in laughter from some game they played.

Lugosi winced his eyes shut and shivered. Revulsion, confusion, and fear warred within his mind. This must all be some illusion, a twisted nightmare. The morphine had never affected him like this before!

Some of the victims had been hung head down, others sideways, others feet down. The stakes rose to various heights, high and low, as if in a morbid caste system of death. A rushing wail of pain swept along the garden of bloody stakes, sounding like a choir.

From the corridor behind Lugosi, a quiet voice murmured. "Listen to them—like children in the night. Do you enjoy the music they make?" Lugosi whirled and stumbled, slumping against the stone wall; the numbness seemed to put his legs at a greater distance from his body.

Behind him stood a man with huge black eyes that reflected tears in the torchlight. His face appeared beautiful, yet seemed to hide a deep agony, like a doe staring into a broken mirror. Rich brown locks hung curling to his shoulders. He wore a purple embroidered robe lined with spotted fur; some of the spots were long smears of brown, like dried spots of blood wiped from wet blades. His full lips trembled below a long, dark moustache.

"What is this place?" Lugosi croaked, then realized that he had answered automatically in the stranger's own tongue, a language as familiar to Lugosi as his childhood, as most of his life. "You are speaking Hungarian!"

The stranger widened his eyes in indignation. Outside, the chorus of moans grew louder, then quiet, like the swell of the wind. "I speak Hungarian now that I am no longer a prisoner of the Turks. We will obliterate their scourge. I will strike such fear in their hearts that the sultan himself will run cowering back to Constantinople!"

One of the vultures swooped close to the open balcony, and then flew back toward its feeding ground. Startled, Lugosi turned around, then back to face the stranger who had frightened him. "Who are you?" he asked.

The Hungarian words fit so naturally in his mouth again. Lugosi had forced his native language aside to learn English, phonetically at first, delivering his lines with power and menace to

American audiences, though he could not understand a word of what he was saying. Understanding came much later.

The haunted stranger took a hesitant step toward Lugosi. "I am ... Vlad Dracula. I bid you welcome. I have waited for you a long time."

Lugosi lurched back and held his hand up in a warding gesture, as if reenacting the scene when Van Helsing shows him a box containing wolfsbane. From childhood, Lugosi had heard horrible stories of Vlad the Impaler, the real Dracula, rumored to be a vampire himself, known to be a bloodthirsty butcher who had slaughtered hundreds of thousands of Turks—and as many of his own people.

In the torchlit shadows, Vlad Dracula paid no attention to Lugosi's reaction. He walked up beside him and stood on the balcony, curling his hands on the stone half-wall. Gaudy rings adorned each of his fingers.

"I knew you would come," Dracula said. "I have been smoking the opium pipe, a trick I learned during my decade of Turkish captivity. The drug makes my soul rest easier. It makes me open for peace and eases the pain. I thought at such a time you might be more likely to appear."

Vlad Dracula turned and locked eyes with Bela Lugosi. The dark, piercing stare seemed more powerful, more menacing than anything Lugosi had mimed in his performance as the vampire. He could not shirk away. He knew now how the Mina character must feel when he said "Look into my eyes ..."

"What do you want from me?" Lugosi whispered.

Vlad Dracula did not try to touch him, but turned away, speaking toward the countless victims writhing below. "Absolution," he said.

"Absolution!" Lugosi cried. "For this? Who do you think I am?"

"How are you called?" Dracula asked.

Lugosi, disoriented yet accustomed to having his name impress guests, answered, "Bela Lugos—no, I am Bela Blasko of the town of Lugos." He drew himself up, trying to feel imposing in his own Dracula costume, but the enormity of Vlad the Impaler's presence seemed to dwarf any imaginary impressiveness Lugosi could command.

Vlad Dracula appeared troubled. "Bela Blasko—that is an odd name for an angel. Are you perhaps one of my fallen countrymen?"

"An angel?" Lugosi blinked. "I am no angel. I cannot grant you forgiveness. I do not even believe in God." He wished the morphine would wear off. This was growing too strange for him, but as he held his hand on the cold stone of the balcony it felt real to him. Too real. The sharp stakes below would be just as solid, and just as sharp.

He looked down at the ranks of tortured people covering the hillside, and he knew from the legends about the Impaler that this was but a tiny fraction of all the atrocities Vlad Dracula had already done. "Even if I could, I would not grant you absolution for all of this."

Vlad Dracula's eyes became wide, but he shrank away from Lugosi. "But I have built monasteries and churches, restored shrines and made offerings. I have surrounded myself with priests and abbots and bishops and confessors. I have done everything I know how." He gazed at the bloodied stakes but seemed not to see them.

"You killed all these people, and many, many more! What do you expect?" Lugosi felt the fear grow in him again, real fear, as he had experienced that war-torn night in the Carpathian Mountains. What would Vlad Dracula do to him?

Some of those victims below were Lugosi's own countrymen, the simple peasants and farmers, the bakers and bankers, craftsmen, just like those Lugosi had fought with in the Great War, just like those who had rescued him after he had been shot in the legs, who had dragged him off to safety, where the nurses tended him, gave him morphine. Vlad Dracula had killed them all.

"There are far worse things awaiting man ... than death," the Impaler said. "I did all this for God, and for my country."

Lugosi felt the words catch in his throat. For his country! His own mind felt like a puzzle, with large pieces of memory breaking loose and fitting together in new ways. Lugosi himself had done things for his country, for Hungary, that others had called atrocities.

Back in 1918, he had embraced communism and the revolution. Proudly, he had bragged about his short apprenticeship as a locksmith, then had formed a union of theater workers, fighting and propagandizing for the revolution that thrust Bela Kun into power. But Kun's dictatorship lasted only a few months, during which Romania attacked the weakened country, and Kun was ousted by the counterrevolution. All supporters of Bela Kun were hunted down and thrown into prison or executed. Lugosi had fled for his life to Vienna with his wife and from there, penniless, Lugosi had traveled to Berlin seeking acting jobs.

And now Vlad Dracula thought he was doing this for his people, to free Wallachia and the towns that would become great Hungarian cities. Lugosi had scorned the weak American audiences because they proved too weak to withstand anything but safe, insignificant frights—but now he didn't believe he could stomach what he saw of Vlad the Impaler.

"I fight the Turks and use their own atrocities against them. They have taught me all this!" Vlad Dracula wrung his hands, then snatched a torch free from its holder on the wall. He pushed it toward Lugosi, letting the fire crackle. Lugosi flinched, but he felt none of the heat. It seemed important for him to speak to Lugosi, to justify everything.

"Can you not hear me? The Turks held me hostage from the time I was a boy. To save his neck, my father Dracul the Dragon willingly turned me over to the sultan, along with my youngest brother Radu. Radu turned traitor, became a Turk in his heart. He grew fat from harem women, and rich banquets, and too much opium. My father then went about attacking the sultan's forces, knowing that his own sons were bound to be executed for it!"

Vlad Dracula held his hands over the torch flame; the heat licked his fingers, but he seemed not to notice. "Day after day, the sultan promised to cut me into small pieces. He promised to have horses pull my legs apart and hold me where I could not struggle while he inserted a dull stake through my body the long way! Several times he even went so far as to tie me to the horses, just to frighten me. Day after day, Bela of Lugos!" He lowered his voice. "Yes, the Turks taught me much about the extremes one can do to an enemy!"

Vlad Dracula hurled the torch out the window. Lugosi watched it whirl and blaze as it dropped through the air to the ground, rolled, then came to rest against a rock. Without the torch, the balcony alcove seemed smothered with shadows, lit only by the starlight and distant fires from the scene of slaughter on the hillside.

"After I escaped, I learned that my father had been ambushed and murdered by John Hunyadi, a Hungarian who should have shared his loyalty! Hunyadi captured my father and my brother Mircea so he could gain lordship over the principalities my father controlled. He struck my father with seventy-three sword strokes before he dealt a mortal blow. He claimed that he had tortured my brother Mircea to death and buried him in the public burial grounds." Dracula shook his head, and Lugosi saw real tears hovering there.

"Mircea had fought beside John Hunyadi for three years and had saved his life a dozen times. When I was but a boy, Mircea taught me how to fish and ride a horse. He showed me the constellations in the stars that the Greeks had taught him." Dracula scraped one of his rings down the stone wall, leaving a white mark.

"When I became Prince again, I ordered his coffin to be opened so that I could give him a proper burial, with priests and candles and hymns. We found his head twisted around, his hands had scraped long gouges on the top of his coffin. John Hunyadi had buried him alive!"

Vlad Dracula glanced behind him, as if to make certain no one else wandered the castle halls so late at night, and then he allowed himself to sob. He mumbled his brother's name.

"Just a few months ago, in my castle on the Arges river in Transylvania, the Turks laid siege to me and fired upon the battlements with their cherrywood cannons. One Turkish slave forewarned me, and I was able to escape by picking my way along the ice and snow of a terrible pass. My own son fell off his horse during the flight, and I have never seen him again. My wife could not come with us, and so rather than being captured by the Turks, she climbed the stairs of our tallest tower overlooking the sheer gorge, and she cast herself out of the window. She was my wife, Bela of Lugos. Do you know what it is like to lose a wife like that?"

Lugosi felt cold from the breeze licking over the edge of the balcony. "Not ... like that. But I can understand the loss."

In exile from Hungary back in 1920, Lugosi had left his wife Ilona in Vienna, while he tried to find work in Berlin in German cinema or on the stage. He had written to her every other day, but she had never replied. He learned later that her father, the executive secretary of a Budapest bank, had convinced her to divorce him, to flee back to Hungary and to avoid her husband at all costs because of the awful things he had done against his own country. In the ten years since, Lugosi had already married twice more, but he still did not feel he had found her match. Dracula's wife had chosen a different way out.

Outside, Lugosi heard distant shouts and the jingling of horses approaching at a gallop. He saw the soldiers break away from their tents, scattering the bonfires and snatching up their weapons. The Impaler seemed not to notice.

"I do not know who you are, or why you have come," Vlad Dracula said. "I prayed for an angel, a voice who could remove these demons of guilt from within me." He snatched out at Lugosi's vampire costume, but his hand passed directly through the actor's chest.

Lugosi shrank back, feeling the icy claw of a spectral hand sweep through his heart. Vlad Dracula widened his enormous dark eyes with superstitious terror. "You truly must be a spirit come to torment me, since you refuse to grant me absolution."

Lugosi did not know how to answer. He delivered his answer with a stuttering, uncertain cadence. "I am neither of those things. I am only a traveler, a dream to you perhaps, from a time and place far from here. I have not lived my life yet. I will be born many centuries from now."

"You come not to judge me, then? Or punish me?" Vlad Dracula looked truly terrified. He looked down at the hand that had passed through Lugosi's body.

"No, I am just an actor—an entertainer. I perform for other people. I try to make them afraid." He shook his head. "But I was wrong. What I do has no bearing on real fear. The acting I do, the frights I give to my audience, are a sham. That fear has no consequences." He leaned out over the balcony, then squeezed his eyes shut at the scores of maimed corpses and those victims not fortunate enough to have died.

"Seeing this convinces me I know nothing about real fear."

In the courtyard directly below, shouting erupted. Marching men hurried out into the night. Someone blasted a horn. Lugosi heard the sounds of a fight, swords clashing. Vlad Dracula glanced at it, dismissed the commotion for a moment, then locked his hypnotic gaze with Lugosi's again. The anguish behind the Impaler's eyes made Lugosi want to squirm.

"That is all? I have prayed repeatedly for an apparition, and you claim to have learned something from *me*? About fear? All is lost. I have been abandoned. God is making a joke with me." His shoulders hunched into the fur-lined robe, and he reddened with anger.

Lugosi had the crawling feeling that if he had been corporeal to the Impaler, Vlad Dracula would have thrust him upon a vacant stake on the hillside. "I do not know what to tell you, Vlad Dracula. I am not your conscience. I have destroyed enough things in my own life by trying to do what I thought was right and best. But I can tell you what I think."

Vlad Dracula cocked an eyebrow. Below, a clattering sound signaled a portcullis opening. Booted feet charged across the flagstone floor as someone hurried into the receiving hall. "My Lord Prince!"

Lugosi spoke rapidly. "The Turks have taught you well, as your atrocities show. But you have perhaps gone too far. You cannot undo the things you have already done, the thousands already slain. But you can change how you act from now on. Your brutal, bloodthirsty reputation is already well-earned, and mothers will frighten their children with stories of Vlad the Impaler for five hundred years! Now perhaps you have built enough terror that you no longer need the slaughter. The mere mention of your name and the terror it evokes may be enough to accomplish your aims, to save Hungary from the Turks. If this is how you must be, try to govern with fear, not with death. Then your God may give your conscience some rest."

Vlad Dracula made a puzzled frown. "Perhaps we are together because I needed to learn something about fear as well." The Impaler laughed with a sound like breaking glass. "For one who has not lived even a single lifetime, you are a wise man, Bela of Lugos."

They both turned at the sound of a running man hurrying up the stone steps to the upper level where Lugosi and Vlad Dracula stood side by side. The messenger scraped his sword against the stone wall, clattering. He swept his cloak back, looking from side to side until he spotted Dracula in the shadowy alcove. Sweat and blood smeared his face.

"My Lord Prince! Why did you not respond?" the man cried. A crimson badge on his shoulder identified him as a retainer from one of the boyars serving Vlad Dracula.

"I have been in conversation with an important representative," Dracula said, nodding to Lugosi. Surprised, but falling back on his training, Lugosi sketched a formal bow to the messenger. But the retainer looked toward where Lugosi stood, blinked, and frowned.

"I see nothing, my Lord Prince."

In a rage, Vlad Dracula snatched out a dagger from his fur-lined robe. The messenger blanched and stumbled backward, warding off the death from the knife but also showing a kind of sick relief that his end would be quick, not moaning and bleeding for days on a stake as the vultures circled about.

"Dracula!" Lugosi snapped, bringing to bear all the power and command he had used during his very best performances as the vampire. Vlad Dracula stopped, holding the knife poised for its strike. The retainer trembled, staring with wide blank eyes, but afraid to flee.

"Look at how terrified you have made this man. The fear you create is a powerful thing. You need not kill him to accomplish your purpose."

Vlad Dracula heard Lugosi, but kept staring at the retainer, making his eyes blaze brighter, his leer more vicious. The retainer began to sob.

"I need not explain my actions to you," he said to the man. "Your soul is mine to crush whenever I wish. Now tell me your news!"

"The sultan's army has arrived. It appears to be but a small vanguard attacking under cover of darkness, but the remaining Turks will be here by tomorrow. We can stand strong against this vanguard—many of them have already fled upon seeing their comrades impaled on this hillside, my Lord Prince. They will report back. It will enrage the sultan's army."

Vlad Dracula pinched his full lips between his fingers. He looked at Lugosi, who stood watching and waiting. The messenger seemed confused at what the Impaler thought he saw.

"Or it will strike *fear* into the sultan's army. We can use this. Go out to the victims on the stakes. Cut off the heads of those dead or mortally wounded—and be quick about it!—and catapult the heads into the Turkish vanguard. They will see the faces of their comrades and know that this will happen to them if they fight me. Find those whose injuries may still allow them to live and set them free of the stakes. Send them back to the sultan to tell how monstrous I am. Then he will think twice about his aggression against me and against my land."

The retainer blinked in astonishment, still trembling from having his life returned to him, curious about these new tactics Vlad Dracula was attempting. "Yes, my Lord Prince!" He scrambled backward and ran to the stone steps.

Lugosi felt the walls around him growing softer, shimmering. His knees felt watery. His body felt empty. The morphine was wearing off.

Dracula tugged at his dark moustache. "This is interesting. The sultan will think it just as horrible, but God will know how merciful I have been. Perhaps next time I smoke the opium pipe, He will send me a true angel."

Lugosi stumbled, feeling sick and dizzy. Warm flecks of light roared through his head. Dracula seemed to loom larger and stronger.

"I cannot see you as clearly, my friend. You grow dim. Our time together is at an end. Now that we have learned what we have learned, it would be best for you to return to your own country."

Lugosi tried to shake the thickening cobwebs from his eyes. "The morphine must be wearing off...."

"And I can barely feel the effects of the opium pipe anymore. But I must dress for battle! If we are to fight the sultan's vanguard, I want them to see exactly who has brought them such fear! Farewell, Bela of Lugos. I will try to do as you suggest."

"Farewell, Vlad Dracula," Lugosi said, raising his hand. It passed through the solid stone of the balcony wall....

The lights flickered around his makeup mirror, dazzling his eyes. Lugosi drew in a deep breath and stared around his tiny dressing room. A shiver ran through him, and he pulled the black cape close around him, seeking for some warmth.

Outside, Dwight Frye attempted his long Renfield laugh one more time, but sneezed at the end. Frye's dressing room door opened, and Lugosi heard him walking away across the set.

On the small table in front of him, Lugosi saw the empty hypodermic needle and the remaining vial of morphine. Fear. The silver point looked like a tiny stake to impale himself on. Morphine had always given him solace, a warm and comfortable feeling that made him forget pain, forget trouble, forget his fears.

But he had used it too much. Now it transported him to a place where he could see only the thousands of bloodied stakes and moaning victims, vultures circling, ravens pecking at living flesh. And the mad, tormented eyes of Vlad the Impaler.

He could not guess where it would take him next, and the possibilities filled him with fear—not the fear without consequences that sent shivers through his audiences, but a real fear that would put his sanity at risk. He had brought it upon himself, cultivated it by his own actions.

Bela Lugosi dropped the syringe and the small vial of morphine onto the hard floor of his dressing room. Slowly, with great care, he ground them both to shards under the heel of his Count Dracula shoes.

His legs ached again from the old injury, but it made him feel solid and alive. The pain wasn't so bad that he needed to hide from it. What he found in his drug-induced hiding place might be worse than the pain itself.

Lugosi opened his dressing room and saw Dwight Frye just leaving through the large doors. He called out for the other actor to wait, remembering to use English again, though the foreign tongue seemed cumbersome to him.

"Mr. Frye, would you care to join me for a bit of dinner? I know it is late, but I would enjoy your company."

Frye stopped, and his eyes widened to show how startled he was. For a moment he looked like the madman Renfield again, but when he chuckled the laugh carried delight, not feigned insanity.

"Yes, I'd sure like that, Mr. Lugosi. It's good to see you're not going to keep to yourself again. The rest of us don't bite, you know. Nothing to be afraid of."

Lugosi smiled sardonically and stepped toward him. The pain in his legs faded into the background. "You're right, Mr. Frye. There is nothing to fear."

Another Tucker's Grove story, also dating back to the founding of the town. One theme you will see in many of these tales is religious intolerance, the danger that lurks in those oh-so-sweet little Protestant churches that grace every Midwestern town. When Garrison Keillor wrote about them in his humorous chronicles of Lake Wobegon, he found irony and humor.

I found something much darker.

Church Services

As his shouted prayer reached a crescendo, Jerome Tucker opened his eyes and watched the demon leave the young man.

Inside the canvas revival tent, the blasphemous thing emerged from the teenaged boy's nostrils and throat like poisonous smoke mixed with a swarm of bees: crackling, buzzing, and writhing. Demonic whispers built to a scream. A trickle of blood followed the thing as it slid and tore its way out of the possessed boy.

The demon had no choice but to obey. Jerome had commanded it with the compulsion of God Himself.

He had lost count over the weeks, but he had summoned and trapped at least a hundred demons on the slow wagon trek through the farmlands of Illinois, across muddy and rutted roads to the wilderness and new homesteads of Wisconsin Territory. In this barely settled land, there were many secrets, many buried shadows of times past. So many demons had been cast out in Biblical times, the evil had to have gone somewhere. What better place to seek refuge than among the heathen in the New World? It made perfect sense.

Inside the large tent crowded with farmers, their wives, their children, and a few shopkeepers from Bartonville (the closest thing that could have been called a town), Jerome raised his hands.

His full, rusty red beard stood out like flames on his chin. "Leave this boy, I command you!"

Even after the demon had fully emerged, the teenager continued to spasm and moan, his jaws clenched, lips drawn back. The audience gasped; several women fainted, while others uttered their own prayers. Two lanky farmers swore with coarse language that would not have pleased an eavesdropping God.

"As Jesus Christ trapped the demon Legion in a group of pigs, so I contain you here, Demon, where you can do no further harm." With an imperative gesture, he stuck out his hand, touched the ornate, pot-bellied clay jar covered with runes and designs—symbols now rusty with dried blood.

The demon struggled and wailed, shifting and convulsing like a tornado of flies, but the crackling black mist was sucked into the containment jar—the holy relic from ancient Egypt, or Babylon, or Assyria (Jerome wasn't exactly sure which). Like smoke swirling up a chimney in a harsh draft, the indefinable thing vanished into the clay vessel with a last alien howl, and when it was trapped in its new prison, the maddening sound stopped with the abruptness of a slammed door.

"Glory to God on high!" called out Jerome's wife, Mollie. She dutifully stood beside him at the pulpit, holding open the tattered Bible, knowing exactly which verses Jerome would need for the next step of the process.

The teenager's weeping mother rushed forward, knocking over one of the thin wooden benches as she came up to throw her arms around her limp son. "Oh, he's saved, he's saved!"

Blood dribbled from the boy's mouth as he groaned; he opened his eyes and stared around with a sparkling awareness, as though he'd been asleep for months. The audience applauded wildly, called out choruses of "Amen!"

Mollie read aloud from the 23rd Psalm, because it was her favorite passage, not because it was especially appropriate. Her high, musical voice gained strength as she read verse after verse.

Jerome was the forceful personality with a passion for his calling, but he couldn't have achieved so much without Mollie's help, without her faith. She had followed him from their home, after his fever, after his parents died, leaving everything behind to journey across untamed country, staking her future on him.

Jerome Tucker had always wanted to be a preacher, but he needed a flock. And with so many homesteaders moving west to stake their claims in uncharted lands, *those* people needed to hear the Gospel. After a near-fatal bout with scarlet fever, Jerome had known exactly what to do. So, he had gathered up whatever money his family had and bought a wagon and horses, a large tent and Bibles, everything he needed.

He went to the land surveyor's office to study maps of Illinois and Wisconsin all the way to the Mississippi River. The owlish-faced clerk had shown him available plots and claimed areas where farmland was being cleared by hardworking pioneers. Jerome did not want acreage for himself; he just needed to find a large enough group of people who required his services.

He knew he would find the right place. He'd been so eager to grab the plat books that he'd cut his finger on the countertop's ragged wooden edge. Sucking on the wound absentmindedly, he had turned pages, following the geography up into south-central Wisconsin. By smeary light that passed through flyspecked windows, he stopped to study farmland, roads, and neighboring towns.

A droplet of blood fell and splashed on one particular area, a bold crimson mark on the map. Jerome considered it a sign, a position chosen by his blood. *That* was where he would go. A place he would call Tucker's Grove.

As they made their way westward while his brother Clancy took care of details back home, he and Mollie preached to crowds, and Jerome had cast out and captured many demons to purify the population along the way, doing God's work. The cross-country journey had taken months, over slushy roads and through falling snow, heavy rainstorms, and a miasma of humidity and mosquitoes. He felt as if he and his wife were required to pass through the very plagues of Egypt to reach this particular Promised Land.

Finally, on a low hill that overlooked recently claimed farmlands, sprawling fields of corn, and uncleared trees that marked land boundaries, Jerome and Mollie erected their big tent for the last time. There, he held nightly services.

When the people began to understand that Jerome could truly cast out demons, that he could take away their sins and purify their thoughts, his flock began to grow....

Now, seeing the teenaged boy get shakily to his feet and collapse in his mother's arms, both crying, Jerome felt tears roll down his cheeks. He had saved at least thirty people in this area already, and they all owed him a great deal. He would forge them into a community, a town, a new place.

Smiling, he lifted his hands and called out once more. The canvas tent was old when he'd purchased it secondhand, patched and stained—by no means was this an adequate house of worship. Now that Jerome knew with all his soul that this was the place ... now that all the people in the revival tent listened to whatever he had to say, he called them together and he made his request.

"I must ask something of you, my friends. This ground has been consecrated with all our prayers. Now, I require your help, your wood, your tools, your labor, and your love. We will build a church here, and then we will establish a town."

During their journey west and north through Wisconsin, at the edge of a river that drained into the Mississippi, Jerome had found the ancient symbol-bedecked urn that changed his life.

He and Mollie had stopped for the night in a small village where flatboats delivered cargo downriver and brought new supplies back upstream. There, they met a man with clumpy brown hair and three fingers missing on the left hand. His face was weathered and more deeply tanned than could be explained by any Midwestern summer, and his eyes had a distant stare, focused on memories rather than the landscape, as if he had already seen more than his share of wonders and nightmares.

The man struck up a conversation with Jerome but did not introduce himself. He explained how he had traveled the Ancient World looking for oddities and treasures.

Interested in the man's experiences, Jerome said, "Pharaoh held the Israelites in Egypt. In ancient times."

"Egypt is an ancient place full of dead things. I'd heard rumors that there were so many treasure-filled tombs scattered across the desert that a man could simply walk along and pick up gold and jewels. There are tombs, all right. The entire land is like a skeleton."

Jerome knew about wealthy Europeans, gentlemen archaeologists, who explored Egypt and returned with mummies and artifacts, telling ludicrous tales of curses and the revenge of ancient gods. Jerome knew all such stories to be false, of course, because he had read the Bible—carefully—several times.

The man held up his left hand, showing the three stumps of his fingers. "A jackal did this. Bit them clean off, when I tried to retrieve a demon jar from a tomb."

"What's a demon jar?" Mollie asked. The man looked at her, surprised that she had spoken.

Jerome had no patience for those who didn't respect his wife. "What's a demon jar?" he repeated.

The man opened the large trunk that held his belongings and moved a rolled rug and some cloth aside to extract an ivory-pale urn made of ancient clay; it looked as if it had been cast from liquefied bone. Its surface was stippled with indecipherable writing, odd designs, one of which Jerome recognized as the Star of David; another, prominent in the center, was unmistakably the Cross.

"Moses wasn't God's only prophet in Egypt," the man said soberly. "This jar was created by one such holy man as a vessel to capture and hold the demons that filled the land." He lifted the lid of the urn and gazed into its dark interior. "It's empty now—either the demons have escaped over the years, or it was never used. But you can tell by the symbols that it must be a sacred relic."

Mollie was more skeptical. "If this was created in ancient Egypt or Sumer, that was many years before Christ died for our sins. How could it carry the symbol of the Cross?"

The man regarded Mollie with no small amount of annoyance. "And what is it, ma'am, that a prophet *does*? Why, he *prophesies!* He knows the future. Wouldn't God's chosen know about the impending arrival of God's son?" He turned back to Jerome. "If you are a preacher, and if you are truly guided by the Holy Spirit, then you must already know how to cast out demons."

In fact, Jerome didn't, though he'd always thought about it.

"Any preacher can *cast out* demons," the man continued. "But then what? They are freed from one host and sent to wander the world, where they continue to wreak havoc. With this urn, however"—the man patted the rough clay surface—"you not only withdraw demons from the possessed, you will also imprison them, seal them in this jar, where they can cause no further harm."

The man sounded tired and disappointed. "To be honest, I have no use for this relic. I am not a holy man." With a smile he extended it toward Jerome. "Take this as my gift. It is better off in your hands, since you can do God's work with it." Suddenly embarrassed or shy, the stranger added, "However, if you could spare some coins, I need to buy passage back home. Thieves in Constantinople took my last money, and I have had to beg my way, working for passage across the sea, on riverboats down the Ohio, then across country, finally to here. My mother has consumption, you see. I am trying to get home, so I can be with her before she dies."

Jerome felt the earnestness in the man's voice, and he knew how much good work he could do with this demon jar.

"Whatever you think the jar is worth ..." The man left the idea hanging.

Mollie shot her husband a sharp glare as Jerome opened his money pouch and withdrew far more coins than they could spare. Jerome was sure, though, that once he began casting out demons, grateful parishioners would quickly contribute to the offering plate.

"How do I use it?" Jerome asked.

The man regarded him earnestly. "You'll know. God will show you."

Late at night, under a buttery-yellow moon, Mollie found Jerome within the framework structure of the nearly completed church. The glass windowpanes had not yet been installed, but the walls were finished, and the roof partially covered. The smell of mingled sawdust and sweat hung in the air, aromas of sweet pine and devoted labor. For the past month, people volunteered their time, several days a week, to finish the great work.

In the large window opening that would soon be filled with beautiful stained-glass panels shipped all the way from Chicago, Mollie could look down the hillside to the silver-lit fields and the small cluster of new buildings, the embryo of the town that her husband had coaxed into existence.

The altar was completed first, covered with an embroidered, lace-edged cloth—a gift from three farmers' wives who had worked their fingers sore to finish it. In the center of the altar lay the large old Bible next to the pale demon jar. Jerome had held regular services here as soon as the framework was erected, and he had packed away his tattered old revival tent for good. He expected his brother Clancy to bring their parents any time now.

Now, he knelt before the altar in the dark. Unlit candles stood in freshly lathed wooden stands. As Mollie entered the skeletal church, her soft step creaked the new-laid pine floorboards, but he did not stop his prayer. Eyes half-shut, he pulled out his knife, touched the razor-edged tip to his thumb, then sliced. The blood looked like black molasses as it welled up.

Mollie stood behind him, bowing her head, not interrupting the sacred ceremony. Jerome extended his thumb and pressed the warm wetness to the cross symbol that stood out in sharp relief among the other designs. The ancient jar seemed to draw the blood and drink it greedily.

"God will protect us from demons," Jerome muttered. "God will contain them inside here."

It wasn't exactly a recitation from the Scriptures, but the demons could hear him. Trapped in their jar, they would be afraid.

The Scripture had a long tradition of blood sacrifice: just as Abraham had been willing to make a blood sacrifice of his son Isaac, just as Moses marked the lintels of the Jews with lambs' blood so that the Angel of Death would pass over their homes, just as God had demanded the blood of his own son Jesus to save humanity. So, Jerome was willing to give up a small amount of his blood to strengthen the demon jar, to keep the evil things inside.

He regained his feet, turned to his wife. "Every demon I've removed and imprisoned is one less soldier that Satan has for the Final Battle. Not only am I making my new town a pure and holy place, I am aiding the whole world."

Mollie, though, was concerned. "All the times in the Bible where a godly man casts out demons, he never tries to *collect* them. He never keeps them like old coins in a purse. And what happens when the vessel is full? Do you know how much evil it can contain? I'm worried about what that jar really does."

"Why, it imprisons demons, Mollie." Jerome leaned closer in the deep shadows of the unfinished church. "And when we bless this new house of worship, when my congregation comes from miles around, they will join together and make a similar sacrifice. We'll purge this area of all sins and evil thoughts. This land, this town of Tucker's Grove, will become a new Eden." His eyes were shining in the moonlight. "Yes, I'm sure, Mollie. I'm sure of our future, I'm sure of this place, and I'm sure of my mission. Not a shred of doubt."

"That's all I wanted to know," Mollie said with a smile, "because I have news for you as well, joyous news." She took his hand and a smear of blood went down the front of her palm. "I'm pregnant, Jerome. I'll have our first child in your new town."

When the church was finished—when all the siding had been painted white, the black shingles laid down, the bell installed in the steeple that perched like a triumphant hand raised toward Heaven—it was time for a great celebration. The three men who had delivered the stained-glass window from Chicago stayed for the festivities; Jerome hoped they would remain permanently, since the town needed glaziers.

Jerome felt that he had lived his entire life for this day. His clothes were freshly laundered, his hair combed, his beard trimmed. Mollie had sewn herself a fine new dress from a bolt of pink fabric she'd purchased at the general store in Bartonville. She left the waistline loose, because now the curve of her belly was becoming noticeable. Jerome thought she looked radiant.

The bell pealed out a shrill, melodic tone as two young farm boys took turns yanking the rope to set up a clangor that rang from horizon to horizon. The people streamed in: more men, women, and families than Jerome had thought lived in the area. They came to dedicate the church they'd helped to build. Though Jerome had not yet secured a piano to lead the music, they would sing familiar hymns in unison. That was all a church really needed.

Jerome spoke up when everyone had squeezed into the pews. "This place of worship stands on holy ground, for I have made it so. All of your crops will be blessed, and all of your children will be strong and protected from evil. I will make it so. *We* will make it so. We will be a community, a bastion against darkness."

He turned to the altar and touched the demon jar. "You have seen me cast out demons. The most powerful and most dangerous of those evil fallen angels are here, trapped inside this urn." He brushed the surface of the vessel. "They are locked there by the grace of God, by the holy symbols ... and by the gift of blood."

Jerome extended his thumb toward the congregation. "Today, we make one grand final summoning to draw out all the evils and ills that permeate this land, that permeate our hearts. We will draw away the pain and darkness, so that Tucker's Grove can be a perfect place, a shining example for mankind."

The people in the church shouted their Amens. Some stood from the pews.

"A drop of blood," Jerome said, "from me, from you—from all of you, and this town will lock away those evil spirits forever." With a flick of his knife, he sliced open his thumb once more, this time a little more extravagantly than he'd expected. The blood flowed, and he touched it to the Cross symbol so that the ancient, mysterious urn drank the scarlet liquid. He held up the knife. "Who will be the first to join me?"

The people in the front pew nearly fell over themselves to come to the altar. Each took up the knife, drew blood, and touched red thumbprints or fingerprints to the pale ivory curves of the ancient vessel.

The second row came forward, jostling and pushing one another. Some wept with joy, while others closed their eyes and prayed as they made their offering. This was not like a somber Communion ceremony: they were an army laying siege to the evil things that had troubled their lives.

With Jerome's command, a great wind of shadows, dark thoughts, evil deeds, frightening memories—the very manifestation of sin—swept up the hills and blew like a quiet winter wind into the church. The congregation could sense how much more darkness the demon jar was drinking, but their blood maintained the seal, trapped the bad things forever.

Jerome felt his heart swell with love for these people, his people. Mollie stood looking preoccupied, maybe a bit worried. He slipped his arm around his wife's waist. "Why are you so quiet, my dear? This is our finest, most perfect hour."

Mollie bit her lower lip and shook her head, afraid to answer at first. Finally, she said, "All that blood ... Instead of trapping the demons, what if it's *feeding* them?"

With a great outcry, the last of the parishioners stumbled back from the urn. The incredibly old Egyptian—or Sumerian, or Assyrian—vessel had begun to glow a faint orange, like fire within an eggshell. The embellished clay walls pulsed in a heartbeat, as if the demons inside were fighting and struggling to break free.

Jerome took a deep breath but could find no words. He had gathered numerous demons from across the countryside on his travels up to Wisconsin, collected them from suffering people over the course of his journey. Victims had come to him from far and wide, and he had torn out the demons and imprisoned them in the vessel, carried them here to his new town.

And they were all furious.

Cracks appeared in the ivory ceramic, then fire belched out of the fissures. The demon jar exploded with a thunderstorm whirlwind of black, screaming voices, buzzing flies. Howling anger and dripping vengeance, they roared out with enough force to snuff a tornado.

Parishioners ducked, throwing themselves onto the pews, onto the floor. The unleashed demons filled the church and swirled around; some streaked through the open front door. A black, smoky jet smashed through the stained-glass window, sending jewel-toned shards flying in every direction.

The evil blackness whistled around Jerome and Mollie. He grabbed his wife, tried to protect her, but he didn't know how. A murky, miasmic face that was made of fangs rose before them, screaming—a scream that sounded more like laughter.

Mollie cringed. The shadows pummeled her, wrapped about her as though she were being sprayed with mud. She collapsed to the floor, crying in terror.

Jerome balled his fists and shouted, "Begone, I command you all! *Begone!*"

And the demons fled the church, racing out and away to find new hosts in the vicinity of Tucker's Grove.

The evil storm subsided just as abruptly as it had begun. The interior of the new church had been shredded, leaving clouds of dust, splinters, and fear. The people were stunned, moaning, touching small cuts and inspecting tattered clothes. As Jerome ran among his people to help, some of them looked away in deep shame, afraid to let him see the shadowed hollows in their eyes, the new darkness that glinted from their gaze.

Jerome felt his bones turn to ice and understood that his dreams were dashed. He had meant to establish a perfect town, to create a new Eden free of sin or evil or hate. Instead, he had brought more darkness to the area and saturated this very place.

He clung to the sharp foundation of his faith. He would not surrender. He refused to leave his town. He had far too much work to do here.

Crumpled and sick, Mollie retched onto the floor, cradling her abdomen. Jerome knelt beside her, helped her to her feet. She swayed against him. "Are you hurt? Are you all right?"

Mollie drew a deep breath. "I'll be fine. I just felt the baby kick, that's all."

He didn't ask her why she was shuddering.

And she didn't tell him that the kick had felt distinctly like that of a cloven hoof.

Every writer has to do a Nazi story at least once in their career. This one is short, and twisted, and it may or may not be just a "crazy person" story. I should note that when I wrote this, my girlfriend's father was a shoe repairman with a small, dingy shop just like the one described here, but he has nothing to do with the character in this story. Honest.

Leatherworks

The frequent puddles were muddying his only other pair of black, patent leather shoes, and the constant gloom outside was making him annoyed by it. He strode across the rain-washed street carrying a briefcase in one hand and wielding an umbrella in the other. His manner, his tie, and his crisp pale-blue suit seemed to shout out "This Man Has A Degree In Business, And Is Damn Proud Of It."

He looked up once to make certain that he had found the proper address on the side street. "Goldmann's Shoe Repair and Leather Artwork." He frowned at the latter part of the sign as he snapped his umbrella shut, shaking loose the excess rainwater and checking that the folds were neat.

"I'm J. Francis Schmidt," he announced as he pushed his way through the door. "And I'm here to pick up my shoes." The jangling of a bell attached to the door almost drowned out his words.

The shop was unlit, except for the small amount of murky light the gloom outside grudgingly allowed through the shop windows. As his eyes adjusted, Schmidt heard a rhythmic tapping which paused briefly, then started again. One quick step brought him to the counter, and one quick slap of his palm struck the "Please Ring Bell for Service" bell. Then he saw the small, wiry man sitting at a workshop area behind the counter, a heavy wooden mallet in one hand, a fistful of gleaming silver tools in the other, and a wallet-sized rectangle of leather spread out on the table before him.

The other man peered up at Schmidt through horn-rimmed glasses, then squinted back at his work. "If you would indulge me, please, for a moment, I will be with you shortly. I need to finish this pattern." The words halted Schmidt's hand on the downsweep of its arc toward the service bell again. He glanced at his watch, saw he still had eleven minutes before his bus would arrive for its customary 4:32 stop.

"Do I recognize you ... Mister Schmidt?" Goldmann—yes, it must be Goldmann—said, without looking up from the leather.

"That would be unlikely. A friend dropped off my shoes, and I have not done business with you before."

"Ah."

Schmidt looked at his watch again, then craned his head over the counter to see if he could decipher the older man's craft. He became caught up in the rapidity with which Goldmann's silver tools flashed in the dexterity of the leatherworker's fingers, only to be returned to the cache of his palm in exchange for another tool. The staccato pounding commanded, and the leather responded by lifting itself, writhing into new forms—a stylized flower, a feathery leaf. With each stroke of the mallet, a vein appeared in a leaf, a seed appeared at the center of a flower, smooth leather became textured, rough edges became smooth.

Purses, wallets, belts, checkbook covers, all lay on shelves or hung on wooden pegs around the walls of the shop. Schmidt looked at the completed items, nodding in approval; looked at the prices, shook his head with a scowl.

"You do nice work, Mister Goldmann, although your prices are unrealistic."

The leatherworker ignored the comment for a moment until he had finished the work he had intended, and stood up from the creaking chair, gathering his mallet, tools, and newly carved leather and bringing them all to the service counter.

"But isn't all artwork expensive, Mister Schmidt?" He dropped his silver tools with a clatter on the glass countertop and beckoned the other man to look at the wallet he was making. "You see, it is almost like sculpture, carving and molding and manipulating the flesh into forms which please me. That is why I call myself a Leather Artist. But still, if you knew anything about leather you would not find my prices out of line. See that purse ... there?"

Schmidt reached for it, grasped the price tag. "Seventy dollars."

"Just the raw leather cost me thirty-five dollars, not to mention the lace, stain, and lacquer ... or the twenty hours of work I spent on it."

Schmidt released the price tag, as if he had grudgingly conceded the point. "Still, it is very beautiful."

Goldmann smiled strangely, and a small fire in his eyes seemed to be focused through the thick glasses for the sole purpose of burning holes in Schmidt's body. "There are others who do not look at leatherwork with such kindness. They see me as something worse than a killer, taking the skins of innocent creatures and—not content with the original murder—warping that flesh to my own ends, contorting it into forms it does not wish to hold. You might think it beautiful, but would the original owner of the skin look at it that way? Tortured flesh ... perhaps that's all it is."

In an effort to make him look less disturbed by the subject matter, Schmidt looked at his watch again. "My shoes, Mister Goldmann, if you please."

Goldmann reached under the counter and found a brown paper bag but failed to extend it across the counter. Schmidt saw black numbers tattooed on the older man's arm and asked, "What's that?" before realizing his mistake.

Goldmann stiffened and recited briskly. *"Bay vier acht comma sieben drei null null eins!* A sample of the leatherwork the Nazis performed." His eyes took on a distant glaze. "They were masters of leatherwork, they were. Making us march up and down, molding our flesh, contorting our minds to the designs which delighted them. Not content with simple death, they had to make soap of our meat, take silver and gold from our teeth, take the souls from our bodies before they took the flesh from our bones!" Goldmann looked at the numbers on his arm.

Schmidt reached for the paper sack; the leatherworker moved it deftly out of reach.

"But even master leather-draftsmen make mistakes. The Nazis made a mistake, yes, they did. They took me for a fine cowhide, but I had the skin from an entirely different breed. They wanted smooth Jew skin, tough Jewish hide—but all they found on the man named Goldmann was a poor Lutheran. Not Jewish, as the name implies—curse my forefathers! I am a Lutheran—I AM NOT A JEW! I tried to tell ... I shouted it over and over again—but the lying Jews shouted the same words, and nobody believed me. I kissed the cross, quoted every passage I knew from the New Testament. It amused them. It did not convince them."

Goldmann glared across the counter at Schmidt, and suddenly his expression changed. "Are you a veteran, Mister Schmidt? Do you remember the war, the camps like Dachau? You do, don't you?"

Schmidt blinked his eyes in confusion. "Why, no. I wasn't even born until ten years after the end of World War Two. Surely I don't look that old?"

Goldmann laughed, "Come now, Herr Schmidt! With a name like yours? Look at you—tall, blond-haired, blue-eyed, fair-skinned! Perfect Aryan material!" He extended his arm in front of him. "*Sieg heil*, Herr Schmidt!"

"Now wait a minute! Just because my name—" He reached forward to snatch the brown-paper bag from the leatherworker's fingers. "I'll take my shoes now, sir, and leave!"

He saw that a large black swastika had been drawn across the back of the bag, and he tore it open. His fine black shoes were mottled with dozens of swastikas cut deeply into the leather. Schmidt looked up in horror at the other just as the heavy wooden mallet crashed into his right temple. He crumpled slowly. The shoes landed on the counter ... he landed on the floor.

Goldmann spat at him, then came quickly around the counter. "Dirty Nazi! You think I wouldn't remember you?" He pulled on Schmidt's limp arms, dragging the blond-haired man into the back room.

He made ready a stretching rack and his tanning materials.

Then he looked around for the skinning knife.

Joe Ledger is a kick-ass action hero in a series of thrillers written by Jonathan Maberry. It's like Tom Clancy meets The X-Files *as Joe and his team fight zombie plagues, UFOs, vampires, or Lovecraftian terrorists. I've read almost the entire series.*

Jonathan opened up his character to other writers for a collection of new Joe Ledger stories. How could I resist?

But when one of your good friends lets you play with his beloved character, you better treat him right. I was determined to write a Joe Ledger story that was as kick-ass as Joe himself.

If you like this story, you can read the rest of the series by Jonathan Maberry, starting with Patient Zero.

Surf's Up
A Joe Ledger Story

—I—

"After what you've been through, Joe, you need a vacation," Mr. Church said. "The DMS can handle world-threatening emergencies without you for a few days."

We could both smell the bullshit. This wasn't a suggestion; it was an order.

An hour later Rudy Sanchez, my therapist and best friend, insisted, "Relax, Joe. Recharge. Blank your mind and just breathe in the salty air, listen to the roar of the surf coming in ..."

"Hold on, let me put on my tie-dyed T-shirt first."

So, for my own damned good, they sent me far away from Washington, DC, to the opposite side of the country: Lincoln City, a tourist town on the Oregon coast. Decent weather, hotel row, seafood restaurants, whale-watching trips, and spectacular headlands where I could watch waves roll in, feel the pulse of the tide, hear the seabirds screech overhead.

I tried Rudy's technique. Don't think about anything. Listen to the surf. No self-reflection. No nightmares. Stay present. It wasn't forgetting all that had happened—just not remembering *right now*. It was supposed to be peaceful.

The first night I walked along the headlands under the full

moon. South, past the main drag and hotel row, I had a good view of the silvery surf, the dark beaches below.

I missed my dog Ghost, a white German Shepard smarter than hell and trained beyond any family Fido's wildest dreams. He'd saved my life dozens of times and had gotten pretty banged up during our last shindig. After specialized vets patched him up, he was healing, relaxing in a doggie hospital—his own little vacation. Just like mine.

I listened to the crash and boom of waves echoing through the night. It was late enough that most restaurants were closed, few people were out. I could be at peace, or a reasonable approximation of it.

With the tide coming in, the sprawl of rocky sand below was shrinking, and before long the waves would be crashing up against the cliffs. Looking down, I could still see a mess of driftwood logs, scattered flotsam, and ropy green kelp strands. Moonlight turned the water and sand into a soothing monochromatic scene.

Which all went to hell when I saw a human body on the beach below.

The dark figure lay face down on the sand, wearing some kind of wetsuit. I couldn't see the head or face. As waves lapped higher on the stony beach, the incoming tide would wash the body back out to sea. If I didn't get to it first.

I dispensed with Rudy's calming techniques. This was no time to be calm. The headlands were high above the water, with rugged sandy cliffs dropping to the beach below. In the town, each hotel had wooden stairs for beach access, but out here I would have to pick my way down. It was about fifty feet down to the rocky beach.

So much for relaxing.

I considered calling the Lincoln City police. What if it was a drowned scuba diver? Sure, there *might* already be search and rescue operations under way. But maybe not. And if I delayed to wait for a response team, somebody's beloved family member would vanish into the sea. I didn't want that on my conscience. Not even on vacation.

I hurried along the cliff's edge and finally found a steep, narrow thread that wound between lumps and outcroppings. I swung my feet over, held onto the sandy slope, and began to descend. The path must have been made by intrepid kids who had no fear, but if they could get down, then so could I.

One crumbling lump broke under my grip, but I caught myself. I didn't want the night to end with two bodies on the beach. I dug my heels in, regained my balance, and scrambled farther down. I hadn't decided how I would retrieve the body once I got there. At full high tide, the water would smash right up against the cliff. Great.

I found a stable ledge and paused there. From my new vantage point the dark form of the body looked ... odd. Even the head and face had a dark, slick covering, not a scuba mask.

My toes slipped as pebbles and sand broke free, and I pressed myself against the rough wall, heart pounding. Now I did use Rudy's calming techniques. I decided I could look at the body when I reached the beach.

The tide kept curling in, but it would take me another twenty minutes or so to get down there. I looked out at the water, the moonlight glittering on the waves.

Four dark figures rose out of the surf and advanced toward the beach and the body.

What the hell?

They were slick and muscular, covered with some kind of oily, full-body wetsuit. I balanced in the notch in the sandy cliff and drew in a breath to shout, but suddenly thought better of it. A chill danced down my spine, and I decided to stay quiet.

The four dark figures marched out of the surf toward the body. Were they some kind of team? A scuba choir?

Maybe the victim had drowned while on a night-diving expedition, and his comrades had come to retrieve him. But how the hell were they going to carry him up the headlands to safety? Call an ambulance and the police?

That wasn't what they were doing. No sir, not at all.

The figures reached the corpse and, working together, they

hefted the slick body. Then they walked *back into the water.* They carried the corpse into the crashing waves.

I really wanted to yell out—and I really wanted to keep quiet.

Lugging the limp body, they waded into the larger breakers and submerged, vanishing into the ocean.

When I finally reached the beach, I hurried to where the body had been. The waves glided higher. The whole area would be submerged soon.

I saw the marks in the sand left by the corpse and the footprints of the retrieval crew.

Webbed feet. The indentation of claws.

Only then did I realize that none of them had worn an air tank.

—II—

I had signed up for a whale-watching cruise for the next morning. The activity wasn't particularly high on my list—especially after what I'd seen the night before—but Top, one of my Department of Military Sciences team members, had recommended it. "Best tourist activity on the coast, especially this time of year."

Since I don't get seasick, I figured why not. A nice, calm outing. Church had insisted that I was on vacation, and I needed to make an effort.

Besides, no refunds.

I boarded the boat at 0700 along with a ragtag group of tourists. As we pulled on clunky orange life vests, some of my companions complained about the early hour. With a wry smile, I recalled the countless times I had started missions at oh dark thirty.

A "three-hour tour." What could possibly go wrong?

The boat headed out to sea. The water was choppy. The other tourists chatted and giggled while they swept the sea with their binoculars. I had bought my own cheap pair from the gift shop at the dock. Always be prepared.

The first mate, who doubled as our tour guide, kept up an inane patter peppered with jokes she had obviously told hundreds of times before. Other vessels dotted the open sea: recreational craft, commercial fishing boats, even enormous container ships far out on the horizon. Now, as I scanned the water for whales, I kept mulling over what had happened the night before.

After I'd made my way back up the cliff, I didn't call the Lincoln City authorities. What would I say? I had no proof, no waterlogged body, and the webbed footprints had long since washed away. I've been considered batshit crazy enough times in my life; I didn't need more of it. So, I kept the incident to myself.

Even so, my spidey senses were tingling.

Although we didn't see any whales, we did encounter something far more interesting.

During the first mate's well-rehearsed patter and dumb jokes, the captain broke in over the intercom in a serious tone. "Friends, I'm afraid there's been a change of plans. That fishing boat out there, not far off the starboard side—that's the right side, for you landlubbers—just sent a distress signal. We're the closest vessel, and by maritime law we're required to offer assistance, like Triple A."

I knew how to change a flat tire. That wouldn't be much help here.

My companions crowded toward the starboard side, orange vest to orange vest, more excited by a potential emergency than by the prospect of seeing whales. Half a mile away, I saw the midsize commercial fishing boat, a trawler with a crew of three or four. Maybe their hull had sprung a leak.

With engines roaring and spray flying, our boat closed the distance. With my whale-watching binoculars, I spotted three people on the trawler's deck waving frantically. Their net dangled from the crane arm, swollen with silvery, wriggling fish. The men seemed alarmed by something they had caught.

My fellow tourists turned their binoculars, and several used their cameras or cell phones. I tightened my focus on the agitated fishermen. In the net, among the fish, was something else ... a figure that was decidedly *not* a fish.

The net swung on the crane, and I tried to follow it, but one of the fishermen walked into my field of view. His expression was drawn and sickly.

My cheap binoculars sucked, but I kept them pressed to my eyes. The fisherman moved aside just as the load of fish shifted, and I realized a human figure had been caught in the net. It was dark, apparently wearing a slick suit. Or maybe it wasn't a suit.

I only got a glimpse of the head—big, round eyes, bony plates like large scales, slits in the neck ... gills?—before the net swung up and out of my field of view.

Was somebody doing a remake of *Creature from the Black Lagoon*?

Our boat approached the fishing trawler, and we could hear the crew shouting, Spanish I think, but the roar of our engines drowned out the words. It sounded like the fishermen were yelling "Monster! Monster!"

Before we got close enough to see clearly, another boat streaked across the waves, much faster and more intimidating than ours. The engine hummed like a fighter jet, and its sharp bow split the water like a shark fin, throwing up a curtain of spray. A maritime horn blatted, as if to scare us off.

Official-looking flags flew from the bow. I focused my binoculars on a government seal I didn't recognize. Office of Oceanic Studies. The new boat sounded its horn again, roaring closer.

The tour boat captain came back on the intercom, sounding relieved. "Well, folks, looks like there's an official response. We'll let the professionals do their thing, and we can resume our tour. Let's go find some whales!"

While my companions cheered, I kept watching through my binoculars as the OOS boat came alongside the trawler. The fishermen seemed more agitated than relieved by the government response. I guessed that some, if not all, of the hardworking crew might be illegals, and being noticed by the authorities was the last thing they wanted.

OOS men in trim, Navy-knockoff uniforms boarded the fishing vessel and went straight for the large net.

Then our captain swung the boat around, sending up a rooster tail of water. Some passengers squealed with delight, while a few groaned from seasickness. Soon, we left the other two boats far in the distance.

I tried to blank my thoughts as Rudy had taught me. I closed my eyes but couldn't get the images out of my head.

—III—

When you're on vacation, you're supposed to do something fun, and I imagined how much I would enjoy getting to the bottom of this. Maybe it wasn't saving the world from rebuilt alien spacecraft or vampire assassins or flesh-eating zombies, but something smelled fishy to me.

I know, I know.

I can't help it.

Back on shore after the whale-watching cruise, I decided to do a little vacation reading. I looked up everything I could find on the Office of Oceanic Studies. Who needs a paperback summer beach read when you can scroll through an official government website?

The OOS was a small department with a mission to enhance our relationship with the seas, yada, yada, yada. I didn't trust a word of their site. I knew the difference between government truth for the public and real truth behind the scenes.

The official boat had responded with lightning speed to intimidate the poor fishermen with their strange catch. "Enhancing relationships" between man and the sea, no doubt.

Their main offices were a "public resource center and Shoreline Encounter Museum" right here in Lincoln City. My vacation was really shaping up. This sounded much more interesting than collecting seashells along the shore.

I strolled along the bustling thoroughfare, the hotel row, the restaurants, used bookstores, souvenir shops, art galleries. Along the Oregon coast the water is too cold and the skies too cloudy to give off a Beach Boys vibe, but the town was pleasant.

I came to the large white building on a small point just south of the business district, with ample parking and a sign with the Office of Oceanic Studies seal I'd seen on the response boat. A large sign advertised "Shoreline Encounter. School Groups Welcome." Everything looked bright and happy, just as official as it should be. Nothing ominous or sinister, which of course raised my suspicions. I'm just that kind of guy.

Attached to the headquarters was a large, windowless annex with a second level that extended down the steep point to a small, sheltered cove and its own dock. I recognized the swift patrol boat tied up there, ready to launch the moment somebody reported a sea monster.

Standing on the edge of the parking lot above, I pulled out my secure phone. I'd promised myself I wouldn't do it, but questions demand answers, and I had seen enough weird shit that I could write my own personal field guide.

I can't do everything myself, though. That's why I had the DMS team.

The voice that answered sounded bright and freckle-faced, with that special patois of "nerd master."

"I didn't expect to hear from you, Joe," said Bug, the Department of Military Sciences' information technology savant. "You're supposed to be on vacation."

"Not supposed to be—I *am*. I'm having fun. I promise."

"Then why are you calling me?"

"More fun—the kind of fun I really enjoy."

"Uh-oh," Bug said. "Extracurricular activities."

"You'll enjoy it, too—I need you to do some digging for me. I'm having some, uh, interesting interactions with an outfit called the Office of Oceanic Studies. I read their web page, but it doesn't really cut the mustard."

"I never understood that phrase," Bug said. He was an expert at going off on tangents. "Why would anyone need to cut mustard?"

"One of life's great mysteries, Bug—just like this one. See if you can find out what the OOS really does. Use MindReader if you have to." MindReader was the DMS's ultrasophisticated, intuitive supercomputer. Every scrap of information stored in the Ark of the Covenant warehouse would have filled only the tiniest fraction of its capacity.

"You're serious, Joe," Bug said. "Talk to me."

"It's going to sound crazy," I warned.

"I already think you're crazy."

"So does most everyone else in the DMS." Maybe they were right. I watched a satisfied family—mom, dad, two kids—emerge from the Shoreline Encounter Museum.

Bug continued, "But we've all seen crazy, and we know not to discount it."

He had me there.

So, I filled him in on what had happened, and when he signed off, he sounded like a kid turned loose in a LEGO store. He promised he'd track down everything he could.

Now it was time for some hands-on investigating. I pulled open the door to the Shoreline Encounter. A volunteer receptionist dressed in a nautical polo shirt and shorts smiled at me, and I purchased a ticket.

I wandered among the exhibits, posters, display cases, and bubbling aquariums, learning about the wonders of sea life, coral reefs, tide pools. I listened to educational messages about humankind's coexistence with the sea. To be honest, the exhibits were small and rinky-dink, especially since tourists could just go down to the shore and see their own tide pools, watch the waves come crashing in ... maybe see strange figures rise up out of the surf and drag bodies away.

Several docents stood like armed guards, ready to answer questions. At a broad set of shallow aquariums, children reached into the water display to pick up starfish, sea urchins, and crabs. Every few minutes a timed wave of salt water gushed over the exhibit to refresh the critters being harassed by the eager kids. By the starfish pool, a sour-faced old woman looked remarkably like my fourth-grade teacher, Mrs. Evans, from Thomas Jefferson Middle School in New Jersey.

Acting like an oblivious tourist, I made my way toward the rear, where the public museum connected with the large windowless annex. A pair of thick steel doors were closed and locked. Hefty security for a small-town aquarium. In contrast to the other friendly museum signs, the barricade was marked AUTHORIZED PERSONNEL ONLY and NO ENTRANCE.

Seeing no OOS personnel, I strolled vapidly up to the back doors, scrutinizing the secure locks and alarm systems. A control pad and ID scanner were on the wall by the door. I guess they didn't want any stray fish getting loose.

"Excuse me, sir," said a stern-looking docent wearing an expression as tight as his shirt. His muscles suggested that he wrestled giant squid for fun. I could tell he was an ex-Marine. His name tag identified him as Hank. "That's our private research annex, not open to the public."

"I, uh, I'm just looking for the bathroom." The old standby—completely lame, but it always works for a second or two. I ambled off without calling any more attention to myself.

"Check out the sea anemone exhibit," Hank suggested. There was no warmth or docentship in his words whatsoever.

My phone vibrated—a text from Bug. *Call me. Secure line.*

I hurried to the front door, and the bright-eyed volunteer seemed disappointed to see me leaving so soon.

"Very educational," I muttered, by way of reparations. "Great sea urchins."

Behind the OOS parking lot at the edge of the land, I looked down at the annex building. It was low tide now, but the water would rise to the level of the annex later that night. On the lower metal walls, I saw what was unmistakably a hatch leading to the sea.

I called Bug back, and he seemed even more excited than usual, though it's hard to tell.

"MindReader found some really interesting details, Joe. Seems like you stepped in a fresh, steaming pile of—"

I cut him off. "Just with the tip of my shoe, Bug. So far. What did you find?"

"Well, the educational *Free Willy* stuff is just a front."

"No surprise there."

"The OOS was connected to a secret military research program, black ops. They experimented with augmenting soldiers for long-term survival underwater."

"*Augmenting them?* You mean like giving them bigger lungs so they can swim farther?" I remembered the clawed, webbed footprints I'd found in the sand.

"Way more than that," Bug said. "The Full Monty! The OOS wanted to surgically adapt volunteers into genuine ... mermen."

I coughed out a quick laugh. "Like *The Little Mermaid?*"

"You told me what you thought you saw. Look, if the military could enhance humans for undersea survival, gills and everything, soldiers could infiltrate harbors, slip into places where even small submarines can't go without being detected. Undersea commandos could place mines on the bottoms of warships."

"And fetch fresh lobster dinner for the generals," I said, the wheels turning in my mind.

Bug continued, "That was five years ago, though. The whole project's been mothballed. The early experiments were failures. The candidates rejected the body modifications and drowned."

I turned to look at the OOS Shoreline Encounter building. "I doubt they're mothballed, Bug. Maybe I'll do some *augmented* investigating and get to the bottom of this."

Bug sounded exasperated. "Or I could put it through channels here. Mr. Church sent you there to take a vacation."

"I *am* on vacation," I said. "*This* is how I have fun."

—IV—

Mothballed, my ass.

I've had experience infiltrating ultra-secure facilities, even end-of-the-world mega fortresses. Breaking into the Shoreline Encounter in Lincoln City, Oregon was a piece of cake. I was supposed to be relaxing, after all.

Behind cloud-scudded skies, the moon still gave enough light to see by. The high tide had indeed submerged the lower part of the mysterious annex, and because there were no windows, I couldn't tell if the lights were on inside.

I made my entry through the roof of the annex, the point of obvious vulnerability. Normally, I'd have my whole DMS team, high-level weaponry, James Bond gadgets. Tonight, I had only my personal sidearm, a Sig Sauer P226 9mm, just a vacation gun, really.

And I had ... me. I'd be able to handle any resistance the aquarium people might offer. I would just have a look around. I could call in the DMS cavalry if we needed to follow up. I didn't intend to get into any trouble.

Who, me?

I pried open one of the four skylights—why is it no one ever sees skylights as a vulnerability?—and lowered myself down. I guess there was a payoff for the hours I spent in the weight room.

My tiptoes barely touched the top of a metal file cabinet, and I let go of the skylight frame, not worrying about how I would climb back out. Any self-respecting evil genius laboratory must have a handy stepstool, right?

The rippled, blue-tinted glass of the skylights gave the lab area a watery glow. The place was hushed except for a low thrum of machinery, power generators, and bubbling water.

I remembered the Shoreline Encounter Museum on the other side, the touchy-feely tidepool tanks where you could pet a starfish or a sea urchin. The Office of Oceanic Studies kept all their

Frankenstein experiments behind security doors, where you needed a special ticket.

Laptop computers and some old-school lab notebooks sat on two government-issue desks. A stainless steel table held dissection trays and surgical implements. In high school biology lab, we dissected frogs or fetal pigs. This was something different—like advanced mad-scientist class.

This main room held aquariums on tables and shelves, bubbling air re-circulators, murky water.

And specimens.

Some people just keep goldfish. The OOS scientists kept *organs*.

The nearest tank held floating eyeballs—large eyeballs, not quite human, with slitted pupils that had a reptilian quality to them. Other tanks contained purplish hearts, and lungs that didn't look right to me, with a branched tube that didn't connect to a windpipe.

One aquarium held an accordion-like stack of pinkish, feathery membranes, and I'd done enough fishing to recognize gills. But these gills were not from any kind of fish I had ever caught.

I remembered the strange, dark figures I had seen on the beach, in the fishermen's net, and what Bug had told me about the "mothballed" OOS experiments.

Creating merpeople?

At the rear of the large, dim room was a connecting door and a ramp sloping down a hall to a lower laboratory. I could hear low voices, the clatter of tools, people moving about.

In a movie, the audience would be shouting at the screen, "No, Joe! Leave it alone! Don't do it!" Wise advice, but this wasn't a movie, and I have been known to possess as little common sense as any teenager in a slasher film. I checked my SIG in its holster, crouched down—because it made me feel sneakier—and slipped down the sloped corridor to the lower chamber. The main event. The place above was just Igor's warm-up room.

The lower lab's brighter light revealed walls covered with

extensive diagrams of human anatomy, as well as modified figures, sketches of fin enhancements, heads with widened mouths and needle-sharp teeth, enlarged eyes, clawed webbed hands.

And gills.

My skin crawled. Three scientists in white coats and surgical gloves were working in the lab. Two were handsome men in their late thirties and looked like they had just walked off the set of a hospital soap opera. An older woman seemed to be in charge, and I recognized the matronly docent from the Shoreline Encounter. She still reminded me of my worst schoolteacher ever, Mrs. Evans.

But this was worse than fourth grade. Far worse.

The two younger doctors leaned over a surgical table on which a humanlike figure seemed to be the subject of an overenthusiastic autopsy. Its greenish-brown skin had been mostly flayed off, spread like a wet blanket on the table beneath the figure. The sternum had been sawed open, the lungs and heart removed and placed in stainless steel trays to be weighed on the scale beside the table.

I wondered if this was the body the OOS had seized from the hapless fishing boat that had caught an unexpected whopper.

One of the surgeons probed the cadaver's chest cavity as the other worked near the throat and head. The thing was not human. Not by a long stretch. The Creature from the Black Lagoon was the best way to describe it. Or, for you kids who don't remember the excellent Universal Studios monster movies, imagine one of the bad guys from *Aquaman*.

But the best way to get distracted from something horrible is to see something even worse. Not very useful advice, I know.

The old schoolteacher scientist stood between two horizontal, transparent coffinlike tanks hooked to burbling oxygenation tubes. The liquid had an unearthly pale glow, enough to illuminate the bandaged horrors inside.

The subjects inside were human, but surgical scars across their chests, arms, and throats made them look as if they'd been sewn up by someone barely qualified to repair upholstery. Jagged fins ran along the forearms and shoulders, augmentations to help them swim through the water. Webbed skin had been grafted onto their split and widened hands. An air mask connected to a breathing tube and a humming respirator covered the lower half of each subject's face.

These plastic-surgery-gone-wrong contestants were far more primitive and slapdash than the specimen on the dissection table. Maybe different phases of the project?

Mrs. Evans held an iPad and took readings from the medical apparatus. Frowning, she adjusted the airflow and looked down. When she moved aside, I could see great gashes in the neck of the nearest patient. Raw, open wounds. Gill slits. They fluttered in an effort to extract oxygen from the fluid in the coffin chamber. The old woman stepped back, humming and nodding. She seemed to be talking to the patients like some fairy godmother.

The nearest patient's eyes were wide open, and even though the mask covered most of his expression, I could read the agony and fear. Even if this guy had volunteered for radical off-the-book experiments, the most naive and patriotic subject would never have imagined this.

I certainly had a vacation story to tell Church.

I heard a familiar *click* and felt the hard steel of a pistol barrel pressed against my temple.

"Still looking for the bathroom?" asked a gruff voice.

—V—

I should have known to expect a fourth person in the lab. Stupid me. It's an unwritten rule that bad guys always come in pairs.

"You're out of toilet paper in stall number two," I said.

It was Hank, the burly guy from the Shoreline Encounter that afternoon.

"Move, smartass." He urged me forward with the gun against my head. It wasn't a good time to argue.

The two soap-opera scientists looked up in alarm, while Mrs. Evans seemed more annoyed than alarmed. "How did he get in?"

"I told you our security is too lax," Hank said.

The older woman sniffed. "It wasn't in the budget. And the new reinforced doors you insisted on didn't keep him out either." She even sounded like my old teacher, especially when she was issuing detention.

"Priorities. We needed to harden the whole facility." Hank glanced meaningfully at a metal hatch on the far wall, which probably led to the sea. It had a submarine-style locking wheel in the center.

Mrs. Evans stalked toward me, iPad still in hand. She spoke to the others as if I couldn't understand English. "Well, what are we supposed to do with him? He's already seen Phase Two." She gestured to the monstrously scarred patients inside the bubbling coffin tanks.

"How about another set of donor lungs?" Hank asked. "Any other organs you need?"

I watched Mrs. Evans's eyes light up at the possibility.

Enough of this.

"Sorry, I never signed the donor card in my wallet," I said. "I'm a Federal agent, investigating the OOS. My department head knows I'm here and so does my team. With one phone call, I can bring in a whole bunch of people from a whole bunch of alphabet government agencies—some you've heard of, some you haven't."

"Then we'd better not let you make that phone call," Hank said.

Not the terrified reaction I was hoping for. He shoved me forward, and I got a better view of the dissection specimen and the surgical subjects.

"Doesn't matter what I've seen," I continued. "We're aware of your covert project to alter human soldiers for underwater survival." I nodded down at the bubbling tanks. "Looks like they're not finished yet. I can recommend a good plastic surgeon."

Mrs. Evans crossed her arms over her chest, deep in thought. The soap-opera doctors looked to her but held their tongues. The dissected body on the operating table made me really uneasy.

I was saved by a knock on the door—cliché, I know, but it's a classic.

The heavy pounding came from the hatch that led to the sea.

—VI—

One of the soap-opera doctors turned white, and terror turned his voice into a strangled squeak. "You said they'd be too afraid to come back!"

Mrs. Evans glared at Hank. "We should have spent our budget on hardening defenses *out there*."

The wheel on the hatch began to turn as if the Incredible Hulk was twisting the lid off a jar. The second doctor ran to grab it, as if he could use brute force to stop the metal door from opening. But the hatch lock clicked and the steel barrier slammed open, smashing the doctor against the wall. A splash of foamy surf pushed in from outside—along with something else.

They seemed to be wearing wetsuits designed by a creature-effects studio—sleek, like seals. Their mouths were seabass-wide and full of teeth. Serrated fins adorned their heads and shoulders, the sides of their faces. Gill slits flapped open and closed, but they hissed through their mouths as they inhaled air as well.

The first one lunged inside. The injured doctor tried to crawl away, but the gill-man stalked forward like a land shark. With a wide, webbed hand he grabbed the doctor by his throat, lifted him off the floor, and raked a clawed hand across his chest.

Two more creatures surged through the hatch, followed by another pair. Mermen, just like Bug had talked about. The Office of Oceanic Studies apparently had a lot more success than the black-budget bureaucrats admitted.

Mermen poured in like walking barracudas. As the first doctor lay dying on the floor, spouting blood from multiple gashes, Hank shoved me aside, no longer interested in a trespasser when faced by an invasion of sea monsters.

Now that the pistol wasn't pressed against my head, I saw he was carrying a Glock 9mm—not much firepower, probably intended to exaggerate the size of Hank's manhood. He didn't threaten, just fired three times in rapid succession, pumping small-caliber bullets into the first merman. The monster grabbed at his chest and collapsed.

Important data point—the things could be killed. Oh happy day!

I pulled out my SIG and stood beside him, though I didn't imagine he would write me a thank you note. But I wasn't ready to just start shooting. The OOS goons wanted to kill *me*, so I didn't have the warm fuzzies for protecting them. Who were the real bad guys here?

And could the mermen tell that *I* wasn't part of the mad scientists' club?

Three creatures darted to the dissection table, and the second dissection doctor panicked and tried to back away. The hissing, sloshing voices of the gill-men sounded utterly inhuman, but rage crosses species lines. Seeing the specimen—their brother—flayed, its organs in trays, one slitted eye floating in a sample container, they went on a rampage. Who could blame them?

Before the doctor took two steps, a pair of mermen seized his arms and spread them apart so another creature could rip him open from his groin to the base of his throat, gutting him like a fish. The doctor's scream lasted far longer than I thought it could. The sound stopped when they yanked his lungs out and plopped them in the stainless steel containers by the autopsy table.

If these things were the result of OOS black-book experiments, why would they turn on their creators? The vicious mermen were clearly superior to the Frankenstein surgical experiments in the coffin tanks, but boy, they certainly held a grudge. Were they the results of "Phase One"?

Hank continued firing his Glock, and more creatures fell.

I kept my pistol raised, trying to keep myself alive without drawing their attack. Then they came at us and, unfortunately, I had to pick sides between sea monsters and monstrous doctors. I chose Team Human.

My modified SIG Sauer had more punch than Hank's

weapon, and I took out three gill-men. It was like shooting fish in a barrel ... but there were a lot of fish.

Half of the creatures headed toward where Mrs. Evans stood with one hand on each coffin tank. She glowered at the mermen as if she could protect her experiments. "No! You can't have my work."

One lunged at her, and I blew it away with a neat hole through the back of its head. The real Mrs. Evans might have given me extra credit.

I shot two more, but the wild army barely noticed.

Hank ran out of bullets, ejected the magazine, slammed another one home. It was his only spare. I had two spare clips—certainly not enough to take on an undersea army. Hell, I was on vacation! I didn't expect to need an arsenal.

One of the mermen loomed over the first coffin tank, where the subject inside was awake. Terrified air bubbles erupted from around the facemask, and his scarred fists battered against the transparent cover. The merman tipped the tank over, shattering the sides. As nutrient fluids gushed out, two creatures hauled the subject through the jagged glass walls, literally ripping him to pieces.

Mrs. Evans shrieked, "No!" She tried her damnedest to protect the second tank. A creature ripped open her lab coat, cutting deep gouges. She fell back, bleeding, but her hands still reached toward the tank as if to save it.

I grabbed her shoulders and dragged her a few feet away. I shot a pair of mermen who pursued us, while others swarmed the second coffin tank, which they smashed open.

Hank charged in like a bull in a China shop, firing his Glock. The shots echoed among the screams and the hissing. His pistol fell silent as he ran out of bullets, then he tried to fight the creatures with his fists. What else was he going to do? Though he looked like a brawler, he was outnumbered and outmatched. Soon his defiant yells turned into screams.

Around us, mermen were smashing and destroying all of the computers, the medical equipment, the diagrams.

I shot the closest pursuing merman, conserving ammunition. Did I want to call their attention to me instead? No, I did not.

The only way out was up the sloped corridor and through the front door. If Hank had indeed spent the OOS security budget on that barricade, maybe it would hold off the sea creatures. Or maybe I was just an optimist.

As I dragged her toward the connecting corridor, Mrs. Evans coughed blood. The claws had missed her throat, but the wounds were deep and bleeding badly. I felt no deep personal obligation toward her, especially since she'd seemed delighted to use me as an organ donor. But if everyone else was dead and the OOS records and systems destroyed, this woman was my only chance at getting answers.

And I liked answers.

She stumbled as I hauled her toward the upper level. Three mermen loped after us. I took one out with a shot to the head, and it collapsed in front of the other two. They hesitated, finally displaying a little caution. Maybe they sensed something different about me. Or maybe it was my deodorant.

I urged Mrs. Evans to the upper-level lab. "Come on, come on!" As I pulled her through the chamber—funny thing—the tanks with the eyeballs, lungs, and gills didn't look nearly as horrifying after what I'd seen below.

I heard the mermen slithering up the corridor after us.

The big security doors were on the far side of the lab, leading into the Shoreline Experience. I hoped we could just push them open from the inside and get out. After all, with budget cuts, why would Hank try to prevent anyone from breaking *out* of the laboratory?

In the chamber below, the creatures continued their destruction of the lab that had created them.

Behind us, five mermen entered the upper lab before I could make it to the security door.

Mrs. Evans picked that moment to collapse with a moan.

So I dragged her.

I slammed my back against the thick door, hoping it operated just like a normal emergency exit. It didn't. Of course, it didn't.

I let Mrs. Evans slump against the door. She was still gurgling, and her breath rattled. Blood soaked her lab coat. I hammered at the door, looked for some sort of activation button. "Open sesame," I yelled. The reinforced doors remained securely locked.

The mermen closed in, their slitted eyes bright. They were all covered in blood and slime, as if they had taken turns with the victims below. They left wet trails behind them, as if a giant snail had crawled along the floor.

I took out one more attacker with my last bullet. I know you're supposed to save the last bullet for yourself, but that's another movie cliché that doesn't always happen in real life.

Then I saw the palm-scanner plate on the side wall.

"Right," I said. "Mrs. Evans, you've got to lend me a hand."

She groaned in pain as I lifted her bloody hand and slapped it against the scanner plate. Somehow the ID reader caught enough of her palm print and the lock clicked.

I shoved the door open as the mermen shambled toward us, picking up speed. I tucked my hands under Mrs. Evans's arms and dragged her through the opening.

Sensing that we were about to escape, the creatures lurched closer. I turned and pushed the heavy door shut. Frantically looking around, I saw the control panel next to the AUTHORIZED PERSONNEL ONLY sign and hit Reengage Security. Good thing the OOS marked their controls with obvious labels.

The locks thunked into place an instant before the first merman hit the barrier. They pounded against it, but I knew the doors would hold for now.

Mrs. Evans lay on the floor in a spreading pool of blood. A lot of blood. My expert opinion, she wasn't going to make it.

I propped her up, which eased her breathing a little. This was my last chance. In many instances when the Grim Reaper is knocking "Shave and a Haircut" at death's door, people get a last statement off their chest, express love for a spouse, apologize for some long-ago regret.

I wanted information.

I leaned closer. "Can you hear me?" Her eyes were glazed. "I saw your surgical experiments, but these mermen are so much better than the ones in the tanks. Perfectly adapted."

She gurgled and coughed. A bubble of blood formed on her lips like the world's most horrific bubble gum.

I had to know. "If you made them, why did they come back and attack you?"

She croaked out words. "So many ..."

"How many did you make? Why did they destroy your lab? Why are they attacking their own creators?"

"Didn't ... create them," Mrs. Evans said. "They are ... *real*."

I wasn't sure I heard her right.

"Tried to study ... specimens from the wild." More blood ran down the side of her face. "Replicate what nature already made." She closed her eyes and a long rattle of disappointment came out of her mouth. "We failed ... failed utterly."

She slumped into final silence.

I sat with the dead woman on the floor of a place that promised an "unforgettable shoreline encounter." A steel security door was my only barrier against an army of sea monsters.

Eventually the battering became halfhearted, then dwindled into silence as the creatures gave up and retreated.

I pulled out my phone and called the special security number I had. A direct line to Church.

"Joe? I'm surprised to hear from you, especially on this line."

"I'm surprised, too," I said. "Send a DMS team out here as soon as you can. I have a cleanup on Aisle Nine."

"Cleanup?" Church asked. "Are you all right? Give me a sitrep."

When I told him the bare bones, it sounded outrageous, even to me—and I had lived through it. A real race of mermen, not just a military experiment after all.

"You'll have to figure out the rest of it, sir," I said. "I'm on vacation."

And one last flash fiction exercise for my Romance class. The assignment was to write a short story with the final line "And they lived happily ever after."

Well, that all depends on whose happiness you're talking about.

Royal Wedding

Bells of rejoicing rang throughout the kingdom. Peasants and townspeople were called away from their tasks to line up and cheer the wedding procession of Prince Derek and Princess Lilac. The people wore their finest clothes and tossed flower petals along the path to the castle. Though they had no coins to spare, they spent time and money cleaning the streets, fixing their roofs, painting their homes, making everything beautiful for the royal couple. They cheered as best they could.

Up in the castle, Hedda had worked in the kitchens since midnight to bake wedding rolls, wedding cake, wedding puddings. The silverware had to be polished until fingers bled. Hedda scowled even though she was supposed to be beaming with joy for what was sure to be the prosperity of the kingdom.

"Come now, all of you!" barked the head cook. "We have to prepare a feast for the eternal happiness of our prince and princess."

"How about our happiness?" Hedda muttered.

"That is not for us to worry about."

Jack, the scruffy young serving boy, came in with an armload of wood for the ovens. "This'll take care of the last breads and pies." He winced as he dumped the wood in the pile. His hands were red and inflamed, and Hedda hurried over to the sweet young man. They had grown up in the village, known each other since they were small children, though neither of them had many prospects.

"Let me see those hands," she said.

His fingers were blistered, every knuckle swollen. "It's the bee stings. Can't help it."

"You could help it if the royal couple didn't insist on honey-drenched bumblebees for an appetizer." On a whim, Princess Lilac had asked for the treat, which meant that someone had to catch jars full of bumblebees, and bumblebees did not like to be caught. Jack had been stung repeatedly, but the appetizers were safe.

With each passing day, Hedda had grown to hate the prince and princess more and more.

"I made a salve for you. I know all the secret recipes." Hedda's mother had been an herb woman, a specialist in medicines and folk remedies, and she had taught her daughter every trick.

She gently rubbed the salve into his fingers. Hedda was sweet on Jack, and each night, the two would find a shadowy alcove in the castle and sit together with a meal scraped from the plates of the decadent nobles. Neither she nor Jack could ever scrounge the coins necessary to pay the marriage tax. The closest they would come to a fine wedding would be to hover in the banquet room and wait for the noble guests to demand more wine or another serving of broiled larks.

Hedda knew the other servants felt the same. Everyone was instructed to keep up appearances no matter how much the prince and princess were despised. But she had had enough, and she saw her opportunity with the wedding banquet.

Nobles from across the kingdom would attend, counts, dukes, barons, other titles that Hedda didn't entirely understand, except they all had to be addressed as "m'lord" and unquestionably obeyed. Hedda was an attractive girl, but too drab and scuffed to draw any nobleman's lusty attention; fortunately, Jack found her pretty. That was all she needed with the thing they had to do tonight.

She had planned for weeks, digging through forest mulch to find the right kind of mushrooms, the orange spiky ones her mother called Death's Daggers. The head cook saw what she carried in her basket, and although the cook knew full well what the mushrooms would do, she turned a blind eye and whistled as she scrubbed a cauldron.

None of the other servants admitted that they knew of the plan, but Hedda didn't need to give them any warning. Finally, when it came time for the meal, the breads, the soup, the roasted boar and venison, every course had a liberal dose of mushrooms, minced up so small as to be unseen. When one serving girl tried to snatch a roll from a basket, the head cook had nearly screamed, swatting the girl's hand and scolding her never to taste the food of her betters.

Hedda, Jack, and the army of castle servants served the well-dressed and perfumed crowd. The handsome prince and blushing bride were too enamored with each other even to think to compliment the meal, which the guests ate with great gusto. Everyone stuffed themselves, but none of the servants tasted a bite, even though the food seemed luscious.

Princess Lilac was the first to groan and cry out in pain as she hunched over with stomach spasms. She spewed vomit into her plate. Her prince cried out for help, then he too doubled over. Very swiftly, all the nobles were retching, writhing on the floor, their skin erupting in boils, their throats constricted.

The servants waited patiently. The process was longer and noisier than Hedda had expected. Her mother had not given her all the details, but Death's Dagger was certainly effective.

Even before the victims all were dead, Hedda and Jack scurried about, pulling rings from fingers, snatching jeweled pendants, prying rubies and sapphires from goblets. Gold coins were piled up as wedding gifts, and Jack stuffed his pockets. Hedda filled a sack with necklaces and brooches, while the other servants scavenged their own riches. They would scatter after tonight.

This castle was dead, but now she and Jack could be free.

They had all the money they could imagine, even enough for the marriage tax, though she had no intention of paying it. They would be married in their own hearts and rich in their own souls.

In the dark of the night they fled the castle and the dead bodies piled in the banquet hall. Hedda didn't think about the people she had just murdered. In her mind, they were a different sort of people anyway.

She and Jack ran off, and they lived happily ever after.

In the first volume of my Horror and Dark Fantasy Stories, "Rude Awakening" used the idea of a vampire waking up, being hunted by a vampire killer, and desperate to know why. This was just too good to do only once, especially when my coauthor, Guy Anthony De Marco suggested a completely different approach. Here again, we meet a vampire feeling secure in his fortress castle, just trying to get a good day's sleep, when an intruder messes everything up.

The Fate Worse Than Death
(with Guy Anthony De Marco)

Lying in the dark in a perfectly restful daytime nap, feeling sated with fresh warm blood (Type O Negative, his favorite), Vlad sensed the intruding presence even before the silent alarm triggered his vibrating watch. The watch buzzed against the mahogany wall of his cozy coffin, warning him.

Always interruptions! Someone was trying to break into his fortress, probably up to no good. "Rest in peace" was harder to achieve than he had ever imagined.

Vlad was a light sleeper, had been for centuries, and even modern sleeping aids like Ambien or Lunesta didn't help. But even with his powers, it was good to remain alert. Careless vampires didn't stay immortal for very long.

He hit the snooze button on the annoying vibrating watch and sighed, not willing to crawl out of the snug coffin just yet. After all, why did he have all those defenses? The intruder should be taken care of without him needing to lift a sharp fingernail.

Vlad couldn't remember the last time someone had bothered to track him down with evil intent, so he doubted this would be a vampire hunter. It was broad daylight, but his mansion was quiet, apparently unoccupied; it was probably a common burglar trying to score some quality electronics. People didn't realize most burglaries happened during the day. And burglars didn't realize how much trouble they would be getting into if they tried to steal from Vladimir Dracul! Especially if they woke him up during daylight hours.

Eight hundred and eighty-two years of existing among those who feared his presence had jaded him. The burglar would be inept, with no idea of the disaster he was about to face. Vlad sighed again and stretched as far as the confines of the coffin would allow. *Too bad,* he thought, *I actually feel depressed that there's nobody left with the guile and fortitude to challenge me.*

He wriggled to a more comfortable position and began to doze. The electric blanket kept him toasty, even though his blood remained cold. The blanket reminded him of his childhood, and he stifled an urge to suck his thumb, remembering the embarrassing previous time, when he'd painfully impaled his thumb on a sharp tooth.

Just as he was drifting off, the alarm watch buzzed again—more urgently this time, to inform him that the intruder had eluded the expensive paramilitary guards and breached the second perimeter of his fortress. Vlad woke further. That was interesting, but the paramilitary guards were flash and dazzle, rather than substance. The intruder was in for an even bigger surprise.

He smiled as he imagined the look of fear and despair that would spread over the hapless thief as he came face-to-face with one of Vlad's *true* guardians. Still feeling sleepy, he settled deeper into his comfortable memory foam. He listened carefully, sure he would hear the sounds of rending and feeding any moment, accompanied by a few delightful screams.

The thought of so much blood and raw meat made him contemplate breakfast after sunset. He didn't always drink blood; that was just a special treat, and—with his vampire metabolism—could actually be fattening. Pork chops, he decided ... yes, he would have pork chops. Maybe with some applesauce and a nice baked potato. He felt blessed that he never needed to worry about high cholesterol. *Blessed!* The thought made him chuckle, which sounded especially loud inside the coffin.

Minutes went by, and he heard no sounds of a struggle, no shouts or growls, no wails of despair. Vlad frowned severely enough that the tips of his fangs protruded from his lips. How had the intruder gotten past his hellhounds? The creatures of the night that prowled his middle sanctum were hungry, fast, and angry at being locked indoors. The three monstrous beasts were the second, third, and fifth most dangerous beings within a mile in any direction (the fourth being the bloodthirsty and sadistic mafioso who lived three estates to the north). Humming the *Jeopardy!* theme song, he cocked his ear to catch any hint of noise from outside his coffin.

Then the lid began to creak open, slowly, tentatively. Startled, Vlad jumped and whacked his head—fine mahogany was definitely a hard wood. Calming himself, he lay back and settled, trying to appear dead and harmless, while he kept his eyes open a slit. The groaning hinges of the lid droned on with painful slowness, and Vlad had to stifle an urge to shout, "Get on with it!" or push the cover open himself.

"Good afternoon, sir," said a lone figure looming over the coffin. "Sorry to interrupt your nap, but we have important business, you and I."

Giving up his slumbering ruse, the vampire sat up to look at his guest while rubbing the small knot growing on his forehead from where he had hit the coffin lid. The intruder was a thick-bodied nerd type with round glasses and a faded Jethro Tull T-shirt. He held a black Evangelion anime backpack in his left hand and wore a black leather belt full of pouches emblazoned with yellow Batman logos.

So, Vlad thought, not the typical burglar—or vampire hunter.

"Good afternoon to you," said the vampire in a thick Transylvanian accent. He had lost his accent over the centuries, but sometimes it seemed appropriate. "Why, may I inquire, are you in my bedchambers at this ungodly hour?"

Usually, when an intruder broke into his fortress, subdued his defenses, and pulled open his coffin, the routine involved sharp sticks and mallets.

The pudgy young man shifted nervously, swung his backpack to one side, and backed away to let the vampire swing his legs out of the coffin. Vlad knew he was intimidating as he stood up to his full six-foot-eight height. He slapped dust from his black tuxedo jacket while observing the intruder.

From behind his round glasses, the man's eyes went wide. "Gosh, you're bigger than I thought you would be." He blinked a few times and then remembered the rest of his manners. "My name is Marvin. Marvin Drake. I'm a computer forensics and security expert. Glad to finally meet you, sir. It was quite difficult to track you down."

Vlad gave a slight bow to his guest. "Then you must know full well who I am. I will, of course, have to deal with you in the usual manner, but your methods intrigue me. I need some answers." He extended a hand, curled the fingers. "I can glamor you into revealing—"

"Oh, that won't be necessary, sir. I came here to talk." Marvin pulled out a gallon baggie filled with a mushed-up yellowish goop. He opened the top to release a pungent smell. "And I did not come unarmed."

Laughing, Vladimir dipped his index finger into the mixture, swirled it around, and pulled out a taste of the garlic and onion. He popped it into his mouth. "*Mmm*, tasty, although it does need some cilantro and a dash of salt. Did you bring any chips?"

Normally, when he demonstrated that he was impervious to the usual defenses against vampires, his adversaries would react with intense fear, but Marvin Drake smiled with delight, showing off crooked, unbrushed teeth. It reminded Vlad of Renfield. Ah, Renfield ... The poor man spent years in rehab trying to kick his habit of eating flies.

"Good, sir. Just checking. How about this?" He yanked out a gold cross from his utility belt and pressed it close to Vlad's face.

Moving faster than humanly possible, since he was no longer human, he snatched the cross out of Marvin's hand and inspected it with a practiced eye, turning it over in his hand. "Gold-plated. I really have to start spreading rumors that only solid gold or silver crucifixes work. At least they're worth something." He tossed the cross back, and Marvin juggled to catch it.

The young man's spreading grin made the vampire pause. There was something wrong with the situation, or with this oddball young man, but Vlad couldn't put a cold finger on what it was. He glanced around at all of the meticulous cobwebs strung along the walls and ceiling—just props, but much easier to maintain than real cobwebs; the ornate candelabras, the suit of armor, the medieval weapons on the wall, all to make his current dank castle feel just like home.

The intruder cast a glance to the heavy, black velvet curtains that hung over the black-painted windows. "Should I even bother opening the curtains to let in the sunlight? I don't suppose that would make you catch fire and explode?"

"No, but the bright light might give me a headache at this hour, and you've been annoying enough already. What is it you want?"

Marvin seemed satisfied to have the preliminaries dispensed with. "May we sit, sir? I really need to have a talk with you." He indicated a small café-style table a few feet away, where Vlad had his coffee after waking up.

The vampire apprehensively took a seat opposite the strange visitor, who was not at all the typical vampire killer. "You're not going to lunge at me with a wooden stake, are you?"

"Would that kill you?"

"No, but it would ruin my favorite ruffled silk shirt, and then I'd have to get truly medieval on you."

"Thanks for the warning, sir. I don't think we have to bother. I have a business proposition for you." Marvin looked puppy-dog hopeful.

"I need answers first." Vlad leaned over. "I want to know how you found me, and how you got in here. Obviously, I have flaws in my security."

Marvin leaned back in his filigree metal chair, adjusted his Jethro Tull shirt. "As I said, I'm a computer forensics and security specialist. I've been tracking you for years. With all of your quirks,

Mr. Dracul, you leave a fairly large data footprint for anyone who knows where to look. Pretty easy, if you know how to do forensic research." He rummaged in the backpack and removed his smartphone.

"For instance, your method of obtaining real estate through a particular set of shell corporations let me keep up with your movements. You typically stay at one location for three to six years before moving on. You tend to stay in Victorian or castle-type estates, which limits your pool of available homes. You prefer colder climates, probably because it resembles the Carpathian Mountains."

"That, and I don't want to get moldy," Vlad said, but he was impressed with what the intruder said. His summation was quite accurate. The centuries had made him complacent, and he forgot that technological advances allowed people to process huge amounts of data in near real-time. "Very clever, Marvin. That explains how you located me. But what about my paramilitary guards? My mercenaries?"

"I was able to track down their personal cell phone numbers and sent them all a YouTube video of a kitten playing with a crocodile. They were so entranced, I walked right past them." He smiled. "You really should watch the clip. It's very funny."

"Seen it already." Vlad frowned. "But my true supernatural guardians are relentless in their pursuit of intruders. How did you get past the hellhounds?"

"Easier than expected," said Marvin. "They're just giant dogs with a bigger appetite. I tossed them each some pork chops laced with LSD and a large ball of peanut butter." He grinned. "Right now, their mouths are stuck shut, and they're watching pink Hello Kittys ride purple unicorns."

"Where did you get the pork chops?"

"From your freezer, sir. They looked fresh."

So much for his planned breakfast.

"And how did you know beforehand that all of the traditional vampire-repelling techniques wouldn't work?"

Eager, Marvin pressed his chest against the metal tabletop,

and Vlad could physically feel the pounding of his guest's youthful Mountain Dew-fueled heart. "I did my homework, sir. Two years ago, when I was bored, I did an analysis of all of the classic books in the public domain. Starting with Bram Stoker, I found that many of the great writers of the last century had some subtle literary commonalities that were statistically improbable. I created a surgically precise literary model that uses a simulated aggregate English professor modeled after personality profiles from more than a thousand arrogant college literary department heads. According to my deep analysis, all of those literary works over the centuries appeared to be written by the same person. I assumed that you were the person who wrote Dracula to feed people the wrong methods to defeat you. But you were writing long before that. You created all those books, didn't you?"

Vlad was embarrassed. "I'm impressed that you could figure it out. The creative writing bug bit me a lot harder than the ancient vampire who turned me. I've been ... dabbling for a while, yes. But I gave up on critique groups back in the eighteenth century."

Maybe this young man would take a look at his poems. No, those were too personal....

Marvin enthusiastically bounced on his chair, his greasy brown hair flapping up and down. "Imagine my surprise when I discovered that my favorite classic stories and novels were actually ghostwritten by an immortal vampire under numerous pen names! Now I know how you can afford all those castles and mansions with all those royalties!"

"All my big sellers are in the public domain," Vlad pointed out.

But Marvin was too excited to hear. "All the top writers in the history of literature were really one ... *ummm*, person. Speculative fiction, romance, erotica, historicals, *New York Times* bestsellers, award winners, and all of them are on my bookshelves."

Vlad felt uncomfortable and exposed. It was hard enough to keep his secret as a vampire, but maintaining a host of pen names was even more of a challenge. He would probably have to kill this intrepid man anyway.

"What's to keep me from reaching across this table and draining you dry?" He felt his senses go alert, his claws itching to tear flesh and spill blood, his fangs ready to plunge into a pudgy throat ... forget the pork chops.

"Nice gambit, but I was the school chess champion from 2006 to 2009. I took precautions. You don't dare harm me."

"And I was the national chess champion in 1782. I played against George Washington, a fellow vampire. He lost a bet and forfeited his fangs, which is why he used wooden teeth." Vlad sneered. "Let me guess, you told a friend where you were going, and they'll call the authorities if you go missing."

Marvin squirmed in his chair, glancing at a large black spider that sat on the table, unmoving. "No, I did something more ... drastic. I have an automated post that will go out on Facebook, Twitter, Pinterest, Tumblr, Reddit, Google+, and every other social media website—including the undead ones like Myspace. The post gives explicit directions on how to find you and where you are now." He nudged the smartphone on the table in front of him. Pointing to a toothy icon on his screen, he said, "Heck, there's even an app for that."

Vlad waved his hand in dismissal, though he was uneasy. "That would only bring a convenient meal for me. I should thank you for arranging breakfast in bed, or casket, as the case may be."

It was Marvin's turn to lean across the small table. "Oh, it's far, far worse than that, sir." He looked into the vampire's red-rimmed eyes and whispered, "Unless you do as I demand, the post will tell everyone that you *sparkle when you sleep!*"

If it was possible for Vlad to look paler than his normal self, he hit a new level of waxy pallor. "You wouldn't dare!"

Marvin flipped the spider over on the table. It had a stamp that said *made in China*. The spider web was nothing but fake Halloween-store cotton strands. Looking around, Marvin indicated all of the faux spooky objects in the coffin chamber. "For you, it's all about appearances, Mr. Dracul. I know that about you, and that's why the sparkly vampire defense is my endgame."

Vladimir sat stiffly in his chair, breathing heavily at the

thought of being chased by every pre-pubescent young lady and their mothers, no matter where he hid. "What ... what do you want from me? You wish me to turn you into an immortal vampire?"

"No, nothing like that." Marvin bent over, reached into his backpack, and produced an enormous stack of dog-eared papers. "Your words inspired me to become a writer. I want you to be my literary mentor." He slid the manuscript across the table. It was titled *The Ears of Argon*, Volume 1 of the "Body Parts of Argon Saga."

Vlad was appalled. "Read amateur manuscripts? I'd rather die —and I have done that already."

"More than that, sir. Let me cowrite a short story with you for my favorite humorous speculative fiction anthology series." Marvin's voice had an edge. "Either you can help me make my *prose* sparkle, or ..."

The vampire shuddered uncontrollably. "You're insane!" He saw with dismay that the manuscript was marked as Part One of Volume 1. The title was in all caps, Old English letters. Marvin's backpack had even larger stacks of paper inside.

Marvin leaned back, looking at him eagerly. "Go on, start reading. I'll sit here quietly, I promise. I just want to watch your reactions."

Vlad picked up the first page, dreading that even an immortal lifespan would not be long enough ... but he would do anything— *anything*—to stop that message from going out.

Where would you go in a zombie apocalypse? Like most horror writers, I've given it a great deal of thought. And yes, I've made up my mind.

The red rock desert in southern Utah is one of my favorite places. I can hike all day in spectacular canyon landscapes and never see another soul. Indeed, the Utah desert is where I'd go if a zombie apocalypse happened.

My wife, however, would not do so well with the isolation, not to mention camping and backpacking.

That was the foundation for this end-of-the-world story, my only real epic zombie apocalypse story (so far).

Social Distance
(with Rebecca Moesta)

—I—
Dale

"This is going to be the most grueling, most difficult survival challenge any of you has ever faced," I said, looking at their faces, a few of them already sunburned and sweaty. I watched the expressions of the nine high school students change as the grim reality washed over them.

We stood together in the Utah desert surrounded by endless blue skies and jaw-dropping stretches of red rock pinnacles, canyon labyrinths, scrub brush, pinon pines, yucca plants. And no people.

"We're on our own here." I shifted the heavy backpack on my shoulders and tightened the strap to carry the weight low on my hips. "We'll give you the skills, but you have to put in the work." I glanced at the other two adult guides for this CanyonTrek adventure. I wanted my introduction to sound like a pep talk. "You're going to love it."

Preston—thin, bookish, and thirty-eight, five years younger than me—wore the most expensive hiking clothes and had the most earnest expression on his face, taking his job as a CT counselor so seriously that even his fellow guides couldn't have fun.

Judy, whose age I put somewhere between sixty-five and infinity, was a leather whip of a woman who had spent twenty years in the army, the rest of her life in the desert, and could probably tie a boot lace with her teeth. She had seen it all and was probably the most competent person in this part of southern Utah.

The nine teenagers looked up to me, though, as the ostensible leader of the expedition.

"Dale's right," Preston said, nodding to me. "These three weeks are going to all be about your personal growth, meeting new challenges, and becoming a better person inside." He pressed his palm to the center of his chest and spread his fingers as if he expected angels to spring out of his heart.

Ophelia, a spunky fifteen-year-old with a dark braid draped over one shoulder, snickered. "Three weeks without cell phones, computers, air conditioning, toilets. Oh, joy." The other kids seemed cautious, still getting a feel for the situation.

"We're good to go," Judy said. "It's time to walk the earth." She strutted out with a trekking pole in one gnarled hand. Her hiking boots looked as old as the Dead Sea Scrolls and yet sturdier than my own.

Our group set off together along the desert path, on our way to the horizon and back. Fortunately, we had topo maps.

Exploring new landscapes and building stronger people was what the CanyonTrek brochure said, and the parents of troubled teens gobbled it up.

As we walked, Bridger and Logan took the lead. Bridger looked like a squeaky-clean Boy Scout, though I knew he had been suspended for bullying his lab partner in chemistry, while Logan had been caught selling alcohol to classmates. Marco, a broad-shouldered Hispanic student who had lost his spot on the varsity soccer team when his grades took a nose dive, hurried to join the other two.

"Ten miles the first day," I said, "while we still have energy."

"Who has energy?" Shaylee asked with a dramatic groan.

I pressed my lips together. I'd hoped to make at least half a mile before the complaints started. "Could be the most beautiful miles you've ever seen," I said. "When we get to the Needles Overlook, it'll take your breath away."

"I can hardly breathe now," panted Noah, a scrawny, freckled thirteen-year-old, the youngest member of our group. He was on the high-functioning end of the Autism Spectrum Disorder, which made him intensely knowledgeable if you were interested in his particular obsessions, or annoying if you weren't.

"As you walk," Preston said, as if reading from a handbook, "be aware of your reactions and consider what you might write in your journals tonight. It's all part of the experience."

"Homework already," Ophelia said. "Oh, joy."

"Personal growth," Preston corrected. "Not homework."

"Can't call it homework, anyway," Noah added in a flat tone. "We aren't going home for three weeks."

"Right," Judy said. "Think of how strong you'll be when you're done." I couldn't tell if she was being sarcastic or not. Her voice was usually a combination of tough chick and prune juice.

CanyonTrek, headquartered in Moab, drew most of its patrons from the troubled teens of wealthy, frustrated parents along the Wasatch Front, hoping to wear down their unruly kids and teach them discipline by sending them on the "experience of a lifetime." There were plenty of reasons these teens ended up on our expeditions. They might be oppositional, blowing off school, drinking, taking drugs, rebelling against stepparents—the possibilities were endless.

By offering fourteen- or twenty-one-day expeditions in the spectacular Canyonlands, CT proposed to *empower students by instilling a perspective of honor, self-reliance, and balance.* The brochure also asserted that participants would *realign priorities and find inner strength through the beauty of nature.*

As far as I was concerned, the arduous job of schlepping a heavy backpack for mile after mile, day after day, should be adequate to settle turbulent or distracted minds. Always worked for me. Preston, though, had planned a curriculum filled with personal-centering exercises, conversation starters, and, of course, the daily journal of their thoughts.

"I thought this was going to be summer camp," said Ava. "Like riding horses, weaving lanyards, singing around the campfire."

"Way better than summer camp," I said.

I liked to be out here, especially in uncertain times. The world seemed nuttier than usual at the moment. The headlines were mostly about some kind of flu epidemic in New York, Los Angeles, and other major cities. In most cases, violence seemed to follow within weeks of each outbreak. Democrats accused Republicans for not offering enough medical and financial assistance, while Republicans blamed Democrats for creating the environments in which the virus flourished. I couldn't stomach the news, which seemed less informative than argumentative day after day.

One more reason to stay away from the cities, if you asked me. I was glad to be out in Red Rocks country, deep in the desert, even with nine surly, difficult kids. It was still better than any normal day in Salt Lake or going to board meetings at the tech center.

This was the fourth group I had led for CT since taking a golden-parachute retirement from my tech job in Salt Lake. The severance package was big enough to keep me in pleasant, comfortable free-fall for a long time until I figured out what I wanted to do next. And I loved the backpacking experience.

My favorite area of the state was this wild segment of Bureau of Land Management canyon country adjacent to the Needles District of Canyonlands National Park. Arches Park was always crawling with tourists, especially this time of year, mid-June, with the kids out of school and the days warm. Before long the desert would show its angry side and temperatures would rise.

I led the group along our planned route, a network of trails and four-wheel-drive roads. Over the three weeks of our character-building expedition, we would go more than fifty miles along with whatever side trips caught my interest. Trekking overland, finding our own campsites, following the maps to little known springs and water sources, and killer views.

Our first main destination was an overlook, a dot on the BLM map with an informational sign and a gravel half circle for parking at the edge of a mesa drop-off. Ahead, we could see the vista of the Needles District and its incredible, surreal formations. In its wisdom, the BLM had installed a metal pipe barricade at the edge of the overlook to keep people from falling off that particular twenty-foot section of the cliff.

"Sure glad they put safety first," Ophelia said, grasping the pipe fence and shaking it. Her parents were intellectual property attorneys, and she was bright and spoiled and a bit of a wiseass.

"Just enjoy the view for a minute," I said, wanting to drink it in myself. It was indeed enough to keep the rambunctious students together and quiet for a minute. I said, "Reminds me of a story about a Scottish shipbuilder named Ebenezer Bryce who became one of the first settlers in all this Utah desert."

"He was LDS—a Mormon pioneer," Shaylee pointed out.

"Bryce Canyon was named after him," Preston added, as if pleased that he knew the answer.

"Bryce Canyon," I agreed, "is one of the most beautiful and complex canyon systems in the state, a wonderland of multicolored rock forma—"

Noah broke in. "Did you know that Bryce Canyon isn't actually a canyon? It's a series of amphitheaters along the edge of a plateau, and they're full of those lumpy rock spires called hoodoos."

I let out a sigh. "Thank you, Noah. Very informative, but back to Ebenezer Bryce. When he came along and found that amazing area, supposedly the first white man ever to see it, you know what he wrote in his journal?" I looked at the nine young people, holding their attention. "He called it 'one hell of a place to lose a cow.' That's it."

Some of the kids dutifully chuckled, while others held onto gloom or aloofness as a matter of pride.

I felt a sudden urge to get through to them. "Don't be a Bryce. Learn how to look at everything around you, not just in terms of the hard work it might represent, but in terms of the wonder—of what *might be*," I said. I was getting a bit zealous, but I couldn't help myself. "Learn to enjoy beauty that's not about entertainment, computer-generated scenes, getting people to like what you post online—none of that. Look at everything around you and realize each sight is a mental snapshot, a moment in time."

With a curt nod, Judy spoke up. "Only guarantee in life is that *things change*."

"Right." I took up the baton again. "Time won't stand still. You'll never see exactly the same thing in the same way ever again. Deserts are different from seashores or rainforests or snowy mountains. They're all amazing, all distinct. Let yourself be enchanted." I scanned the group for any reaction.

Ophelia rolled her eyes and Logan made a scoffing sound. While Ava and Isabel looked attentive, Noah watched a lizard sunning itself nearby. Bridger and Shaylee were whispering to each other, and Marco folded his arms across his chest, while Zane seemed to be playing a drum solo in the air.

I took a deep breath before plunging in again with a stern tone. "This adventure may not be your choice, but there's no opt-out button. You're here. You'll learn survival skills and how to work as a team. You'll get sweaty and sunburned. Your feet'll be sore and you may discover some muscles you never knew you had until they started aching. But you'll be proud of what you accomplish. By the time three weeks in the wilderness are up, you'll be stronger, braver, and more resourceful than ever."

"And more in touch with your inner selves," Preston said.

Judy hooked her thumbs into her belt loops, and her eyes narrowed as she stared out at the vista, nodding in appreciation.

That was before we ran into the first zombies.

Kevin J. Anderson

Ophelia Journal

Day 1. Is there any more ridiculous assignment than journaling? My shrink makes me do it. Won't work any better here than it does at home, but here goes.

I'm trapped in the wilderness with eight other students and three counselors who think they own us for the next few weeks.

Dale acts like the chief. Okay-looking for an older guy, but he must be like forty-five. Pretty sure of himself and definitely on the bossy side. I like it when he jokes.

Preston's on the wimpy side. He actually meditates. So dorky. Says he was an Eagle Scout. No surprise there. His clothes look more stylish than practical, like he's posing for a magazine. Talks in that annoying super-friendly voice that therapists use.

Judy is a tough lady. Not sure she was ever fifteen like me. Looks like a piece of beef jerky with a chunk of dandelion fluff stuck on top. Says what she thinks but keeps it short and snappy. Some people would call it rude; I call it refreshing. If we say "shit" or whatever she always says "language!" meaning not to use bad words, but I'm pretty sure she's got some "language" in her, too, depending on the situation. I'll wait and watch.

This morning's first lesson was "hygiene." Beyond embarrassing. Who wants to talk about digging catholes to poop or bury blood? Yich. Plus, the spot has to be just right. Seriously. Six inches deep, at least two hundred feet from any water sources, trails, or camp. Use hand sanitizer. Blah blah blah. Hope my period doesn't arrive while we're still out here. But it will. Insanely awkward. Anyway, we already had that mortifying lesson. Ach. Ick. Ew. Backpacking is hard enough without adding that extra serving of torture for us girls. Whyyyyyyy?

Day 2. This is so not a vacation. Why would anyone choose to camp? I. Would. Not. *Everything* takes ten times as much work as at home. We have civilization for a reason, so why put ourselves through this by choice?

We can't just go to bed. No. We have to put up tents. We can't just nuke food and eat it. Again, no. We either have to build a fire or use those dumb little gas stoves. Then add water to dry food that all joy has been drained out of. Don't even get me started on doing dishes, either. Everyone has chores every day. That's on top of ten or more miles of hiking! It's impossible to get a minute to ourselves, and then we have to journal.

And Utah in June? June! Whose brilliant idea was that?

Today's main lesson: protecting the environment. We can't just throw stuff away when we're done with it. No, no, no. Whatever we "pack in" on our trip, we have to "pack out," including trash. WTF?

Next lesson was finding and purifying water with our portable filters.

Day 3. The lowdown on my fellow inmates.

Bridger is LDS, which means Mormon, but he doesn't like to be called that. Says he loves to read, and plays guitar, drums, and piano. Weren't allowed to bring books or instruments, so I bet he's frustrated. I hear him humming a lot.

Noah is only 13—youngest in our whole group. Pretty sure he's high-functioning on the Autism Spectrum and klutzy like my cousin. His aunt's a veterinarian, so he knows a lot about animals. He drones on and on about them. All. The. Time. Plus he blurts stuff out at random times and doesn't notice if we look confused or shocked or whatever. He doesn't pick up on social cues. His mom teaches special ed, which is probably a good thing, considering.

Marco is tanned and decent-looking. I approve. Why is he on a CanyonTrek? Got suspended from the varsity soccer team when his grades did a swan dive in the winter. Didn't say why. He's obviously smart. I mean, he speaks three languages fluently, but he mostly talks about movies and tv shows.

Logan generally keeps to himself. He's an Army brat and moves around a lot, so maybe not good at making friends? Tall with lanky shoulder-length hair, so I thought he was a stoner, but I could be wrong. He obviously works out because, well, muscles. Really nice muscles.

Zane is hard to sum up. Straight dark hair that falls across his blue eyes. Dimples that make me stare like an idiot. Kind of like that actor on *Vampire Diaries* that I've been watching for the past few years. He gives me a strange feeling when we talk, like he *thinks* a lot more than he says. He's kind and helpful but not in obvious ways. He just glides in and does things without being told and then he goes right back to what he was doing. What's that about?

Day 4. It's totally quiet on the trail. No music, no tv, no phone. Can't even text Skye and Maren. So boring here that even writing in a journal seems interesting. Preston and Judy read everything we write (seriously? when??). Preston is going to start helping us "process" our thoughts starting tomorrow. So ... there's that humiliation to look forward to.

We did lessons on stuff they called navigation and orienteering, or just "nav." Reading topographical, aka topo, maps, using a compass, remembering shapes and markers in the land around us, judging directions and time by the sun. Useless stuff like that. I mean, we've all got GPS on our phones, right? (If they would let us *have* our phones.)

Day 5. The staff focused on more "outdoor living" skills. (For the record, I refuse to ever get into outdoor living.)

Agh! They teach us stuff and then make us practice. Like we're little kids taking piano lessons. When they test us at a skill, Dale always asks, "Can you do that?" in kind of a drill sergeant voice. I learned fast to just answer "I can do that." Because if we don't say it, Dale makes us practice again about twenty bajillion times. So no thanks. From now on, "I can do that." Even if I can't.

There are only four girls in our group including me.

Ava is an airhead, but I like her. Not everyone can be brilliant like me. She's fourteen and nice—maybe too nice. Marco told me her parents sent her on a CT expedition because some jerkfaces at school convinced her to steal test answers for them. She got caught, of course. She has a pretty voice and wants to sing as a pro. Maybe she and Bridger should put together a band.

Isabel is such a Goody-Two-Shoes I don't know how she got sent here. St. Isabel does everything the counselors tell her to without complaining. I don't trust people who are too good. They're usually judgy as hell.

Shaylee is LDS like Bridger, but they never met before this trip. She's my age but does acting, dances ballet, plays flute and piccolo, blah blah blah. Oh, and writes poetry. Give me a break. What is it with these LDS kids and "The Arts"? I just added her to the pop band in my mind with Bridger and Ava.

Last: I'm me. My parents are IP attorneys and they're always away. Even though a TV practically raised me, I've made straight As since middle school. No tutors. Just me. But that didn't seem to warrant my parents' attention, so I developed an unhealthy interest in murder scenes and decided to be a forensic scientist. CSI stuff. Instead of worrying, my parents arranged for me to watch some autopsies in person. Huh. Turns out I can handle seeing real dead people, so that works out. Yay, me. The parents didn't even notice I was rebelling, so I cranked it up a notch. Started raiding the liquor cabinet regularly, then bought Adderall from school friends to keep my grades up. Brilliant, right? Eventually (better late than never) my parents caught on, and here I am.

Day 6. Almost every day Dale finds a time to say, "That's what adventuring is all about: solving problems." (Or you can insert traveling or navigating or cooking or getting along in place of "adventuring.") So apparently *everything* is all about solving problems.

Dale: Can you solve problems?
Me: I can do that.

Hah. We'll see.

Day 7. Hike. Sweat. Learn to act as a team. Sing. Hey, I'm not half-bad at this singing stuff. Maybe I'll learn to play bass and join the rock band. In my head, I've named it Cat-hole Daze.

Days 8–14. Blah blah blah. You get the idea.

—II—
Dale

When I trained to become a CanyonTrek counselor, they supposedly prepared me for any emergency situation—which meant I'd taken a first aid course and sat through PowerPoint presentations on various scenarios.

Fifteen days into our three-week adventure, Judy, Preston, and I had made some progress filing the rough edges off our teen adventurers. The most drama I expected was minor personality clashes, blisters and scrapes, inadvertent dehydration, wishing for the comforts of technology, or missing their families. Most of them had begun to appreciate what they had in their homelife.

I never expected Preston to get bitten by a rattlesnake.

In late June, Utah's canyon country was getting hot, and our by-the-book counselor decided to wear shorts, low-cut socks, and trail runners for comfort, leaving his legs exposed from knee to ankle. Preston took the lead, enjoying the morning vistas, while the rest of us followed by twos and threes, with Judy at the middle of the group and me bringing up the rear with Noah.

Preoccupied by the view, Preston didn't see the rattlesnake sunning itself on the red rocks. The snake did see Preston, though, and was so startled that it bit him on the calf. His yelp was high-pitched, like a girl getting free tickets to a Taylor Swift concert.

Zane bounded forward as the rattlesnake slithered into a wide crack between the rocks. "Shit, that's a big one!"

"Language," Judy shouted automatically, running toward our colleague faster than I thought she could move.

Noah assured me he was fine, so I ran to the front of the group.

Preston collapsed to the ground, sagging onto his overlarge backpack. "It attacked me! See where I'm bleeding? Oh, it hurts."

Judy instantly dropped next to Preston.

As I arrived, I glanced at Zane. "Did you see what it was?"

Before he could answer, Ava, the most delicate of our girls, answered helpfully. "It was a snake!"

"It bit me!" Preston said, although we had already established that.

"I'm pretty sure it was a rattler," Zane said. "I saw the diamond patterns on its back. But it could have been a gopher snake."

"It wasn't a fucking gopher snake!" Preston cried.

"Language!" Judy snapped. She had shucked her backpack and was frantically opening the zippered compartment to get the first aid pack and snakebite kit.

I slung my pack off as well.

Not at all squeamish, Ophelia knelt beside Preston, wiped away a trickle of blood, and turned his leg to expose the bite marks. Two neat little punctures, with the skin around them already starting to swell.

Zane investigated the crack in the rock where the snake had disappeared.

Bridger joined him and poked at it with his trekking pole. "Want me to get the snake out, just to make sure?"

"No!" both Judy and I said.

"Can't risk two snakebites," I added. "Treat Preston on the assumption that it was a rattlesnake."

Noah ran up to stand near Bridger and Zane, breathing hard.

Ophelia frowned. "But aren't rattlesnakes rare out here?"

"Somewhat," Noah agreed, trying to get a look at the snake in the crack. "Statistically, injuries by bee sting are way more common. And only about five people have died from snakebite in Utah in the whole past century."

"So this is a once-in-a-lifetime thing?" Ava asked.

"Sure," Noah answered. "I'd say this definitely qualifies as a special event."

"I'm not *feeling* exactly special," Preston said. "This is really starting to burn and it feels like needles are stabbing me!"

"I think I see the snake!" Bridger said.

Marco came up behind Zane and Bridger. "Hey, I'm pretty sure rattlesnakes are protected under Utah law."

I opened my pack and dug down to the bottom to get out the emergency sat phone we affectionately called "the bat signal." Out here in the Canyonlands wilderness, not even within the boundaries of the national park, a mobile phone wouldn't get a signal at all, but CanyonTrek—"safety is our number one priority for the protection, comfort, and education of our young adventurers"—assigned one expensive satellite phone per group, and I carried it.

We were just over two-thirds of the way into our trip, so I knew our exact location: as far from help as we could possibly be. Fortunately, out of caution and common sense, we had filed our route map in the Moab offices. With one call I should be able to summon a search and rescue helicopter team. CanyonTrek was a card-carrying member of Utah Search and Rescue Assistance, so the rescue team would come in like the cavalry. I knew the admins carried pricey insurance and made regular donations to USARA in case some troubled teen went off the trail and broke an ankle.

I switched on the sat phone and waited while it searched the sky for a signal. The bars danced and blipped. Apparently, the satellites were shy today.

Meanwhile, Judy deployed our snakebite kit. Her brows were drawn together, her gaze intense as she used a plastic disposable razor to scrape the fine hair off Preston's leg around the bite marks. "Next we clean."

"I can do that," Ophelia said, opening the sterile alcohol wipes, and lightly swabbed away the blood and dirt from the area.

"Now for the handy extractor pump," Judy said. She pulled out a plastic tube like a large syringe, fitted a suction cap on the end, and positioned it near Preston's leg.

"Snakes," Marco quoted. "Why did it have to be snakes?"

Preston glowered at him. "This is not a stupid movie. I can feel the venom working."

"When you panic, your pulse races," Judy said. "And that just spreads the poison around—so calm down. Somebody sing 'Kumbaya,' okay?"

I thought she was being sarcastic, but Ava took Judy's words to heart. Sitting behind Preston, Ava put a hand on his arm and sang softly. Shaylee stood close by and hummed along.

Noah approached and looked over Judy's shoulder, as if this were one of their lessons. She pressed the extractor against the lower of the punctures, but Noah grabbed the syringe away from the wound. "That's the old way. It's not how they treat snakebites anymore."

Judy gave him a shrewd look. "This has been SOP—standard operating procedure—for as long as I can remember."

Noah shook his head. "No tourniquets. No cutting. No sucking."

"Really?" Ava sounded disappointed.

"Why listen to him? He's just a kid," Preston objected. "Read the instructions in the kit!"

"How'd you hear about the changes?" Judy asked Noah.

Ophelia spoke up. "His aunt's a veterinarian, remember? He knows endless mind-numbing details about animals and medicine."

While they went back and forth, Isabel, the quiet girl, got out Preston's water bottle and gave him a few careful sips.

Just then, my sat phone locked onto a signal, and I punched the preprogrammed number for CanyonTrek HQ. It rang eleven times without being answered. "So much for emergency preparedness." I was starting to sweat myself.

Several of the teens looked at me with concern. I hit redial, and the bat signal rang seven more times before someone finally picked up.

"Thank god!" I said. "This is Dale from Group One. We've got an emergency situation. Preston got bitten by a rattlesnake.

Please send the rescue chopper immediately." They would acquire our location from the bat signal's built-in GPS, so I didn't waste time giving directions. "I'll get our group to an open area and set out some signal flags."

Over the phone, I could hear shouts and havoc. Maybe they were having a rowdy party at CT headquarters.

The answer I got was not at all what I expected. A strained, feminine voice shouted in my ear, "Who is this? Where are you? Can you send help?"

I was pretty sure it was Desiree, the office manager, but I'd never heard her sound so ragged.

"This is Dale—and you're mixed up. *I* called *you* for help. I need an urgent medical evac for a snakebite victim."

"Snakebite?" Desiree's voice rose with hysteria. "A snakebite! Are you crazy? That's the least of our problems." Something was definitely wrong. Desiree was usually so poised and cheerful.

"Can you put Bob on?" I said. "This is an emergency."

"Stay where you are," she said. "You're better off." It sounded like total chaos around her.

Her voice came through so loud over the sat phone that our whole group could hear her. "Moab is overrun! The epidemic spread. People from the big cities, trying to escape that virus a couple weeks ago? They swarmed out here and *brought it with them*! They're going crazy!" In the background I heard shouts, furniture being knocked over, a great crash, and the distinct crack of gunfire.

"Oh god, they smashed right through the door!"

"What is going on over there?" I said, pressing the bat signal to my ear.

"Bob!" Desiree screamed. I heard more gunshots, splintering wood, shattering glass, simultaneous yells. When I heard Desiree's voice again, it was a hopeless wail that abruptly changed to shrieks of agony. The phone fell to the floor with a clunk, and then I couldn't tell what the sounds were: Some kind of scuffling. Panting. Wet noises ...

My throat went dry. What could I do? The students around

me were staring, puzzled, and not nearly as terrified as I thought they should be. I switched off the bat signal.

Judy looked up from the snakebite wound. "Are they coming? What did they say?"

I tucked the bat signal back inside my pack. "I think we're on our own."

While Judy reread the instructions with the snakebite kit, Noah rattled off a list at breakneck speed. "Step one, move a safe distance away from the snake. Step two, have the victim rest on the ground. To slow the spread of venom, keep the bite at or below heart-level and keep the victim still and calm. Step three, get medical help as soon as possible. Antivenom is the primary treatment."

"Which we don't have," Judy said, looking at me. "I guess we can't count on anyone coming to help, huh?"

I shook my head. "Sounds like folks in Moab are worse off than we are. So what comes next?"

Noah continued with his list, as if it were a first aid spelling bee. We covered the snakebite wound with a clean, dry dressing, even used a Sharpie to outline the discolored area and write the time, so we could track the spread of the damage. Preston groaned.

Noah finished, "Step eight, if medical help can't reach the victim, do not wait: take the victim to medical assistance. Left untreated, damage may be permanent or fatal."

"That sucks," Logan said.

"Sucking is obsolete," Noah said.

"No undoing a snakebite," Marco observed. "You need antivenom. It's a race against time."

"That's it then," said Zane. "We take Preston somewhere that has real medical help."

"It's always something." Judy set her jaw. "We'll handle it."

"That's what CanyonTrek is about: learning to solve problems," I agreed.

Sweat stood out on Preston's forehead and he didn't seem to be following the conversation. "You're just going to leave the venom in me?"

"Whatever's necessary to get you help, buddy, that's what we'll do," I said, starting to choke up. How often had I been annoyed with Preston, taking him for granted instead of treating him like my friend? I gave myself a mental kick. No time to agonize about my feelings. We had to get going.

Ophelia got out a roll of stretchy white bandage.

I pulled out the topo map and unfolded it on the rocks. Logan, who had proven excellent at map reading, came up beside me and Bridger joined us a moment later. I showed them the area we had been exploring and the trail of faint dots, which indicated a mere "suggested route" marked by occasional rock cairns. We were in the deepest desert wilds with the darkest night skies and the greatest solitude. Also the farthest from help.

"Now I know where we are," muttered Bridger. "We're screwed. That's where."

Logan gave a soft laugh but did not let himself be distracted. "Judging by the terrain, we must be here." He pointed to the map and traced the faint dots.

"Good. I agree," I said. "That means it's about five miles total from here to these four-wheel-drive roads." I ran a finger from our position to our first goal. "We have to move Preston. With some help, he should be able to walk on his injured leg. Camping's free-range on BLM lands, so let's hope we find somebody with a vehicle."

"No helicopter?" Preston moaned, leaning against a rock while Ophelia and Judy finished securing the bandage around his calf. "Shouldn't I just lie here and rest?"

"*Pfft*," Shaylee said. "You told us we couldn't stop and rest just because we were tired."

"You weren't bit by a rattlesnake!" Preston said. "Damn kids are so spoiled!"

I frowned at him, because this certainly wasn't Preston's usual philosophy of how to deal with reluctant young people. "You *could* stay here," I agreed, "but since there's no helicopter coming, it'll take forever to bring help. We may arrive too late. If we get you to those Jeep roads, you'll be better off." It wasn't exactly ideal, but we were SOL regarding the speedy rescue we'd expected in an emergency.

I was haunted by what I had heard on the sat phone. None of it made sense. I put away the map in my heavy backpack and zipped up the saddlebags. "Okay, everyone. We've got to move out. Empty Preston's pack and distribute the items amongst yourselves. No telling what we might need."

While several of the kids darted off for hygiene breaks, very careful to watch for snakes, Zane and Ophelia emptied Preston's backpack and distributed the weight evenly among the hikers. Judy helped Preston lace his hiking boot. "We want to support your foot, but not too tight. That thing's going to swell like a sonofabitch," she said, then caught herself. "Language, sorry."

Ava and Judy helped Preston to his feet. He looked wan but determined to hobble. Judy offered him the option of using her sturdy trekking pole in addition to his own, like crutches.

"We can make a human crutch," Logan said. "You put one arm around my neck and my arm goes around your back. We'll need someone to help from the other side."

"I can do that," Marco said.

Preston agreed, so the young men put on their packs and supported him, one on either side. "Okay, let's blow this joint," he said.

Feeling the urgency, I set off, raising an arm to get everyone's attention. "This'll be tough, but necessary. Today we keep up a fast, steady pace, eat some miles. I believe you can do it. We need medical help for Preston, so let's get out to where we can be found."

The whole group murmured their agreement. No complaints. They understood the seriousness.

Before long, the hike turned arduous, although the map rated it as "easy." Up to that point, the days had been pleasant enough, with highs around eighty degrees. Today, Mother Nature chose to throw ninety degrees at us.

We wound our way through the slickrock, yucca, and saltbush, disappointed that we couldn't take the time just to enjoy the alien-looking hoodoos, red rock mounds striped with white frosting. This area had always held a primeval wonder for me, but now it felt like a nightmare landscape.

Finally, when we found the four-wheel-drive road, I realized that the term "road" was gracious and optimistic. The red powdery soil was punctuated by boulders, ruts, and deep washouts. On the bright side, I could see tire tracks, so someone had driven here since the previous rain ... whenever that was. We were forty miles from a paved highway, but we knew the way out.

By late afternoon, Preston was getting more and more miserable, his face gray and sweaty, his lips drawn back in pain. He finally insisted that we rest. Leaning on a rust-colored boulder and propping up his foot, he fumbled with the bandage.

Judy clucked her tongue. "Better leave it alone. That sucker is swelling up."

"I want to see," Preston said and unwound the fabric to expose his leg—angry red and swollen, with scarlet lines tracing up past his knee. "Oh, this is bad. I'm going to die of a snakebite! This is ridiculous."

"Wrap it up again," I said. "Keep it clean, and let's get going. We'll find somebody."

Marco patted Preston's shoulder. "Bro, in the words of the philosopher Dory, 'just keep swimming.'"

The sun was low on the western horizon and the temperature was already beginning to cool, mercifully. "We can make a few more miles down the road before nightfall." I tried to sound hopeful. "If someone is camping out here, we'll see the lights or the fire."

"Great, we can roast marshmallows," Preston groaned.

Two students chuckled despite the seriousness of the situation.

Marco tried to stay upbeat. "Come on, champ. Never give up. Never surrender."

We moved down the 4WD road, and within an hour we crossed a low swell, and I could see across the desert ahead. I was overjoyed to see a battered recreational vehicle parked off the road in one of the makeshift distributed campsites. "There, Preston! See, I told you."

"Woohoo!" Ophelia said. "First time I've ever been thrilled to see a Winnebago. We're usually stuck behind one on a slow mountain road."

We moved forward with a target now and with hope, plodding along, each of us taking turns shouting, trying to get the attention of the campers. "Hello!" I shouted. "We need help."

"Help," Shaylee cried.

Isabel and Ava added their voices, and soon we were a chorus. No one stirred in or around the RV, though. Perhaps the people had gone backpacking somewhere and left their campsite for a while.

In a low voice Judy asked me, "What do we do if no one's home?"

"Break in and take what we need." I mentally estimated a 50/50 chance that at least one of these teens knew how to hotwire a vehicle.

"Help!" Zane yelled toward the RV. Then he, Marco, Noah, and Logan bellowed greetings and pleas for help, trying to outdo each other, while Preston cringed at the noise.

As we hiked closer and the late afternoon shadows grew longer, we heard faint noises inside the Winnebago, beyond the curtained windows. The flimsy door swung open.

"Help!" we yelled again.

We were close enough to the campsite that I could make out something on the ground—was it a person? It was. A body, actually. Or what was left of one. A large portion of the skin and muscles had been ripped away in ragged chunks.

The two figures that emerged from the RV no longer appeared fully human. They had pale, blotchy skin, wild hair, blood-smeared faces. And they were naked.

That was when the shit really hit the fan.

—III—
Dale

The two sickly things that lurched out of the Winnebago came at us fast. Their bodies were discolored, and we could see far too much of their skin, as if they had shambled out of a nudist colony for leprosy patients. They made wild, inhuman, and *hungry* sounds.

The hope of the RV, the campsite—any sign of life at all in the vast empty desert—juiced Preston with adrenaline. Always annoyingly optimistic, he ignored the warning signs. While the rest of us hesitated, he broke away from Zane and Logan and lurched forward, waving his arms. "Help! I've been bitten by a snake. We need to get to a doctor."

He certainly drew their attention. Both of the things were male, embarrassingly so. Even without clothes or weapons, they had clutching hands and menacing teeth—and they weren't afraid to use them.

The older male charged Preston and drove him to the ground. The counselor fell hard on his back and cried out, "My leg!"

Working his jaws, the scarecrowish creature pinned Preston down and bit into his face, before using skeletal hands to tear at his throat and chest. Each wound drew a wordless shriek from Preston. The sound of it was appalling, almost inhuman.

Backing up toward me, Ava screamed, and several of the others decided that was the appropriate response.

Everything happened so fast. The second creature came at us, wild and moaning. It launched itself toward me, eyes blazing, hands outstretched. Its ragged nails clawed at the space between us, reaching toward me. I swung my trekking pole so hard it made a whistling sound in the air. I was just trying to batter away the grasping hands, but I brought it down so hard, the fingers snapped like hollow sticks.

Finished killing Preston, the first attacker turned and ran straight into our group.

Zane wielded his walking stick like a tae kwon do master. Logan and Marco waded in, while Noah, Bridger, Ava, and Isabel clustered together, raising their makeshift weapons.

"Och. This is like *Night of the Living Dead!*" Ophelia blurted.

Hearing her, Marco called out, "Original George Romero version, or the remake?"

"Can't go wrong with George Romero," Ophelia answered, dodging the thing that had killed Preston.

I kept fighting away at the ghoulish man who was trying to rip my throat out. I whacked again with my walking stick, this time with more practice, more confidence, and more urgency. I struck my attacker full in the eye, and he didn't even flinch. After all, what was one more wound or gash on his already ravaged body?

Ophelia swung her walking stick, still jabbering in her fangirl fascination. "Now, the *Return of the Living Dead* movies were funny." She whacked at the older creature, Preston's murderer. Blood streamed from the hideous mouth down to his chest. "That's where we got used to the idea that zombies eat brains." To my surprise, Ophelia did not look fazed.

My attacker continued to flail and scrabble, for some reason fixated on me, even though there were plenty of other choice morsels around. At least three of the kids had bolted off into the desert. Good call.

Zane smashed the first creature and yelled for Ophelia to run. She made a break for it, but her diseased attacker sprang forward and clutched her overstuffed backpack, clawing and ripping, as if it were filled with internal organs rather than pack food. She tried to get loose.

I stumbled on something and tripped backward, instinctively rolling to the side, so I wasn't like a turtle turned upside down with my heavy pack. I saw that I had tripped over the gnawed, stripped remains of a third person—the bloody body I had seen from a distance. Wisps of long hair clinging to the skull implied it was an older woman.

I kicked out, knocked the attacker back, and lurched to my feet. As he came at me again, I extended my trekking pole and jabbed as hard as I could with the pointed metal end. I stabbed him right through the neck, like a gladiator with a spear. I shoved again and again, until the point came out the thing's back and blood spouted out. I twisted and wrenched, realizing that my pole was now stuck in the body. The attacker flailed, then collapsed. His snapping jaws slowed as he died.

All the screaming confused the details of what was going on, but the loud gunshot was unmistakable, then a second one. Expecting another attack, I turned, only to see Judy holding a pistol in a cool firing stance, like an Old West gunfighter at high noon.

My jaw dropped.

The older thing attacking Ophelia's backpack gurgled and let go so suddenly that Ophelia lurched forward and landed on her hands and knees. The creature staggered sideways, fell, and rolled face down on the ground with two gunshot wounds in his back.

"Och!" Ophelia brushed gravel from her hands, and Zane helped her to her feet. They scrambled away from the dead corpse, or whatever you call it. Ophelia blinked in surprise. "I guess you don't have to shoot these things in the head to kill them. So, not real zombies."

I wrenched my bloody trekking pole from the neck of my own attacker. "Whatever works," I said.

"What the hell was that all about?" gasped Bridger, then reconsidered. "What the *fuck* was that?"

Judy didn't correct him for his language, although it shocked me, especially coming from one of our straightlaced Mormon kids. Ava, Noah, and Shaylee had rushed over to Preston to give first aid, but he lay unmoving, his face and throat ripped open.

"He's dead," Ava groaned. "They killed him!"

Tilting his head to study Preston, Noah said with odd inappropriateness, "Well, at least he didn't die from the snakebite."

"I may put that in my journal tonight," Ophelia said. She looked over at me and Judy. "Do we still have to do our journals?"

Neither of us answered.

Judy still held her pistol, then slowly lowered the weapon, visibly winding down.

"We aren't supposed to have guns," I said. "CT's pretty strict about that."

She gave me a withering look. "Not *supposed to*." She sniffed. "I signed a contract to protect these kids. It's a Glock 21, .45 caliber. But CT also says that counselors must be prepared for any circumstances."

"You kidding me? Even from a zombie invasion?"

Judy shrugged.

"Och. Please don't," Ophelia said. "Don't say zombies. It doesn't feel appropriate to me—so trite, so *fictional*. These were real. Are we sure what they really are? What if we called them living dead—LDs for short?"

I looked over at the murdered counselor. "Preston didn't like to use terms that made people uncomfortable. Something about being politically correct."

Ophelia nodded. Turning abruptly, she went over to Preston's body, sat beside him, and took his bloody hand.

Judy strode toward the Winnebago. "Preston would also have wanted us to understand what's happening and take stock of our resources."

The vehicle's flimsy door had flapped shut. She yanked it open and stepped into the RV, cautiously extending her pistol. "Nobody's home. And nobody's housecleaning, either."

As I followed Judy inside, I could tell that the Winnebago had never been nice, but now it was a disaster, a combination of hoarder and homeless camp under a bridge. Cans of beans, chili, and soup had been pried open somehow, scooped out—with bare fingers, I assumed—and strewn on the floor. Ramen noodle packets had been crunched and devoured, sometimes with half the plastic wrapper.

"Guess they don't just eat brains," I said. "Oh, that's right, they aren't 'zombies.'"

Tucked on a shelf beside the small cupboard, I found two

copies of the *Salt Lake Tribune*. I pulled them out, unfolding the front pages.

"Jackpot," I said, showing Judy.

By now, several of the teens had ventured into the RV with us. Others milled around the campsite. Zane was apparently standing guard in case more of the living dead marched across the open desert.

I read the lead story out loud about a viral epidemic that had surged through the nation's largest cities and soon spread to Salt Lake City. Even smaller areas like Moab suffered unexpected outbreaks, as people fled the cities to isolate themselves from the virus, bringing it with them. I thought of Desiree screaming over the sat phone, and the sound of gunfire at CanyonTrek HQ.

Beside me, Judy shook her head. "This is messed up."

"Hey, look," said Marco. He held up a couple of postcards from the windowsill by the Formica dinette table. "They were going to mail these when they got to the Needles Outpost." He squinted to make out the handwriting. "I think they were an older couple, Linda and Frank, and their son Owen. A couple of weeks ago when people started getting sick, they drove out here to hole up. Frank thought the desert was the best place. They were going to get more supplies from the Needles Outpost before it was too late." Marco shook his head. "The last line says, 'Owen isn't feeling well.'"

I glanced out the open door of the RV. "I guess he got worse."

The mangled body outside must have been Linda. Now we knew who our two attackers were.

Noah came through the door, ignoring everyone, and said, "You probably want these." He handed me a set of keys with a metal fob marked Winnebago and ducked back out the door.

A plan was coming together in my mind. I looked around at the mess inside the RV. In addition to eating most of mom, Frank and Owen had ransacked the Winnebago's supplies. But our group still had a week's worth of pack food—two weeks if we stretched it, since CT always overplanned. I remembered complaining a few times about the extra weight in emergency supplies. The old me was an idiot. Now I don't mind at all.

The rest of our teen wards clustered around the door looking in.

What could I say after all we had just been through?

I took a deep breath and spread my arms. "Now we have a vehicle."

Ophelia Journal

Day X. I've lost track. Maybe it doesn't matter.

Hi Preston. This one's for you, even though we don't have to journal today. See, I'm still doing my assignments.

I stayed by you for a long time today and said a lot of bad words. A bit inappropriate, but I know you wouldn't have minded.

I can't believe you're gone. Dead. And what an awful way to die. You were really nice, except toward the end and that was really the snakebite's fault. Sorry you went through so much pain.

I don't know what happens now. Wherever you are, I want you to know that I won't forget you, no matter what. I don't think any of us ever will. Personal growth, meeting new challenges, and becoming a better person inside.

—IV—
Dale

In the aftermath at the campsite, we took care of clearing out and cleaning the Winnebago with plenty of Windex and Pine-Sol and using up a jumbo bottle of hand sanitizer. Everyone read the newspaper stories, so we were up to speed on the end of the world —at least out here. Many of the larger cities were still intact, but hospitals were overwhelmed. The *Salt Lake Tribune* didn't give us the answers we really needed, though—like what the hell we should do now.

We pitched camp as usual to sleep outside—no one was ready to take advantage of the RV yet. In the morning we took turns digging graves, not much more than uneven divots in the rocky ground. We needed to bury Preston, and it seemed appropriate to do the same for whatever was left of Linda, Frank, and Owen. This part definitely wasn't in the CT manual. In the end, we wrapped the bodies in old blankets we found in the RV, put them in the shallow trenches, and piled rocks on top of them.

As the students picked up the heavy stones for the cairns, Ophelia called, "Watch out for snakes. They can kill you just as dead as the LDs."

Next to her, Zane raised his eyebrows. "LDs?"

The two of them were spending a lot of time together. She smiled. "Yeah, it's short for *living deads*."

"Why not call them zombies?" asked Noah.

"Because they're not exactly dead and rotting. You saw them—they're diseased. It's a virus, a plague."

"They were naked," Shaylee said.

Ophelia rolled her eyes. "After all we went through, *that's* what you noticed?"

"Well, they were *really* naked," she said.

"LDs?" Bridger frowned. "Sounds like LDS."

"Not meant as an insult," I said. "We just need something to call them."

"Exactly," Ophelia said. "Especially if a whole herd of LDs comes shambling across the desert to get us. It'd be stupid to waste time arguing about terminology."

"Why would we? You're the only person who objects to calling them zombies," Logan observed. Before Ophelia could answer, he raised his hands in surrender. "Never mind. I'm not objecting. LDs it is."

"*Pfft*," Shaylee said.

Several of our group turned nervously, shading their eyes to look across the expanse of hoodoos and red rocks, the rills of canyons, as if scanning for LDs.

"I have to get home," Isabel said.

"We all do." I assured her. I wanted to offer hope, but should I? So far the bat signal hadn't been able to reach anyone who could help us. It was a bad sign for civilization. "We'll find out just what's going on in the world. Meanwhile, it's tight but we can all fit inside the Winnebago. We can go somewhere."

My announcement was greeted with genuine cheers.

I climbed into the driver's seat, took a deep breath, uttered a prayer to any higher power that might be listening, and turned the key.

The engine started right up. It puttered a little, one of the pistons firing erratically, but it seemed to run fine. My joy lasted only a moment, though. I was dismayed to see that the fuel light was on. "Great. They came all the way out here and were about to run out of gas."

Judy leaned in the window, concerned. "Highway 191 is about forty miles, and another fifteen or so to Monticello." Monticello was a small farming community that had a few amenities—gas station, general store, cafés.

Who knew how long the fuel light had been on, or how much remained in the tank? I shook my head. "Not sure we'd make it that far."

Logan came forward holding a map and plopped himself down on the passenger seat beside me. "That Needles Outpost thing isn't very far, though. It's on the park-access road."

I felt a glimmer of hope. I'd been there once, a campground, gas station, cutesy tourist teepees, souvenir shop, and general store on private land just outside the boundary to Canyonlands National Park. "That might do it. We can at least fuel up there, stockpile supplies. No telling how long we might have to stay out here in the desert keeping our distance from people with the virus."

"But I've got to go home," Logan said. "What if my family is in the middle of this? They may need help."

"Mine too," said Ava.

Noah echoed the sentiment.

"It's a safe bet that they're all in the middle of it," Judy said, "and there's nothing you can do to help. Sorry, kids, but they'd want you to stay safe, and the safest place is out here with us."

"Tell that to Preston," Ophelia said.

"Everybody climb in," I said, conscious that the engine was gulping fuel every second I left it running. "We'll get to the Needles Outpost and figure out what to do from there. Maybe they'll have a more recent newspaper."

Leaving the four fresh graves behind, including our lost counselor, everyone piled into the RV. The teens argued over seats. Logan called shotgun, but Judy overruled him, shooed him away, and swung herself into the passenger seat beside me. "You good at maneuvering on four-wheel-drive roads?"

"That's not the question so much as is the Winnebago good on them?" I said. "We know it got this far." As we moved away from the nightmarish campsite, twenty-five miles an hour seemed like reckless speed. We rattled over washboard ridges, hit potholes, swerved around boulders. I was amazed the big recreational vehicle had made it out here, but Frank, Owen, and Linda must have really been determined. I kept glancing at the fuel light.

Right now I could have been in a conference room at my software company headquarters or reading over budget documents or flying to a trade conference. After my early retirement, I'd stashed my savings and lived on a minimal budget. Spending my days walking around slickrock country had seemed like the perfect idea. I wasn't prepared for anything like this!

And yet if I had been at my normal job, I would surely be in a worse situation now. Our software engineers worked hard, lived in the office, put in ridiculous hours, but were never obsessive about personal hygiene. The epidemic would surely have raged through the offices, and employees-turned-LDs would have torn through the cubicles, smashed computer terminals, and eaten their coworkers in favor of the stale donuts left in the breakroom. I remembered my ex-wife saying that my midlife crisis was going to kill me. But maybe it was the only thing that had kept me alive.

The Winnebago bounced and rattled along the rough road for nearly an hour. I was sweating about the fuel, and my neck and shoulders were stiff with tension, but at least they had been toughened from carrying a heavy backpack. The students tried to play games to distract themselves. Sometimes they bickered, other times they fell into a nervous silence.

We saw smoke, and I slowed down to see another campsite on an offshoot pullout. A small pop-up camper and a tent had been set on fire and actually flipped on its side.

"I don't see any LDs around," Zane said. "Should we have a look?"

"Don't stop," Judy said. "Just get to the outpost."

I agreed.

After what felt like forever, we finally left the Jeep road and hit the patched and pitted access road that dead-ended into the national park. The feeling of tires humming on actual asphalt was heaven.

The engine began to putter and cough more, and I recognized the signs of a near-empty gas tank. "We're on fumes," I announced.

I knew we would make it, though, when we saw the turnoff for the Needles Outpost. I pulled down the road surrounded by desert scrub and rock formations, the type of scenery postcards and tourist brochures are made out of. A rustic wooden sign said *Needles Outpost*, as if it had been carved by some old pioneer.

The campground seemed sparsely populated: a handful of RVs interspersed with white teepees, a few parked vans, a dozen miscellaneous tents.

"Look, there's people!" Shaylee said. "We're saved."

Something set off my alarm bells. Figures moved aimlessly around. Then I noticed that a couple of tents were torn and collapsed, the windows on a van were smashed open, the sliding side door yanked off its tracks. The figures that emerged from some recreational vehicles were pale-skinned, blotchy, and naked.

"No!" Ava said in a plaintive voice.

"They're LDs," Ophelia confirmed.

I glanced at the fuel gauge, then ahead to the general store and its line of gas pumps. The Needles Outpost store was a single large building, set away from the main campground. I hoped we'd have enough time.

"No choice. We've got to do this." I accelerated toward the gas pumps. "Soon as I pull up, break into the same teams we used this morning. Can you do that?"

A chorus of voices behind me said, "I can do that."

"Good. We've got several things to do. This is what teamwork is all about: solving problems. Team one, with Judy: work the pumps and fill us up with gas. Team two, stand watch and fight off any LDs that come close. Team three, you're with me. We have to get inside the general store, load up with as much food and supplies as we can possibly grab."

"Don't forget toilet paper," said Logan.

Gasping on its last fumes, the Winnebago pulled into the outpost.

Judy looked at me and said, "This is going to be fun."

—V—
Dale

Even though we saw jerky, uncertain figures in the campground, the general store and outpost building looked quiet and abandoned. That could be a good thing or a bad thing.

The outpost building had mirrorlike solar panels on the roof, and three large sausage-shaped propane tanks sat in the rear of the building. I pulled the Winnebago up to the bank of gas pumps, choosing one in the open on the opposite side of the general store.

Judy looked around with the thousand-yard stare of a battle-hardened veteran. "You could get closer."

"I want some room for movement," I said. "Just in case LDs come boiling out of that trading post, too." The thought of a horde of cannibalistic zombies surging out of the souvenir shop in new tee shirts and chintzy dude-ranch hats almost made me smile. Almost.

"Good thinking," Judy said with a curt nod.

Figures were starting to move in from the group campsites and the cute tepees. "Ready teams?" I said. "Get in and out as fast as we can. Be flexible. This is a fluid situation."

"Mmm, fluids," Shaylee said. "We need to grab some soda, too."

"We'll need to grab some of those camper propane tanks for the Winnebago," Logan said, pointing to a rack of stubby tanks on the side wall of the store. "You know, to heat up our Ramen noodles and Chef Boyardee."

Chef BAD? I hoped the apocalypse wasn't quite that bad yet. "Ophelia, Zane, Shaylee—you're with me in the general store to grab supplies. Judy, you've got Ava, Logan, and Noah to fill the gas and grab propane. Bridger, Marco, Isabel, take your hiking sticks or whatever you need and guard the perimeter. Keep watch."

"Can I keep watch from inside the RV?" asked Isabel in a quavering voice.

"I know it's hard, but I need you with your team," I said. "Remember how we said this experience would teach you survival skills? I expect you *all* to survive, damn it."

Marco's eyes widened, and he nodded. "I can do that." Several of the others echoed his words.

Zane popped open the Winnebago's door, and we rushed out all at once. The fresh, hot air struck me, making me realize how close and stinky the inside of the RV had been.

"Ooh look. They have showers," Ava said, pointing toward a side building.

A sigh of longing rippled through the group, and I felt it, too. We had more than two weeks of sweat and trail dirt on us.

"No time," I replied. "Better grungy than dead."

"Yeah, it's a tough choice, but ..." Zane turned his cocky grin toward Ophelia. I'd seen the two flirting with each other.

Judy headed to the gas pump with Ava and Noah, while

Logan ran to the rack of small propane tanks. The three guards fanned out, looking nervous—the most skittish sentry ring I'd ever seen, but I couldn't blame them.

We ran to the trading post. The operating hours were conveniently listed, but the glass doors were locked, the interior dark.

"They're not open," Shaylee said in dismay.

Ophelia pointed to the hours posted on the door. "According to this, they should be."

"That could be a good thing. Maybe it means the store hasn't been ransacked by LDs," I said.

Shaylee rattled the door, as if a few more attempts might magically open the outpost for business. She made a *pfft* of annoyance.

Ophelia pressed her face to the glass and shaded her eyes to peer inside. "Nothing moving in there," she said. "But I see potato chips ... and they have a special on Cherry Coke."

"We've got to get inside," Zane said. Before any of us noticed what he was doing, he picked up a decorative rock and smashed it into one of the thick glass doors, producing a hole surrounded by pointed shards and spiderweb cracks. "Now it's ready for customers."

Ophelia scowled at Zane. "Och. Couldn't you have found a side window? LDs probably aren't good at getting through windows. But with the front door broken—what if we need to barricade ourselves inside against an army of living dead?"

"Oh." Zane looked crestfallen, not just because of what he'd done, but because of Ophelia's disappointment.

"You probably don't watch enough movies," Ophelia grumbled.

I pushed a loose fragment of glass away to clear the hole and reached inside to click open the deadbolt. "Let's go."

"Isn't this stealing?" Shaylee said sounding uneasy.

It wasn't anywhere in the CT playbook, but I wasn't going to argue. "Desperate times," I said. "We'll pay for any damages later, when things go back to normal. But we need supplies now."

At the gas pumps, Judy had yanked up one of the nozzles and tried all the buttons. Ava removed the gas cap from the RV. Logan had a camper propane tank in each hand and was lugging them from the rack to the Winnebago.

I entered the dark general store. "Hello?" I called out. "Anybody here? We need help."

My words echoed among the well-stocked metal shelves and displays. I was relieved to see that other scavengers hadn't already taken everything.

"OK, quick, grab what you can," I said. "This might need to last us for a long time." Saying this gave me a chill. Since Preston's snakebite, we had been reacting from gut instinct, not thinking more than an hour or two ahead. Now I was planning for a crisis that might last for weeks or even months. I was acknowledging that we would not simply be met at the pickup point by Bob in a CT van that would take these kids back to clean clothes and showers, then into the appreciative arms of their families. That wasn't going to happen.

"Cherry Coke or regular?" Ophelia called out. "They're both on sale."

"Cherry," said Zane.

"Decaf," said Shaylee, then made a *pfft* sound. "No—make mine regular after all."

I glanced outside, where gaunt, hungry-looking figures were moving closer. I counted maybe twenty LDs coming in from the campground, all naked. Strange. Had they come here to "get back to nature," or was nudity a *thing* that all LDs did?

Bridger, Noah, and Isabel had spread out beyond the RV, holding their hiking sticks. Bridger had picked up some egg-sized rocks and crouched, ready to throw them.

With jerky awkward movements the LDs came closer. Yup. Might turn out very much like a scene from *Night of the Living*

Dead, and my mind made no distinction between the original, the remake, or even the spinoffs.

In frustration, Judy slammed her hand against the metal side of the gas pump. She sent Ava on an urgent dash back to the general store. I met her at the door, suddenly struck by the possibility that the gas pumps might not be working at all. "What's wrong?"

Ava was out of breath and panted for a few seconds before saying, "Judy needs your credit card. Hers was declined."

I fished out my wallet, pulled my Visa from its slot, and handed it over. As Ava ran back to Judy with my card, I yelled toward the gas pumps, "Helluva time not to pay your monthly minimum!"

Judy spread her hands in apology.

I ducked back into the shadowy store. The lack of lighting must have been intentional, because the outpost was solar powered and off the grid.

Zane and Ophelia had shopping carts, while Shaylee carried a basket, running up and down the rows. Ophelia started with candy and chips.

"Get the cool ranch ones," Zane said. "Way better than chile verde."

"Roger. Also getting all kinds of cookies," Ophelia said.

"Remember, this is survival," I called to them, "not snack time. Think nutrition. We need protein."

"I found the Spam and Vienna sausages!" Shaylee said. "Ooh, and Slim Jims."

I shrugged "That's definitely closer." I checked outside again.

Judy was pumping gas now, filling the Winnebago's tank. Ava had gathered several large red gas cans and was filling them at another pump.

"Better hurry," Noah yelled. "They're getting closer."

"Gas doesn't pump itself," Judy said. "It takes as long as it takes." She looked around warily, and I saw that her Glock was now holstered at her side. Good.

Dozens of LDs were swarming from the campground, as if

someone had rung the dinner bell. The Needles Outpost campground must have been pretty full, and I imagined plenty of people had come here to avoid the viral apocalypse. Of course, it only took one bad zombie to infect the whole barrel.

Inside the store, I grabbed a shopping cart and threw in protein bars, electrolyte drinks, and bottled water. I made the mistake of thinking this was all going smoothly.

That's when I heard the distinctive click and ratchet of a shotgun slide being racked, followed by the clink of something small hitting the floor. We all froze. I turned toward the noise and saw a gray-bearded man in a plaid shirt and bib overalls. He pointed a shotgun at me, then swung it around to aim at the kids. "Who the hell are you, and what are you doing in my store?"

With a clank, Ophelia dropped a can of chili on the floor. "Uh, shopping?"

I raised my hands. "We just needed supplies."

"Can't you see we're closed?" His face was drawn and his eyes wary as he stepped closer. "And you smashed my damn door!"

He must have locked himself inside the outpost for days, hiding in the dark so the LDs wouldn't notice him.

"My name is Dale," I said, consciously using a calm, friendly voice. A Preston voice. "I'm here with a group of CanyonTrek students. We were out in the BLM lands at the edge of the Needles and came back to ... all this."

"How do I know you're not infected?" the old man demanded.

Shaylee made a *pfft* sound. "How? We've been out in the middle of nowhere."

I slowly reached for my pants pocket. "Look, we're not stealing. I can pay for everything. We just need to load up our RV and get back into the desert to wait this thing out." I slid out my wallet, opened it, and saw the empty slot where my credit card usually was. I opened the cash section and pulled out a couple of twenties. Normally I carried more ... but who needs cash on a Needles backpacking trip?

Judy shouted from outside. "Dale, speed it up! We've got

company." Through the open doors I saw her hand the gas pump to Logan. "Finish this," she said and stalked off, pulling her pistol.

Ava filled up another red gas can, returned the hose to the pump, and frantically screwed on the caps.

"Well, now you caught the attention of the campers," the old man snorted. "Nothing worse than dissatisfied campers."

The LDs were rushing toward the Winnebago now. Marco and Isabel swung their trekking poles back and forth, driving a few of the diseased victims back. Bridger hurled stones, smacking one LD in the center of her forehead.

Judy strode up beside him, raised her Glock, and fired with a loud crack. She shot the nearest pale and bloody figure in the center of his naked chest.

"Dale, I did not bring enough bullets for the Alamo here!"

I pleaded with the old man. "Look, we have to get out of here. If you think you're safe, stay." I reached a decision and blurted out. "Or you're welcome to come with us and get far away ... but you've got to run now."

"Name's Wendell," he said, lowering the shotgun. "And I'll give us some elbow room." He slipped past us and rushed out the door.

I yelled at the three kids in the store. "Come on, all of you. Take what you can and get back to the RV."

Zane and Ophelia ran up and down the aisles with their shopping carts rattling, while and Shaylee set her overfull basket by the door and grabbed a new one. I added all the emergency supplies I could grab to my cart. As I passed the cash register, I swept a pile of batteries in with the mix and trundled out to the RV.

Logan hooked the gas nozzle back in place on the pump and whirled to screw the cap back on the tank.

Wendell stepped next to Judy and discharged his shotgun with a loud boom. The buckshot dispersed wide enough to blast two of the oncoming LDs and knock them flat.

"Back into the Winnebago, everybody!" I yelled. They didn't need to be told twice.

Wendell chambered another round, ejecting the spent shell, and shot again.

I leaped into the driver's seat, jammed the keys into the ignition. Judy fired her Glock twice more, and then the rest of our group piled aboard the RV. Wendell followed them into the back, while Judy hopped in through the passenger door.

"Don't worry, I got your credit card, Dale," said Ava with earnest diligence.

"Thank you," I replied and started the engine.

"Did anyone get toilet paper?" Logan asked.

"*Pfft*," Shaylee said, slapping her forehead, at the same time as Ophelia said, "Aargh!" and Zane said, "Uh-oh!"

"*Not* going back," Judy said sternly.

The big RV rolled forward not much faster than the living dead could shamble. I stomped on the accelerator. The Winnebago was a workhorse, slow and heavy, but it did pick up speed, eventually. I was glad we'd used one of the outer gas pumps, because the behemoth couldn't maneuver in tight quarters. I swung a wide U-turn.

Wendell was trying to situate himself on one of the seats in back.

"You might just have to hold on," Ophelia told him.

About ten LDs that must have wandered over from the campground blocked the exit road.

"Crap!" Zane said. "Can you dodge them?"

"Is there another road out?" I barked at Wendell.

"Only one road in and one road out," he said. "Never been a problem before."

"Straight through it is," I muttered. No point in trying to dodge any LDs. I accelerated toward the bottleneck that limited our escape. I braced myself, gripping the steering wheel.

Shaylee screamed, "Look out!"

"Don't worry, they'll jump out of the way," I said, not believing it for a moment.

They didn't. The Winnebago struck a few LDs, scattered the

rest, and kept going even as we felt a sickening bump under our tires.

"Just a pothole," Judy said. "Nothing to worry about."

I raced along the bumpy, patched road.

"Just a pothole," I agreed.

—VI—
Dale

We were home free. More or less. Our RV had a full gas tank and a couple of spare cans. We had food. We had water. We had propane. And we had no idea where to go.

"I want to get home," Shaylee said.

"Forget Moab, just head straight up to Salt Lake," Bridger piped up from the back. "My family's there." He looked around at the other eight students. "Most of our families are there, right?"

"I miss them." Marco's voice cracked. "I never thought I'd say it ..."

Into a rising chorus of excited voices and worried demands, Wendell spoke. "That's the least safe place to be right now! I watched the TV until most of the stations went off. Salt Lake is burning. There's a virus spreading. Hospitals are overflowing with flu patients. On top of that, those infected *things* are everywhere."

"We call them LDs," Ava said, trying to be helpful. "It stands for 'living dead.'"

"You can't know what's happening everywhere," Zane insisted. "We should see for ourselves."

"What I do know is this: driving toward an infected city is the opposite of wise," the old man said. His shoulders sagged. I could see him in the rearview mirror. "Five days ago my wife took the truck into Monticello to get our monthly delivery. She called to tell me our delivery didn't come, and there were *riots* in the streets. How? There's only a couple thousand people in the whole town, and none of them are the rioting type. She said 'Don't come anywhere near town—it's not safe.' That was when the call got cut off, and phone service has been down ever since." His voice wavered on the verge of weeping. "Next day, a young couple with a baby stopped here for gas. They *came* from Monticello, said there were stark-naked people and fires and murders all over town. They escaped. My wife never came back. And I know damn well what's happening out there."

I turned on the radio and scrolled through the stations, getting mostly static except for, oddly, a station that blared brassy Mexican music and another with a vehement preacher railing about the end times. I switched it off.

"It's probably going to get worse before it gets better," I said.

My heart felt heavy for these teens. They were unwillingly participants in CT because their parents thought they needed behavior modification, boot-camp counselors to toughen them up and straighten them out. Before our three-week expedition, Judy, Preston, and I had met with all of the parents and learned about the home situations so we could understand the special problems these kids might pose. Some of the parents probably just wanted to breathe a sigh of relief at getting the unruly teens out of their hair. Ava had naively thought she was coming to a summer camp.

I'd been through this before. The parents expected miracles from a few days out in the Canyonlands hiking and tent camping. They wanted us counselors to force an epiphany, make their almost-adult sons or daughters appreciate the things they had, learn a new work ethic, develop respect and civility. All in three weeks or less. We did accomplish some of those things. Their nightly journals were a good tool to help us assess their progress, but it wasn't magic.

These kids all wanted to go back home, because most of their problems paled in comparison to a deadly epidemic. But having heard Desiree on the sat phone, I could guess what had happened at CanyonTrek HQ in Moab ... and maybe all of Moab. We'd read the papers, and we knew what to expect in Salt Lake. These kids couldn't go home. They couldn't help.

As I maneuvered the Winnebago along the narrow winding road through the red rock desert, I said, "I think we should stay here on the BLM lands for a while. We've got food and supplies.

We have our packs and tents. The smartest thing is to wait this out, and I'll keep trying to reach someone who can tell us when it's safe."

"That's what we need to do," said Wendell. "Plenty of places to get lost out here. We could hunker down."

"That's my vote, too," said Judy, "so it's unanimous."

"Hey, we didn't get a vote!" Ophelia and Zane chimed in at the same time.

"This isn't a democracy," I said. "It's an oligarchy." I paused for a second then said, "Look it up."

"There's no dictionary," the kids grumbled. "We should have a say."

I took a turnoff and left the pavement for another dirt road. A brown Forest Service sign with white letters said Overlook 15 miles. It seemed a good place to start, to get a feel for where we were.

The road was rough, and its washboard surface rattled our teeth. If Preston were still alive, he probably would have started a group song, like "Ninety-nine Bottles of Soda on the Wall." As it was, most of the young people sat in confusion and sadness, trying to absorb what was happening. The RV gave us countless options of where to camp. There were plenty of firepits and open parking areas, no traffic that we could see.

"I made a promise to keep all of you safe," I said to the group.

Judy nodded. "Me too. I just wish I'd managed to pick up more rounds for my Glock."

After the long rattling drive I finally pulled the Winnebago to a stop at the abandoned, nameless overlook. From a high point on the edge of a mesa, it offered a view out across an endless wonderland of hoodoos, rust red pinnacles, and deep-cut canyons.

We all climbed out.

"I found a picnic table!" Isabel said.

I drank in the desert scenery, using it to find a tiny speck of calm deep inside me. Even in a world with a spreading epidemic, upheavals in society, and living dead roaming the streets, I felt a sense of satisfaction. I was taking care of the people I was responsible for. We were safe. For now.

Looking at the landscape, I said to myself, "One hell of a place to lose a cow."

Standing nearby, Ophelia flashed me an odd smile. "But maybe a good place to lose the LDs."

I drew in a deep breath of the warm, dry desert air and nodded slowly. "I agree."

Ophelia Journal

Day 1. I'm starting over. I'm not who I was a few weeks ago.

So this is for me.

Sounds corny, but this is true: We morphed into a family of sorts, with a mom, dad, grandpa, and nine kids. Well, except for one thing. None of us are kids anymore.

Life is harder than before. Gritty. Backbreaking. We all have jobs every day—guard duty, cooking, foraging, inventing, sanitation. There's no choice. We don't argue about it. Who else would do the work?

We solve problems, pretty much around the clock.

Me? I wait, and hope for a future when I can maybe see my parents again. Meanwhile, I'll live the life that I have, not the one I wish for.

I can do that.

When I was in college, I took a family vacation with the neighbor family, the McGlauchlens—mom, dad, three kids, and me. As a young man eager to see the country, I tagged along when they loaded up the woody station wagon with suitcases and sleeping bags, and we did a great American road trip from Wisconsin all the way out to Seattle, then up into British Columbia. I wanted to see the country beyond the rural Midwest and couldn't pass up the opportunity, and the McGlauchlens were happy for the extra driver and an extra hand setting up camp each night.

Among the many wonderful places we stopped was the Custer Battlefield National Monument in Montana. The National Park Service ranger took us on a guided walk through the grassy hills, and he explained step by step the catastrophic events that converged in the massacre of Custer's last stand. Being in that old battlefield site was a profound experience for me, and I became interested in the history of the event. I knew I had to turn it into a story somehow.

"Last Stand" is also loosely connected to the Tucker's Grove series.

Last Stand

```
                    Massacred
        Gen Custer and 261 Men the Victims

    3 Days Desperate Fighting by Maj. Reno and
              Remainder of the Seventh
```

— *Bismarck Daily Tribune* [Dakota Territory]:
July 6, 1876

"The [steamer] Far West arrived this morning, bringing terrible news from the expedition and 38 wounded men for treatment in the hospital. Genl. Custer with his command met an overwhelming force of Indians on the Little Big Horn ... and five companies ... were completely cut to pieces, not one man being left....

"This has been a very gloomy day at the post. There are 24 women here who have been made widows by the disaster."

— Medical Journal of Assistant Surgeon J.V.D. Middleton, Fort Abraham Lincoln, Dakota Territory. July 6, 1876

K enner is coming back from the dead to kill me. Tonight. And I can do nothing but wait. The vengeful sorcery which animates my former comrade has already slaughtered the other three, one by one, during the rotten core of the night.

Tucker, the first, knew nothing of his fate and lay mangled by the riverbank with his face a frozen expression of soul-bursting fear. But at least he did not have to endure these hours of horrified waiting. Darby is murdered. Barrett is murdered. How am I to fight against an obsidian-clawed ghoul turned against his friends by Sioux hatred and magic?

I can hear the hushed expectancy of the river, feel the lulling sway of the Far West as it fights against the ropes tying it up during the blackest hours of night. The pungent smell of old, rain-soaked hay seeps into the night, placed on the deck here to "brave fighters." I don't complain—after that night on Reno Hill surrounded by screaming victorious Sioux, feeling our parched and festering throats and having nothing but horse blood to drink ... how could I complain about mere crowdedness?

Captain Marsh has pushed the Far West admirably, but I doubt if any steamer could move faster than Kenner's murderous spirit. I could have fled the boat this morning at the Powder River Depot. Hoping for safety. No, not even the massive stockade of Fort Pease had stopped Kenner from shredding Darby like confetti.

So I wait, awake in the darkness on the Far West, knowing that I have not run far enough or fast enough. Tomorrow, perhaps, the steamer will reach Bismarck and civilization ... but by then my body will have been rended by obsidian claws.

And Kenner is coming.

```
"After we gained the bluffs we could look
back upon the plains where the Indians
were, and could see them stripping and
scalping our men, and mutilating the
bodies in a horrible manner. The prairie
was all afire."
```

> — John M. Ryan, survivor of the Reno Hill battle,
> as recollected in the *Hardin* [Montana] *Tribune*,
> June 22, 1923

Details regarding events on Reno Hill, submitted to Montana State Historical Society by Lieutenant Edgerton. Ultimately rejected, August 1896, "due to obvious implausibility."

"God, I'm thirsty!"

Three hundred and fifty beaten men huddled in the darkness atop Reno Hill, waiting in baffled terror and wondering when the thousands of vengeful Sioux warriors would finally swoop down to complete the massacre.

"Goddamn Indian cowards!" Kenner cursed, digging his knife into the baked ground. He probably would have spat in disgust, as was his habit, if his throat hadn't been so parched.

Murderous shadows hid in the wicked moonlight; huge bonfires burned in the village below, and capering warriors shouted and danced their victory.

"If they'd come here one at a time I'd take them all on, man-to-man, and see who's the better fighter!" He stuck his knife up to its hilt into the ground.

"They don't have to," Barrett said, more calmly than any of them felt. "They can just wait us out. We're almost out of ammunition. Almost out of water. All they have to do is watch the creek. With this heat we'll be dead in a few days."

"God, I'm thirsty," Tucker whined. His thin and skittish voice matched his physical build exactly.

"Shut up, Tucker!" Kenner growled at him.

"You're only making it worse." Edgerton spoke soothingly, as if to make up for Kenner's anger. "Maybe Custer'll still come."

Kenner laughed. Barrett frowned skeptically. Tucker didn't seem to hear. Darby, once so proud of the tomahawk he had taken from a dead Indian, now sat in silence, hammering the tomahawk at the ground as if he could kill a Sioux with each blow to Sioux land.

Custer had charged off with his own battalion early in the afternoon, ordering Reno to attack the village which turned out to be ten times larger than any of them had suspected. Reno had charged into the howling hornet's nest of Indians, expecting aid from Custer ... aid which never arrived. Custer had disappeared. Reno had fallen back into the forest beside the creek, and, when that proved untenable, he had led his men in a desperate charge across the creek to the dubious safety of the bluffs on the other side. A costly retreat, leaving the bodies of many fallen soldiers behind.

Now, at night, the outnumbered survivors cringed like animals waiting to be slaughtered, each dealing with the terror in his own way. Some wailed, some prayed to God, some cursed Him for allowing this to happen, some curled up on the ground and did nothing.

"Wilson's dead by now," Edgerton said flatly, letting the words hang in the air. "When Weir retreated, I left him wounded and hidden in a gully. I promised we'd organize a skirmish to come back and get him. I promised. We never did. And I promised." The silence sobbed around him for a moment.

"We were supposed to be the Romans, bringing civilization to this Godless land. But now the barbarians are destroying us."

Barrett smiled wryly. "Not godless—they've probably got their own demons to pray to." He paused, and continued quietly. "Judging from their success so far, the Indian gods seem to be more effective than our own." He removed his spectacles and vigorously polished the dry dust from them. Firelight glinted on the lenses.

"Doesn't anybody have anything to drink?" Tucker said in a cracking voice.

Kenner banged his empty canteen as evidence. "You're welcome to make a run for the creek if you want to fill it up."

Tucker swallowed hard and sat back in silence. Darby whacked his tomahawk on the ground, gouging out a deep chunk of dirt. In the distance, the Indians let out a loud whooping cheer, and the victory fires burned brighter. Moans from the wounded drifted on the sluggish night air, and dying animals uttered sounds which made the pain of the men seem like nothing.

"Doc Porter's keeping all the water for the wounded." Barrett's nonchalant tone was taut with strain. "Doesn't matter. We're all going to die anyway."

"Shut up, Barrett," Edgerton and Kenner snapped in unison, then glared at each other. Edgerton had never gotten along well with the burly Kenner—to him, the often brutal and over-zealous trooper was one small step above a savage. Edgerton was educated, had a family back in Bismarck, and kept himself scrupulously honest. Kenner, on the other hand, couldn't read, claimed to have a woman waiting for him at every fort along the Yellowstone, and did everything he felt he could get away with.

"There's juice in the tins of fruit on the pack mules," Barrett continued. "But Reno said he'd shoot anyone who tries to get them. It's only a matter of time." No one had the energy to tell him to keep quiet.

"They say the Indians drink blood." Darby finally spoke up, holding his tomahawk so tightly his knuckles whitened.

"Plenty of that around here," Edgerton mumbled.

"Yes, there is, isn't there?" Kenner said quietly, with disturbing sincerity in his voice.

The maniacal silence of the night filled their ears for a long time.

"You're crazy," Edgerton finally said.

"Ah, the trappings of civilization cling to the very end, don't they?" Barrett looked directly at Edgerton. Edgerton knew that Barrett considered himself well-educated in his own right, but instead of feeling close to the spectacled man, he felt an uneasy sense of competition.

"Oh, Lordy, I'm almost thirsty enough to do it. I wish I was home."

"Well, go home then, Tucker! It's only a year's walk to Wisconsin," Kenner snapped.

"I'd love to try this on the neck of one of them Sioux horses." Darby swung the tomahawk again. "Bet it'd bleed like hell."

Barrett licked his dry lips.

"Is ... is anybody else gonna drink if I do?" Tucker asked.

"Shit! I'm gonna drink even if you don't." Kenner grabbed an empty cooking pot from one of the packs.

"You're crazy...." Edgerton said, less forcefully now. It felt as if the sun itself burned down his throat.

The troopers normally killed a wounded horse to put an end to its misery. But since this horse had been owned by a Sioux, a Sioux responsible for the deaths of at least two white men, some of the soldiers insisted that the horse be left to die in its own long and painful fashion. Several bullets had shattered its spine, and it moved sluggishly with its forelegs, dragging the useless hindquarters behind in a slow madman's trail in the dust. It had finally collapsed near the perimeter in the dying heat of the day, not knowing that its bulky body made an effective barrier for the crouching men.

Kenner and Darby crept up to the horse, eager with the cooking pot and tomahawk; Tucker, Barrett and Edgerton followed closely behind. The horse knew they had come for blood, as if it could smell the intent on bodies too parched even to sweat. In the awkwardly reflected firelight, Edgerton caught a glimpse of the horse's wide and defiant eye. It was green and reptilian with a slit pupil, like the eye of a poisonous snake just waiting to give the gift of venom. Edgerton suppressed a shudder.

The horse glared at them but lay still as Kenner carefully placed the pot next to its heaving neck. Darby grinned and swung the stone hatchet, chopping through veins and laying open all the liquid any desperate man could hope to gorge himself on. Tucker scrambled forward eagerly, and bright foaming blood sprayed in his face, dripping warm and wet down his chin. Crumbling remnants of civilization tugged at his instincts, making him spit the blood from his mouth.

"Jeezus!" Kenner shouted.

"Quick! Get that pot under it before it stops spurting! You're gonna lose all of it!" Barrett seemed to be trying to control the excitement in his voice as he sat back and watched the others.

The horse made no sound as its life gushed from the wound. Its reptilian eye seemed to focus on all of them at once.

In the village below, the Indians suddenly fell silent. The victory fires continued to burn, sending demon-smoke writhing up into the shining night.

Kenner slurped from the pot, drinking deeply as if to show he had no qualms whatsoever. He passed it to Darby, who closed his eyes as he drank. Tucker snatched the pot and gulped, letting a thin, clotting trickle run across his razor stubble. Barrett drank, watching Edgerton as if this were a challenge for the two of them to meet. Edgerton finally took the near-empty pot, hesitated, looked at the remaining pool of blood as it oozed from the open wound on the now-dead horse. Thirst clawed at the inside of his throat. He couldn't be expected to put up any kind of fight against the Sioux if all he could think of was his miserable thirst. His very survival depended on this. Survival.

He held the warm metal to his lips and sipped at the stale-copper taste.

"Hey! Anybody religious? We got one hell of a communion going here!" Kenner shouted.

"Keep quiet, you bastard!" Edgerton growled.

But Kenner seemed to be possessed, as if distant lightning were coursing through his veins. He leaped to his feet, straining against the shackles of his body and baring his teeth as he faced the silent burning fires in the Indian village. His eyes seemed filled with molten lead, and a bizarre energy surged through him.

"Dammit!" he howled, "I could run down there right now and kill them Indians with my bare hands!" He clawed at the air in a disturbingly animal gesture.

"Kenner, would you keep down! Shut up!" Barrett hissed.

Edgerton could feel the hot blood he had drunk, like glowing iron piercing his gut. He wanted to vomit, but couldn't.

Another trooper, a Captain, parted the shadows and came forward, calling to no one in particular. "Doc Porter says we have to have water. Major Reno is asking for volunteers to make a dash to the creek. Anybody interested?" His voice sounded tired, as if he were asking only in order to fulfill a duty and did not expect an answer.

"Hell, yes!" Kenner jumped toward the Captain, startling him. "What a way to get even with those Indian snakes! Gimme two pots and I'll fill 'em! Hurry!"

Kenner grabbed the pots and made a dash for the edge of the bluff as if he needed to burn away the energy bubbling through him. For an instant, Edgerton thought the burly man would leap headfirst off the bluff, but then Kenner found the steep and narrow buffalo trail worn down the river bank. He disappeared into the shadows below.

A few moments later Darby stood up. "I'm going, too."

The Captain looked as if both men had lost their minds in the hot battle that afternoon; but he gave Darby a pot and sent him down the trail as well.

Tucker scrambled to the edge and lay on his stomach, peering over into the darkness. "Holy cow! Kenner's at the creek already!"

A few scattered gunshots rang out down below. "They missed him. He's got the water, and he's coming back up!"

"He probably wouldn't feel it even if they did hit him," Barrett said to Edgerton. Blood dried around the spectacled man's lips. Self-consciously, Edgerton wiped his own mouth.

"Is Darby to the creek yet?" Edgerton asked.

"Can't see him."

Kenner appeared at the top of the bluff and handed two

brimming water pots to the dumbfounded Captain. "Don't just stand there! Get me two more pots—come on!"

The Captain scrambled to obey.

Impatiently, Kenner picked up a large rock and hurled it over the rim into the night. At that moment a shooting-star blazed overhead, and it seemed almost as if Kenner had thrown it.

Kenner snorted. "Ain't anybody else coming?" He took two more pots and scrambled down again. More frequent gunfire bounced and skittered along the creekbed below.

"Darby's coming up," Tucker announced. A few moments later the other man lurched over the rim carrying a canteen filled with barely a cup of water.

"Good thing those Sioux are lousy shots," Darby gasped. Edgerton noticed a bleeding wound on the man's arm where a bullet had grazed him. "I'm not going down there again."

"They're just toying with us," Barrett mumbled. "Cat and mouse. Isn't it fun?"

"That idiot!" Tucker gasped. "Kenner's down there, up to his knees in the water, jumping up and down and cussing at the Indians!"

"What the hell!" Edgerton, Barrett, and Darby knelt beside Tucker, searching for the burly man somewhere below. The gunfire had stopped, but they could hear the sudden intakes of silence, the quiet patter on stone as the Indians shot arrows. Below, Kenner stopped shouting. He jerked and fell backward into the water.

The Captain stood at the rim. "Is anybody going to go down and get him? See if he's still alive? Or, for the sake of mercy, rescue his body from the Indians? You saw what they did to the ones we left behind this afternoon!"

"Why don't you go get him, Captain?" Barrett asked. "He fetched your water."

"He was your friend," the Captain snapped.

"I'm not going down there again!" Darby insisted.

"He wasn't my friend," Barrett said.

"You're not making me do it!" Tucker whined. "I'm too scared.

If you threw me over the edge I wouldn't even fall down there 'cause I'm so scared."

"He wasn't my friend either," Edgerton mumbled.

"It's ironic, even laughable now. But at the time we could imagine no greater terror than that night on Reno Hill.... Our imaginations have grown since then."

— Lieutenant Edgerton's journal.

In the back of my mind I believe I had always known this war to be far more than a mere conflict between two armies. No, it was a battle of trained soldier against painted warrior, civilization against bloodthirsty savagery, modern military techniques against arrow and tomahawk.

By all rights we should have won!

Perhaps civilization just doesn't belong here.

There are those who claim the Indians have a right to commit their atrocities. But you would be hard-pressed to find one such man among the survivors of Reno Hill, the ones who watched in the settling dust of a bloated afternoon as the Sioux women gleefully ran over the battlefield, slitting the throats of wounded troopers. Or the warriors who stripped and mutilated the bodies of our comrades so that—as the Sioux believe—the spirits of the fallen enemy will find no peace in heaven.

Before any man tells me the Indians have a right to do this, I will tell him to go back and look at the graves, to reflect for a moment that not one unmutilated body lies buried there, thanks to the cruel knives of the bloodthirsty Sioux. I will ask him to believe that the souls of hundreds of American soldiers now wander *aimlessly and in anguish because the doors of heaven are closed to them.*

He will not believe me.

He hasn't seen Kenner.

Nor has he seen Darby's murdered body within the *security of Fort Pease, with the heavy doors ripped apart and bullet holes from Darby's pistol dotting the walls ... and not one man at the Fort having heard a sound all night long.* Nor does he have Barrett's flag-wrapped body here beside him on the deck of a haunted boat in the middle of the night. Barrett's eyes had been torn out, perhaps so he couldn't see his own blood spilling over the deck rail into the quiet river. But his gleaming spectacles remained completely untouched on his face, as if for an ironic joke. Tomorrow, when the *Far West* reaches Bismarck, they are going to give Barrett a full military burial.

Put a man through all this, and then ask him to be objective about the Indians.

I took Darby's tomahawk with me, perhaps to give to his sister as a keepsake, if ever I see her, and if I survive. I have my pistol loaded at my side, but it gives me no comfort because I remember how effective Darby's own pistol must have been in Fort Pease.

I am sweating.

On the riverbanks all the insects suddenly stifle their sounds, extinguished like a fire. The river fails to make any sound against the *Far West*. The quietly snoring troopers on deck cease to breathe.

Kenner has drawn a curtain of night silence around us, to shelter himself from any prying eyes.

A loud thump strikes the deck behind me, as of something heavy settling there.

"Your turn, Edgerton," Kenner says.

"The nightmares of children are as nothing compared to the

nightmares of men ... and at times even the nightmares of men pale before reality."

— Lieutenant Edgerton's journal

June 27, 1876: explanation of Walter Tucker's death, as told by Lieutenant Edgerton. "Purely conjecture, and purely preposterous!"

— evaluation by Montana State Historical Society, written in red ink.

They stared at each other, quivering like pudding as the aftershocks of terror ran through them and then vanished. Tucker looked at Barrett, Darby, and Edgerton—the four of them had survived. Many of the other men were weeping. The Sioux had fought for most of the following day and then, after setting the prairie afire, they took their women and children and departed.

Brigadier General Terry's rescue column arrived the next morning, too late to do much more than help find and bury the mutilated dead. Custer's entire Seventh Cavalry lay among those dead, but Tucker was hard-pressed to consider himself "fortunate."

All fighting had stopped, but still it felt like a battlefield. The dry grass moved in the silence, suggesting that there must have been a breeze although the hot sun denied it. Flies and stench hung in the sluggish air as hundreds of bodies began to bloat. Terry's men were appalled, and many of them would sleep with their noses on the wet river bank to distract them from the smell.

Terry had offered a hundred-dollar bonus to any volunteers willing to carry a message downstream to the Far West, asking Captain Marsh to prepare to receive casualties.

"I'm going to see if I can find him," Tucker said. He had rinsed his mouth with fresh water again and again, but still the hot coppery taste of stolen blood clung to his tongue.

"Who?" Edgerton asked.

Barrett scowled at him. "Who the hell do you think?"

"You weren't too anxious to go looking for him two nights ago, Tucker," Darby remarked.

"Well, neither were you!"

"Let him go. If he can't find Kenner, maybe we'll help look," Barrett suggested.

"I, for one, don't know if I can stand the sight of another corpse today. Besides, it's almost dark," Edgerton said.

"Scared of the dark, are you?" Barrett asked sarcastically.

"I don't know what I'm scared of anymore."

"Well, I'm going." Tucker gave a disgusted snort. "That bastard made us drink blood—now we're no better than the damned Indians." He turned his back on the other three and began picking his way down to the riverbank.

The sun hung close to the horizon, tingeing the sky and shadows with a coppery color. The creek bed was rocky and filled with broken brush, and the shallow, slow-moving water had succeeded in washing most of the battle from its memory. The landscape looked dry-brown and barren, with rises and dips affording hundreds of hiding places for hostile Indians. Arrows, tattered shreds of uniforms, personal possessions dropped in panic as Reno's men had furiously splashed across the creek to the safety of the bluffs, all lay scattered on the riverbank. And a few bodies. One of them would be Kenner's. Tucker felt sick inside; tomorrow, Terry would want them to spend hours in the hot and stinking sun identifying and burying the hundreds who had fallen. Tucker didn't know if he had the stomach for it.

He slogged up the creek to where he had seen Kenner fall, and began to dart his eyes into the shadowy corners where a dead man might hide. Within a few moments Tucker found him, halfway up the bank as if he had crawled there to outrun death. Kenner's body lay in the gray outline of a shadow, one shoulder up against a rock and the other arm stiff and outstretched. His blue uniform was torn, and his mouth had been bruised and smashed, grinning with jagged, broken teeth. Both of Kenner's eyes were gone, taken away by the birds or the Sioux, and the torn-meat sockets stared at Tucker like gaping, blood-filled mouths.

"Serves you right, Kenner," Tucker sneered, alone with his bravado. Of the soldiers, Tucker believed he disliked Kenner the most. "Ah, the times you poked fun at me, beat me up, pushed me around, made me feel like a worm in front of the others, but you got yours. Now who has the last laugh?"

Tucker kicked the dead trooper and forced a high-pitched nervous laugh. Suddenly his flesh crawled on his spine, and it seemed as if Kenner's head had moved just the slightest bit, focusing the torn and empty eye sockets on him. Around him all noises seemed vanquished, and even the water in the creek ceased to move; he had the strangest feeling that the sun had stopped setting. Then he noticed that Kenner's nails were black and glassy, curved into claws like knives.

"I've got the last laugh, Tucker," Kenner said, as he sat up and reached out with a fistful of obsidian claws.

When they found Tucker's flayed and staring body the next morning, somebody said the Indians must have gotten him. And nobody ever found Kenner.

"Don't tell me it's not possible! You weren't there! You sit behind your desks and think your civilized preconceptions had significance then. Well you're wrong, gentlemen. Dead wrong."

— Letter from Lieutenant Edgerton to Montana State Historical Society, September 1896.

All through the blistering heat of the afternoon the following day, Terry's men and Reno's survivors did their best to identify and bury the dead. An almost maniacal gloom hung over everyone, and most of the soldiers worked slack-jawed and glassy-eyed, as if their brains refused to accept what their eyes told them.

Anxious to flee the battlefield, Terry ordered the men to set out at 6:30 that evening, trudging along and carrying the wounded on hand-litters. They struggled and gasped and sweated. In five and a half hours they had covered four miles.

The next day, some of the more resourceful troopers helped design and construct both mule-litters and travois. The others tried to find shade and rested as sweat-beads popped out on their foreheads, waiting for the heat of day to fall into death.

"What do you suppose really happened to Tucker?" Barrett asked.

"Indians got him," Darby answered automatically.

"Don't be ridiculous. We all know the Sioux trotted off into the hills a day before Terry even got here. There weren't any Indians by that creek." Barrett wiped the lenses of his sweat-streaked spectacles.

"Nobody ever found Kenner," Edgerton whispered.

Darby and Barrett held their silence. Barrett took a flask of whiskey and drank deeply. He wiped his mouth, then spat. "Even whiskey doesn't burn the taste from your mouth." He drank again, offered it to Darby (who refused), and then tossed the flask to Edgerton, taking him by surprise. Edgerton fumbled for a moment but caught the flask. He drank, too.

They set out again at 5:30, after the waves of heat had wakened heavy thunderheads in the sky. Nightfall came with the fanfare of thick rain and pitch darkness. They slogged through the water and muck, carrying the wounded and pressing forward as if they were enjoying the clean rain. Shadowy couriers found their way through the storm, bearing the message that the Far West lay ready and waiting for the soldiers. But the rain turned to hail and showered them as heavily as Indian arrows. The hail lay on the ground in white stinging pellets, like dead men's teeth.

And through it all, Edgerton felt an oppressive fear prickling at the back of his neck. Some deadly leviathan stalked them through the darkness, biding its time, waiting. "Do you feel it?" Edgerton called to Darby as quietly as he could through the storm.

"You better believe it. God, I can't wait until we get to Fort Pease. I'm gonna crawl under a bed and hide for a week."

Kenner found Darby at Fort Pease, ripping the door to shreds in the middle of the night. Darby's hand still gripped his empty pistol even though his knuckles had split. Bullet holes burned into the walls, but Edgerton and Barrett found no indication of any blood on the floor other than Darby's own.

Two days later, after Captain Marsh had launched the Far West on its breakneck journey to Bismarck, Barrett lay draped almost casually across the deck-rail, with his face mutilated but his spectacles remarkably clean and untouched, still resting on the stubs of his ears.

That left Edgerton all alone. And terribly afraid.

"Mister Edgerton, our very detailed records of the Battle of the Little Bighorn make no mention whatsoever of the grisly murders you describe, or of a soldier named 'Kenner.' You are obviously given to unfortunate flights of fancy. It was for this reason two years ago that I refused to let the Society publish your own Sioux War memoirs. Even the name of the villain in your fantastic story is a rather clumsy attempt to discredit me personally. Be warned

> that any further communication from you will be viewed upon as slander."
>
> — W. B. Kenner, director, Montana Historical Society

Kenner stands in front of me on the silent deck of the steamer, staring at me with gaping eye sockets which see more than his eyes ever could. He rips away the tattered top of his blue uniform and casts it over the deck rail, as if it pains and offends him. He does not taunt me, as I had expected him to do, but comes forward with a confident, wickedly rolling stride.

"You always were a bloodthirsty one, Kenner. This doesn't hardly surprise me at all." I can barely believe the words which come from my lips—this is the last statement from a man doomed to suffer a horrible death?

The words bring Kenner up short, and he stops.

I hold my pistol rigidly in front of me, though I suspect the bullets will have no effect. Darby was a good shot. But here I must make my last stand. Maybe I can club Kenner with the gun.

"Is it going to stop with me, or do you plan on ripping apart every trooper you can find, and from there go into Bismarck and prey upon shopkeepers and their wives?"

"Bloodthirsty," Kenner said. "An interesting choice of words."

I can see him clearly in the moonlight, and his outline has a vague and wavering quality, as if my eyes are not able to see him completely. I say nothing more. He still hasn't answered my question.

"It'll end with you, Edgerton. And I will end as well."

"What do you mean? Aren't you enjoying yourself enough?" My instinct tells me to keep him talking, that perhaps he must depart with the dawn or something. But then I remember that time has stopped around us. It is useless.

"No! I have no part in this."

"Then why are you doing it? You murdered Tucker —and Darby—and Barrett! Do you hate us so much? Because we didn't risk ourselves to go down and rescue your body? Is that it? Well, I am sincerely sorry. If we thought you were still alive, maybe one of us would have tried. But even you cannot be foolish enough to expect us to get killed for a man who was already dead. You wouldn't have done it yourself."

My voice cracks a few times, and I doubt if I will ever fully believe the bravado that has come over me.

"No, I wouldn't have done it myself. Nor do I blame you."

My delicately constructed rationalization of irrational events tinkles and breaks around me. Kenner continues to speak, and for that I am thankful.

"There's a different war going on here, Edgerton. Civilization is poking its nose in where it has no business being. We're pulling our way of life up like a weed and trying to transplant it here. It's not just the Indians who are fighting—it's the animals, the plants, the water, the insects, the land itself! Can't you hear how everything has hushed in anticipation of our meeting? Even time is holding its breath. You have stolen something and are trying to flee to the boundaries of civilization with it. I can't let you do that."

My mind reels—what is it he wants? I look at Darby's tomahawk at my belt, and I can think of nothing else I have taken from the wilderness. Those men died because of a tomahawk? But why didn't Kenner take it from Darby's room at Fort Pease?

*"It's the blood, Edgerton. We all drank the blood of a Sioux horse. While it pulses through your veins, I can't let you leave here. I can't let you pass across the boundary into civilization. Even now I can feel the blood screaming, crying out to be released from the body it finds so abhorrent. The pull was so strong it set fire to my veins and pulled me back to the borderland of life. The blood has a soul of its own, and it beseeches me to free its kindred from the bodies of civilized men. I must pour your blood back to the earth so that the wilderness may reclaim what you have taken. And when I have done my work, the blood will burn out of my own vessels, turn

my heart into a lump of ash, and leap from my body back into the embrace of the land."

He steps forward, holding forth the knives of his hands in an almost placating gesture. I shout and shout for help, but rouse no one. My grip on the pistol becomes steadier.

"You were always something of a milksop, Edgerton. Frankly, I'm surprised you are going to resist. I had expected you to whimper, like Barrett did."

My fingers clench convulsively, and the pistol fires. The bullet ricochets off one of the rails behind Kenner. I could not have missed. I fire five times in all. The shots wake no one. And Kenner walks through the bullets. I hurl the pistol at him and watch as it passes through his chest and clatters on the deck.

"My body does not recognize your civilized weapons. The burning blood will have nothing to do with them. Relax, Edgerton. I still remember you—the death itself will be quick. And perhaps this time the blood will not demand mutilation."

I remember the bullet holes in the walls around Darby. And I remember how Darby's battle had ended. "Barrett's spectacles! That's how you clawed his eyes but didn't so much as scratch the lenses." I hope this will make him pause. It doesn't.

He draws back an arm, preparing to swipe at me with his obsidian claws.

The self-preservation drive bursts within me, breaking down the walls of reason and unleashing purely animal instinct. I tear Darby's tomahawk from my belt and howl maniacally as I lunge forward, splitting Kenner's breastbone and driving the primitive stone axe into his dead heart. The tomahawk strikes something as firm as gelatin, and hangs suspended in Kenner's flayed chest.

Kenner stops cold and begins convulsing like a man in contact with a Galvanic battery. Beads of red sweat burst from his pores and begin trickling together, running in rivulets up his chest, against the pull of gravity. The blood reaches his forehead and leaps into the night air like a narrow river of fiery droplets, whirling together in a cyclone of blood as it moves against the night toward shore.

Kenner falls over the deck rail and lands in the silent river with a splash like a thunderclap. Suddenly I can hear the night sounds again; the river laps up against the sides of the Far West.

I collapse to the deck, shaking, drenched with sweat, and feeling utterly ill. Kenner is gone, and I have survived. But he, and the bloodthirsty wilderness, have had their victory as well. No logic, or careful planning, or rationalization has saved me this night—it was pure animal instinct. I butchered a former comrade by swinging a stone hatchet into his chest and reveled in the feeling of conquest.

Never again will I consider myself a civilized man.

Sickness rises up explosively in my gut, and I lurch to the rail. Bending over, I retch so violently that small blood vessels burst in the whites of my eyes.

Red wetness spews from my mouth and vanishes overboard into the night.

Blood.

I've written a lot of stories to celebrate the holiday season. For several years I was part of a group of writers who gathered every Christmas Eve to read our new stories aloud as we sat around the fireplace. Some of mine were warmhearted and charming.

Some were not.

Santa Claus Is Coming to Get You!

'Twas the night before the night before Christmas, and all through the house little sounds were stirring ... creeping, whispers of noise, echoes of things better left unseen in the darkness, even around the holiday season.

Jeff stared up at the bottom of his little brother's bunk. Ever since Stevie had gotten rid of the night light, he always feared that the upper bunk would fall on top of him and squish him flat.

A strong gust of wind rattled the windowpane. Wet snow brushing against it sounded like the hiss of a deadly snake, but he could hear that his brother was not asleep. "Stevie? I thought of something about Christmas."

"What?" The voice was muffled by Stevie's ratty blue blanket.

"Well, Santa keeps a list of who's naughty and nice, right? So, what does he do to the kids who've been naughty?" He didn't know why he asked Stevie. Stevie wouldn't know.

"They don't get any presents I guess.... Do you really think Mom and Dad are that mad at us?"

Jeff sucked in a breath. "We were playing with matches, Stevie! We could have burned the house down—you heard them say that. Imagine if we burned the house down ... Besides, it doesn't matter if Mom and Dad are angry. What'll Santa think?"

Jeff swallowed. He had to get the ideas out of his head. "I gotta tell you this, Stevie, because it's important. Something a kid told me at school.

"He said that it isn't Santa who puts presents out when you're good. It's just your Mom and Dad. They wait until you go to sleep, and then they sneak out some presents. It's all pretend."

"Oh, come on!"

"Think about it. Your parents are the ones who know what you really want." He pushed on in a whisper. "What if Santa only comes when you're bad?"

"But we said we were sorry! And ... and it wasn't my idea—it was yours. And nothing got hurt."

Jeff closed his eyes so he wouldn't see the bottom of the upper bunk. "I think Santa looks for naughty little boys and girls. That's why he comes around on Christmas Eve.

"He sneaks down the chimney, and he carries an empty sack with him. And when he knows he's in a house where there's a naughty kid, he goes into their bedroom and grabs them, and stuffs them in the sack! Then he pushes them up the chimney and throws the bag in the back of his sleigh with all the other naughty little boys and girls. And then he takes them back up north where it's always cold and where the wind always blows—and there's nothing to eat."

Jeff's eyes sparkled from hot tears. He thought he heard Stevie shivering above him.

"What kind of food do you think Santa gets up there at the North Pole? How does Santa stay so fat? I bet all year long he keeps the naughty kids he's taken the Christmas before and he eats them! He keeps them locked up in icicle cages ... and on special days like on his birthday or on Thanksgiving, he takes an extra fat kid and he roasts him over a fire! That's what happens to bad kids on Christmas Eve."

Jeff heard a muffled sob in the upper bunk. He saw the support slats vibrate. "No, it's not true. We weren't that bad. I'm sorry. We won't do it again."

Jeff closed his eyes. "You better watch out, Stevie, you better not cry. 'Cause Santa Claus is coming to get you!"

He heard Stevie sucking on the corner of his blanket to keep from crying. "We can hide."

Jeff shook his head in despair. "No. He sees you when you're sleeping, and he knows when you're awake. We can't escape from him!"

"How about if we lock the bedroom door?"

"That won't stop Santa Claus! You know how big he is from eating all those little kids. And he's probably got some of his evil little elves to help him."

He listened to Stevie crying in the sheets. He listened to the wind. "We're gonna have to trick him. We have to get Santa before he gets us!"

On Christmas Eve, Dad turned on the Christmas tree lights and hung out the empty stockings by the fireplace. He grinned at the boys who stared red-eyed in fear.

"You guys look like you're so excited you haven't been able to sleep. Better go on to bed—it's Christmas tomorrow, and you've got a long night ahead of you." He smiled at them. "Don't forget to put out milk and cookies for Santa."

Mom scowled at them. "You boys know how naughty you were. I wouldn't expect too many presents from Santa this year."

Jeff felt his heart stop. He swallowed and tried to keep anything from showing on his face. Stevie shivered.

"Oh, come on, Janet. It's Christmas Eve," Dad said.

Jeff and Stevie slowly brought out the glass of milk and a plate with four Oreo cookies they had made up earlier. Stevie was so scared he almost dropped the glass.

They had poured strychnine pellets into the milk and put rat poison in the frosting of the Oreos.

"Go on boys, good night. And don't get up too early tomorrow," Dad said.

The two boys marched off to their room, heads down. Visions of Santa's blood danced in their heads.

Jeff lay awake for hours, sweating and shivering. He and Stevie didn't need to say anything to each other. After Mom and Dad went to bed, the boys listened for any sound from the roof, from the chimney.

He pictured Santa Claus heaving himself out from the fireplace, pushing aside the grate and stepping out into the living room. His eyes were red and wild, his fingers long claws, his beard tangled and stained with the meal he'd had before setting out in his sleigh—perhaps the last two children from the year before, now scrawny and starved. He would have snapped them up like crackers.

And now Santa was hungry for more, a new batch to restock his freezer that was as big as the whole North Pole.

Santa would take a crinkled piece of paper out of his pocket to look at it, and yes, there under the "Naughty" column, would be the names of Jeff and Stevie in all capital letters. He'd wipe the list on his blood-red coat.

His black belt was shiny and wicked looking, with the silver buckle and its pointed corners razor-sharp to slash the throats of children. And over his shoulder hung a brown burlap sack stained with rusty splotches.

Then Santa would go to their bedroom. Jeff and Stevie could struggle against him, they could throw their blankets on him, hit him with their pillows and their toys—but Santa Claus was stronger than that. He would reach up first to snatch Stevie from the top bunk and stuff him in the sack.

And then Santa would lunge forward with fingers grayish

blue from frostbite. He'd wrap his hand around Jeff's throat and draw him toward the sack....

Then Santa would haul them up through the chimney to the roof. Maybe he would toss one of them toward the waiting reindeer who snorted and stomped their hooves on the ice-covered shingles. And the reindeer, playing all their reindeer games, would toss the boy from sharp antler to sharp antler.

All the while, Santa stood leaning back, glaring, and belching forth his maniacal "Ho! Ho! Ho!"

Jeff didn't know when his terror dissolved into fitful nightmares, but he found himself awake and alive the next morning.

"Stevie!" he whispered. He was afraid to look in the pale light of dawn, half expecting to find blood running down the wall from the upper bunk. "Stevie, wake up!"

Jeff heard a sharp indrawn breath. "Jeff! Santa didn't get us."

They both started laughing. "Come on, let's go see."

They tumbled out of bed, then spent ten minutes dismantling the barricade of toys and small furniture they had placed in front of the door. The house remained still and quiet around them. Nothing was stirring, not even a mouse.

Jeff glanced at the dining room table as they crept into the living room. The cookies were gone. The milk glass had been drained dry.

Jeff looked for a contorted red-suited form lying in the corner —but he saw nothing. The Christmas tree lights blinked on and off; Mom and Dad had left them on all night.

Stevie crept to the Christmas tree and looked. His face turned white as he pulled out several new gift-wrapped boxes. All marked "FROM SANTA."

"Oh, Jeff! Oh, Jeff—you were wrong! What if we killed Santa!"

They both gawked at the presents.

"Jeff, Santa took the poison!"

Jeff swallowed and stood up. Tears filled his eyes. "We have to be brave, Stevie." He nodded. "We better go tell Mom and Dad." He shuddered, then screwed up his courage.

"Let's go wake them up."

This is another early story, written while I was taking medieval history classes. I had done a term paper on the Wars of the Roses, and I was also fascinated by various legends of the Grim Reaper and the Danse Macabre. Since I had done all the research, I figured I had to put it to good fictional use. And I was obviously listening to Blue Öyster Cult and Kansas at the time.

This story was lost for years in my archive boxes, and I had entirely forgotten about it, but I discovered "Deathdance" again while sorting through contributor copies to prepare the materials for these collections. I hope you enjoy it.

Deathdance

The afternoon lasted an eternity, or perhaps time just passed more slowly on the battlefield. All the sounds were a dull roar in Daniel's ears: he no longer heard the monotonous clash of metal, the redundant screams of dying men, the confused cries of wounded horses. He fought mechanically, keeping his face passively grim. He flicked blood and sweat out of his eyes. If he let himself believe how exhausted he was, he knew he would meet Death very swiftly.

By now, his sword had become only a dull notched edge from hacking through leather, chain mail, and bone. He had at last become accustomed to using a weapon, but Daniel found it little different from the sickle he had used during all his years of hard peasant labor, and this battlefield was little different from a wheat harvest ... except that the wheat stalks never fought back.

Beside him, one of his comrades fell to the mud with a mortal wound to the throat.

"For Lancaster!" The victorious enemy soldier raised his sword in triumph, and Daniel thrust into the opening, sinking the tip of his own blade home.

"And that one's for York," he muttered, withdrawing his blade and letting the enemy fall.

At least Daniel *thought* they were fighting for York this week

—his lord Braxton had changed sides often enough to make a bumblebee dizzy. Braxton believed that the safest course lay in switching allegiance each time the tides of England's civil war changed. The higher politics didn't matter much to Daniel, since neither outcome would change his life.

Daniel looked to the lord sitting astride his gray-and-white horse, keeping to the fringes of the battle. On Braxton's shield, he could see the white rose of York boldly standing out; but the shield had been repainted so often that the old paint had begun to peel, revealing chips of the red rose of Lancaster beneath so that the white petals looked flecked with blood. Daniel knew Braxton would never come close enough to the battle to let real blood spatter his shield. But the lord paid him his livery, and so Daniel did as he commanded. And in Braxton's service, Daniel found a better life than working on his family's small patches of marshy farmland three days a week, then working on Braxton's demesne the rest of the time. Not long ago, he had swung a sickle, cutting the wheat after it had dried in the sun. But Braxton needed more fighting men, and now Daniel swung a sword instead.

Above him, looming over the battlefield, gray clouds strangled the sky. In the minstrels' tales that Daniel enjoyed so much, he'd heard that the skies were sunnier over distant lands, over Rome, but he knew only England, with its rain and its toils and its wars. The field on which they fought was muddy, moistened by clotting blood and churned by stomping feet—a wheat field, recently reaped, with broken shafts of straw standing skeletal and alone until trampled by charging warriors. A dark line of forest surrounded most of the field, setting it off as a fighting arena.

Braxton fed his men well, gave them shelter, and even allowed them a certain amount of freedom. Daniel had companions, too; he called them friends, but did not think of them as such. Although he did enjoy a good joke or good wine, Daniel had learned the virtues of keeping to himself, remaining quiet, and thinking about things that interested him, but rarely concerned the others. Sometimes he felt barricaded within a self-built wall thicker than the stones of Braxton's castle. Since last winter's fever and the death of his younger brother Jack, Daniel found it safer to live without friends.

Work never ended, whether it be farming or fighting, unless one had somehow managed to enter the world through a noblewoman's womb. The plodding battle continued. Daniel defended himself against another soldier who was far inferior in fighting skill and found time to look for Artis, the minstrel.

The thin minstrel seemed small and weak on the battlefield, but he fought doggedly against a man much larger than himself. Artis's opponent didn't appear to be much of a fighter either, though—perhaps a cook for the Lancaster army—by the clumsy way he handled his sword.

Daniel liked Artis, though he never admitted as much to the minstrel, or even to himself. Artis had often entertained Braxton's men on the eves of battles such as this one, singing them songs of distant lands, wondrous places, and exotic legends. Before, Daniel never troubled himself to imagine what lay beyond the storm-gray ocean, or what had taken place in the world before his own birth. Artis had touched off a spark of imagination in him, opening up a small release from his life's rut.

While the other fighters had laughed and talked and eaten during the performance, Daniel had—more often than not—simply listened to the minstrel's songs. Then Artis's eyes would catch his, and Daniel would quickly look for more wine or suddenly remember a joke that he needed to tell the others. Out of the corner of his eye, Daniel sometimes saw Artis smile to himself as he continued playing.

The minstrel sang songs to rouse the men's spirits as they sat around the fires in the courtyard, watching plumes of white breath rise from mouths warm with wine. Artis had sung songs not two weeks before about how Queen Margaret had bravely driven away the would-be usurper Richard of York. But now, since Braxton had changed sides again, the songs told of how only Richard of York would free them from the insane King Henry VI.

During one of the war songs, someone had asked Artis how he'd gotten his firsthand knowledge of great battle deeds, how a simple minstrel could ever know what it was like to fight in a war. Now that he thought about it, Daniel should have wrung the other soldier's neck, ally or not—and so it was that the untrained minstrel had brought himself to the battlefield in order to experience the war he would later sing about. Daniel knew grimly that Artis would probably never walk away from this battle.

Trumpets sounded in the forest. Fresh foot soldiers swarmed through the trees, accompanied by archers and mounted men. Reinforcements—but whose? Daniel squinted his eyes, saw the shields of the horsemen.

Red roses.

The men for Lancaster cheered, and Daniel angrily slashed at one of them, changing the man's triumphant cry into a hollow death rattle. He saw Braxton turn his horse and ride, leaving his warriors behind and melting into the dark web of the surrounding woods. Daniel continued to fight. Braxton hadn't been much help to his soldiers anyway.

Heedless of all around him, Artis the minstrel continued to press his opponent, both of them fighting clumsily but determined. The big man slipped in the mud a little and, almost accidentally, the minstrel thrust his sword into the other's stomach. The cook screamed.

Artis tried to withdraw his blade as the big man fell, but the sword was pulled from his hand. Blood poured from the wound, spilling over the minstrel, and Artis shuddered violently, sobbing. The cook screamed and screamed. Artis stabbed him twice more, desperately, until the man stopped crying out. Artis fell to his knees.

Daniel realized he had stopped fighting as his entire world focused on the minstrel; he remembered the first man *he* had killed. His breath ran cold in his nostrils as he felt deep empathy for the singer. Somehow, Daniel felt that Artis would never again sing of brave deeds in battle, or the glory of slaying one's foes. A part of the Artis that Daniel had known had already died.

Trumpets sounded again, and horsemen charged onto the

battlefield. Many men began to flee. Lancaster archers rained arrows into the fray.

Artis hunched over the dead cook, and Daniel watched the ripples of convulsions run down his shoulders as he vomited in revulsion of what he had done. Then, Artis's eyes bulged wide and white in a comical expression of astonishment as he stared down at the pointed tip of an arrow that had plunged through his back and sprung miraculously from his chest. He fell forward on top of the cook.

Daniel stood helpless on the battlefield. His sword felt limp and impotent at his side. The veins stood out on his neck as he yearned to scream at the soldiers on the field, but no words came. He thrust his sword into the air in silent challenge but could not take his eyes off the fallen Artis. A horseman charged across the field, trampling the minstrel's body without notice. Tears blinded Daniel's eyes.

He didn't hear the pounding hooves, didn't sense the rider coming behind him until it was too late. Out of the corner of his eye he saw the flicker of a blade's glinting downsweep, and his battle-strung reflexes took over. He tried to leap forward, to dive away from the rider—but he felt the steel strike the flesh of his neck, felt the blade cutting into the bone of his spine.

And then as he fell, he felt nothing, not even pain.

Numbness ... emptiness, neither hot nor cold. Daniel knew he wasn't falling, though he could not feel the ground beneath him. His eyes remained open and staring, and from his odd perspective on the muddy field, he could still watch the battle.

All motion had ceased. The soldiers stood poised, frozen as if caught in a bizarre painting. The downsweep of a sword was caught in the grip of timeless air, its wielder's arm petrified. Wounded men hung by a thread of their pain, in mid-fall, somehow ignoring the tug of gravity. The air itself had congealed into a surreal gray prism, as if even beams of light had paused on their headlong flight from the sun.

The silence drummed heavily on his ears.

He could see the horseman behind him: the horse with one hoof off the ground, another barely touching ... the enemy soldier's blade frozen in the follow-through of his stroke. Droplets of blood —Daniel's blood—hung motionless in the air like glistening red jewels.

A tingle ran through him, as if a thunderstorm were coming, as if every hair on his body had stiffened. Behind him, he heard soft footsteps and the rustle of cloth. He smelled the sudden stench of mold, dampness, and decay. He tried to turn, but his muscles refused to respond.

"So Daniel, we meet at last." The cold dry voice reminded him of wind blowing through a cave.

A shadow ran across his face, then a figure shrouded in black stepped into his limited field of view. A death's-head with empty, honeycombed eye sockets leered out from the cavernous shadow of a billowy black hood.

"Don't fear me," said the Reaper.

The silence flowed back into Daniel's ears, as vacuum swallowed the dark angel's words.

"You know who *I* am, of course. All men recognize me in their own way. I'm glad we may finally have a word together."

Daniel tried to speak, but his throat remained locked. Death nodded toward him, and suddenly the words spilled out. "Am I dead, then?"

"No, not yet. The instant of a man's death is timeless. You may take all the time you need to decide."

"To decide?"

"Whether you wish to come with me or not." Daniel was taken aback, struck into silence.

"But if you *are* Death—who stole my brother Jack from me last winter, who snatches children from their cradles, lovers from each other's arms—"

"Yes, I *am* Death," the Reaper interrupted. "I can obliterate kings, emperors, empires! Mountains turn to dust before me—the seasons, the sun, the stars in heaven all fall at a gesture from my hand." His voice dropped low. "Yet, still, I have come here to *ask* ... will you come with me?"

Daniel blinked his eyes, unable to move more than that. He felt utterly helpless lying in the cold mud. Once more, he found his voice.

"And if I *refuse*?"

Death's response was not an answer. "Unlike many, you *do* have a choice. Of course, I wouldn't ask you to decide so quickly, Daniel. I have more than eternity to await your decision. But first, let me give you a few details—your spine has been severed, and you are left here helpless. You cannot move your arms or legs. You cannot eat, you cannot speak. Anyone who finds you, here among the other slain of the battle, will take you for dead. You will lie here, unable to move as the crows peck at your eyes—and, blind, you will slowly starve until at last you call for me to return. Surely, Daniel, this is not the death you desire? Far better that you be slain in battle, now, fighting for your lord, is it not?"

Daniel didn't answer.

"Come, I will show you something first." Death motioned for him to follow.

Daniel walled himself off with suspicion, and hesitated. "This is some manner of trickery."

For the first time, he heard a tinge of anger in the Reaper's hollow voice. "Daniel, I could crush your very soul out of existence with the tip of one finger. I have no need of tricks."

Daniel felt as if a hand had been lifted from his chest, and he stood up to walk beside Death on the battlefield. He felt strangely lightheaded, ethereal, as if walking without touching the ground.

"I think you have already guessed how this battle will end, Daniel ... but would you be interested to know that this war will bring itself to a panting halt, many years from now, more out of exhaustion than victory?"

Daniel paused a long time, then shook his head. "No ... I honestly don't think I'd be interested."

The Reaper laughed with a dry, rattling chuckle. "I should have expected such a reply! But rest assured, I take no sides."

They paused before the motionless figure of a large grubby soldier engaged in a frozen duel with a younger fair-haired man.

"This man was one of your comrades. You remember him well as a friendless, unpleasant, and foul-mouthed man."

Death clapped a bony hand on the man's shoulder, then moved away with a rustle of musty black shadow-garments to stand by the fair-haired soldier.

"And this man has a wife and three daughters. He is hardworking and well liked, but he is poor." The Reaper traced a line on the young man's cheek with a long skeletal finger. "And after he has died today, his wife and daughters will go hungry and slowly starve this winter, until I come for them one by one. Is that fair enough for you?"

Daniel gazed into the hollow sockets where eyes should have been, wondering if they stared back at him. "Death, you are *cruel.*"

"Cruel? You misunderstand. Sadness, hunger, disease, and pain are trademarks of *life*, not Death. I am an option—a way out. I am fair to all people."

Daniel turned to point at the horseman still holding his blade, dripping Daniel's blood.

"Then Reaper, if you are indeed fair, strike me down that man who hacked me from behind. You need only to touch him. Grant me vengeance."

Death laughed again, lightly moving through the motionless battlefield and forcing Daniel to dance quickly in order to catch up.

"Daniel, if I granted each man vengeance upon his killer—you yourself would have been dead many times over! But rest assured, this man already carries his own death within him, drawn from a whore he visited in London. It will fester within him and he will also pass it to his wife, and to his daughter in incest. He *will* die, and his death will not be remembered as a valiant one."

Daniel allowed himself a satisfied smile. The Reaper stopped and turned to him. "I believe I have said all that is necessary. But before I ask for your decision, I'd like you to speak to someone."

"Daniel!"

The man turned to see the thin minstrel coming toward him, dodging the petrified soldiers as a deer might slip around trees in a forest.

"Artis!"

The minstrel came up to Daniel, smiling almost sheepishly. "It appears my career as a great warrior ended a little sooner than I anticipated."

Daniel laughed a little, uncomfortable with himself as he realized how glad he was to see Artis. "No sooner than *I* expected."

Artis looked deeply into the other's eyes, silently altering the subject. "You were careless to turn your back on a naked blade, if only to gawk at me."

"You saw that? Even after you had fallen?"

The minstrel drew a mouthful of air. "I stood here when Death touched your shoulder."

Daniel stiffened. "And the Reaper has sent you here to convince me to die."

Artis smiled, shrugging. "One does not wish to make an enemy of Death. Daniel, please don't resist, don't *want* to resist—you don't know what it's like here. It is fascinating, enthralling, even grander than the grand things I sang about. Do you know the things we can do now that we could never do before? We stand here unhindered by *life!* We can go anywhere, be anything, see everything!" Artis's voice dropped. "Do you know how beautiful a storm is once you can stand and watch without having to fear if it will destroy your fields or ruin your home?"

He looked at Daniel. "The Reaper told me everything about you I didn't already know. What does your life have to offer you that you can't have here? Women? They didn't mean that much to you, Daniel, but here you can have every woman that ever lived—see Helen of Troy, Cleopatra, see the Lady Guinevere, all the beautiful goddesses I've sung about!

"What else? Gold? What good is gold to you now? All the gold in the world wouldn't buy you a minute from Death if he truly insisted on taking you. We are *dust*, Daniel, dust in the wind ... nothing. And yet, Death comes to us all, one by one, talks to us, coaxes us, takes none against his will. Not even your brother Jack."

Daniel faltered. "Don't—"

But Artis's eyes shimmered with the rapid words almost singing from his throat. "Come with me, Daniel! Think of what we can do. We can travel to lands never before seen by Christian men! We can pass through the thickest forests in the blink of an eye, ignore the fiercest beasts. We can visit Rome, and even Constantinople without fearing the Turks. We can stand on a mountaintop and look down on eagles' nests, look down upon all the land! Come with me, Daniel—we have a world to explore."

Daniel stood as still as the other frozen soldiers on the battlefield, letting the incredible silence engulf him. It was a silence not broken by a single heartbeat or breathing ... not even Daniel's.

"Jack is here?"

"Yes. And so am I."

He had no idea how long he stood in the silence. Then slowly, almost imperceptibly, he nodded.

The Reaper appeared before him. "Shall we seal this deal with a handshake?"

Death held out his bony hand, and Daniel shuddered but slowly extended his own. He expected the grip of Death to be cold—but it was warm and firm, reassuring.

Daniel felt no change.

Artis smiled. "Come on, Daniel! Where shall we go first? You pick!"

Death turned, letting his black cowl ripple like liquid shadows pouring into the air. Daniel could almost imagine a grin on the leering skeletal face.

"I will leave you two now. This is a battlefield, and I have much work to do." The Reaper flowed back into the frozen melee as the battleground slowly came back to life.

A large grubby soldier failed to dodge as a sword plunged into his chest; he fell with a grunt as his slayer—a young fair-haired man with a wife and three daughters—choked on an arrow that had pierced his throat.

Daniel looked around once at his old comrades and wondered how many of those pitiful soldiers would speak intimately with Death today. He realized now that they had never truly been his friends. He felt a rising excitement inside as he and the minstrel departed. They had decided to go to see Rome.

And no one on the battlefield noticed his passing.

Another Dan Shamble story, one of my funniest.

"Fire in the Hole" was inspired by a great piece of artwork. For decades, I've been a judge of the Writers of the Future contest, and I gladly accepted when they asked me to write the lead story for Volume 39 of their annual anthology. I knew I wanted to do a Dan Shamble story, always looking for an opportunity to play with one of my favorite characters.

There was one catch, though. My story had to be inspired by the cover painting, an original work by Illustrators of the Future judge Tom Wood. I didn't think that would be a problem, since I could put Dan Shamble in any strange scenario.

When I saw the painting, though, I could only scratch my head. It was a truly spectacular work, and Tom is a genius artist. But how was I going to write a noir zombie detective story that featured a huge Asian fire dragon in the air above a pagoda?

Well, nothing can stop a persistent zombie private investigator ... or the writer of same.

Fire in the Hole
A Dan Shamble, Zombie P.I. Adventure

—I—

The slime on the amphibian's face glistened in the office lights, but I could still see the tear spill out of his yellow eye. It ran slowly down the spots on his cheek.

I hate to see a salamander cry.

"It'll be all right, young man," I said, ushering him into Chambeaux & Deyer Investigations. "Tell us about your case."

Feeling supportive, even paternal, I put an arm around his small shoulders. That was unfortunate, because it left a sticky smear on my sport jacket sleeve, but the client always comes first.

"Come in," said Sheyenne, my ghost girlfriend, as she flitted forward from the reception desk. "You're safe here. What's your name?"

The young salamander walked upright, balanced by the thick tail that protruded through the rear of his patched trousers. Frayed old tennis shoes barely covered his webbed feet.

"I'm Syl." He sniffled, and the slime made a thick liquid sound in his sinuses. "I can't stand it anymore at home." His black forked tongue flicked in and out of his wide mouth, and another viscous tear rolled down the opposite spotted cheek. "I need to be emancipated!"

Sheyenne used her poltergeist powers to close the door, so he had an added measure of safety. His slitted eyes flicked back and forth like a hunted animal. His head was slung low, as if he'd been browbeaten too many times.

Robin Deyer, my firebrand human lawyer partner, emerged from her office, straightening her trim business suit and ready to dive headfirst into the case. "It's our mission to help Unnaturals everywhere," she said, her dark brown eyes already flashing. "Don't you worry, Mr., uh, Syl. Come into the conference room. We want to hear all about it."

"I just don't think I can face him alone," Syl said. "He's such a domineering presence." He hung his head even lower.

"Who?" Robin and Sheyenne both asked in unison, as if they meant to tag-team strangle whoever was picking on this endearing new client (although when dealing with monsters, strangling isn't always an effective option).

"My Pa!" Syl said. "If he knew I was here, he would whup the spots right off my hide."

A girl's cheery voice came from the back of the office. "Oh, he's so cute!" Alvina, my adorable vampire half-daughter, skipped out of the kitchenette, where she had been playing a slow game of tic-tac-toe with the sentient kitchen mold growing on our wall.

Startled, Syl spun about, thrashing his thick tail, but then he saw only a ten-year-old girl, although now that she had turned into a vampire, Alvina would never grow up. She came right up to Syl and reached out to shake his webbed hand. "Oh, it's sticky and slimy."

Syl nodded. "I put on a fresh coat so I'd look presentable. I wanted to make a good impression, so you'd take my case."

Robin gestured to the open door of the conference room. "Let's get all the details." She carried a yellow legal pad as well as the magic pencil that would transcribe her notes.

Even if this sounded like a strictly legal matter, I liked to sit in on intake meetings. Cases often spiraled out of control, and we might need my skills as a zombie detective.

Over the years, Chambeaux & Deyer Investigations had seen

many unusual cases. There was no shortage of work since the Big Uneasy—when an unusual alignment of planets, the correct phase of the moon, and the accidental spilling of a virgin's blood (a fifty-year-old clumsy librarian, but a virgin nevertheless) on the original Necronomicon brought back all the mythical monsters, ghouls, ghosts, vampires, werewolves, mummies, demons, etc. At first there had been a great uproar, but eventually all the Unnaturals settled down in the Quarter and just tried to live their lives and get along.

I'd been a down-and-out P.I., and I set out my shingle here because I had no better place to go. When a case went sour, someone came up behind me in a dark alley and shot me in the back of the head. But after the magic of the Big Uneasy, you can't keep a determined detective down. I clawed my way back up out of the grave as a zombie. Back from the dead, and back on the case.

Now, Sheyenne drifted into the conference room with a pitcher of water, green tea for Robin, bad coffee for me, and a juice box (special blood-orange blend) for Alvina. Syl took the pitcher of water and slurped some with his forked tongue and smeared more over his drying slime.

After bracing himself, he began to explain. "It's my Pa." He put his slimy elbows on the table surface. "He constantly criticizes me, crushes my spirit, makes me work sixteen-hour days. He locks me in my muddy tunnel room ... and he yells a lot."

Robin's expression darkened with anger. "Does he beat you?"

"Sometimes with a belt, though he usually wears bib overalls. There are patches on my back where he really did knock the spots right off." Then something changed in the salamander's demeanor, and he sat up straighter. He squared his shoulders. "But I'm learning how to find my inner spirit, how to be strong, and how to stand up for myself! I've been taking self-esteem lessons."

"Good for you," Sheyenne said.

Alvina's grin showed her baby-teeth fangs as she slurped her juice box. Robin's enchanted pencil furiously took notes all by itself on the legal pad.

"I never would have been able to get this far without my guru," Syl said. "I know I can be brave. I can find the backbone because—" He pounded the conference room table with a small fist. "I may be an amphibian, but I am also a vertebrate!"

I wanted to cheer him on. "Indeed you are."

Then Syl lowered his spotted head again. "But I don't know the legal details. I want to be emancipated from Pa so I can live my own life, but I'm not considered an adult." He sniffled again, and two more gelid tears rolled down his face. "I'm too young."

"How old are you?" Robin asked.

"Ten."

"He's my age!" Alvina chimed in.

Robin clucked her tongue. "I'm afraid that's too young for the law. Ten years old is still considered a child."

Syl flicked his forked black tongue out of his mouth. "But I'm not a child! The expected lifespan of a common salamander can be twenty to thirty years, so I've lived at least a third of my life. Surely that means I'm an adult? Relatively speaking?"

Alvina, who spent far too much time on Wikipedia, said, "Well, it depends on what kind of salamander. The giant Chinese salamander can live up to two hundred years."

"Then I'm screwed," Syl moaned. "I'll just have to go back to the ashram and keep learning how to be strong."

Robin considered. "Hmmm, I can make that argument. An Unnatural salamander is a different creature altogether, and the law is vague. I think I can make the case that you qualify as an adult, subjectively speaking."

Syl beamed with renewed hope. I folded my gray hands on the table. "I can arrange for protection, if you do need a zombie private investigator."

"Oh, thank you!" Syl pressed his hands to his heart. "That helps me gain the confidence to find my inner me."

He had a decided spring in his step as he glided out of our offices.

—II—

That night I went out for a quiet midnight walk in the Unnatural Quarter. It was long after dark with the moon just rising—the busiest time for people and monsters to be out and about. The Talbot & Knowles Blood Bars did a brisk business, and the nightclubs were open and noisy. Little shops of horrors, as well as groceries, served plenty of customers.

I wore my sport jacket with the clumsily stitched bullet holes across the front, and my fedora tilted just enough to cover the bullet hole in my forehead. I had recently been freshened up at the embalming parlor, and I felt good. I take great pains to maintain my appearance, mostly for the benefit of my ghost girlfriend. I'm not one of those rotting shamblers who eat at fast-food restaurants and refuse to take care of themselves.

The energy of the Quarter always helps me concentrate. As a detective, I could learn many details about cases and contacts just by wandering around, picking up the vibe. Besides, it kept the rigor mortis out of my joints and made me limber.

I bumped into Officer Toby McGoohan in his blue patrolman uniform standing on a street corner. All week he'd had the midnight shift. I raised my hand in a wave. "Hey, McGoo." He's my best human friend.

"Hey, Shamble." A wide grin spread across his freckled face.

Nearby, under an ornate wrought iron lamppost slouched a skeleton saxophone player with the instrument pressed against his teeth. He attempted to blast out a mournful, if cliched, rendition of "Feelings" although the sax remained mercifully silent, because the skeleton had no lungs.

"Do you know how many lawn gnomes it takes to screw—" McGoo began, but before he could finish laying out his joke, we were interrupted by a huge fire dragon that suddenly appeared overhead. Its breathy roar was accompanied by the crackling sound of serpentine flames. The thing looked like a reptilian inferno in the air.

All activity stopped in the streets. Several people screamed. Vampires and werewolves ducked for cover, and a considerate hunchback threw a flameproof tarp over a terrified mummy so his bandages would not catch fire.

The enormous flame dragon was diaphanous, constructed entirely of fire, smoke, and burning gases. It roiled along above the rooftops in the Quarter, its long tail thrashing, its fiery jaws opening to exhale a gout of orange fire. The dragon was full of fire and menace, shooting sparks and cinders as it drifted overhead like a low-flying aircraft. Fires began to spread from rooftop to rooftop. It was a disaster.

On the other hand, McGoo hadn't finished his dumb joke, so I would count that as a small victory.

"What is that thing?" McGoo cried, one hand on each of his service revolvers, but neither the regular bullets nor the silver bullets would have any effect on this elemental creature.

"It's a *fire dragon*, obviously," I said. "But let's not worry about genus or species right now."

"Thanks for the help, Shamble," McGoo said, and we both started running.

The panicked people ran for shelter, though there was little to be had. A quick-thinking frog demon was resourceful enough to pop open a manhole. "Down here, down here!" he shouted, ribbiting like a frog. He leaped into the sewers with a loud splash, and a crowd of terrified pedestrians followed him.

The fire dragon moved like an alligator cruising through a swamp. It flapped its enormous flame wings, shot sparks in all directions, and ignited more fires.

McGoo was on the radio. "Call out the fire department. All divisions!" He listened to a squawk of static and yelled back, "It's a fire dragon! Better send the special unit!"

Taking our cue from the clever frog demon, the two of us popped more manhole covers, directing the evacuation down below. We sent as many people as possible into the flowing tunnels of sewage, where they would be safe and comfortable.

Even as shockwaves of panic spread, the elemental flame

dragon seemed unaware of the destruction and terror it was causing. Instead, it just drifted over the rooftops as if it, too, was out on a quiet midnight stroll.

I had no idea how to fight it or scare it off. The fires were spreading from roof to roof, and if something weren't done soon, the whole Quarter would become an inferno.

Then the creature flapped its wings and rose higher into the sky. As we watched, it simply dissipated into wisps of flame and thinning smoke. Neither McGoo nor I had done anything to drive it off, but we would shrug and share credit for saving the world.

But even though the threat was gone, the fires still raged. We heard a wailing, ear-splitting siren as the fire truck rolled up, a bright red tanker vehicle. A pale-skinned banshee with dark stringy hair clung to the side of the truck and let out a warbling wail that cleared all traffic and shattered many windows. As soon as the driver screeched to a halt and the banshee stopped wailing, the tank hatch popped open. From inside, silvery frolicking water sprites burst upward as if they were riding a geyser. The water sprites giggled, playing together and dancing in the air as they pulled the water from the tanker and spread it out into streams.

"We've got this, hee-hee!" said the lead sprite, a chubby, silvery-skinned woman who flicked her fingers and sprayed water everywhere.

Other sprites reached to the sky and called in clouds, which came galloping from the horizon. The water sprites circled around each other as if playing ring-around-the-rosy, spraying water onto the burning rooftops.

Steam filled the air as the fires were extinguished. The playful sprites swooped down, chattering and spreading more water. Soon, a downpour burst out of the first black thunderhead, and the sprites jabbed each other, as if it were just horseplay in a swimming pool.

"It's great to see people who love their jobs," I said to McGoo.

The water sprites swept over the burning rooftops and extinguished all the fires. In fact, the giggling creatures seemed disappointed that they were so swift and effective, which ended their play too soon.

Drenched, McGoo and I stood in puddles on the street. The water sprites spun around together and then sullenly returned to the tank in the back of the fire truck.

Next to us by the lamppost, the skeleton jazz musician continued swaying with his saxophone, playing his imaginary tune. We looked at the blackened rooftops, saw wisps of smoke still roiling up, but the fires were out.

"That could have been a great inferno, Shamble," McGoo said.

"Instead, it's just a scorch—at least this time." I shook water from the brim of my fedora. "Let's hope that fire dragon never returns."

—III—

Sometimes clients need more than our usual services—instead of offering protection or investigating nefarious activities, we can also provide moral support. When Syl the salamander asked if we would stand by him for his graduation/ascension ceremony at the Wham-Bam Ashram, how could we refuse? The slimy little kid already had self-esteem issues.

"My Pa won't support me," Syl said on the phone to a very warm and understanding Sheyenne. "And I wouldn't want him there. He'd just complain and ruin everybody's state of bliss."

Sheyenne and I agreed to go to the ashram, while Robin burned the midnight oil (and the morning oil), studying case precedents for the emancipation of Unnatural youths and larvae.

Alvina bounced up and down and really wanted to go, but it was McGoo's night to watch her—he's her other half-daddy, and since neither of us actually knows who her real father is, we take turns—Sheyenne and I decided it might not be a good idea to have the bubbly little vampire girl there. If there was going to be a lot of meditation and nirvana and bliss, it would be too much for a rambunctious kid.

We arrived at the Wham-Bam Ashram just after dark, with the full moon rising. Surrounded by beautifully landscaped gardens, it was a perfect peaceful setting for quite an elaborate structure set on a hill—and hills are hard to come by in the Unnatural Quarter, which is surrounded by swampland. The ashram was an elaborate and impressive Asian pagoda with curved, pointy roofs and an open area at the bottom. The zigzag walkway up the hill was marked by a string of paper lanterns, illuminated by a whole swarm of rent-a-fairies.

Although the architecture was non–culturally specific, it seemed just the right place to study enlightenment. I'd heard that before the Big Uneasy, the ashram was a high-end tea house that had gone out of business.

Sheyenne glowed with satisfaction as she drifted beside me. I walked under the archway into the grand open area of the Wham-Bam Ashram. Incense rose from fragrant torches burning in wall sconces.

I picked up a program sheet.

Enlightenment Ceremony
Graduation and ascension of our karma-positive students
Hosted by Guru Grbth

We entered, not sure where to go or what to do. Ahead, dozens of people were gathered in concentric circles around a central dais. Around the edges were parents, spouses, and demonic symbiotes who had come to show support for the graduates. I saw two proud-looking vampires, a scaly water creature who spritzed himself from a mister, and even a nervous-looking older woman who seemed to be the aunt of one of the students.

On a raised central platform sat an enormous, burly ogre whose shaggy head was the size of a suitcase, covered with dreadlocks and fur—Guru Grbth, I assumed. His thick lower lip was like an inflated firehose. His eyes were as big as dinner plates.

He wore a loose robe comprised of at least two bedsheets' worth of tie-dyed material, pastel pinks and blues and yellows. Somehow, perhaps with the aid of a forklift, he had lowered himself into a lotus position on a bamboo mat. He rested a huge spiked club the size of a telephone pole on one knee.

Seated in circles on the floor were the ashram students, wearing white robes that covered their hairy, scaly, slimy, or pallid bodies. The students bent close to one another, whispering in barely contained excitement.

Syl sat in the outer ring, his slime glistening in the torchlight. He turned his head with unexpected flexibility and spotted us. He sprang to his feet and scampered over to us, his big tail waving from beneath the white robe. "You came! You really came to support me!"

"Of course we did, Syl," said Sheyenne.

"Oh, this means so much to me!" He reached out and shook my hand in a grip that felt like a glove filed with mucus.

"We'll help you stand up for yourself, kid," I said.

His tongue flicked out. "Oh, Guru Grbth is already teaching me how to find my inner strength and delve to the depths of my soul. By meditating and using magic, I can find my true inner salamander."

Wind chimes tinkled and jangled, adding to the mood. The spectators around the room muttered in building suspense, or maybe it was boredom because they had waited so long for the ceremony to begin. On the dais, the guru shook his shaggy head and let out a belch.

"That's Guru Grbth?" I asked. "A little hard to pronounce, isn't it?"

Syl nodded. "When you reach a certain stage of enlightenment, you no longer need vowels in your name."

"Really? What's the next stage?"

"Then you don't even use consonants." Syl tightened the sash of his white robe, keeping his voice low. "I've been sneaking out and taking these classes, and I've learned so much. I'm so proud of my classmates, too. We've had werewolves with hair-loss problems, vampires with hemoglobin intolerances, ghosts who are frightened of their own shadows." He nodded to the other graduation candidates sitting in the circle, patiently waiting for the ceremony to begin.

"Even some mummies, I see." Sheyenne indicated a pair of old cloth-wrapped bodies that looked like dried collections of twigs.

"Oh, those two—some of Grbth's most famous students. They've attended for five years running."

"It takes that long to graduate?"

"Not really. They just got down into the lotus position and have never been able to get up again."

In the back of the room an Igor assistant swung a mallet and bashed a large copper gong, which nearly deafened us. It did accomplish its aim of hushing the audience. Syl shook my hand again, then scurried back to his place among the students.

Grbth's deep and resonant voice rumbled out. "We begin with a brief meditation." He lifted one massive hand and curled his thumb and forefinger together in an O. With his other hand, he raised the spiked club and bashed it on the floor while humming a drawn-out, thunderous "BOOOOOOOMMM!"

All of the students repeated the same sound, and the ogre bashed his club again, calling out the meditation syllable. "BOOOOOOOMMM!"

I turned to Sheyenne. "I thought they were supposed to chant *Om*."

"This sound is more definitive," she said.

After several minutes of this, the Wham-Bam Ashram was shaken to its foundations, and I worried the tall pagoda would come tumbling down. Finally, the ogre guru stopped. With astonishing nimbleness, he unfolded himself and rose to his feet, letting the tie-dyed robe hang around him like the tent of a Woodstock ghost.

"We are gathered to celebrate the graduation of a new group of students. I taught them the ways of enlightenment, inner peace, and strength. They have unlocked the true potential of their souls, and tonight they will each be presented with ... the Amulet of Importance."

In his sausage-like fingers Grbth lifted a tiny gold chain with a little locket in the middle.

The enlightened students tittered and gasped. The other spectators, including myself and Sheyenne, were both impressed and confused.

The ogre swung his large eyes over the gathered students, peaceful yet extremely proud. "You have all learned how to be your true selves. I know you will do great things for monsters everywhere."

"BOOOOOOOMMMM!" yelled a werewolf student, whose fur bristled in many different directions.

"BOOOOOOO!" yelled a ghost, drawing the sound out to a pleading moan good enough to haunt a castle.

"Boooooooommm!" squeaked a lawn gnome, wobbling back and forth.

The petrified mummies rasped out the cheer themselves, and soon everyone joined in. Syl seemed delighted.

Grbth called up the students by name, and each filed up to the central dais. Uniformed Igors stood at the base of the dais and handed each graduate a printed certificate and a little gold chain.

Syl was one of the last, swelled with pride and confidence. He swiveled his spotted head to reassure himself that we'd stayed through the ceremony. I gave him a congratulatory nod.

The little salamander stepped up to the dais, leaving faint slime tracks from the holes in his tennis shoes. The guru ogre bowed his wagon-sized head. "You, Syl, are one of my greatest students. You have truly learned from me. You already have the power within yourself." Grbth took the gold chain from the nearby Igor and draped it over the narrow amphibious head. "With this Amulet of Importance, I say that you are ready for the world. Go face whatever challenges arise."

The gold chain slid down the slime-coated neck. Syl's forked tongue flicked in and out, then he danced off the stage, letting the next enlightened graduate come up behind him. He scuttled back to join us, glowing with excitement.

"We're very happy for you," said Sheyenne.

"Congratulations. You did real good, kid," I said. "I'm sure your father would be proud of you, too."

Syl's head drooped. "I have to change into street clothes. My Pa would say it's all a waste of time. He doesn't know this is how I spend my allowance."

I felt sad and disappointed to hear this. "It'll get better. We'll help."

—IV—

Even after Syl the salamander had graduated into self-confidence and the next stage of enlightenment, complete with his Amulet of Importance bling, his life was still downtrodden drudgery.

I came upon the poor slimy kid just after I had finished serving an eviction notice to a rowdy frat-boy poltergeist. He had died of alcohol poisoning during a college party and was still so spiritually inebriated he didn't even know he was dead—nor was he happy to get the eviction notice. Nevertheless, the unpleasant deed was done, and Sheyenne could send a bill to the client. I felt as if a burden had been lifted from my shoulders.

And then I saw Syl slogging along the streets in his patched pants and tattered sneakers. His body was splattered with mud, which did not actually look out of place among the spots. He pushed a wheelbarrow piled high with thick mud, head down, forked tongue lolling out with exhaustion. As he drove his load down the street, some of the mud dribbled off the sides and splattered onto the pavement.

"Hi, Syl," I said. "Looks like you're hard at work."

The young salamander looked up at me. "Sorry I can't stop and talk, Mr. Chambeaux. I have to haul two more loads of mud today or my Pa will get mad."

He was not at all the bright and confident salamander I'd seen the night before in the Wham-Bam Ashram. I tried to sound encouraging. "My partner is still researching the age requirements for a sentient salamander to apply for emancipation from an abusive parent. But seeing this ..." I shook my head. "We might have an argument both ways. If the court insists that you're underage, then we can charge your father for violating child labor laws."

"Just doing my chores," Syl said as he plodded along, and I shambled beside him. "It's not a job, because he doesn't pay me. Except my allowance. That's how I paid for my teachings from Master Grbth. Worth every penny."

The overburdened wheelbarrow creaked. "Where are you taking this mud?" I asked.

"I'm hauling mud from the swamp on the west side of town to the swamp on the east side of town."

"And why would you take mud from the west side?" I asked, wondering if it was a better quality of muck.

Syl kept trudging along. "To make room for the mud that I carry back from the eastern swamp. My father says the swamps are due for a full-fledged mud exchange, and I'm the one who has to do it. I've been at this for two years now."

My heart went out to him, and I knew Robin would be furious when she heard this. "Not today, kid. We'll dump this load and then go home. I want to meet your father." As a zombie I can be looming and intimidating, though I prefer not to be confrontational. I decided to make an exception for stern salamander parents, though.

We walked along, chatting, and I tried to lift his mood. Syl was very proud of the tiny gold amulet dangling from a chain at his neck.

When we got outside of the Quarter to the eastern swamp, I helped the salamander push the heavy wheelbarrow next to where a long shovel had been stuck between mangrove roots. Together, we dumped the mud into the murky swamp with a big brown plop.

Syl looked forlornly at the shovel. "I've got to load up again and head back to the west side. Five loads each day. That's my quota."

"Today we're changing the quota," I said. "Leave the wheelbarrow here. I want to have words with your father. I'll take the heat if he gets upset."

Syl's tongue flicked in and out. "Mythical salamanders had a lot of heat, but my Pa and I are just mud salamanders."

"You're not 'just' anything, kid. We're getting you out of this mess."

Agitated and uneasy, Syl led me along a well-worn path until we reached the dreary mudflats, the neighborhood where he had grown up and where his father—whose name was Neb—had built a hovel. It was all they could afford, since Neb was lazy and refused to work.

The hovel was a rounded hummock of mud covered with moss and dead patchy grass. Empty cans of beans and Vienna sausages were scattered around the lawn; the most prominent feature was an old rusty wheelbarrow propped up on cinderblocks, its axle broken.

The muddy mound reminded me of an English barrow, but I had seen some of the nice, remodeled barrows that a group of entrepreneurial wights were offering for short-term rentals on AirBNBarrow. This one, though, did not look like that.

"That's my home," Syl said. "A nasty, dirty, wet hole, filled with the ends of worms and an oozy smell." He blinked his yellow eyes. "Not like the comfortable holes I read about in *The Hobbit*."

It was made even nastier by the surly-looking salamander who sat in an old metal lawn chair on the front porch next to the round door. Neb was dressed in a pair of faded bib overalls with no undershirt so I could see the spotty flesh in his armpits. His spots were gray and leprous looking, and his eyes blazed with a tinge of red.

The pudgy salamander let out a grumbling hiss, then wrenched himself out of the chair, smashing his thick tail back and forth. "What are you doing home, boy?" His forked tongue lashed out of his mouth. "You ain't put in a sixteen-hour day yet!"

"I wanted you to meet somebody, Pa." Syl clutched the arm of my sport jacket and tugged me forward.

"Don't want to meet nobody, and I warned you never to make friends."

I loomed in front of him as best I could. "I'm Dan Chambeaux, private investigator."

"You're a zombie," Neb snapped.

"And you're very observant," I said. "We're looking into your son's welfare and possible abuse. Slavery isn't a sign of being a good parent."

"I'm his guardian. The boy has to earn his keep." Neb lurched closer, trying to be menacing, but I can be menacing too. I held my (muddy) ground.

Neb glowered. "I've taken care of that boy since he hatched. His mother abandoned the whole clutch of eggs after she spawned. No-good whore! Left me with barely enough of our eggs to eat, but I missed this one." He nudged an elbow toward the sulking and intimidated Syl. "So, he hatched, and I had to take care of him. I raised him to do a good day's work and to take care of his Pa." He snapped at the spotted young salamander. "Go crawl into the hole and lock yourself in your room. You're grounded!"

Syl's eyes lit up. "Really?" The delight was plain in his voice. "Then I can finish reading *The Hobbit*!" He ducked through the round door and slithered into the tunnel beneath the hovel.

Neb glared at me. "And you mind your own damn business!" He slouched back down into his metal lawn chair.

I certainly knew my own damn business. I turned away, thinking of the additional details I could report to Robin so she could file amended paperwork for Judge Hawkins.

—v—

That night as Sheyenne and I were reading Alvina a bedtime story after she crawled into her large cardboard coffin box—the little vampire girl had asked for *Children's Selections from the*

"*Necronomicon*"—the enormous fire dragon appeared again over the Quarter, even larger than the first time.

When I looked through the dingy windows of my upstairs apartment, I could see the blazing reptilian entity rising over the rooftops.

Alvina peered next to me. "Oh, it's like a nightlight!"

Fire alarms rang throughout the city, and police sirens wailed, including the banshee. At least the water-sprite firefighters were going to have fun tonight.

"Keep Alvina safe," I said to Sheyenne as I hurried for the door. "I better go see if I can help. I'm sure McGoo is already running to the scene."

"What can you do about it?" Sheyenne asked, clearly concerned.

"Well ..." I paused and pondered. "McGoo and I stood there and watched last time, and that proved pretty effective."

I was out the door before she could make a counterargument.

I lurched off at full speed, slipping into "fast zombie" mode. The elemental dragon beat its blazing wings like huge sails. It craned its serpentine neck, opened its jaws, and coughed out even brighter fire. Sparks flew from its lashing tail.

The ethereal creature circled overhead, bellowing, but it didn't attack. A monster of such great size could have blasted the whole Quarter into cinders. But when the fire dragon trumpeted out a call and blasted flames up into the sky, the sound didn't seem angry or vengeful. Rather, it was more triumphant, like a celebration of freedom or confidence (not that I'm an expert on elemental dragon sounds).

I could see where the creature was heading—straight toward the tall pagoda tower of the Wham-Bam Ashram.

While the rest of the UQ emergency response teams raced to quench fires and rescue innocent victims, I decided to head the thing off at the source.

After seeing the powerful guru ogre, a guy so enlightened he no longer needed vowels in his name, I wondered if Grbth could help.

As I raced up the steep, zigzag path to the tiered pagoda, I wished the ashram had simply chosen a straight line instead of a sidewalk that symbolized the winding journey of life. The paper lamps along the walkway were dark, since the rent-a-fairies apparently weren't working tonight.

The fire dragon circled high above, bellowing out more fire, thrashing sparks from its tail. I could hear the furnace crackling of its passage.

I ducked into the open pavilion, which was nearly empty. On his bamboo mat on the raised dais, the huge ogre again sat in a lotus position, holding the spiked club.

"Hello!" I called out. "Mr. Grbth, there's a fire dragon overhead! Better get out before it destroys the whole ashram."

The ogre raised his head. Despite the crisis going on throughout the Quarter, he seemed utterly at peace, content with his role in the universe. His heavy-lidded eyes opened and closed with the deliberate slowness of an electric garage door. His voice rumbled out. "I am aware of all things. That is one of the benefits of achieving nirvana. I no longer need security cameras."

I felt suddenly suspicious. "Do you have something to do with that fire dragon?"

Grbth hung his huge head. "Yes, I am partly responsible. I must take care of this unsettling ripple in the stream of peaceful consciousness." He looked toward the roof of the pagoda and the many levels of the pavilion above. "Sometimes my followers don't even know their own strength, once it's unlocked."

"Your followers?" I asked. "One of your students is doing this?"

"No—one of my graduates. Now I must meditate." Grbth closed his eyes again and raised the spiked club. He pounded the floor with a resounding thud. From the depths of his solar plexus emerged a low rumbling meditative sound. "Boooooommm! Boooooommm!"

The vibrations did something strange to the air, and I felt dizzy. I backed away, worried that the fire dragon would incinerate the ashram at any moment. The unfazed ogre had fallen into a deep mediative state, and I could see there would be no convincing him. Since he was the size of a small automobile, I certainly wasn't going to move him against his will.

When I dashed outside, I looked up to the pinnacle of the pagoda, where the fire dragon hovered in the air. Elsewhere in the Quarter, emergency crews had responded, and the water sprites worked with conventional fire suppression crews to extinguish the flames as fast as possible. But unless it was stopped, the restless elemental creature could keep spreading fire wherever it went.

But as I stared up at the dragon, another figure rippled in the air. A huge intimidating form rose up through the pavilion's open windows and balconies, until it coalesced in the sky to become a misty but terrifying manifestation of Guru Grbth.

The huge ogre had created an astral projection of himself and now hovered in the open air to face off against the dragon. Planning ahead, Grbth also carried an astrally projected spiked club. It was just like a scene from one of those Godzilla versus Monster of the Week movies, and I prepared myself for a smackdown.

The fire dragon flapped its enormous wings, scattering sparks and little flames. The spectral ogre loomed closer, reached out a muscular arm.

I cringed, looking for cover.

And the shimmering guru patted the fire dragon on its flaming head.

Astral Grbth mumbled a soothing meditative sound, and the elemental dragon circled closer, thrashing like a dog wagging its tail. The ogre stroked down the dragon's spine.

"There, there ..." boomed Grbth's voice. "Focus. Find your center. You have unlocked your inner strength. Now you must control it."

The fire dragon flapped its wings and rolled in the air, so the astral ogre could scratch its scaly belly. More sparks flew. The flickering dragon rumbled and purred, then pulled away, drifting higher. It flapped giant incandescent wings and rose into the air where it spread out, faded, then dissipated into mere curls of smoke.

The astrally projected ogre nodded in satisfaction, grumbling, and then he, too, dissipated into nothingness.

I bolted back into the ashram to find Grbth stirring on his bamboo mat, standing up with a groan and a grumble. He placed a hand against the small of his back as if he had pulled a muscle.

"All taken care of, for now," said the guru ogre. "Sometimes they get excited once they reach enlightenment, but with great power comes great responsibility." Grbth scratched his shaggy beard and belched. "I need to have my students start meditating over comic books."

"What are you talking about? Who was it?" But I already knew. "It's Syl, isn't it?"

The big ogre nodded. "Yes, poor boy. Terrible home life. He needed self-esteem and self-protection. Here at the Wham-Bam Ashram, I teach my students to find the strength within. Syl discovered and released his inner salamander."

—VI—

I couldn't do this alone. After rushing back to the office, I rounded up Robin, who was now armed with all the paperwork she had filed—as well as an emergency protective order she had just received from Judge Hawkins. That would help poor Syl even more than his Amulet of Importance.

As we set off for the salamander hovel in the mudflats, Sheyenne demanded to go along. And since Alvina was not technically able to stay by herself (and it was far too late to get an emergency babysitter), my half-daughter tagged along as well, even though sinister swamps and fire dragons and abusive amphibious fathers weren't exactly the best things for a little kid to be exposed to. She promised to take pictures for her Monstagram and SickTok accounts.

When we got to the barrow-shaped hovel, it was clear we had found the right place. On the ground, the slurry of stagnant water and brown ooze bubbled like volcanic mudpots. The air sparkled and flashed overhead, manifesting just a hint of the fire dragon. Alvina looked up at the light show and grinned with fascination.

With her ghostly speed Sheyenne drifted ahead of us. "Hurry, Beaux!" she called back. "I hear shouting! I don't want Syl to get hurt."

Robin stalked forward, clutching the legal briefcase against her side. "That Neb Salamander is going to be in more trouble than he can imagine. We'll sue every last spot off of him."

A geyser erupted in the mudflat, and sulfurous steam hissed out. The fiery dragon flickered in the air again. We reached the round door set into the grass-covered mound just as another mudpot burbled open and swallowed the broken old wheelbarrow propped on cinderblocks.

Behind the sealed round door, Robin and I could hear shouting. "Get to your room, you worthless slimy son of a—"

I pounded on the door. "Neb, open up! Zombie detective!" It wasn't as intimidating as yelling "Police!" but at least he would know we weren't door-to-door salespeople.

The shouting stopped, and I heard squishy sounds approaching. Robin opened her briefcase and pulled out the legal document, holding it like a battle-axe.

The round door swung inward and we could see the dank, muddy tunnels inside. "What do you want?" Neb demanded. He still wore the same old bib overalls.

"This is a legal decree." Robin thrust the protective order forward. "Your son Syl has requested emancipation from you. He is to be cut loose immediately. You no longer have any parental rights."

"Emancipation!" Neb growled. "That's too damn many syllables. Let me see that." He grabbed the document out of Robin's hands, leaving slimy prints on the paper.

"We also have it digitally recorded," Sheyenne added.

From the back of the tunnel, Syl slunk forward. Seeing us, he seemed to find inner self-confidence. "I hired them, Pa, because I don't want to live with you anymore. You don't treat me right. I'm my own person."

Neb crumpled the emancipation decree and threw it into the mud outside. "I am his guardian. He's mine to do with as I please. He's too young to face the world alone."

"He was old enough to face you," I said. "Syl is stronger than you can imagine."

"I found my inner salamander!" Syl clutched the little gold Amulet of Importance around his neck.

Overhead, the sparks and wispy flames coalesced, creating the fire dragon. "That's me." He jabbed a webbed hand toward the astral manifestation. "That's who I am inside—a fire dragon! And I'm not afraid of you anymore."

Neb was certainly afraid, however. "Why you ungrateful little—"

The fire dragon roared, and a whoosh of diaphanous flames swept across the mudflats. Neb ducked back into the tunnel.

Robin extended a hand and took Syl's slimy fingers, pulling the young salamander out into the night, while Sheyenne and Alvina came closer to support him. Robin said, "You can start over, Syl. You're legally and completely free. The judge agreed with our case."

"What am I supposed to do?" Neb squirmed. "Haul all that mud myself? Wheelbarrow after wheelbarrow, from one swamp to another? It's ridiculous."

"It's ridiculous," I agreed.

"But Syl won't be part of it," Robin said.

Sheyenne drifted down and picked up the wadded emancipation decree. "I did mention that we also have a digital copy."

I said to surly Neb, "Maybe if you went to the Wham-Bam Ashram, you could work hard, meditate ... and find your own inner *worm*."

"Wait, there's something I need." Syl withdrew his hand from Robin's and ducked back into the dank tunnel.

While we waited, we faced off against Neb, but the abusive

amphibian didn't have the vocabulary to express what he really felt.

Syl emerged a moment later holding a beloved battered paperback copy of *The Hobbit*. "Now we can go," he said.

We walked proudly away from the mudflats, and Alvina skipped along next to the young salamander. I could tell they would be close friends. Syl was so happy, he even managed to whistle a cheerful tune with his forked tongue.

"We'll set you up temporary lodgings, and I'm sure you can get a job. You have countless opportunities," Robin said.

"I'm a salamander," Syl said, taking it as a badge of honor. "The future is bright as mud."

As we strolled along, the fire dragon appeared again, glowing bright and happy. Golden sparks flew in all directions. With a companion like that, I knew Syl wouldn't have any trouble at all.

In a Japanese history course, I closely studied the the samurai, and because I was a bloodthirsty young man, I was particularly interested in the practice of seppuku—quite different from the portrayal of "harey carey" in bad films and TV shows.

In a story, you might start with one idea and run it into the ground, but what really makes a plot expand into something remarkable is what I call a "collision idea," a completely unrelated concept that lights the story on fire. Take the idea of cloning dinosaurs, for instance, and add the collision idea of an amusement park. What could possibly go wrong?

When I realized that the last days of the samurai overlapped with the early days of Hollywood, and the discovery that actual snuff films had been made almost as early as film was produced, that became the perfect collision idea for "Redmond's Private Screening."

Redmond's Private Screening

Sharper than any barber's straight razor, the edge of the samurai blade nicked the skin, drew blood. The director hissed in surprise, frowning at his cut finger, then laughed at himself. "How'd you like to slice *that* across your belly, Mikey?"

As his assistant Michael Kendai watched, Redmond held the blade up to the bright California sunlight that streamed into the makeshift studio though open windows and a cobwebbed skylight. "The katana is real, sir, a century old. More than just a prop."

"Forged in 1811, eh?" He didn't sound impressed. "It's just a sword."

Outside, the muffled sounds of motorcar traffic echoed along the dirt streets. One of the rattling vehicles backfired, and someone shouted obscenities in coarse Italian. Horses clopped by, pulling a late-morning milk cart. In his tiny warehouse studio, Michael knew that Redmond never noticed any outside distractions. He was too caught up in finding interesting things to shoot with his motion-picture camera, and he would never believe the doomsayers who claimed that nickelodeon audiences were tired of seeing marvels on celluloid film.

"Where did you get this samurai Taka-what's-his-name?" Redmond spoke as if the young Japanese man and his elderly parents weren't already right there beside him. The immigrants spoke no English, remained apart from the conversation; but they knew full well the business matters being discussed. "And how did you talk him into doing Harry Carry in front of the motion picture camera?"

Michael folded his hands together, frowned at Redmond's unkempt appearance, mussed red-brown hair, and pungent cologne. He gave the director a look that plainly said *Not many people try my patience, but you are one of them.* "Akira Takahashi came to me of his own free will and volunteered his performance of *hara-kiri*."

He looked around the small back-room studio, not eager to begin, but they would lose the best sunlight soon. The glass cyclopean eye of his hand-cranked movie camera stood watching the young samurai. A spare camera (which didn't work anyway) leaned against a corner.

Takahashi sat in bright robes, cross-legged on the white blanket he had spread out for him on top of the sour sawdust. His pate had been shaved in the traditional fashion, his straight black hair gathered in a ponytail at his neck. The old father, holding a worn, nicked sword of his own, squatted stony-faced beside his son, staring straight ahead. Only the wrinkled mother showed fear and anger, flashing tears at Redmond.

Michael explained, "Mr. Takahashi wishes to book steamer passage back to Japan for his parents, and he can think of no other way to raise the money. He considers it a fair exchange."

Redmond laughed nervously. His face had too many freckles, his skin was too pasty, his personality too slippery. "A lot of people are trying to get into this new movie business, but not usually by killing themselves on film." He sheathed the blade and handed the slim katana back.

Michael frowned at how low he himself had fallen, how disappointed the spirits of his own dead family must be. "Most directors do not wish to photograph such a spectacle either, and most patrons do not wish to see the result. But there are exceptions everywhere." He gave Redmond a cold stare. "You and I know how to find them."

The director raised his chin, pontificating. "Fifteen years ago, people flocked to nickelodeons to see a man sneeze, to watch a waterfall or a running horse. Today, we've got to give them something more for their money, eh?"

"I'm sure we do."

With a deaf ear for his assistant's sarcasm, Redmond strutted around the floor, looking at the natural light, at the position of the white blanket, but Michael had already set everything up perfectly. The three Japanese followed the director with their eyes, like animals in a cage.

"If they liked it so much in Japan, why'd they come to Hollywood in the first place, eh?" Redmond whispered, as if he didn't want the family to hear.

Michael drew a deep breath. "Many well-to-do samurai families were ruined in the overthrow of the last Shogun in 1868. Akira's father tried to earn a living in the new Japanese National Army, but he could not tolerate the army's lack of traditional honor. His eldest son, Akira's brother, entered the Japanese navy and was killed five years ago in the Russo-Japanese War. Akira and his parents then fled to America, but they found no opportunities here. Now they are destitute and wish only to go home to die."

"Well, we'll help them out then, eh?" Redmond removed a folded piece of paper from his trouser pocket. "I drew up a simple contract for Mr. Samurai. Get him to sign it, and we can start shooting." He looked critically at the slanting daylight in the studio. "Read it to him, if you like."

Michael glanced over the contract; it looked as if Redmond had done the typing himself. He formally presented the samurai with his sword, then spoke rapidly in Japanese, explaining the contract and its purpose. The young man drew himself up, glared at Redmond, and answered Michael sharply.

"He doesn't understand the need for a contract." Michael

turned to Redmond. "He asks if you are questioning his honor, if you doubt he will do as he has promised."

"What?" Redmond was oblivious to nuances. "The contract's for his protection, not mine."

Michael relayed the information. The old mother spoke quickly, while her son stared down at the curved sword in its sheath. "They ask why they should not trust you. Are you not an honorable man?"

Redmond made an exasperated sound. "Mikey, just explain to them I need to have it in writing that he's fully aware of what he's doing, that he offered his services willingly, and that I did not seek him out. What does he care anyway, eh? He's going to be dead."

Michael considered for a moment, then spoke in Japanese again. "I told him it was our custom to require such agreements. They have a great respect for customs and traditions." Finally, Takahashi took the contract and signed.

Redmond rolled his eyes and tucked the signed paper into his pocket. He clapped his hands for attention. "Okay, let's get this show on the road."

Michael took up his position behind the tripod, checking the lens, making sure the celluloid reel was loaded properly. Due to the questionable legality of his projects, Redmond involved as few people in the productions as possible. Michael had become accustomed to cranking the camera himself.

Sunlight poured through the flyspecked skylight, flooding the blanket spread on the floor. Akira Takahashi blinked in the glare. The handle of the katana looked like molten silver. Redmond didn't have to tell anyone what to do.

The old mother moved out of the light to where she could watch. The elder Takahashi drew himself taller, holding his own sword in one hand. He waited just behind and to the right of his son.

"Mikey, what's the old guy doing with a sword?" Redmond asked.

"He is the *kaishaku*." Michael paused just long enough to

emphasize how little Redmond understood about what was going to take place. "During *hara-kiri*, a samurai is permitted to have a close friend stand beside him. Once he has succeeded in cutting open his belly, the friend is allowed to strike off his head, releasing him from the terrible pain."

Redmond's eyes widened. "You mean the old man is going to chop off—oh, fantastic! You didn't tell me that before."

Michael scowled, then erased the expression. By participating in this heinous act, he felt as if he was betraying the Takahashi family—but he was giving them what they wanted. Even with his rationalizations, he disgusted himself.

Michael looked through the camera and signaled to Takahashi that everything was ready. The young samurai held the gazes of his parents for a long moment, then he took up the sword. Michael began to turn the crank, recording every second on the clicking ribbon of film.

Takahashi pulled the katana from its sheath, never taking his eyes from the steel. The traditional samurai sword had been crafted by one of the finest Zen sword makers, displaying an edge that consisted of half a million layers of folded steel, so sharp it seemed to slice rays of sunlight.

Takahashi took a white cloth from his father and wrapped it around the blade close to the hilt, leaving five inches of naked metal. He placed the wrapped katana on the blanket in front of him so he could proceed without taking his eyes from it. He never blinked while he undid the sash of his ceremonial robe, baring his chest. His stomach muscles were firm and tense.

Maintaining an even, smooth motion, Michael turned the camera crank as queasiness built within him. If a blade had plunged into his own belly, a swarm of butterflies would have emerged....

Takahashi stared into space. Moving by itself, his hand picked up the katana again, flipped it around so that its point rested against his abdomen. Michael saw the smallest of tremors in his throat, as if he were trying not to swallow.

For long moments he did not breathe. Everything stopped,

like a still from a motion picture. The father stood like a statue behind his son, sword raised and waiting. The ancient mother stared wide-eyed but made no sound.

Redmond fidgeted. "What's he waiting for?"

"Shut up, Redmond."

Takahashi uttered an animal sound and thrust five inches of the blade into the left side of his abdomen. He made an astonished, coughing sound. He sat rigid, frozen again.

Crimson soaked into his bright robe, dribbled onto his leg. Spasms flickered across his face, betraying the pain. Takahashi's hands became slippery with blood, but he managed to keep his grip on the handle.

He used both hands against the back of the blade to push the cutting edge across his stomach in a gash that grew wider like a grotesque smile. His face turned gray and wet, and his breathing had no rhythm at all.

Michael continued to turn the camera crank. Redmond stared, silent with awe and fascination.

Takahashi's body shuddered as the blade cut below his navel. He gave another, weaker cry and wrenched the blade the rest of the way across.

Michael's world turned red and fuzzy. Black things swam in his stomach and his eyes; sweat trickled down his forehead. His knees turned to water, but at least he didn't topple the camera. Redmond saw him faint, muttered a curse, and pushed him out of the way. He began cranking the camera himself.

Takahashi's body convulsed as if he were trying to vomit, and intestines spilled out into his lap like gray, white, and red eels. His eyes pushed away their glassy bleariness and widened upon seeing all that had been kept neatly inside of him. He made a gurgling sound.

"*Seppuku!*" the old man cried and brought down his sword, striking off his son's head. The dead samurai collapsed into a heap of blood and mismatched flesh. The old man fell to his knees.

"Perfect!" Redmond said and stopped filming.

Two days later, Michael found Redmond waiting for him in a booth at the back of the café, adding too much sugar to his mug of coffee. Michael felt bone-weary and ragged. "The funeral pyre was very difficult to arrange, Redmond."

The director scowled up from his plate of fried eggs. "I don't care how hard it was, Mikey, you're not getting any more money for it. We've got a written agreement."

Michael let out a disgusted sigh as he sat down. "I was merely stating a fact." Seeing Michael's Japanese features, the waiter ignored him.

Redmond stirred his coffee, oblivious to how his spoon clanged against the mug. He whistled for the waiter to bring coffee for Michael. "So why did you go to all that trouble, if it was so difficult? That part wasn't written into the contract."

The waiter brought a silver pot over, then left scowling when Michael ordered tea instead. Michael leaned across the sticky tabletop. "Redmond, we killed their son. We owed it to them."

"What is someone with a conscience doing in this business?" Redmond tried to laugh, then took a bite out of his jam-smeared toast. "Besides, *we* didn't kill the guy. If his parents didn't want him to do it, they could have stopped him at any time." He slurped his coffee, then spooned in more sugar.

"Not in Japanese culture, Redmond. Once a son comes of age, the parents must follow his wishes. Mr. Takahashi decided to send his mother and father home. They had no choice in the matter." The waiter returned with Michael's tea. Absently, after the man had left, he took a sugar cube and laid it on his saucer, crushing it with the rounded bottom of his spoon, then tapped the sugar into his tea. "Their steamer should have departed for Japan at dawn today."

"You haven't heard yet, eh?" Redmond snickered, another bite of toast poised halfway to his mouth. "The old man was so excited that he dropped stone dead on the dock. Spilled Junior's ashes all over the place. Can you imagine the expression on the old lady's face?"

Michael stopped stirring his tea and looked straight into Redmond's muddy green eyes, searching for some sign of a practical joke. "How do you know this? Why did no one tell me?"

"Nobody could find you! As far as I know, you disappear off the face of the Earth when you don't want to be found. I got a telegram from a flustered delivery boy. Seems he'd been running all over Hollywood looking for you."

Michael remained silent for so long that Redmond began to fidget. The family had already been through so much. Michael finally muttered, as if speaking to himself, "Their eldest son died fighting the Russian navy for Liaotung Peninsula. On his last birthday, after he'd been gone for months on the battleship *Miyako*, the family set out an extra bowl of rice to honor him. And the son sent his spirit across the sea to join them for the meal. They laughed and talked, but with moonrise the spirit returned to the ship." He lowered his voice to a whisper. "That night, the *Miyako* struck a mine in the Sea of Japan and sank."

Redmond took another bite of his runny eggs. "You mean the ghost appeared even *before* the son was killed? Just what were they doing for their little celebration? Smoking opium pipes?"

"Opium is from China, Redmond, not Japan." With an effort, Michael regained his patience. "Vengeful ghosts are common in our tradition. Anyone who dies violently is certain to haunt those who caused him to suffer. But the Japanese don't believe a person needs to be dead to send his spirit wandering. The family Takahashi truly believes they dined with the elder son on the eve of his death."

"Aww, tug my heartstrings." Then Redmond narrowed his eyes at Michael. "Oh, I see, you're trying to scare me that Mr. Samurai's ghost is coming to get me. Forget it, Mikey. He volunteered. *You* brought him to me."

Michael didn't bother to respond. He stood up, leaving Redmond to pay for his unfinished tea. "Is that all you wanted to see me about?"

Redmond smiled. "I'll be screening my samurai picture in three days, and I need you to run the projector. I've found a private room and five men sufficiently bored with the nickelodeons. They'll pay ten dollars each, if I can deliver what I've promised. Some are worried it might be trick photography, like George Meliés might do."

"Meliés never showed a man disemboweling himself." Michael let no ironic expression show. "Besides, Redmond, who could question your honesty?"

Redmond grinned, then scowled, then drank his coffee.

Redmond insisted on keeping the door locked and the screening room dim, lit only by tasteless red lights behind incense burners. Even more tasteless was his decision to use Takahashi's white blanket—laundered to remove most of the bloodstains—as a projection screen.

Michael mounted the single celluloid reel on the projector as Redmond ushered his clients to flimsy wooden chairs in the room. The director wore a ridiculous Japanese robe, as if to create the proper ambiance.

Michael inspected the five men, who didn't bother to notice the Japanese-American assistant. One looked bored, two were fidgety (wearing obvious disguises); the remaining two frowned with skepticism while tugging on their identical muttonchop whiskers.

Michael wondered what type of lives these men led. Did they beat their wives, or harm their children, or frequent prostitutes—or did they derive enough pleasure just from watching gruesome motion-picture shows?

Of the six pictures on which he had worked with Redmond, this had been by far the most dissatisfying. The first had been a beautiful study of a ballerina's dance; then he had photographed sultry naked women. What might come next after ritual suicide—

Redmond killing a baby, perhaps? Michael felt the shame in his involvement, even if Redmond didn't care.

After this evening's spectacle, Michael had made up his mind to disappear, as he had done so many times before, simply cover his tracks. He had enough skill and connections to find work elsewhere, even with his Japanese heritage. Perhaps he would go to New York City, though the majority of filmmaking had shifted toward the Los Angeles area with its variety of scenery....

As Michael fed the celluloid film into the projector and checked the bulb, Redmond began to explain, inaccurately, the traditions and lore behind *hara-kiri*. Michael considered leaving the room after he started the projector, just to avoid seeing Takahashi die yet again, but decided against it. He would see this project through to the end, then be away from Redmond for good.

"Gentlemen, please enjoy the first screening of Redmond's *Scarlet Sword*." The director placed his hands together to imitate a Japanese bow, then stepped away from the bloodstained screen. As the projector began to flicker and whir, a sepia image of Akira Takahashi appeared on the screen. Michael focused quickly.

The five men in the audience watched as the grim young man sat cross-legged in his robes, staring at his sword. The film was intensely sharp and remarkably clear, showing too many details.

Takahashi withdrew the katana from its sheath and took the cloth from his father's gnarled hand. The clicking projector made the only noise in the room. The men leaned forward to watch; Michael was reminded of crocodiles lurking on riverbanks, alert for prey.

Takahashi placed the point of the sword against his stomach. He drew a deep breath, ready for the thrust.

Along the top of the screen appeared a deep crimson line, startling in its intensity against the black-and-white world. The red line widened, covering about a quarter of the screen before it began to drip like thick blood down the screen.

The five men muttered in amazement at Redmond's technique, how he'd been able to superimpose such a brilliant color onto the dull sepia tone.

"Mikey!" Redmond said, his voice a confused growl.

On the image, Takahashi stared down at the curved sword, oblivious to the thick red streams oozing across the screen and obliterating everything.

Feeling a growing horror, Michael tapped the projector lens. A shadow of his fingers should have fallen across the stained-blanket screen, but it didn't. Droplets popped out of the movie reel itself, like juice from a pomegranate seed. Michael touched the film feeding into the projector. His fingers came away wet and sticky.

The five men in the audience began to grumble. The crimson blot prevented them from seeing what the samurai was doing. Redmond swallowed several times; his freckled skin looked a sick gray in the red light.

The curtain of blood spilled to the bottom of the screen and covered the entire picture.

A roaring wind numbed Michael's ears, making him giddy. His vision went fuzzy, and then an empty coldness swept over him. The wind stopped abruptly, and a surreal fuzziness filled the screening room.

"Mikey!" Redmond's voice cracked like a pubescent teenager's.

The projector had stopped, though the screen still glowed like a window onto a scarlet landscape. Michael stood beside the motionless reel of film, but he could not move. Neither did the men seated in the wooden folding chairs. It was as if time had stopped, as if the apparatus projecting their lives had frozen on a single frame.

Except for Redmond, who stormed back and forth. "What the hell is going on here?" He seemed to know the answer, but could think of nothing else to say, no other way to pretend having command of the situation.

Will Vengeance suffice? It wasn't a voice. It wasn't even words. Michael heard Japanese, but the other men in the room seemed to understand as well.

Redmond made a strange sound between a gulp and a scream.

"What do you mean? I did everything I promised!" He paused, as if spinning through his memories of everything Michael had told him. "I kept my honor!" Michael could not react, or move, or say anything to help him.

You are a man fundamentally without honor. Writing promises on paper to ensure that you will keep them, profiting by the suffering of others. These five will receive enough blood for their tastes, and my own. Such men deserve to die as common criminals.

The men sat frozen in their seats, but Michael watched as their heads slumped, one by one. He thought he heard a squelching sound and then a haunting series of screams echoing in the air. Michael felt like a helpless bystander, watching and wondering if he himself might be next.

Redmond, you shall have an opportunity to regain your honor.

The crimson covering the screen thinned and began to drip away, revealing a new image of a freckled man dressed in gaudy Japanese robes. He sat cross-legged and holding a samurai sword against his bared abdomen.

"You can't do this!" In the room, Redmond swatted at his robe as if trying to knock away the touch of a phantom sword. The image of Redmond on the screen sat contemplating the blade about to pierce his stomach. "We had a contract!"

I made no contract with you.

"Yes! You signed it, and I fulfilled my part, just like I promised. I didn't cheat you. Look, I'm sorry your father died, but I had nothing to do with that. I can't help it he spilled your ashes on the dock. Please!"

Michael tried to call out to Redmond, but his vocal cords had snapped like so many spiderwebs.

You have me confused with my son, fool. He is content with the bargain he made and with the price it cost him. I am the one who demands vengeance.

On the screen, another robed figure stepped behind the image of Redmond, holding a second sword. Takahashi's old mother, taking up her position to be Redmond's *kaishaku*.

I am the one suffered most. My sons both gone, my husband. I am left with nothing, and I demand retribution.

"You can't be a ghost. You're not even dead!"

On the screen, the old woman smiled and raised the sword. *Why must a body be dead for the spirit to roam free?*

She nodded to the image of Redmond in the film. He looked into space as if in a trance, then drove the sword into his belly.

The film broke, and the projector bulb burst at the same time. Michael snapped off the machine, and as silence returned he heard a brief remnant of a scream disappearing into time. It sounded like Redmond's voice.

He fumbled for the main light switches. Redmond sprawled on the floor clutching his stomach. The other five men slumped in their folding wooden chairs, arms dangling at their sides.

Michael touched Redmond. The director's skin was cold and rigid. He checked the businessmen, and they were dead as well. He could find no blood anywhere. The sticky redness had vanished even from the film and the projector.

The shock crept up on him, paralyzing him. Why had the old woman's ghost spared him? He himself had arranged for her son's death. But Michael had not deviated from the old woman's conception of honor, as Redmond had. That did not mean Michael was an honorable man. He still had to deal with his own shame.

Shame. The traditions of Michael Kendai's culture had taught him how to cope with shame. Was the old woman's ghost expecting him to follow the traditional course? Redmond had the excuse of ignorance; Michael did not. Would she come after him if he did not kill himself to atone for his crime? But he was too much of a coward.

He rewound the film before he removed the reel. He vowed that no one else would ever watch *Scarlet Sword.* He would destroy it. He knew where Redmond kept prints of his other films, and he mounted the ballerina reel onto the projector. The police would be very confused.

Michael would be long gone before anyone discovered the

bodies and turned their eyes toward a convenient Japanese scapegoat. Michael could cover his tracks. He was good at that.

New York looked better and better.

Fighting down the feelings of fear and shame within him, Michael left the screening room. He tried to keep from running as he fled into the street.

And now for one last Tucker's Grove story, drawing on my high school memories. The rural culture where I grew up was straight out of a Ray Bradbury short story, and it had both charms and horrors for an imaginative young boy who wanted to be a writer. My childhood was a combination of Norman Rockwell and Norman Bates.

I remember spending a lot of time walking along the railroad tracks out in the country, looking at discarded junk along the siding, letting my imagination wander.

This story is about a demon-possessed train....

Loco-Motive

My best buddy Alan got killed yesterday, demolished by a hit-and-run train. They found Alan's car smashed to pieces, scattered all up and down the embankment like wrapping paper on a Christmas morning.

The Locust Road intersection is well marked. I know that, drunk or not, Alan would never have driven into a goddamn freight train. According to the railroad company's schedules, no real train was even *close* to the crossing at that time of night.

Imagine, coming back from college to be pall bearer for a closed coffin—that's the part that really sucks. Goddamn it, Alan— you were supposed to be best man at my wedding if I ever got married....

But it gives me an excuse to come back home. To see for myself if that awful train has returned for one last run. How visible would an all-black locomotive be if it shut off its one-eyed headlight, slavering oil and grinding red-hot coal in its belly, waiting to pounce on Alan's car as he drove home?

Alan and I were kids together. We did all that stuff like running across the fields, hiding between the rows of corn, daring each other to climb just one rung closer to the top of old man Pickman's silo.

Alan collected wheat pennies; I collected silver Mercury

dimes. I've still got my heavy ceramic mug half-full of those dimes, up in my room at home somewhere. We used to spend hours and hours each summer on our bikes, riding down the country roads to the bank in Tucker's Grove, where we'd exchange one roll of coins for another and then eagerly scavenge in the new rolls for our individual treasures: my dimes, his pennies.

We watched superhero cartoons together on Saturday mornings, usually at my house because we had a big color TV; my parents would get crabby when we'd wake them up so early in the morning. Then it was outside in the snow or the sun, talking about how much we preferred *Lost in Space* and "Voyage to See What's on the Bottom" to *Star Trek* because those shows had better monsters (though we both got *heavily* into *Star Trek* in high school).

There's usually one day every summer, somewhere in the middle, when you get so bored you *almost* wish it was time for school to start again. Of course, I never said anything like that to Alan because he probably would have punched me in the stomach even for *saying* such a stupid thing. That was when we decided to head off for the railroad tracks.

The tracks were about a mile away, but you could see them across the fields, riding high on their isolated embankment and cut off from the world by rickety barbed-wire fences. The fences didn't prove to be any obstacle at all for us, aside from the occasional sissy fear of getting lockjaw if you scratched yourself on one of the rusty barbs.

Out on the tracks we felt *away* from everything, kings of the mountain, just Alan and me. The twin steel tracks stretched away for the longest distance before they curved sharply toward Bartonville, which we couldn't even see on account of the low hills in between.

Aimlessly, I walked along, stretching my legs to step on one crosstie, then the next. Alan tried to balance on the thin steel rail, but he kept falling off after four steps or so. Once, we placed a couple of Alan's wheat pennies on the rails just before a train came, and afterward we had looked in awe at the shiny, squashed copper disk—you could barely see the ghost of Lincoln's face smeared long and flat from the thunderous passage of the train.

The spaces between the ties were filled with gravel, cinders, and other junk. Two tall, silver-painted towers stood on either side of the tracks, one facing each way down the line, with dead green and red lights that would shine a warning when trains came.

Off in the distance, in the opposite direction from Bartonville and the big curve of the tracks, we could see old man Pickman and his ancient tractor pulling the disks across the field and chewing up dirt. The firing of the tractor sounded like toy gunshots in the empty air; apart from that, we could only hear a couple of birds, and the wind. Pickman pulled his muddy tractor up on Locust Road, trying to cross from one field to the next, but the tractor sounded like it couldn't go on with life anymore. It popped and backfired before it gave up completely, right near where the tracks crossed the road. We could barely hear the sound of Pickman's shouts as he got off the tractor, jumped up and down, and kicked one of the machine's huge back tires. Alan and I both giggled and watched for a long time as he stomped off down the road to his big white farmhouse.

The old farmer got boring after a while, though, and Alan changed the subject. "Where do you suppose all this *junk* comes from?"

He indicated the embankment by the tracks, and I noticed all the debris scattered up and down the fence line. A refrigerator door, a broken and rusted plow, an automobile fender, some hubcaps, the top of a stove, and more—it was the oddest assortment of ruined things you could imagine. I had never really paid much attention before, thinking it as natural as the long grass and the wild roses along the fence line. But Alan was right—there wasn't a logical explanation for why that kind of junk would all be there, a mile away from the nearest farmhouse.

I shrugged, but Alan kept thinking aloud. "Do you suppose a *train* put it there?"

"You mean hobos? Why would they want to throw junk like that?"

"No, I mean a *train*! Like, a *live* train that comes out after dark and attacks cars and things. What if there's a big, black locomotive, you know, and it grabs stuff, tears it apart, and throws the pieces all up and down the tracks." Alan's eyes were glistening with his own imagination.

"That's dumb, Alan." It was one of the only times I made fun of his ideas. "Why would it do that?"

But he seemed emphatic, and I could see he really wasn't kidding. "Maybe it's angry, *really* angry because ... well, because it's a *train*—it's stuck on the rails, and it can't go anywhere else. It's trapped. A car can drive wherever it wants, you know, and so can a tractor. But not a train."

It made sense to me, and Alan didn't pull my leg often. I found my mind wandering, imagining, seriously considering the idea—and it was just exotic enough to capture my imagination. While lying in bed, trying to sleep at nights, I *did* hear trains all the time, some of them with odd whistles, and it seemed to me I heard too many crashing and rattling sounds to be explained by the clatter of a simple passing train.

On hot summer nights when the sheets were sticky from the humidity, I slept in my underwear and left my window open to listen to the crickets and the grasshoppers ... but just when I was finally dozing off, I could sometimes hear that one special train, the vengeful locomotive that was angry because it could never get off the tracks. It was a really spooky idea, just the type of thing we needed to improve a boring summer day. "But where does it come from?" I asked.

Solemnly, Alan turned to point at where the curve of the tracks swung behind the hills and vanished from our sight. "There."

"Where? In Bartonville?"

"No, stupid. See where the tracks disappear? It doesn't just go around the curve to Bartonville—*maybe* sometimes that curve is something else. Like a doorway into another dimension. You know, like the *Twilight Zone*." Alan said this with great seriousness, and to us—after years of watching fantastic TV shows—the idea was eminently reasonable.

 I couldn't argue with that. Enchanted, I stared down the tracks, and then slowly, trying to appear nonchalant, I stepped off the crossties and onto the cinder bed at the edge of the embankment. I didn't want Alan to think I was chicken. But I saw that he was anxious to get away from the rails, too.

 Of course, we had to see if it was all true. We double-promised to come back that night, sneaking out after dark and after our parents had gone to sleep. Since it was summer, it didn't get dark until late, so I set my alarm clock for 11:15 and put it under my pillow.

 I didn't plan to go to sleep, but with two hours of lying there in the humid summer heat, I ended up having the most vivid nightmare: the giant black locomotive, murderous and wanting to destroy machines and people, waiting for me, burning not coal but human bones. Luckily, the muffled alarm brought me out of it before I could wake up yelling for my parents. I was shaking in the darkness, and I almost didn't dare to get up. I lay there looking up at the ceiling. The sluggish breeze moved the curtains so that they sounded like slithering ghosts against the windowsill. But I knew what Alan would think if I didn't show up, so I got dressed and sneaked out of the quiet house, being careful not to let the screen door slam shut.

 Alan was waiting for me at the end of our driveway, and we walked down Locust Road without saying anything until we were out of earshot of the houses. The road stood out plain in the moonlight, but we didn't want to cut across the fields in the dark. Raccoons and skunks and possums come out into the fields at night, and other things you don't even want to imagine. The moon was full and high up in the sky, and we would get to the tracks around midnight—it was going to be so perfect.

 "I dreamed of the train," I told Alan.

 "So did I." We didn't say anything else until we reached the railroad crossing. Old man Pickman's tractor looked like a sick mechanical cow standing half in the ditch and half on the road where it had stalled.

"Let's walk down a-ways."

I followed Alan out onto the tracks, stepping from crosstie to crosstie, as we walked farther from the road. The bugs in the grass seemed very loud that night, and the noise hung in the air. We kept walking, oddly silent but neither of us willing to admit we were scared.

The insect buzzing stopped abruptly, as if someone had switched off a radio. We heard a distant grating sound as one of the tall signal towers swung its colored glass lens into place. A red light stabbed at us like a bloodshot eye. A train was coming! Then, a moment later, the *other* signal tower, the one facing the opposite direction, swung its light into place and shone the red light the other way.

I couldn't say anything. Alan gasped, "This is it! This is it!"

We heard a sound like a muffled roar, and then, emerging from around the Bartonville curve, crawling out of another dimension where it could sit and brood on its vengeance day after day, we both saw a gleaming yellow headlight. The light was like a spear pointing at us, charging down at us, and all we could do was stand there, hypnotized.

I jerked on Alan's arm. "Come on! Get off the tracks!"

We both tumbled down the embankment and scrambled for cover in the thick wild rose bushes. We would have a bad time explaining all our scratches to our moms the next day, but I was too scared to care right then. The black locomotive came on, relentlessly charging down the tracks that chained it to its never-changing route. Dark smoke belched from its smokestack and was swallowed up by the night and the stars. The locomotive's one-eyed headlight, a searchlight, poked ahead, looking for victims. The thing wasn't like a passenger train, or even a freight train, but like something out of a cowboy movie, an old coal-burning locomotive—just exactly the way I had pictured it. Two large wheels under the empty engineer's compartment clattered powerfully, heaving a gleaming brass piston back and forth, driving the entire train. The wide, triangular cowcatcher in the front of the locomotive looked like a guillotine blade. Seven cars, all black, trailed behind the locomotive—it reminded me of a giant metal caterpillar, with each black car one of its segments.

I wanted to blink my eyes and make it go away. It's not real! We just made it up! But how can you deny a couple million tons of hot, angry steel charging down the tracks in front of your very eyes?

The black train chugged and clattered past our hiding place, and we could feel the heat of its big coal-burning furnace. I wanted to cry then, even in front of Alan. But the big yellow eye of the locomotive didn't see us—instead it focused on new prey. It paused, hissing steam like a fighting cat, seemed to tense and coil its mechanical muscles, and then *lunged* forward—toward old man Pickman's stalled tractor.

The tractor didn't move, of course—it was just a tractor. But the locomotive reared up off the tracks, and it struck. Its shining pistons detached themselves and reached forward like steel mantis arms to grasp the heavy old tractor and pull it onto the tracks. The steam hissed and built up; black smoke poured out of the smokestack, and the wheels churned backward. The locomotive took its mechanical victim, dragging it along the tracks like a spider returning to its lair.

The locomotive stopped right in front of us and proceeded to *tear* Pickman's tractor apart. Wheel guards, the two small headlights, parts of the engine, the rusty and uncomfortable seat on its thick spring—all were shredded by invisible steel jaws under the locomotive itself. We could feel the heat, smell the oil and the hot steel of an overworked engine.

As it destroyed the tractor, the black train tossed the scrap metal along the embankment, like you would throw chicken bones after a barbecue. One of the huge black tractor tires crashed down right by us, almost smashing me, and I yelled out loud. In a second, I was up and running toward the barbed wire fence, not caring at all about skunks or possums or raccoons in the soybeans. Alan shouted at me to get down.

The locomotive let out the most horrible roaring explosion I've ever heard in my life, like it was *really* angry at us for having discovered it. I dove over the fence, bouncing on the wires, not thinking about scratches or cuts or even lockjaw. Alan was right on my heels. Behind me, the locomotive reared up off the tracks again, keeping its back seven cars firmly on the rails. It was like a snake, a big black cobra maybe, trying to strike, trying to smash us. It came down hard on the embankment, and the bladelike cowcatcher made a deep smoking impression in the dirt.

But it missed us, and we were out in Pickman's soybean field running like hell, not even trying to dodge the rows. The locomotive bellowed in anger, trapped on the rails but promising to get us both someday. We ran and ran, and after a while the locomotive turned back to destroying the poor old tractor.

Neither Alan nor I went back to the railroad tracks again all summer, no way. That autumn my dad had us pack up and move back into town, since he'd grown tired of the country life by then. Alan and I drifted apart, now that we weren't constantly in touch with each other; sure, we were still friends, but it wasn't the *same*.

Then in high school we rediscovered our friendship, falling back into the best-buddies bit. Since Alan was almost a year older than I, he got his driver's license first and took me all over the place, and because he turned eighteen first, he could get me all the beer I wanted. I remember spending many a weekend afternoon on his back porch, shootin' the breeze with the stereo turned up, and looking across the fields at the distant railroad tracks.

After graduation, I went off to college; Alan went instead to a local technical college where he picked up a something-or-other degree in electronics. He ended up working as a manager for a chain restaurant in Bartonville and partying a lot.

Meanwhile, I was doing the typical college stunt of waiting until Friday night to start a term paper that was due on the following Monday. Last week, I had planned on doing an all-nighter, but spent most of my time feeling stupid and miserable because the girl I'd been chasing all semester still wouldn't go out with me. I finally gave up on the term paper an hour or so past midnight and flopped on my unmade dorm bed, going to sleep with all my clothes on....

Even after so many years, I dreamed of the black locomotive again, slavering thick oil from its mechanical jaws, searching for us with its one yellow eye. It charged at me and I ran, but I couldn't get off the tracks—I was trapped, and the train was gaining on me, wanting to grind me to a pulp beneath its crushing wheels and scatter my limbs all up and down the embankment. I woke up drowning in sweat.

And that was the night Alan got killed in his car by the Locust Road crossing. Demolished—parts of his car thrown gleefully all along the tracks....

When I heard, and when I figured it out, I went into the bathroom for almost an hour, bent over the John, trying to be sick, sick at myself. I think it might have hardened me up inside, so I could face going back home.

Alan's funeral was like a regular class reunion. Everybody was there, all the people who ever knew him. Even the freaks and the jocks came, the ones who would never sign your yearbook or bother to talk to you in the halls. Now they couldn't even look Alan in the face because of the closed coffin. I think I held up pretty well, even though I was distracted. What kind of jerk gets *distracted* at the funeral of his best buddy?

Afterward, back home, I went alone to my old room and closed the door. Mom and Dad seemed willing to let me work it out for myself. I found the old ceramic mug half-filled with my silver Mercury dimes; it had been buried in the junk on one of my closet shelves. I sat down on the neatly made single bed that had been mine for so many years, but my bedroom became a guest room when I moved out. I looked out the window and waited for sunset to come.

I had to drive to the Locust Road tracks this time, telling my parents I wanted to go cruising for a little bit, to clear my head. Dad warned me not to drink too much—he spoke out of habit, I think, from all the times I had gone out cruising with Alan. But partying wasn't what I had in mind at all.

I pulled my car over on the shallow, rutted ditch next to the railroad crossing, shut off the headlights, and got out. I had some time yet before midnight, and the moon shone full again. I walked out into the brisk autumn night. I could see my breath, like the smoke coming out of a black locomotive.

I stared at the tracks a long while before I got up the courage to step between the iron rails. In the moonlight down the embankment I saw something glint, and when I looked closer, I realized it was the broken rearview mirror from Alan's car.

The vengeful black locomotive wasn't *real*—it was all made up, just a fantasy shared between us two kids. There's a certain power in naïveté, I think, and if you believe in something with all your heart, all your terror ... well, who knows? Maybe there really *is* a Santa Claus or an Easter Bunny or a Boogey Man, from all the children in the world believing in it with pure unquestioning faith that only a kid can have. Alan and I had *believed* in the killer train, and we had challenged its reality by going to see, to prove it was only imaginary—and the nightmare had called our bluff.

Now, I had to *believe* I could destroy it. But I was a lot older and a lot more cynical this time.

I started to walk down the tracks again, all alone, listening to the coins jingle together in my pocket. I headed toward the Bartonville curve, away from the road and all hope of rescue.

The darkness made the ground hard to see, and I stumbled more than once on a broken crosstie. But I walked until I got between the two skeletal signal towers on either side of the tracks, then I put my hands on my hips, trying to look defiant, and shouted into the night.

Kevin J. Anderson

"Come on, you son of a bitch! Come get me!" The words echoed out, and the insect noises paused a moment before starting up again; when nothing happened, I felt belittled and stupid. "What's the matter? Are you *chicken*?"

A loud, unearthly bellow exploded from the darkness far ahead. The furnace in the black locomotive was stoked up with a little bit of Hell itself, and a blast of heat forced the steam to surge upward and scream through its whistle. I thought everyone in all of Rutherford County must have heard that noise.

Then its eye suddenly appeared, a round yellow bullet coming straight at me from around the curve and out of its unreal dimension. I was flooded with light, transfixed. I heard the rattling rhythm of the locomotive's wheels, the clatter against the tracks, the chug of its pistons. Smoke spurted from its stack as the train charged toward me, thinking only of murder.

My hands were shaking as I dug around in my pockets. Trying to keep cool, I pulled out two of my special dimes, my silver Mercury dimes, and stooped down to lay them on the tracks, one on each steel rail. I stepped back, remaining between the tracks, not even thinking about trying to run. Silver dimes ... everyone knew that *silver* was deadly to supernatural things. What would the horror movies be without silver bullets, silver crosses, silvered mirrors? I tried not to think about it too much because I had to *believe* this game would work. And these silver dimes were special, cherished from childhood. I cursed myself over and over again for having majored in science, for insisting that things had to make *sense* before I could believe in them.

But this would work. I knew it would work. I *knew* it would work. How come you can remember all sorts of stupid things from your childhood, but you can't remember what it was like to *believe* in something? I crossed my fingers, and then I double-crossed them. That might help.

The locomotive's cowcatcher looked like a spearhead as it came at me. I could see the engine's brass pistons grabbing forward and back, reaching out to stab me. Its eye never blinked, but I could see the slavering oil dripping from its mechanical jaws, and I definitely felt the heat pouring off of it. The base of its smokestack had begun to turn a cherry red from its exertion. And in the engineer's compartment, I could see a figure. Alan. Riding the train, unable to get off. I knew he saw me waiting for him. The train blasted its steam whistle.

    The black locomotive came down the tracks at me like a cannonball. I stood there petrified, looking at the pitifully small coins resting on the tracks as if they were really supposed to protect me. The train didn't pause—I knew it wouldn't; it didn't want to give me a chance to jump off the tracks. But I felt calm inside—at least I knew what was going to hit me; Alan hadn't even had that much warning. I had a terrible urge to shut my eyes, but I couldn't. The nightmare was real now, and I couldn't hide under the covers.

    Then the black locomotive struck the little circles of silver, but it seemed to impact an invisible wall of concrete. The locomotive smashed together, splitting into ribbons of iron. The boiler burst, and orange flames erupted from splits in its iron-plated side. The wheels ground to a screaming halt as the other seven cars piled up; and then the whole train exploded again, blasting up into the silent starry sky in a rain of hot shreds of metal. I never saw what happened to the shadow of Alan on the train—maybe he was never there in the first place.

    I felt the heat and the push of the shockwave. I stood unmoving, waiting for a big chunk of shrapnel to come down and kill me after all. But nothing did, and I stared at the wreckage for a few minutes, listening to the *patter* and *thunk* of broken iron falling to the ground.

    After a pause, the insects started singing again.

    I bent to pick up my dimes and found that both had been flattened by the locomotive's momentum, smeared out into gleaming silver ovals. I pocketed them with reverence, as if I were holding talismans, splinters of the cross—they would always be special, a part of unreality that would ruin my chances of a career in science.

Kevin J. Anderson

I barely remembered walking back to my car, but as I drove back to town, I got the shakes really bad. Nobody noticed the difference later, though I found I could face Alan's death, now that I had done something about it. Later on, I realized how you selectively learn to forget the things you can't explain.

There's always junk scattered along the railroad tracks—discarded bits of twisted metal, rusted pieces of machinery—but nobody knows what it is or how it got there. Someday I'm probably going to come back to the Locust Road crossing, and I'll look for a piece of that black locomotive, to keep with my souvenirs of Alan.

I opened this collection with a story written with Neil Peart, and also included a rock-inspired horror story written with Janis Ian. I'll end the book with another one written with Neil Peart, our first.

Not long after I met him, Neil bicycled around Africa on several epic trips, often on his own. e would send me lavishly detailed travelogues of his journeys, the sights he saw, the villages that welcomed him, the people he met. He even self-published some of those accounts in very limited books for his friends.

I had an idea for an ominous, atmospheric story featuring a rock drummer taking a similar bicycle trip across Africa, but I had never seen it for myself and I didn't have the descriptions I needed. After brainstorming with Neil, I wrote this story and embroidered it with all the amazing details he had so meticulously documented in his essays. Everything came together smoothly.

"Drumbeats" is one of my favorite stories.

Drumbeats
(with Neil Peart)

After nine months of touring across North America—with hotel suites and elaborate dinners and clean sheets every day—it felt good to be hot and dirty, muscles straining not for the benefit of any screaming audience, but just to get to the next village up the dusty road, where none of the natives recognized Danny Imbro or knew his name. To them, he was just another White Man, an exotic object of awe for little children, a target of scorn for drunken soldiers at border checkpoints.

Bicycling through Africa was about the furthest thing from a rock concert tour that Danny could imagine—which was why he did it, after promoting the latest Blitzkrieg album and performing each song until the tracks were worn smooth in his head. This cleared his mind, gave him a sense of balance, perspective.

The other members of Blitzkrieg did their own thing during the group's break months. Phil, whom they called the "music machine" because he couldn't stop writing music, spent his relaxation time cranking out film scores for Hollywood; Reggie caught up on his reading, soaking up grocery bags full of political thrillers and mysteries; Shane turned into a vegetable on Maui. But Danny Imbro took his expensive-but-battered bicycle and bummed around West Africa. The others thought it strangely appropriate that the band's drummer would go off hunting for tribal rhythms.

Late in the afternoon on the sixth day of his ride through Cameroon, Danny stopped in a large open market and bus depot in the town of Garoua. The marketplace was a line of mud-brick kiosks and chophouses, the air filled with the smell of baked dust and stones, hot oil and frying beignets. Abandoned cars squatted by the roadside, stripped clean but unblemished by corrosion in the dry air. Groups of men and children in long blouses like nightshirts idled their time away on the street corners.

Wives and daughters appeared on the road with their buckets, going to fetch water from the well on the other side of the marketplace. They wore bright-colored *pagnes* and kerchiefs, covering their traditionally naked breasts with T-shirts or castoff Western blouses, since the government in the capital city of Yaounde had forbidden women from going topless.

Behind one kiosk in the shade sat a pan holding several bottles of Coca-Cola, Fanta, and ginger ale, cooling in water. Some vendors sold a thin stew of bony fish chunks over gritty rice, others sold *fufu*, a doughlike paste of pounded yams to be dipped into a sauce of meat and okra. Bread merchants stacked their long *baguettes* like dry firewood.

Danny used the back of his hand to smear sweat-caked dust off his forehead, then removed the bandanna he wore under his helmet to keep the sweat out of his eyes. With streaks of white skin peeking through the layer of grit around his eyes, he probably looked like some strange lemur.

In halting French, he began haggling with a wiry boy to buy a bottle of water. Hiding behind his kiosk, the boy demanded 800 francs for the water, an outrageous price. While Danny attempted to bargain it down, he saw the gaunt, grayish-skinned man walking through the marketplace like a wind-up toy running down.

The man was playing a drum.

The boy cringed and looked away. Danny kept staring. The crowd seemed to shrink away from the strange man as he wandered among them, continuing his incessant beat. He wore his hair long and unruly, which in itself was unusual among the close-cropped Africans. In the equatorial heat, the long, stained overcoat he wore must have heated his body like a furnace, but the man did not seem to notice. His eyes were focused on some invisible distance.

"*Huit-cent francs,*" the boy insisted on his price, holding the lukewarm bottle of water just out of Danny's reach.

The staggering man walked closer, tapping a slow monotonous beat on the small cylindrical drum under his arm. He did not change his tempo but continued to play as if his life depended on it. Danny saw that the man's fingers and wrists were wrapped with scraps of hide; even so, he had beaten his fingertips bloody.

Danny stood transfixed. He had heard tribal musicians play all manner of percussion instruments, from hollowed tree trunks, to rusted metal cans, to beautifully carved *djembe* drums with goat-skin drumheads—but he had never heard a tone so rich and sweet, with such an odd echoey quality as this strange African drum.

In the studio, he had messed around with drum synthesizers and reverbs and the new technology designed to turn computer hackers into musicians. But this drum sounded different, solid and pure, and it hooked him through the heart, hypnotizing him. It distracted him entirely from the unpleasant appearance of its bearer.

"What is that?" he asked.

"*Sept-cent francs,*" the boy insisted in a nervous whisper, dropping his price to 700 and pushing the water closer.

Danny walked in front of the staggering man, smiling broadly enough to show the grit between his teeth, and listened to the tapping drumbeat. The drummer turned his gaze to Danny and stared through him. The pupils of his eyes were like two gaping bullet wounds through his skull. Danny took a step backward but found himself moving to the beat. The drummer faced him, finding his audience. Danny tried to place the rhythm, to burn it into his mind—something this mesmerizing simply had to be included in a new Blitzkrieg song.

Danny looked at the cylindrical drum, trying to determine what might be causing its odd double-resonance—a thin inner membrane, perhaps? He saw nothing but elaborate carvings on the sweat polished wood, and a drumhead with a smooth, dark-brown coloration. He knew the Africans used all kinds of skin for their drumheads, and he couldn't begin to guess what this was.

He mimed a question to the drummer, then asked, *"Est-ce-que je peux l'essayer?"* May I try it?

The gaunt man said nothing but held out the drum near enough for Danny to touch it without interrupting his obsessive rhythm. His overcoat flapped open, and the hot stench of decay made Danny stagger backward, but he held his ground, reaching for the drum.

Danny ran his fingers over the smooth drumskin, then tapped with his fingers. The deep sound resonated with a beat of its own, like a heartbeat. It delighted him. "For sale? *Est-ce-que c'est a vendre?"* He took out a thousand francs as a starting point, although if water alone cost 800 francs here, this drum was worth much, much more.

The man snatched the drum away and clutched it to his chest, shaking his head vigorously. His drumming hand continued its unrelenting beat.

Danny took out two thousand francs, then was disappointed to see not the slightest change of expression on the odd drummer's face. "Okay, then, where was the drum made? Where can I get another one? *Où est-ce qu'on peut trouver un autre comme ça?"* He put most of the money back into his pack, keeping 200 francs out. Danny stuffed the money into the fist of the drummer; the man's hand seemed to be made of petrified wood. *"Où?"*

The man scowled, then gestured behind him, toward the Mandara Mountains along Cameroon's border with Nigeria. *"Kabas."*

He turned and staggered away, still tapping on his drum as if to mark his footsteps. Danny watched him go, then returned to the kiosk, unfolding the map from his pack. "Where is this Kabas? Is it a place? *C'est un village?*"

"*Huit-cent francs,*" the boy said, offering the water again at his original 800 franc price.

Danny bought the water, and the boy gave him directions.

He spent the night in a Garouan hotel that made Motel 6 look like Caesar's Palace. Anxious to be on his way to find his own new drum, Danny roused a local vendor and cajoled him into preparing a quick omelet for breakfast. He took a sip from his 800 franc bottle of water, saving the rest for the long bike ride, then pedaled off into the stirring sounds of early morning.

As Danny left Garoua on the main road, heading toward the mountains, savanna and thorn trees stretched away under a crystal sky. A pair of doves bathed in the dust of the road ahead, but as he rode toward them, they flew up into the last of the trees with a *chuk-chuk* of alarm and a flash of white tail feathers. Smoke from grassfires on the plains tainted the air.

How different it was to be riding through a landscape, he thought—with no walls or windows between his senses and the world—rather than just riding by it. Danny felt the road under his thin wheels, the sun, the wind on his body. It made a strange place less exotic, yet it became infinitely more real.

The road out of Garoua was a wide boulevard that turned into a smaller road heading north. With his bicycle tires humming and crunching on the irregular pavement, Danny passed a few ragged cotton fields, then entered the plains of dry, yellow grass and thorny scrub, everywhere studded with boulders and sculpted anthills. By 7:30 in the morning, a hot breeze rose, carrying a honeysuckle-like perfume. Everything vibrated with heat.

Within an hour the road grew worse, but Danny kept his pace, taking deep breaths in the trancelike state that kept the horizon moving closer. Drums. Kabas. Long rides helped him clear his head, but he found he had to concentrate to steer around the worst ruts and the biggest stones.

Great columns of stone appeared above the hills to east and west. One was pyramid-shaped, one a huge rounded breast, yet another a great stone phallus. Danny had seen photographs of these "inselberg" formations caused by volcanoes that had eroded over the eons, leaving behind vertical cores of lava.

Erosion had struck the road here, too, turning it into a heaving washboard, which then veered left into a trough between tumbled boulders and up through a gauntlet of thorn trees. Danny stopped for another drink of water, another glance at the map. The water boy at the kiosk had marked the location of Kabas with his fingernail, but it was not printed on the map.

After Danny had climbed uphill for an hour, the beaten path became no more than a worn trail, forcing him to squeeze between walls of thorns and dry millet stalks. The squadrons of hovering dragonflies were harmless, but the hordes of tiny flies circling his face were maddening, and he couldn't pedal fast enough to escape them.

It was nearly noon, the sun reflecting straight up from the dry earth, and the little shade cast by the scattered trees dwindled to a small circle around the trunks. "Where the hell am I going?" he said to the sky.

But in his head he kept hearing the odd, potent beat resonating from the bizarre drum he had seen in the Garoua marketplace. He recalled the grayish, shambling man who had never once stopped tapping on his drum, even though his fingers bled. No matter how bad the road got, Danny thought, he would keep going. He'd never been so intrigued by a drumbeat before, and he never left things half-finished.

Danny Imbro was a goal-oriented person. The other members of Blitzkrieg razzed him about it, that once he made up his mind to do something, he plowed ahead, defying all common sense. Back in school, he had made up his mind to be a drummer. He had hammered away at just about every object in sight with his fingertips, pencils, silverware, anything that made noise. He kept at it until he drove everyone else around him nuts, and somewhere along the line he became good.

Now people stood at the chain link fences behind concert halls and applauded whenever he walked from the backstage dressing rooms out to the tour buses—as if he were somehow doing a better job of walking than any of them had ever seen before....

Up ahead, an enormous buttress tree, a gnarled and twisted pair of trunks hung with cable-thick vines, cast a wide patch of shade. Beneath the tree, watching him approach, sat a small boy.

The boy leaped to his feet, as if he had been waiting for Danny. Shirtless and dusty, he held a hooklike withered arm against his chest; but his grin was completely disarming. *"Je suis guide?"* the boy called.

Relief stifled Danny's laugh. He nodded vigorously. *"Oui!"* Yes, he could certainly use a guide right about now. *"Je cherche Kabas—village des tambours.* The village of drums."

The smiling boy danced around like a goat, jumping from rock to rock. He was pleasant-faced and healthy looking, except for the crippled arm; his skin was very dark, but his eyes had a slight Asian cast. He chattered in a high voice, a mixture of French and native dialect. Danny caught enough to understand that the boy's name was Anatole.

Before the boy led him on, though, Danny dismounted, leaning his bicycle against a boulder, and unzipped his pack to take out the raisins, peanuts, and the dry remains of a baguette. Anatole watched him with wide eyes, and Danny gave him a handful of raisins, which the boy wolfed down. Small flies whined around their faces as they ate. Danny answered the boy's incessant questions with as few words as possible: did he come from America, did black boys live there, why was he visiting Cameroon?

The short rest sank its soporific claws into him, but Danny decided not to give in. An afternoon siesta made a lot of sense, but now that he had his own personal guide to the village, he made it his goal not to stop again until they reached Kabas. "Okay?" Danny raised his eyebrows and struggled to his feet.

Anatole sprang out from the shade and fetched Danny's bike for him, struggling with one arm to keep it upright. After several trips to Africa, Danny had seen plenty of withered limbs, caused by childhood diseases, accidents, and bungled inoculations. Out here in the wilder areas, such problems were even more prevalent, and he wondered how Anatole managed to survive; acting as a "guide" for the rare travelers would hardly suffice.

Danny pulled out a hundred francs—an eighth of what he had paid for one bottle of water—and handed it to the boy, who looked as if he had just been handed the crown jewels. Danny figured he had probably made a friend for life.

Anatole trotted ahead, gesturing with his good arm. Danny pedaled after him.

The narrow valley captured a smear of greenness in the dry hills, with a cluster of mango trees, guava trees, and strange baobabs with eight-foot-thick trunks. Playing the knowledgeable tour guide, Anatole explained that the local women used the baobab fruits for baby formula if their breast milk failed. The villagers used another tree to manufacture an insect repellent.

The houses of Kabas blended into the landscape, because they were of the landscape—stones and branches and grass. The walls were made of dry mud, laid on a handful at a time, and the roofs were thatched into cones. Tiny pink and white stones studded the mud, sparkling like quartz in the sun.

At first the place looked deserted, but then an ancient man emerged from a turret-shaped hut. An enormous cutlass dangled from his waist, although the shrunken man looked as if it might take him an hour just to lift the blade. Anatole shouted something, then gestured for Danny to follow him. The great cutlass swayed against the old man's unsteady knees as he bowed slightly—or stooped—and greeted Danny in formal, unpracticed French. "*Bonsoir!*"

"*Makonya,*" Danny said, remembering the local greeting from Garoua. He walked his bike in among the round and square buildings. A few chickens scratched in the dirt, and a pair of black-and-brown goats nosed between the huts. A sinewy, long-limbed old woman wearing only a loincloth tended a fire. He immediately started looking for the special drums but saw none.

Within the village, a high-walled courtyard enclosed two round huts. Gravel covered the open area between them, roofed over with a network of serpent-shaped sticks supporting grass mats. This seemed to be the chief's compound. Anatole held Danny's arm and dragged him forward.

Inside the wall, a white-robed figure reclined in a canvas chair under an acacia tree. His handsome features had a North African cast, thin lips over white teeth, and a rakish mustache. His aristocratic head was wrapped in a red-and-white checked scarf, and even in repose he was obviously tall. He looked every bit the romantic desert prince, like Rudolf Valentino in *The Sheik*. After greeting Danny in both French and the local language, the chief gestured for his visitor to sit beside him.

Before Danny could move, two other boys appeared carrying a rolled-up mat of woven grass, which they spread out for him. Anatole scolded them for horning in on his customer, but the two boys cuffed him and ignored his protests. Then the chief shouted at them all for disturbing his peace and drove the boys away. Danny watched them kicking Anatole as they scampered away from the chief, and he felt for his new friend, angry at how tough people picked on weaker ones the world over.

He sat cross-legged on the mat, and it took him only a moment to begin reveling in the moment of relaxation. No cars or trucks disturbed the peace. He was miles from the nearest electricity, or glass window, or airplane. He sat looking up into the leaves of the acacia, listening to the quiet buzz of the villagers, and thought, "I'm living in a *National Geographic* documentary!"

Anatole stole back into the compound, bearing two bottles of warm Mirinda orange soda, which he gave to Danny and the chief. Other boys gathered under the tree, glaring at Anatole, then looking at Danny with ill-concealed awe.

After several moments of polite smiling and nodding, Danny asked the chief if all the boys were his children. Anatole assisted in the unnecessary translation.

"*Oui,*" the chief said, patting his chest proudly. He claimed to have fathered 31 sons, which made Danny wonder if the women in the village found it politic to routinely claim the chief as the father of their babies. As with all remote African villages, though, many children died of various sicknesses. Just a week earlier, one of the babies had succumbed to a terrible fever, the chief said.

The chief asked Danny the usual questions about his country, whether any black men lived there, why had he visited Cameroon; then he insisted that Danny eat dinner with them. The women would prepare the village's specialty of chicken in peanut sauce.

Hearing this, the old sentry emerged with his cutlass, smiled widely at Danny, then turned around the side wall. The squawking of a terrified chicken erupted in the sleepy afternoon air, the sounds of a scuffle, and then the squawking stopped.

Finally, Danny asked the question that had brought him to Kabas in the first place. "*Moi, je suis musicien; je cherche les tambours speciaux.*" He mimed rapping on a small drum, then turned to Anatole for assistance.

The chief sat up startled, then nodded. He hammered on the air, mimicking drum playing, as if to make sure. Danny nodded. The chief clapped his hands and gestured for Anatole to take Danny somewhere. The boy pulled Danny to his feet and, surrounded by other chattering boys, dragged him back out of the walled courtyard. Danny managed to turn around and bow to the chief.

After trooping up a stairlike terrace of rock, they entered the courtyard of another homestead. The main shelter was made of hand-shaped blocks with a flat roof of corrugated metal. Anatole explained that this was the home of the local *sorcier*, or wizard.

Anatole called out, then gestured for Danny to follow through the low doorway. Inside the hut, the walls were hung with evidence of the *sorcier's* trade—odd bits of metal, small carvings, bundles of fur and feathers, mortars full of powders and herbs, clay urns for water and millet beer, smooth skins curing from the roof poles. And drums.

"*Tambours!*" Anatole said, spreading his hands wide.

Judging from the craftsman's tools around the hut, the *sorcier* made the village's drums as well as stored them. Danny saw several small gourd drums, larger log drums, and hollow cylinders of every size, all intricately carved with serpentine symbols, circles feeding into spirals, lines tangled into knots.

Danny reached out to touch one—then the *sorcier* himself stood up from the shadows near the far wall. Danny bit off a startled cry as the lithe old man glided forward. The *sorcier* was tall and rangy, but his skin was a battleground of wrinkles, as if someone had clumsily fashioned him out of papier mâché.

"Pardon," Danny said. The wrinkled man had been sitting on a low stool, putting the finishing touches to a new drum.

Fixing his eyes on his visitor, the *sorcier* withdrew a medium-sized drum from a niche in the wall. Closing his eyes, he tapped on it. The mud walls of the hut reverberated with the hollow vibration, an earthy, primal beat that resonated in Danny's bones. Danny grinned with awe. Yes! The gaunt man's drum had not been a fluke. The drums of Kabas had some special construction that caused this hypnotic tone.

Danny reached out tentatively. The wrinkled man gave him an appraising look, then extended the drum enough for Danny to strike it. He tapped a few tentative beats and laughed out loud when the instrument rewarded him with the same rich sound.

The *sorcier* turned away, taking the drum with him and returning it to its niche in the wall. In two flowing strides, the wrinkled man went to his stool in the shadows, picking up the drum he had been fashioning, moving it into the crack of light that seeped through the windows. Pointing, he spoke in a staccato dialect, which Anatole translated into pidgin French.

The *sorcier* is finishing a new drum today, Anatole said. Perhaps they would play it this evening, an initiation. The chief's baby son would have enjoyed that. From the baby's body, the *sorcier* had been able to salvage only enough skin to make this one small drum.

"What?" Danny said, looking down at the deep brown skin covering the top of the drum.

Anatole explained, as if it was the most ordinary thing in the world, that whenever one of the chief's many sons died, the *sorcier* used his skin to make one of Kabas's special drums. It had always been done.

Danny wrestled with that for a moment. On his first trip to Africa five years earlier, he had learned the wrenching truth of how different these cultures were.

"Why?" he finally asked. *"Pourquoi?"*

He had seen other drums made entirely of human skin taken from slain enemies, fashioned in the shape of stunted bodies with gaping mouths; when tapped a hollow sound came from the effigy's mouths. He knew that trying to impose his Western moral framework on the inhabitants of an alien land was hopeless. I'm sorry, sir, but you'll have to check your preconceptions at the door, he thought jokingly to himself.

"Magique." Anatole's eyes showed a flash of fear—fear born of respect for great power, rather than paranoia or panic. With the magic drums of Kabas, the chief could conquer any man, steal his heartbeat. It was old magic, a technique the village wizards had discovered long before the French had come to Cameroon, and before them the Germans. Kabas had been isolated, and at peace for longer than the memories of the oldest people in the village. Because of the drums. Anatole smiled, proud of his story, and Danny restrained an urge to pat him on the head.

Trying not to let his disbelief show, Danny nodded deeply to the *sorcier*. *"Merci,"* he said. As Anatole led him back out to the courtyard, the *sorcier* returned to his work on the small drum.

Danny wondered if he should have tried to buy one of the drums from the wrinkled man. Did he believe the story about using human skins? Probably. Why would Anatole lie?

As they left the *sorcier's* homestead to begin the trek back to the village, he looked westward across the jagged landscape of inselbergs. At sunset, the air filled with hundreds of kites, their wings rigid, circling high on the last thermals. Like leaves before the wind, the birds came spiraling down to disappear into the trees, filling them with the invisible flapping of wings.

When they reached the main village again, Danny saw that the women had returned from their labor in the nearby fields. He was familiar with the African tradition of sending the women and children out for backbreaking labor while the men lounged in the shade and talked "business."

The numerous sons of the chief and other adults gathered inside the courtyard near the fire, which the old sinewy woman had stoked into a larger blaze. Other men emerged, and Danny wondered where they had been hiding all afternoon. Out hunting? If so, they had nothing to show for their efforts. Anatole directed Danny to sit on a mat beside the chief, and everyone smiled vigorously at each other, the villagers exchanging the call-and-response litany of ritual greetings, which could go on for several minutes.

The old woman served the chief first, then the honored guest. She placed a brown yam like a baked potato on the mat in front of him, miming that it was hot. Danny took a cautious bite; the yam was pungent and turned to paste in his mouth. Then the woman reappeared with the promised chicken in peanut sauce. They ate quietly in a circle around the fire, ignoring each other, as red shadows flickered across their faces.

Listening to the sounds of eating, as well as the simmering evening hush of the West African hills, Danny felt the emptiness like a peaceful vacuum, draining away stress and loud noises and hectic schedules. After too many head-pounding tours and adrenaline-crazed performances, Danny was convinced he had forgotten how to sit quietly, how to slow down. After one rough segment of the last Blitzkrieg tour, he had taken a few days to go camping in the mountains; he recalled pacing in vigorous circles around the picnic table, muttering to himself that he was relaxing as fast as he could!

Calming down was an acquired skill, he felt, and there was no better teacher than Africa.

After the meal, heads turned in the firelight, and Danny looked up to see the *sorcier* enter the chief's compound. The wrinkled man cradled several of his mystical drums. He placed one of the drums in front of the chief, then set the others on an empty spot on the ground. He squatted behind one drum, thrusting his long, lean legs up and to the side like the wings of a vulture.

Danny perked up. "A concert?" He turned to Anatole, who spoke rapidly to the *sorcier*. The wrinkled man looked skeptically at Danny, then shrugged. He picked up one of the extra drums and ceremoniously extended it to Danny.

Danny couldn't stop smiling. He took the drum and looked at it. The coffee-colored skin felt smooth and velvety as he touched it. A shiver went up his spine as he tapped the drumhead. Making music from human skin. He forced his instinctive revulsion back into the gray static of his mind, the place where he stored things "to think about later." For now, he had the drum in his hands.

The chief thumped out a few beats, then stopped. The *sorcier* mimicked them and glanced toward Danny. "Jam session!" he muttered under his breath, then repeated the sequence easily and cleanly, but added a quick, complicated flourish to the end.

The chief raised his eyebrows, followed suit with the beat, and made it more complicated still. The *sorcier* flowed into his part, and Danny joined in with another counterpoint. It reminded him of the Dueling Banjos sequence from *Deliverance*."

The echoing, rich tone of the drum made his fingers warm and tingly, but he allowed himself to be swallowed up in the mystic rhythms, the primal pounding out in the middle of the African wilderness. The other night noises vanished around him, the smoke from the fire rose straight up, and the light centered into a pinpoint of his concentration.

Using his bare fingers—sticks would only interrupt the magical contact between himself and the drum—Danny continued weaving into their rhythms, trading points and counterpoints. The beat touched a core of past lives deep within him, an atavistic, pagan intensity, as the three drummers reached into the Pulse of the World. The chief played on; the *sorcier* played on; and Danny let his eyes fade half-closed in a rhythmic trance, as they explored the wordless language and hypnotic interplay of rhythm.

Danny became aware of the other boys standing up and swaying, jabbering excitedly and laughing as they danced around him. He deciphered their words as "White man drum! White man drum!" It was a safe bet they'd never seen a white man play a drum before.

Suddenly the *sorcier* stopped, and within a beat the chief also quit playing. Danny felt wrenched out of the experience, but reluctantly played a concluding figure as well, ending with an emphatic flam. His arms burned from the exertion, sweat dripped down the stubble on his chin. His ears buzzed from the noise. Unable to restrain himself, Danny began laughing with delight.

The *sorcier* said something, which Anatole translated. *"Vous avez l'esprit de batteur."* You have the spirit of a drummer.

With a throbbing hand, Danny squeezed Anatole's bare shoulder and nodded. *"Oui."*

The chief also congratulated him, thanking him for sharing his white man's music with the village. Danny found that ironic, since he had come here to pick up a rich African flavor for his compositions. But Danny could record his impressions in new songs; the village of Kabas had no way of keeping what he had brought to them.

The withered *sorcier* picked up one of the drums at his side, and Danny recognized it as the small drum the old man had been finishing in the dim hut that afternoon. He fixed his deep gaze on Danny for a moment, then handed it to him.

Anatole sat up, alarmed, but bit off a comment he had intended to make. Danny nodded in reassurance and in delight he took the new drum. He held it to his chest and inclined his head deeply to show his appreciation. *"Merci!"*

Anatole took Danny's hand to lead him away from the walled

courtyard. The chief clapped his hands and barked something to the other boys, who looked at Anatole with glee before they got up and scurried to the huts for sleeping. Anatole stared nervously at Danny, but Danny didn't understand what had just occurred.

He repeated his thanks, bowing again to the chief and *sorcier*, but the two of them just stared at him. He was reminded of an East African scene: a pair of lions sizing up their prey. He shook his head to clear the morbid thought and followed Anatole.

In the village proper, one of the round thatched huts had been swept for Danny to sleep in. Outside, his bicycle leaned against a tree, no doubt guarded during the day by the little man with the enormous cutlass. Anatole seemed uneasy, wanting to say something, but afraid.

Trying to comfort him, Danny opened his pack and withdrew a stick of chewing gum for the boy. Anatole spoke rapidly, gushing his thanks. Other boys suddenly materialized from the shadows with childish murder in their eyes. They tried to take the gum from Anatole, but he popped it in his mouth and ran off. "Hey!" Danny shouted, but Anatole bolted into the night with the boys chasing after.

Wondering if Anatole was in any real danger, Danny removed the blanket and sleeping bag from his bike, then carried them inside the guest hut. He decided the boy could take care of himself, that he had spent his life as the whipping boy for the other sons of the chief. The thought drained some of the exhilaration from the memory of the evening's performance.

His legs ached after the torturous ride upland from Garoua, and he fantasized briefly about sitting in the Jacuzzi in the capital suite of some five-star hotel. He considered how wonderful it would be to sip on some cold champagne, or a scotch on the rocks.

Instead, he lifted the gift drum, inspecting it. He would find some way to use it on the next album, add a rich African tone to the music. Paul Simon and Peter Gabriel had done it, though the style of Blitzkrieg's music was a bit more … aggressive.

He would not tell anyone about the human skin, especially the customs officials. He tried without success to decipher the mystical swirling patterns carved into the wood, the interwoven curves, circles, and knots. It made him dizzy.

Danny closed his eyes and began to play the drum, quietly so as not to disturb the other villagers. But as the sound reached his ears, he snapped his eyes open. The tone from the drum was flat and weak, like a cheap tourist tom-tom, plastic over a coffee can.

He frowned at the gift drum. Where was the rich reverberation, the primal pulse of the earth? He tapped again, but heard only an empty and hollow sound, soulless. Danny scowled, wondering if the *sorcier* had ruined the drum by accident, then decided to get rid of it by giving it to the unsuspecting White Man who wouldn't know the difference.

Angry and uneasy, Danny set the African drum next to him; he would try it again in the morning. He could play it for the chief, show him its flat tone. Perhaps they would exchange it. Maybe he would have to buy another one.

He hoped Anatole was all right.

Danny sat down to pull the thorns and prickers from his clothes. The village women had provided him with two plastic basins of water for bathing, one for soaping and scrubbing, the other for rinsing. The warm water felt refreshing on his face, his neck. After stripping off his pungent socks, he rinsed his toes and soles.

The night stillness was hypnotic, and as he spread his sleeping bag and stretched out on it, he felt as if he were seeping into the cloth, into the ground, swallowed up in sleep....

Anatole woke him up only a few moments later, shaking him and whispering harshly in his ear. Dirt, blood, and bruises covered the boy's wiry body, and his clothes had been torn in a scuffle. He didn't seem to care. He kept shaking Danny.

But it was already too late.

Danny sat up, blinking his eyes. Sharp pains like a bear trap ripped through his chest. A giant hand had wrapped around his torso and would squeeze until his ribs popped free of his spine.

He gasped, opening and closing his mouth, but could not give voice to his agony. He grabbed Anatole's withered arm, but the boy struggled away, searching for something. Black spots swam in his eyes. He tried to breathe, but his chest wouldn't let him. He began slipping, sliding down an endless cliff into blackness.

Anatole finally reached an object on the floor of the hut. He snatched it up with his good hand, tucked it firmly under his withered arm, and began to thump on it.

The drum!

As the boy rapped out a slow, steady beat, Danny felt the iron band loosen around his heart. Blood rushed into his head again, and he drew a deep breath. Dizziness continued to swim around him, but the impossible pain receded. He clutched his chest, rubbing his sternum. He uttered a breathy thanks to Anatole.

Had he just suffered a heart attack? Good God, all the fast living had decided to catch up to him while he was out in the middle of nowhere, far from any hope of medical attention!

Then he realized with a chill that the sounds from the gift drum were now rich and echoey, with the unearthly depth he remembered from the other drums. Anatole continued his slow rhythm, and suddenly Danny recognized it. A heartbeat.

What was it the boy had told him inside the *sorcier's* hut—that the magical drums could steal a man's heartbeat? *"Ton coeur c'est dans ici,"* Anatole said, continuing his drumming. Your heartbeat lives in here now.

Danny remembered the gaunt, shambling man in the marketplace of Garoua, obsessively tapping the drum from Kabas as if his life depended on it, until his hide-wrapped fingers were bloodied. Had that man also escaped his fate in the village, and fled south?

"You had the spirit of a drummer," Anatole said in his pidgin French, "and now the drum has your spirit." As if to emphasize his statement, as if he knew a White Man would be skeptical of such magic, Anatole ceased his rhythm on the drum.

The claws returned to Danny's heart, and the vise in his chest clamped back down. His heart had stopped beating. Heart beats, drumbeats—

The boy stopped only long enough to convince Danny, then

started the beat again. He looked with pleading eyes in the shadowy hut. *"Je vais avec toi!"* I go with you. Let me be your heartbeat. From now on.

Leaving his sleeping bag behind, Danny staggered out of the guest hut to his bicycle resting against an acacia tree. The rest of the village was dark and silent, and the next morning they would expect to find him dead and cold on his blankets; and the new drum would have the same resonant quality, the same throbbing of a captured spirit, to add to their collection. The sound of White Man's music for Kabas.

"Allez!" Anatole whispered as Danny climbed aboard his bike. Go! What was he supposed to do now? The boy ran in front of him along the narrow track. Danny did not fear navigating the rugged trail by moonlight, with snakes and who-knows-what abroad in the grass, as much as he feared staying in Kabas and being there when the chief and the *sorcier* came to look at his body in the morning, and no doubt to appraise their pale new drum skin.

But how long could Anatole continue his drumming? If the beat stopped for only a moment, Danny would seize up. They would have to take turns sleeping. Would this nightmare continue after he had left the vicinity of the village? Distance had not helped the shambling man in the marketplace in Garoua.

Would this be the rest of his life?

Stricken with panic, Danny nodded to the boy, just wanting to be out of there and not knowing what else to do. Yes, I'll take you with me. What other choice do I have? He pedaled his bike away from Kabas, crunching on the rough dirt path. Anatole jogged in front of him, tapping on the drum.

And tapping.

And tapping.

Previous Publication Information

"Bad Water," copyright © 2016, WordFire, Inc., first published in *The Book of the Emissaries*, ed. Emily C. Skaftun, Every Day Publishing, 2016.

"Bump in the Night," copyright © 2022, WordFire, Inc., first published in *Pulphouse #19*, 2022.

"Church Services," copyright © 2009, WordFire, Inc., first published in *Dark Delicacies III: Haunted*, ed. Del Howison and Jeff Gelb, Running Press, 2009.

"Dark Carbuncle," with Janis Ian, copyright © 2010, WordFire, Inc. and Janis Ian, first published in *Blood Lite II: Overbite*, ed. Kevin J. Anderson, Gallery Books, 2010.

"Deathdance," copyright © 1988, WordFire, Inc., first published in *Haunts*, Spring/Summer 1988.

"Drumbeats," copyright © 1994, Kevin J. Anderson and Neil Peart, first published in *Shock Rock II*, ed. Jeff Gelb, Pocket Books, 1994.

"The Fate Worse Than Death," with Guy Anthony de Marco, copyright © 2014, WordFire, Inc. and Guy Anthony de Marco, first published in *Unidentified Funny Objects 3*, ed. Alex Shvartsman, UFO Publishing, 2014.

"Fire in the Hole," copyright © 2023, WordFire, Inc., first published in *L. Ron Hubbard Presents Writers of the Future Volume 39*, ed. Jody Lynne Nye and Dean Wesley Smith, Galaxy Press, 2023.

"Last Stand," copyright © 1991, WordFire, Inc., first published in *Weirdbook 26*, Autumn 1991.

"Leatherworks," copyright © 1984, WordFire, Inc., first published in *The Horror Show*, Fall 1984.

"Loco-Motive," copyright © 1987, WordFire, Inc., first published in *Amazing Stories*, 1987.

"Much at Stake," copyright © 1991, WordFire, Inc., first published in *The*

Previous Publication Information

Ultimate Dracula, ed. Byron Preiss, David Keller, and Megan Miller, Dell, 1991.

"Notches," copyright © 1985, WordFire, Inc., first published in *The Horror Show*, Winter 1985.

"Redmond's Private Screening," copyright © 2001, WordFire, Inc., first published in *Realms of Fantasy*, April 2001.
"Royal Wedding," original to this collection, copyright © 2018, WordFire, Inc.

"Santa Claus Is Coming to Get You," copyright © 1991, WordFire, Inc., first published in *Deathrealm*, Fall⁄Winter 1991.

"Scarecrow Season," copyright © 2011, WordFire, Inc., first published in *Tucker's Grove*, Arc Manor, 2011.

"Social Distance," copyright © 2021, WordFire, Inc., first published in *We Shall Rise*, ed. John Ringo & Gary Poole, Baen Books, 2021.

"Surf's Up," copyright © 2023, WordFire, Inc. and Jonathan Maberry Productions LLC, first published in *Joe Ledger: Unbreakable*, ed. Jonathan Maberry and Bryan Thomas Schmidt, Journalstone Publishing, 2024.

"We Get What We Deserve: The Pickpocket's Tale," with Neil Peart, copyright © 2015, WordFire, Inc. and Pratt Music, Inc., first published in *Clockwork Lives*, by Kevin J. Anderson and Neil Peart, ECW Press, 2015.

About the Author

Kevin J. Anderson has published more than 180 books, 58 of which have been national or international bestsellers. He has 24 million copies in print in 34 languages.

He has written numerous novels in the Star Wars, X-Files, and Dune universes, as well as the unique Clockwork Angels steampunk trilogy with legendary Rush drummer Neil Peart. His original works include the Saga of Seven Suns series, the Wake the Dragon and Terra Incognita fantasy trilogies, the humorous Dan Shamble, Zombie P.I. series and The Dragon Business series.

He has edited numerous anthologies, written comics and games, and the lyrics to two rock CDs as companions to his Terra Incognita trilogy.

Anderson is the director of the graduate program in Publishing at Western Colorado University, and he and his wife Rebecca Moesta are the publishers of WordFire Press.

If You Liked ...

If you liked *Horror and Dark Fantasy Stories: Volume 2*, you might also enjoy other WordFire Press titles by Kevin J. Anderson

Our list of other WordFire Press authors and titles is always growing. To find out more and shop our selection of titles, visit us at:
wordfirepress.com

Milton Keynes UK
Ingram Content Group UK Ltd.
UKHW042113111124
451073UK00015B/348/J